Praise for the Retrievers novels of

laura anne gilman

Staying Dead

"An entertaining, fast-paced thriller set in a world where cell phones
and computers exist uneasily with magic, and a couple of engaging
and highly talented rogues solve crimes while trying not to
commit too many of their own."
—*Locus*

Curse the Dark

"With an atmosphere reminiscent of Dan Brown's *The Da Vinci Code* and
Umberto Eco's *The Name of the Rose* by way of Sam Spade, Gilman's
second Wren Valere adventure (after *Staying Dead*) features fast-paced
action, wisecracking dialog a

"Ripping good urban fantasy, fas
mystery and magic…this is a pa
avoid roman ce, and the entire series is worth checking out.

"This fourth book in G
relationship, as usual
an unexpected directi
the
—*Ro*

"An intel
by far th

Retrievers novels
from

laura anne gilman

and LUNA Books:

And coming in 2010, the first in her new series:
PSI: Paranormal Scene Investigations

Hard Magic

laura anne gilman

blood
from
stone

LUNA™
www.LUNA-Books.com

5/09 9⁰⁰

LUNA™

Recycling programs
for this product may
not exist in your area.

First trade printing May 2009

BLOOD FROM STONE

ISBN-13: 978-0-373-80297-5
ISBN-10:   0-373-80297-8

Copyright © 2009 by Laura Anne Gilman

First trade printing May 2009

Author photo copyright © by Peter R. Liverakos

This is a work of fiction. Names, characters, places and incidents are
either the product of the author's imagination or are used fictitiously, and
any resemblance to actual persons, living or dead, business establishments,
events or locales is entirely coincidental.

This edition published by arrangement with Harlequin Books S.A.

® and TM are trademarks of Harlequin Books S.A., used under license.
Trademarks indicated with ® are registered in the United States Patent
and Trademark Office, the Canadian Trade Marks Office and in other
countries.

www.LUNA-Books.com

Printed in U.S.A.

AUTHOR NOTE

Blood from Stone was an easy book to write—and a difficult one at the same time.

Easy, because I've lived with these characters, their personalities and problems, for the length of six books now. We've been together for the long haul, and each book is like visiting with old and dear friends.

Difficult, because with this book their story comes to a (temporary) close. The Cosa Nostradamus universe continues with *Hard Magic,* but Wren and Sergei will be taking a short break to let Bonnie and her crew take center stage. While I'm sad to see them go, I'm thrilled that Bonnie's getting her chance to shine. You can read a teaser for that book at the end of this one.

Meanwhile, you have *Blood from Stone* yet to read, wherein Wren and Sergei are faced with a new challenge—one that involves Wren's sidekick P.B. and the fate of all demon-kind!

Enjoy!

Laura Anne Gilman
May 2009

There's only one person this book could be dedicated to: my editor, Mary-Theresa Hussey, who has put up with this entire crew and their writer for six books now, and come back and asked for more....

And maybe that's all that we need
is to meet in the middle of impossibility.
—"Mystery"
Indigo Girls

prologue

"Why do you think you need it?"

"I..." He wants to say that he doesn't know, but that's already been established as a cop-out. He may not know, but there is a reason. There is always a reason. So he says what he already knows. *"It feels good. The pain. But it's not about masochism. It's about trust."* That was true. It *felt* true. *"The pain means that something bad is happening, but I trust that nothing will go wrong."*

"But things do. You're damaging yourself. Every time you do it, you're hurting yourself."

"I didn't...I don't care. I still need it." A pause, because he has always been honest in his own way. *"I don't need it. I want it. I want it enough to risk everything. And it* will *cost me everything. That's why I'm here."*

"It" was current, magical energy. Talent could use it, manipulate it. To a Null like himself, it was deadly, screwing with the internal organs. Being caught in a current backlash was like being repeatedly hit with lightning bolts. Nobody in their right mind would find it a turn-on.

It wouldn't be the first time he'd wondered if he was crazy.

"What do you what to accomplish here? Do you want to not want it?"

That was the damned thing about therapists. They ask the kinds of questions you don't want to think about, much less answer. He shifts in the chair, his legs suddenly too long for comfort, his hands too large, his skin too tight around his frame.

"What do you want?" The voice probes again, soothing but insistent.

"I don't know. That's the problem."

"Indeed."

"I hate it when you say that. I hate everything about this."

"Then why are you here?"

Sergei shifts again, wishing desperately for his cigarette case. He hasn't had a cigarette in years, but right now, the feel of the thin cylinder in his fingers would be just as soothing as the hit of nicotine ever was. Because he doesn't know why he is here, doesn't know what he is supposed to do or say, or bring out of it.

"I don't know."

Except he does know. Wren. Always, ever, Wren Valere. Partner, lover, best friend…the source of his addiction, and the thing he would lose, if he couldn't get it under control.

He just doesn't know how to do that, without walking away from her, too.

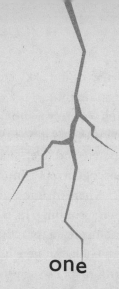

one

In the middle of a copse of trees, bordered on one side behind her by a dry creek bed and on the other in front of her by a low stone wall covered with moss and bird shit, Wren Valere crouched, her backside an inch off the leaf-strewn ground, her palms resting on her knees, and her knees complaining about the whole situation. She was tired, sweaty and pissed-off at the universe in general and one person in particular.

"Annoying, ignorant woman," she scolded that person, hidden inside the house on the other side of that wall. "You couldn't have taken the kid to Boston, or Philadelphia, or somewhere semicivilized? No, you had to go all bucolic and pastoral and…leafy." Wren reached up to pull another twig out of her braid, and wiped sweat off her forehead with the back of her hand. It was a lovely, autumn-crisp day, pale blue skies overhead, and she was sure that there were hundreds of people driving up and down the winding county road a few miles back for the sole purpose of enjoying the scarlet-and-orange display of the maples and oaks and whatever else those trees were. More power to them.

Wren Valere was not a nature girl. The leaves were pretty, and she was glad it was a nice day, but she wanted to be home, on concrete and steel, surrounded by the familiar and comforting hum of current running through the city. Home was Manhattan, where magic fed on and was fed by the torrents of electricity running in the city's veins. A Talent like her—a current-mage, a practitioner of modern magics—had no business being out here in the woods, miles from anything more powerful than a solar powered bug-zapper.

Genevieve, you're exaggerating, she heard her mother's voice say, exasperated. All right, she admitted that she might be overstating things slightly. It still felt like middle-of-nowheresville to her: too quiet, too green and too still, electrically speaking.

The thought made her reach instinctively, a mental touch stroking the core of current nestled inside her, deep in a non-existent-to-X-rays cavity somewhere in her gut, just to make sure it was still there. Like a bank, you could overdraw and forget to refill, and even though she *knew* she had enough in there, it was a nervous twitch, obsessive-compulsive, to make sure, and then make sure again.

Current was similar to—but not quite identical to—the electrical energy the modern world had harnessed to do its bidding. They were, so far as anyone could determine, generated off the same sources, and appeared in the same natural and man-made situations, but with a vastly different result when channeled by their natural conductors. Metal, in the case of electricity: Talent, in the case of current.

The more abstract and technical distinctions between current and electricity were lost on most of the *Cosa Nostradamus*, the worldwide magical community, except those very few who made an actual study of it.

Wren wasn't one of those few. She wasn't an academic; she was a Retriever. She came, she stole, she went home, with no interest in the whys, so long as it worked. Although she freely admitted that the feeling of it simmering inside was nice, too. Some Talent described their internal core of magic, the power they carried with them at all times, as a pool of potent liquid, or birds flocking together, their feathers rustling with power. For her, it was a pit of serpents, thick-muscled neon beasts sliding and slithering against each other. The touch filled her with a quiet satisfaction, a sense of power resting under her skin, ready if she needed it.

Reassured, she moved forward through the trees, only to be pulled up short by something tugging on her braid, before realizing that it wasn't an attack—or at least, not one she needed to worry about.

Reaching back, Wren removed her braid from the grasp of a branch and scowled at it, as though it alone were responsible for her bad mood. "I hate camping. I hate bugs. I hate trees."

She didn't really hate trees—Borani, one of her oldest friends, was a dryad in fact, which made her an actual, honest-to-God tree hugger. Wren had never needed to go camping to know how she felt about it. She preferred luxury hotels to sleeping on the ground.

She did hate bugs, though. Wren grimaced, and reached a hand down the back of her outfit, scratching at something irritating her skin. She pulled her hand away and made a face, shaking the remains of the unidentifiable insect off her fingers. She especially hated bugs that kept trying to crawl under the fabric of her slicks to reach the bare skin underneath.

"Ugh." She wiped her fingers on the grass. "Next job? High-rise. Climate controlled. Coffee shop on the corner." She kept her voice low, more from habit than belief that there was anyone around to hear her. "God, I'd kill for a cup of halfway decent coffee...."

She really shouldn't be in a bad mood at all, even with bugs and twigs. Coffee and the rest of civilization would be waiting for her when she got home, same as always. This was just a job, and it would be over soon. And money in the bank made every job better, in retrospect.

Tugging the hood of her formfitting black bodysuit over her ears, making sure that the braid was now tucked comfortably inside the fabric, Wren kept crawling forward until she reached a low hedge of some prickly-leaved bushes. Rising up to her knees, she scowled over the shrubbery at the perfectly lovely little cottage on the other side of nowhere.

All right, she told herself, enough with the griping and the moaning. Showtime.

She let herself reassess the scenario, just to get the brain in the right place. The area was on the grid. She could feel the quiet hum of electrical wires—man-made power—overhead, not far away. There wasn't a lot, but if she suddenly had a need it was there to draw down on. Comforting. And the house wasn't totally isolated—despite the screen of trees, a half-hour hike would bring her back to the highway, and it was probably only a few minutes' drive from the front door to the nearest coffee joint. If, of course, you had a car.

The job had specified no traces, though, which meant that renting a car, even using one of her many fake IDs, was out. Frustrating, but manageable. The client was paying large sums for this to be a spotless, trouble-free Retrieval, and that was what The Wren would deliver. No muss, no fuss, no anything the courts could use at a later date against the client. Everything had to be perfect.

It was more than just ego at stake, that perfection, although she was always about that. This particular job had come to Sergei, her partner/business manager, not through the usual route of the *Cosa Nostradamus* or his art world contacts, but through a retired NYC cop now living upstate, a guy named McKierney who moonlighted as a bounty hunter. The client had gone to him originally, but this kind of grab wasn't McKierney's scene. He had heard about The Wren through his own contacts, and had given the client her name and Sergei's contact number as the go-to girl for this particular job.

She didn't get many jobs out of the urban areas, where most of the *Cosa* congregated. A satisfied client here, among human Nulls, could open up a whole new market for her, and there was no way she was going to give less than everything to it, even if it involved trees and bugs and crawling around in the dirt. Sergei had drummed that career advice into her head years ago: you never knew when the next client was going to be the million-dollar meal ticket.

Yeah, the job stank, on a bunch of levels. Money—and clients with money—got her into a lot of situations she didn't enjoy. But this job had something even better than money to offer: there was absolutely no stink of magic to the Retrieval. After spending a year of their lives immersed in a literal life-and-death struggle, when what seemed like half the city suddenly set out to wipe the streets clear of anything that looked as though it might be magical, and then having to give over another nine months to the job of cleaning up the aftermath—and getting her own life back into some kind of order—Wren was more than ready for something distinctly unmagical. Even a be-damned custodial he-said-she-said, with a four-year-old kid as the prize.

That was the job she was on, right now. Mommy had

grabbed the kid and run. Wren was here to Retrieve him for Daddy, who was the client.

Wren shifted on her haunches, still feeling the creepy-crawling sensation of bug legs on her skin. That was the real reason she was griping, not the green leafy buggy nature thing. Live Retrievals were a bitch. She'd only done two before, and both of them had involved adults. One she'd been able to reason with, the other she'd had Sergei along to help conk the target over the head when the reasoning didn't work.

She steadfastly didn't think of the third live Retrieval she had done. That had been different. That…hadn't been her, entirely.

Hadn't it?

Nobody had judged. Nobody had said anything after, except thank you. She had restored a dozen teenagers to their family, broken the spine of the anti-*Cosa* organization, the Silence. But Wren didn't list that Retrieval in her nonexistent CV. She didn't talk about it. She tried not to remember anything about it, the hours of cold rage and hot current spinning her out of control, making her—for the second time in her life—into a killer, however justified those deaths were, to save the lives of others. No matter that she hadn't been entirely sane at the time.

Inanimate things were easier to Retrieve, every way up and down. Adult live retrievals were bad enough: seriously tough to stash a four-year-old in your knapsack. They tended to squirm.

And yet…the challenge was irresistible. The benefits for a job well done were deeply rewarding. So here she was.

Wren didn't let herself think about the morality of the Retrieval, either way. If possession was nine-tenths of the law, The Wren was the other tenth. Not that she didn't have standards about what was just or fair; she just didn't let them get in the way of an accepted job. If something set off Sergei's well-honed antenna for fishy, she trusted him to say no before she ever knew the offer had been made. That was his job.

"And you need to be getting on with yours already," she muttered, annoyed at herself. Taking a deep breath, she felt her annoyance, acknowledged it, and then let it go, slipping away like water down a drain.

Shifting to rise up a little more, risking exposure, she reached into the pouch strapped to her ribs, pulling out a pair of tiny, old-fashioned binoculars. She raised the 'nocs to her eyes and looked at the target. The lens allowed her to zoom in, picking up the details that blueprints and aerial shots couldn't give. Nothing like on-the-spot reconnaissance, no matter what the tech-types might claim.

The cottage was a build-by-numbers kit, probably prefab. Nice, though. One story, with a half attic, and windows designed to let in light without giving a direct view in. Brown wood and shingles with blue trim, and an off-white matte roof that, she had been told, was supposed to be more fuel-efficient than the traditional black ones. So, new, or at least with a newish roof. A roof, she noted, that overhung the windows just enough to allow someone with a decent amount of agility to drop down and reach those windows. Bad architect, and worse contractor, to let that get past.

Someone hadn't considered the landscaping from a security angle, either. The cottage faced into a small lawn and a gravel road that led down to the main road, but the back was set into a copse of mature trees. The contractor had managed to build into the existing site, rather than bulldozing and replanting. Pretty. Lousy security, but pretty.

She lowered the binoculars and looked at the cottage unaided. It still looked like an invitation to larceny. Perfect. Now she just had to find a way in, and the job was halfway done. Unfortunately, the hard half was still to come.

Dropping back down behind the hedge entirely, Wren settled herself into a more comfortable crouch on the damp soil, and let herself sink into fugue state.

It used to take her the count of five-seven, when she was still in training. Now, the thought was no sooner thought than it became action. The outside world didn't fade so much as become irrelevant; she could still see and hear and sense everything that went on around her but it was less real than the world she could "see" inside. In that world, every living thing was colored with vivid current, from the shadowy, flickering purple of the insects around her to the solid, slow-pulsing silver of the trees, and the passing bright red of something the size of a large cat, or maybe a fox. Stronger flickers up in the branches suggested that there might be piskies in the area. No other Fatae, not even the hint of a dryad or wood-mocker. Interesting. Not indicative, necessarily, but...interesting.

Everything carried current within itself; sliding into a fugue state allowed a Talent—a witch, a mage, or a wizard, if you liked the older terms—to find, access and use it more efficiently. Strong Talent—traditionally called "Pures"—could sense and use more current; weaker Talent, obviously, less.

Wren had always been strong, with little interrupting the flow of current in her veins. Last year, she had become—however temporarily—the recipient of current gifted by the Fatae, the nonhuman members of the *Cosa Nostradamus*. That blast had temporarily unblocked every channel in her system, kicking her from mostly Pure to too Pure. Talent bodies might be able to handle that much magic, but human brains weren't designed for it. She had been able to work amazing things in the short term, but it had also screwed with her in ways she was still discovering.

One of those new long-term results was that, once in fugue

state, she could sense the presence of current in almost every animate thing, and a few inanimate things, as well.

A nice little side effect, yeah. She could, if she had to, find a refueling station almost anywhere. Unfortunately, using fugue state now also gave her cramps that made PMS feel like a walk in the proverbial park. Everything had a price.

So don't linger. Get it done and get out she reminded herself even as she reached out to gather as much information as she could about the structure in front of her. Just because there was no visible sign of defenses, either physical or magical, didn't meant they weren't there. Careless got you dead or caught, and both were bad news.

She pulled current from her core, shaping it with her will and intent until greedy tendrils of neon-colored power stretched outward, touching and tasting the air, searching for any hint of either current or electricity.

Nothing. A void stretched in front of her: no defenses, and no house, either. Nothing but trees. Impossible, if she believed what her eyes told her. Even if they had built a house without any electrical wiring whatsoever, she should have been able to sense the natural current within the wood, stone and metals, much less the flesh-and-blood entities moving within those walls.

Some Talent trusted their magical senses more than their physical ones. Wren wasn't that arrogant, or that dumb. When the two senses disagreed, something was hinky. Either the house itself was an illusion, or something she couldn't sense was blocking it from being found by magic. Both options were…disturbing.

Giving her Talent one last try, she stretched a tendril of current out, not toward the building, but down, sinking it deep into the soil and stone, reaching for anything that might have been laid in the foundations, deep enough to be hidden to even a directed search. Wren felt a cramp starting, low in her belly, and ignored it, extending herself even as she remained firmly grounded in her body. Sink and stretch, just a little more, just to make sure…

What the…? She touched a warmth—a hard, sharp warmth—tucked underneath the crust, deep in the bedrock where there should only have been cold earth. It spread beyond the house, covering a wider range, suggesting that the house was only secondary, protected as an afterthought. Was that what was blocking her? She pushed a little more, trying to determine the cause. Wh—

At her second touch, something shoved back at her, hard. Unprepared, the magical blow almost knocked her over, physically.

The hell? she thought, pissed off as much at being caught by surprise as at the assault itself. She touched it again with a handful of current-tendrils, not quite a shove in response, but not gentle, either.

That something in the bedrock expanded, filled with thick, hot anger and a wild swirling sense of frustration swamped her own current and tendrils. Angry, yes, and sullen, all that and a feeling of bile-ridden resentment that threatened to consume her, and something worse underneath, something darker and meaner and rising fast.

Yeeeah, outta here, she thought in near panic. *Outta here* now.

Dropping out of fugue state, Wren blinked a few times to let her eyesight return to normal, and then moved away from the hedge as carefully and as quickly as she could manage. A branch crackled underfoot, and she froze, and then moved backward again. Too clumsy, she was making too much noise. Damn. Her skills as a Retriever were legend, but moving invisibly through an occupied house was a different kind of ability than being able to move silently through trees and shrubs, complete with a carpeting of annoyingly crunchy leaves underfoot.

She was shaking, and sweating, and it annoyed her.

Once her nerves told her that she had gotten far enough away to feel secure, she dropped to the ground, placing her bare palms flat against the soil, letting the extra current in her system run off into the earth, grounding herself, bringing everything back into balance and soothing the restless, roiling shimmer of her core.

"Jesus wept," she whispered, too shaken to really care if a squirrel or Piskie or too-curious wood-knocker heard her at this point. "What the *hell* was *that?*"

two

The sound of her own voice seemed to shock the air around her, like chemicals dumped into a pond, because she could swear that she saw it shimmer around her. In the branches far overhead a bird of some kind chirped, and something else squawked in response, and a third, deeper voice chattered a command for them both to shut it. Wren could relate to that third voice.

After a few minutes of waiting nervously for something—anything—to come raging out of the trees or rising up from the soil after her, Wren gathered her legs underneath her more comfortably into a cross-legged position in the dirt. Her palms now rested flat on her knees, and she pushed back, feeling her spine unkink and straighten, and her heart slowly return to a more normal beat, while her skin slowly lost the warm, red flush of fear.

Think, Valere. Don't just react. She had been caught in current backlash before—she had been the *cause* of current backlash before—and it had never felt like that. And yet it was, undeniably, current that she had felt. Thick, angry current, black like tar and strangely familiar...

Black tar. Angry.

Her heart stilled, but her body shivered in recognition. She had felt that combination before, yes. Inside herself, in her core, in her veins and under her skin, like sludge instead of blood and bone. She had felt it inside herself when she wizzed last year, when the pileup of trouble, cumulating with several Nulls trying to rape and murder her had sent her into current overload. The greatest fear of any and every Talent, to be so lost to the current inside and out that all sense of self-control disappeared into the storm. It had been days before she realized what was happening, and once she did, the situation had gotten so bad that insanity had been all that allowed her to survive and do what needed to be done.

In the dark hours of the Blackout, when she had been the focal point of the Fatae-donated current, when she had led the *Cosa* in striking back against their enemies, sanity would have gotten her killed.

Nobody came back from wizzing. Not ever. She should have been lost in that abyss, too, driven by despair, overwork and too much current use. Instead, her partner, Sergei, and the demon P.B. had dragged her back out of the abyss, barely and by the skin of their teeth. It had taken a magical bond P.B. had created—or allowed to be created—between them, and by extension, between P.B. and her partner/on-again-off-again lover; a bond that had never before—so far as they knew—been attempted, much less established.

That triangular bond of friendship had saved her sanity, and her life. Whoever she had touched out there just now wasn't so lucky. It was still lost within the maelstrom, howling and alone.

Had it been alone? She remembered feeling something deeper, below the blast, like the echo of a scream....

The feel of that anger made her start to shake all over again, and she backed away, retreating to a safer distance from even the memory. *Jesus wept. He wept for the sinners and blessed them in his name.* She wasn't religious, her upbringing casually Protestant and left behind when she went to college, but those two words, *Jesus wept*, had resonated with her, curse and prayer all in one. And in this case, both curse and prayer were wholly appropriate.

Wizzarts were dangerous. Not just because the overload made them crazy, but because crazy made them—what was the word Sergei used? Feckless. Without control, without any concern for their own well-being, they could access more current than was safe...and that much power in the hands of a madman—or woman—was never a good thing.

She brought the shaking under control, schooling her body into obedience. That wasn't her, hiding her essence deep within the earth's crust. That wasn't her core, so dark and tarry, rather than clear and sharp. She wasn't wizzed. She was in control, damn it. She wasn't a danger to herself, or anyone else, not any more.

Whatever—whoever—had snapped at her back there *was* a danger. And yet, the wizzart hadn't hurt her, even though he—definitely he, she thought, remembering the taste of the current's signature—he had been angry enough to do some serious damage. Angry and frustrated and quite mad.

But he hadn't hurt her. She kept coming back to that, above and beyond the anger and the crazy; that and the inescapable fact that that current-signature had been oddly, confusingly familiar. How could she know...?

Wren swallowed hard, a sick queasiness rising in her gut that had nothing to do with fear. "Oh damn it to hell and back. Max?"

It was half question, half realization, and it had the unexpected, unplanned, and unwanted result of bringing him to her.

Unlike the last time Max appeared, there was no blowout of electronics, no sudden windstorm of energy. He was just *there*. Older than she remembered him being, still dressed in his usual sloppy sweatshirt and khaki shorts showing off knobby knees, but his face was even more like a dried apple, surrounded by a mane of shaggy, white hair. His blue-green eyes were still bright—too bright, and too wild to trust. She could feel the current crackling within him, making him unsafe to touch, unsafe to be near.

This time, though, his body shimmered outwardly, too; the current visibly feeding on him even as he fed on it, some unholy symbiotic frenzy. It was terrifying, and terrifyingly beautiful, like a fire raging out of control. Which, she supposed, it was. An electrical fire, destroying him from within. Destroying anything too close.

Some part of Wren's mind that wasn't busy panicking wondered if he had always been like this, if everyone who wizzed looked like that, and her descent into the same maelstrom was what allowed her to see it now—and if she, too, looked like that to his eyes.

Those bright eyes stared at her without blinking. "Hey hey hey, brat. Hey, little girl." His voice was rusty, as though he hadn't used it in a long time.

Wren took a deep breath, and calmed down. For the moment, at least, Max seemed to be, well, not sane, but in control. She hadn't been a little girl in years—decades—but he had been a friend to her mentor for decades before she was born, and would probably always see her as a thirteen-year-old with braids and no brains.

Right now, she was okay with that. It was probably why she wasn't dead, those few random, faded, fond memories still caught somewhere inside the crazy. Just don't rely on it, Valere, she reminded herself. Don't assume a damned thing. He could and probably will snap at any instant.

"Max." Her voice sounded surprisingly calm, considering how her insides were churning. "It's really not so good to see you."

He cackled at that, a scary-ass sound. "You've been busy, brat."

Stewart Maxwell, also known as The Alchemist for reasons that she'd never had explained. Every time she encountered him she barely got away with her life. Not that he had any grudge against her specifically—he was fond of her, the girl-child she had been—but wizzarts just naturally tended to the homicidal. So far he'd tried to pitch her over a cliff—seven years back—and then brought up a current-storm to wipe her off the face of the earth a few years ago. She didn't really want to know how he'd think appropriate to kill her this time. Or what she might be capable of now, to try to stop him.

Try, and fail. She had no illusions about that. She was good. He was crazy. Crazy trumped even very good, every time. But they could do significant damage to anyone caught up in the area during the battle. Better not to get into it at all.

There was a reason nobody in their right mind stayed near a wizzart. Their entire maddened existence was dedicated toward channeling the energies, feeling them as completely as possible, every living cell turned toward the goal of becoming the perfect, one hundred percent Pure magical conductor. And that included their brain cells.

Because of that, wizzarts lived in the moment, the instant of action, without any thought to consequences or responsibility, only more and more and more of the lovely, seductive, orgasmic power. There was never enough to satisfy, and chasing it made them irascible, ornery, obnoxious, and deeply dangerous. She had to get away; but carefully, carefully.

"What happened to the dog?" she asked, trying to buy time, figure out how she was going to get out of this without further head-butting.

The last time she had seen him, he had a dog with him. Big, floppy-eared mongrel. He had named it Dog, of course. Even sane, she didn't remember Max having much in the way of imagination.

A look of something sad and hungry passed over Max's face, and was gone.

"Killed him," he said without inflection, dismissing man's best friend that easily.

Wren almost laughed. Of course Max had. Poor Dog. She hoped it had been quick.

Those bright eyes squinted, and Max scowled at her. "You can't be here," he said with obvious irritation.

All right, that was not what she was expecting to come out of his mouth. Although what she had expected, Wren didn't know. She didn't know why he was here, miles and miles away from the last place she had seen him, right in the middle of her damn job, or why he was so pissed off, not that wizzarts needed a reason for anything.

"You should have gone away when I told you to," he said, his hair sparking with agitation. His hands weren't moving yet, though. It was when his hands started to move that the storm was about to hit. Assuming that telltale sign still worked, anyway.

"When you told…" she started to say, then stopped. Oh. The void covering the area where the house should have been. Right. Suddenly the twigs and bugs and dirt-sore knees seemed the least of her problems. Was he tied up somehow in this job? But how? No, that didn't…feel right. There was something else underlying it all, something she could almost taste, almost recognize, but it slipped away when she tried to chase it. Why was he here? Why now? Why had he bothered to show himself?

"Shoved you away," he muttered. "Don't go poking where you've been told off, like you got no manners. Be smart, stupid brat. For your own good."

He was making a faint bit of sense, which worried her even without understanding it. If she were smart she'd nod her head, pack up, forget about the job, and listen to the not-so-nice, very crazy man.

She *was* smart. She was also stubborn. And, according to one of P.B.'s favorite new rants, she had developed a recent and rather disturbing case of can't-kill-me-nyah-nyah. And nobody told her to do something for her own good, not without telling her *why*.

Wren stood up, her five-foot-and-no-inches barely noticeable against Max's sinewy height, and pulled down enough current to make her own flesh sparkle. A statement: *Don't push me, old man.* Maybe P.B. was right to worry.

"I'm on a job, Max. A job that's got nothing to do with you." That she knew of, anyway. *Shit, let it have nothing to do with him, please. No such thing as coincidence, but let it not be connected.* "Let me get it done and we're out of your hair. But you will let me get it done."

Her voice stayed even and low, even as everything inside her was turning into wobbling Jell-O. She was stronger than she had ever been, stronger than she really wanted to be. Maybe one of the strongest, Purest Talent of her generation, no lie. But the thought of going against a full wizzart scared the shit out of her.

That fear was reassuring, actually. It meant that she was still sane.

"You can't be here" he said again, as though her defiance hadn't even happened. To him, it probably hadn't. He could be a single-minded bastard.

The wind rose around them, filled with static and dry leaves.

Him or her, she wasn't sure who was doing it. Reaching down into the core, where her own reservoir of current seethed like a pool of dry-scaled, neon–colored snakes, she soothed it, coaxed it back under her control. Controlled herself, which meant controlling her core. Control had been what saved her. It made her weaker than Max, able to channel less current through her body, but she could direct it better, focus her strikes.

She let that knowledge show on her face. "I can and I will. Max. Max!" She shouted his name, seeing his eyes glaze over, and was relieved when they focused back on her. Having a wizzart's attention was unnerving, but letting him go spastic was when it got deadly. Suddenly the words tumbled out of her, desperate to be heard while she still had his mostly sane attention. "Max, there's a way out. To unwiz. To come back. I did it. You can, too."

She actually didn't know if there was, if it had been too long, was too late for him. Once you wizzed, you never went back, that was what everyone knew. Except she had. Sort of. Because of P.B. There was only one P.B. Would she share? *Could* she? Would *he?*

Wren shoved that doubt back into a box in her mind and latched it shut. Never mind that boxing difficult things up had probably led to her wizzing in the first place; it was still a useful tool. No time, no place for doubts. She was fine, she was functional, and she owed it to Max—to Neezer, her long-gone mentor, who had introduced them—to try. To at least pass the knowledge on. And if the possibility distracted him from his you-can't-be-here shtick, so much the better.

"Way out? I'm already way out, brat." He grinned at her, a death's-head grin, and the hair rose on the back of her neck even under the slicks that covered her head to toe. The light-absorbing, water-repelling, tear-resisting material was great for avoiding cameras, motion detectors, nosy guards and aggressive tree branches, but it didn't do a damn thing against the heebie-jeebies.

This wasn't the Max she remembered. That Max was unnerving, dangerous, his hair trigger halfway pulled. This Max was…

Scared.

Jesus wept. The concept made her sweat. Anything that scared a wizzart…

Wren swallowed, and went for broke. "Max, what aren't you telling me?"

His voice dropped into a growl. "I'm telling you to go. Don't be here. You don't want to be here, not…not here. Not here."

She was definite about her first impression, now. He was scared, and he was hiding something. From her. Scared, and trying to get rid of her, rather than tell her. Something he didn't want her near, didn't want her to know about. Why? What was hiding down there, deep in the bedrock?

Did it really matter? It did not.

"I'll go as soon as I get what I came for, Max."

The static was crackling in her hair now, making her eyes itch. The song of it was alluring, enticing. She could tell him endless years that there was a way back from the edge, and he wouldn't hear because he wouldn't *want* to hear. That was the thing about wizzing that the others—the ones who hadn't been there—didn't realize: it's so damn dangerous because it feels so damn fabulous. You really don't care that the cost is your sanity.

And she couldn't honestly tell him it was better on the sane side of the street.

"Go away *now!*"

His hands flickered, a tiny sprinkling-of-water motion. She didn't have time to brace herself before the blast threw her backward, landing her hard on her ass, knocking her head against a tree and stealing the air from her lungs. She rolled even as she hit, expecting a bolt of current to follow, to finish her off.

Another gust slammed into her, bruising her from hip to rib, but no bolt.

Run run run the voice inside her head was chanting, the natural, smart, sane response when dealing with a pissed-off wizzart. Max might be scared, but he wasn't scared of *her.* Wren kept rolling, coming up on elbows and knees, her head still ringing from the blow but her senses clear enough to know exactly where the old bastard was. A thick rope of current, dark purple and scarlet, uncoiled from her core and lashed out. She felt the hit more than saw it, felt Max's shock and anger recoil back through the connection. How dare she strike at him?

"You're the one who attacked *me,* you stupid wizzed son of a bitch!" she yelled, not caring if the target, the state troopers, and half of Saratoga County heard her.

Another blast was his only response, still not a bolt but a cold, salt-filled wind, shoving her hard enough to send her back on her ass and scoot her a half-dozen feet farther into the woods. Leaves and branches scratched at her slicks, and the hard roots bruised her ass and elbows.

"*Go!*" echoed in her head, a roar like a waterfall, a jet engine, a lion in full fury.

Scrabbling to her feet, Wren fled deeper into the trees.

It took her three hours and seventeen minutes after she stopped running to work up the nerve to head back to the target site. This time she came in from the opposite direction, circling around and coming up along the access road. The approach wasn't as good for a Retrieval—the road was public access, and anyone might come along at exactly the wrong moment—but with luck maybe Max wasn't watching there, or didn't care so much about it. Maybe whatever it was that he was hiding, or protecting, was only on the other side of the woods.

Maybe was a pretty flimsy word, when it came to wizzarts.

She tried to focus on the job and only the job—timing and distance, plus the approximate weight of the Retrieval as given by the client, equaling effort to get back to the road and across the state line—but her brain kept skittering back to Max's words.

No, not his words. His emotions. The bastard had been angry, and he was crazy as a sewer rat with rabid mange, but unless he'd dropped way under the wizzart sanity range, such as it was, in the past year, he'd been overreacting. Last time she had gotten full warning before he went psycho on her. This time he came in primed at the pump. Why? What had scared him enough that he came out specifically to scare her, to *warn* her?

Enough she thought. *It doesn't matter why, not right now. Focus. Job.* With Max possibly still in the neighborhood, she didn't dare draw down current, for fear of alerting him to the fact that she'd come back. That meant changing more than the direction of her approach; she had to change the mode, too.

Walking up to the pull-off to the house, Wren made sure that her thigh-pack was securely fastened, drew in a deep breath, held it for a moment, and then exhaled. Calm. Calm and collected and loose and all those other things that made you aware of every inch of your body but not so aware that you were distracted by it. Normally she would have invoked her no-see-me, that inner and innate skill of deflecting attention that made her a natural Retriever, but she wasn't sure if even that would be enough to trigger Max's return.

Instead, she had to do it the old-fashioned way, crawling through the shin-high grass toward the house, keeping herself as low-profile as possible, alert to every sound and smell that might mean danger or discovery.

Breaking into a house in the middle of the day was something best left to either rank amateurs or seasoned pros. She
enjoyed it, herself—during nighttime most people tended to
be paranoid, and early morning or dusk was tricky—the few
times she'd gotten shot at, it was at dusk. Daylight, targets were
relaxed, less likely to start at an unexpected noise or shadow,
less likely to call the police or trigger an alarm.

"Hi." A voice piped a greeting unnervingly close to her ear.

Plus, people tended to be a lot more understanding of someone
caught in their backyard midday, as opposed to midnight.

"Hi," she said back after she got her heart down from where
it had lodged in her throat, rolling onto her side but staying
down and as relaxed as possible. The grass—probably not mown
all summer—tickled her nose.

"Whatcha doin'?"

Her interrogator was blond, blue-eyed, and two feet tall. All
right, maybe three. Shorter than she was, but since she was lying
down, it was hard to judge for sure by how much.

"Your dad sent me to get you." Sometimes honesty was so
startling, it worked.

"Oh." The target considered that for a moment, thankfully not sucking his thumb or whatever else disgusting or
otherwise unhygienic that small children did, and then
nodded. "Okay."

He dropped to his own stomach and looked at her as though
expecting something.

Well, she thought, amused. *If it's as easy as that, who the hell
am I to argue?* She tilted her head to indicate the way she had
come, and he nodded, getting up on his elbows and knees,
echoing her posture. She turned, keeping him in sight out of
the corner of her eye, and they started to snake-crawl back
through the grass. Kid was a pretty good wriggler, although he

kept his butt too high in the air. His cute little denim coveralls were going to be ruined, though.

"Marc? Marc, where are you?"

A woman's voice, clear and far too close: coming from inside the house. Back of the house, through an open window, Wren estimated. The voice was slightly concerned, maybe a little annoyed, but not really worried. Not yet. Damn. From the way the target froze, it was mommy dearest. His blue eyes flicked toward the house, and then back to her, clearly looking for guidance. His skin was milk-pale, as if he never got much sun and would burn badly if he did.

"She won't let you go back to your dad," Wren whispered, feeling like several different kinds of sleaze. Never mind who the actual custodial parent was—she hadn't bothered to ask Sergei— Daddy was the client and she worked for the client and anyway, the court would decide eventually unless Daddy did a runner with junior, too, and she was thinking too damn much again.

"I don't like either of them right now." Such a serious little voice, confiding such a huge secret. Wren swallowed, and forced herself to meet that blue gaze.

"Wiggle this way, and keep your butt down," was all she said.

Once she had gotten the kid away from the house and down the road a bit, she coaxed him back to his feet, and they had headed back to the main road. Only one car had driven past them, heading toward the house, and Wren made sure the kid was tucked against her side, barely visible against the deflecting properties of her slicks, unless you were looking specifically for a wee one. From there, it was a relatively easy walk to her job-cache, an abandoned tree house in the back of someone's summer home, where she had stowed her regular clothes, wallet, and other forms of identification and civilization. Her slicks packed away securely, they walked on toward the previously arranged rendezvous site. The kid had kept up reasonably well, staying quiet and only needing to be carried the last mile into town. He didn't whimper, sniffle, or pick his nose, for which Wren was endlessly thankful.

As they walked she tried to sort through everything that had happened in some kind of calm and distanced way. It was no use: whatever had happened back there needed more thought and calm than she had right now. Finish the job, then worry about crazy Max.

To that end, now dressed in a pair of jeans and a white T-shirt under her leather jacket, her hair pulled into a careless ponytail, Wren looked to the casual observer like a young mother out for an afternoon with her offspring, waiting for Daddy. The thought made her cringe, but she had to admit that it was perfect camouflage in this SUV-and-picket-fence town.

By the time she found a pay phone and checked in with her partner back in Manhattan, her sense of humor about the entire situation had returned, and she could—almost—laugh about it. Her partner wasn't quite so sanguine.

"Max? Stewart Maxwell? Our least favorite loon of all the loons we know?" Sergei's normally calm and crisp voice was less doubting than exasperated.

Wren kept most of her attention on the kid sitting on the curb eating an ice-cream cone with both hands and his entire face. "Yeah. That one."

"You're sure? Of course you're sure. Never mind. Damn. I'd hoped he was dead already."

There was no love lost between her partner and Max. In fact, they pretty much loathed each other.

"He was acting pretty weird," she continued, ignoring Sergei's last comment.

There was a telling silence at the other end of the phone line, and Wren leaned against the open booth and grinned despite herself. "Weird even for wizzed," she clarified.

"I don't like this," Sergei was saying, back in his office in the city. She pictured him, sitting behind his huge wooden desk, the one he wouldn't let them have sex on, even though he got a glint in his eye every time she brought it up, surrounded by paperwork and expensive artwork, and the lovely hum of the city outside the gallery's door.

"You and me both, partner," she responded. "But I finished the job, and as soon as I drop off the package, I'll be on my way home, away from whatever it was Max was so wound up about. Which should make him happy, for whatever values of happy he understands. I'm keeping low-profile until then." She paused, wondering if she should ask, then plunged in. "How are you doing?"

There was a faint hesitation on the other end of the line. "I'm fine."

Like hell he was. They had been partners too long for her not to pick up the signs. There was tension in his voice that had been there even before she dropped her little Max-shaped bombshell, and she could practically feel how tight he was holding the phone from her end of it. Something was up. Something had gotten him seriously wound. She made herself drop it, leave it alone, for now. Anything that made him that tense would probably make her unhappy, and getting a Talent upset while using the phone usually resulted in bad things for the phone. Current and electricity traveled along the same paths, and current trumped electricity every time.

"All right." She started to say something else, feeling the urge again to dig a little around the topic, then shut her mouth with a snap. If there was anything seriously wrong, he would tell her.

Or not. Wasn't as though she could do anything about whatever it was from here, anyway. "I'll see you tonight."

She hung up the phone, but despite their mutual reassurances of all-rightitude, Wren still felt uneasy. It had to be Sergei affecting her. Job was almost done. Money was in the bank. She should feel calm and satisfied, not wound like a damned spring. Please *let it be Sergei's mood affecting me...*

"Hey."

The kid looked up from his seat on the curb, his entire face covered with chocolate ice cream, those blue eyes still totally wide and innocent.

"You're a mess. Go over to that water fountain and wash your face."

"I don't have a towel," he protested.

"Use your sleeve."

The thought seemed to astonish him. Or maybe it was the fact that an adult was giving him permission to do it. Wren didn't know and honestly didn't care. The hair on the back of her neck was flat, but she still had the sense of something hinky in the air, even now. This was where they were supposed to be, when they were supposed to be there—early, even. Everything should have been fine, and yet...

She trusted her instincts. She just didn't know what to do with them, in this case.

Obeying her order, the kid walked across the street to the park, where there was a stone structure with three water fountains—one adult-sized, one kid-sized, and one down so low to the ground that Wren stared at it for a moment before realizing that it was for animals, operated by a paw-pedal on the ground.

Kid went to the kid-sized one, and seemed to be trying to puzzle it out, as though he had never used one before. Wren frowned. Okay, he was a little kid, and maybe not all that bright, but there was something seriously off about him. Almost as though he'd lived his entire life, if not in isolation then damn near close. Trusting a total stranger enough to come with her? Not knowing how to use a water fountain?

"Drop him off and walk away," she told herself sternly. "Wondering about shit, getting involved, is never a good idea. You should have learned that, if nothing else, by now."

Getting involved led to things like politics, and betrayals, and pitched battles where people—friends—died. Enough already. She had done enough. Back to the lonejack creed: self first, second and third, and the devil take the hindmost.

"Hey kid, get a move on!" she shouted. He turned his blond head, and as he did so a Frisbee came soaring out of the park, arching on a downward motion that, Wren realized, was going to collide directly with the kid's head.

Oh hell. Visions of a concussion, a hospital trip, questions about parental authority and authorization…. Without thinking, she used just a thread of current to knock the projectile off course, but by the time her touch got there, the Frisbee had already been knocked down out of the air, landing at the kid's feet.

Wren tensed. Someone else had used current on the disk to knock it away, she could feel it. *Fuck.* It might have been a Good Samaritan, looking out for a toddler. Or it could have been someone letting her know that she was under observation, for a range of possible reasons, only some of them positive. Until the kid was handed over, she was still on the job; she couldn't afford to relax, or make any dangerous assumptions.

Wren looked around as inconspicuously as she could, trying to catch anyone who might be paying the kid—or her—unwanted attention. Mothers playing with their kids, a couple of teenagers shoving each other on the sidewalk, the kids who threw the Frisbee in the first place, coming to get their toy, an old man—or maybe a woman—sitting on a bench a block away. None of them gave off any kind of vibe, good or bad. She felt hamstrung, frustrated, blind in both eyes without current to inform her other senses. Damn Max and damn caution. She opened up, just a sliver of a slice of access.

The kid reached down to pick up the Frisbee, and as he did so the skin on her arms prickled, reacting to current still in the air, crackling around the rim of the toy.

The kid had done it. The kid was Talent.

Damn it, this sort of shit was supposed to be in the briefing!

three

Wren didn't normally curse—much—but in her head she was running through every single rude and offensive word she knew, in three different languages, English, Spanish and Russian.

Goddamn briefing. Khrenoten *briefing.*

The briefing Sergei gave her before every job was based on a combination of the client's own details and—assuming that the client either lied, was an idiot, or withheld "didn't think it was important" information, all things that had proven true in the past—all the Intel Sergei himself had been able to dig up. Before Wren ever looked at a single blueprint or plotted a basic approach, she knew what she was dealing with.

So much for no damn magic in this job.

A target who was also a Talent—even if just a kid—should have been in the damn dossier. Not because it would have made the job more difficult, but because it would have made the entire damned thing that much easier! Talent generally meant a certain understanding of things, up to and including—

as she had just seen—the ability to defend yourself when attacked. That was how most Talent discovered themselves at first, reacting in a way that they or their parents or their friends know wasn't possible, and trying to do it again. It also created a bond among Talent—at least until they got to know one another.

Jesus wept, if I'd known he was a Talent, I could have called the damn kid from the edge of the yard, lured him out that way! Although if he had panicked, things could have gotten ugly. Four was too young—by about eight years—to have started any kind of real training, even if it was obvious that the kid did have enough ability to protect himself....

But who would have trained him? Incomplete dossier aside, Wren was pretty damn sure neither parent was a Talent—in fact, mommy dearest had to be damn near Null, not to have been able to set up a security cordon, or track her kid—her *stolen* kid—leaving the yard. Unless she had…unless Max had been part of it after all…

Wren was checking the street even as she crossed it, her senses working overtime. Damn it, damn Max and the paranoia he left her with; if she'd been using current she would have *known* for a fact if anyone was on their tail and could have dealt with them, and now they were blind, blind and exposed, because the kid using current could have called Christ-knew-what down on them, even if she didn't think Max would care what one kid did—but then, why had he cared about what *she* did?

Her head hurt, inside and out.

"Kid, get over here!" she barked, stopping him from picking up the Frisbee. Those innocent blue eyes blinked, as if he was about to cry, but she didn't care. She dived down into her core and grabbed the first strand she could find, letting it crawl up her arm like a boa constrictor until it flowed out, separating into a dozen, then a hundred strands, invisible to the eye but there nonetheless. ★Find,★ she told them. ★Find and bind.★

There was a black-paneled van down the street, the engine off and cold, two bodies motionless in the back. Alive and breathing regularly, she noted with relief. Sleeping off a big lunch, maybe. Two cars farther down, one of them parked illegally, engines still warm, drivers behind the wheel. She didn't have even a smidge of empathy or true telepathy—she didn't know anyone who did, actually, those skills were so rare they might be myth only—so the thoughts of those drivers were hidden from her. But the electrical signals she could pick up said that the muscles of the guys behind the wheel were slack, waiting but not tense, and didn't seem to pose a threat. They might have been part of the pickup, but she didn't think so. The agreement had said a Jeep—anything else and she had no requirement to hand the kid over.

She might not like kids, or care who had actual legal custody, but she wasn't going to hand him over to someone without the proper cues and codes. And not just because it would be bad business. Lonejacks—the freelancers and independent contractors of the *Cosa Nostradamus*—might not play together well, traditionally, but kids got breaks adults didn't. Survival of the species, if you were being blunt about it.

That motivation—that need—had sent Wren into the proverbial, nonactual dragon's lair to rescue teenagers last summer, and she had almost died because of it. This sweet-eyed kid could have—probably would have—been one of them, if he were a decade older—lost, disenfranchised, unaffiliated Talents in their teens, looking for the brass ring. She could have been one, if John Ebeneezer hadn't grabbed her ear in a candy store one day almost fifteen years ago and read her the riot act about using Talent for shoplifting. There was a reason Talent used the one-on-one mentoring system—okay, mostly it was because of hidebound issues of paranoia and security. But also because you needed to care about your student to keep them safe, and you had to care about your teacher in order to learn. This kid didn't have anyone.

Kid She risked pinging him, the current so soft as to barely reach across the street. It was easier if you had a sense of the person you were trying to reach—if you knew them personally, or had a blood-tie to them—but line of sight was almost as good.

Confusion flooded into her brain, answering at least one question—the kid was acting purely on instinct, not a scrap of training in him. And if she wasn't careful, she could send him into panic. Not good. Wren pulled back the ping, raising a careful barrier between the two of them. If he tried to reach out, he'd encounter null space, and think that he had just imagined the call. She hoped.

She calmed herself, pasted an open, reassuring expression on her face. "Come on, kid. Time to hook up with your dad."

His hand was still wet, but she took it anyway, feeling the little fingers curling into her palm. His little legs had to walk twice as fast to keep up with hers, but she resisted the urge to pick him up, just in case she suddenly needed her arms free, for whatever reason.

God, please, let this transfer go smoothly. She really just wanted to go home and have a drink.

An hour later, she was willing to forgo the drink, just to be home without a sticky little paw or pair of big, blue eyes anywhere near her. The kid was cute, but enough was enough. Where the hell was his pickup?

"Daddy was a blond, huh?"

Wren turned to face the man who had spoken.

"I beg your pardon?" She and the kid had walked a circuit of the park, and were now sitting on the swings, as per instructions. Or she was, anyway. The kid had taken one look at the swings, far too high up for his little legs, and promptly sat down in the dirt at her feet, scratching at it intently with a stick.

"His coloring and yours, they don't quite match up. So I figured Daddy was a blond." The voice was friendly, even jovial, but the face—surprisingly round—was set in grim lines. Mocha-colored skin and black walnut eyes, shaved head, full lips, and artificially whitened teeth. He did not look like a man who would ordinarily care about genetics, kids, or the combination thereof, not even to hit on their supposed momma.

"I don't know," she said. "It was dark."

Spoken, the code exchange sounded even worse than it had on paper. But the words matched. This was the handover.

"Hey, kid."

Kid looked up at her, then looked at the man, doubtfully.

"He's going to take you to your dad," she told him.

"No he's not." Kid sounded pretty damn definite about that.

The guy laughed. Not nervously, not overconfidently. It sounded as though he really was honestly amused.

Wren looked at the kid again. Talent. Untrained, possibly totally clueless, and four years old. His judgment wasn't to be trusted.

Except that it was marching with her own. Something about this guy was off. Damn it, and things had been going so well until now. For her usual values of "going well," anyway.

"Is there a problem?" the guy asked her, not sitting down on the swing beside her, but standing, not quite too close, next to the kid. His body language was calm, open, and approachable. He could be grim because he didn't like little kids. Or because he didn't like her. Or maybe he had trouble finding a parking space. Maybe he was just a grim but otherwise likable guy.

"No. No problem." The code phrases matched. Her part of the job was over. Wasn't that what she had wanted?

Grim-faced guy looked down at the target. "Marc junior, is there a problem?"

Kid looked up at the man, his expression still blandly innocent, and said "No sir. No problem." He had the slightest lisp when he said 'sir.' His hand was clammy, reaching up and gripping her hand again. Great.

"Then let's get this done," the guy said. "The kid goes with me."

Wren wasn't a precog, but she did have a significant skill in psychometry. Touching something, especially something with a lot of emotional importance, gave her the history of the object. Sometimes a little, sometimes a lot, but always accurate.

Moving swiftly, letting go of the kid's hand, she stood and shifted so that the guy had to pivot to follow her As he did so, her now-free hand darted out under his sports coat, slipping his wallet out of his back pocket even as she opened up to her current, letting the information flow into her brain.

The images were clear: Guy had bought the kid, cold hard cash. Wren didn't know if the seller was Mom or Dad but she did know that both had been approached, by either this guy or his employer, and both Mom and Dad had been willing to listen. One of them had closed the deal, probably Dad, and now Wren was being used to deliver.

Kid was right. She didn't like either one of his parents, either.

The moment her hand let go of the leather of his wallet, she was in motion, grabbing the kid up and running like hell, expecting any minute to hear the sound of a gun being cocked, feel the burning sensation of bullets entering her skin, or the shouts for her to stop, the claims of child-napping, or something else that would galvanize other people in the park against her.

Damn, what she wouldn't give to be able to Translocate right now!

The swings were just off the paved walkway, barely inside the park proper, along with one of those round whirling things, a slide, and a couple of seesaws. There was maybe a hundred yards of grass ahead of that, then a grove of trees. Too mani-cured to be really useful, but it was the only cover around.

The gunfire came just as she started to think that they were going to make it to that relative safety. The screams of parents as kids scattered off the playground made her heart jump into her throat, but she didn't stop running. The kid was a heavy weight under her arm, but she didn't dare put him down. Her legs were short but his were even shorter, and there was no way he'd be able to keep up.

A bullet zinged past her ear—from the front. "Oh, fuck this," she muttered, realizing that the guy had brought backup. Would they risk hitting the kid?

No more time to worry about maybes and mights, she decided. Nulls with guns now scared her more than the risk of Max at his worst.

Without missing a stride, she reached down with two mental hands and dragged up current, spinning it with a thought into a tent of magical energy deflecting not only bullets but eyesight from finding them.

Once, she would have needed a cantrip or spell to help focus her thoughts and direct the current. If she'd had time, she still would have used one, just to make sure her intent was clear and focused. But her ability to channel was greater than it had been then, and she didn't *need* words any more than she needed hand-waving or a wand.

She found, channeled, and created, all in one swoop. Wizzing did have its perks.

Then the cramps hit her, and she almost dropped the kid as she doubled over in agony. *Perks, my* ass. She managed not to drop Marc Jr, mainly because his arms were wrapped around her neck.

"We gotta run," a soft, serious voice piped near her ear.

"I know, kid, I know."

But she couldn't move, not for all the little hands tugging at her. The pain was too intense; it took all her energy to keep the shield up and still remain functional. They were going to have to hope that the shield was enough, that they could outlast the threat, hope that once they started attracting attention, the bad guys would give up and go away.

"Over there!" A voice shouting, alerting: bringing danger. Backup troops, she had been right, the guy wasn't alone. And nobody seemed to be willing to get involved, not that she blamed them. Gunfire sent smart people for the general direction of down and away. The only people crazy enough to get involved—heroes, professional or otherwise—were not the sort she wanted involved in this, either. Best case scenario, they'd ask to see ID, and the kid didn't have any. Nor did she have any proof he belonged with her. That would lead to…questions.

A guy came running up, gun in hand, his face red with the exertion of chasing after her, and the first guy, the contact, was close behind. They weren't giving up—they knew she was there, somewhere.

Her shield wasn't going to be enough. If these guys were aware, and trained, they might even be able to see through her shield. You could fool all of the people some of the time, but not if they knew what they were looking for. Not even she could do that. Or at least, she thought, she never had been able to *before*. …

Wren reached deep inside herself for another double handful of current. Dark blue and reds, a shimmer of orange, an etching of silver, all coiling around her hands, sliding up her shoulders, setting fire to her bones. The power that possessed her almost overwhelmed the cramps, reminding her of how good it could feel to simply let go, to let the current run through her.

Kill them.

The thought—an echo of her own voice, her own memory—shot through her like a lightning bolt, familiar and terrifying. Suddenly she was no longer in a green suburban park, but surrounded by concrete and metal, pressure slamming against her brain, her pulse racing, the weight of an entire city crushing her with the need to strike, to destroy, to kill any and everything that stood against her, that threatened her and hers.

No. No more. Never again. The thought was hers, supported by deeper, masculine voices.

She could kill. She had killed. She had been backed into a corner and struck out, and destroyed those who threatened her and hers.

The knowledge no longer devastated her. She had killed. She was not a killer. She was not. She would not allow that reaction, that desire, to rule her, to control her. She would *not*.

The current scorched her skin, but she controlled it. Controlled herself.

Survive. Do not kill. Survive. The two warring instincts—the two opposing needs—battled for primacy over her reactions.

Idiot female.

The roar of words in her head was fire and brimstone, treacle and mud, coming down over her barriers like brackish high tide over the breakers.

Max? A mixed wash of relief and fear. She had been right; her current called him, even here. He scared the hell out of her, but hell was what she needed to get rid of, right now. Better the devil in someone else than the devil in you?

Max, I…need help

Admitting that to anyone was difficult for her. Admitting it to a crazy man, a fellow lonejack who had just tried to run her off the job, who was as likely to kill them both as help them, to a wizzart who might do anything, or nothing, in response to her plea…

Let me in

Oh God. What a very, very, very bad idea that was. She had no choice. There wasn't anyone strong enough, near enough. Trust wasn't an issue in the face of survival.

She grabbed the kid more tightly, and let down her barriers just enough to let Max slide in.

Given access to her inner self, he swept up and over her like a storm front, his intent rising up before her, his intent to do what she could not. His tarry current was vile and yet beautiful, black lightning sparking and flashing inside a dark storm cloud of his awareness. Battered, barely holding herself together, somehow she fought it.

No! No killing.

His disgust at what he saw as her weakness was a physical blow in a psychic battle. Wren took it, absorbed it, did not strike back but merely—merely!—demanded that he adhere to her command.

She was not strong enough to command a wizzart, not without going there herself. Not without losing her own tenuous control. But he could allow himself to be directed, if he chose.

If he chose.

Hurt them, she suggested. *Scare the shit out of them. But don't snuff them.*

He resisted, and she pushed harder. *Harder to scare away

than to kill* she challenged him, risking the taunt to get his dander up and aimed where she needed it. *Just keep the kid safe.* She hesitated, then added *and me, too!* just in case he was unclear on the concept of "help."

Push and shove, push and shove, an endless space of a second, and then she felt his reluctant acquiescence, felt the brimstone and treacle mass sweep around until her current and his slammed against each other, their differing masses and density creating virtual thunderclaps where they came into contact. The kid shuddered, caught between them, racked by the current. She didn't dare reach down to comfort him, all of her focus on keeping Max with them and in the game plan.

Follow me A visual with the words, a thick black anvil of a storm cloud opening up, a stovepipe chimney down into the heart of the storm, swirling around her with all the power of The Alchemist's overpowered, overfull brain.

She grabbed the kid with both hands, keeping him down on the ground with her, trying to send some reassurance, and leaped into the maelstrom.

Inside, there was a second of calm, the winds howling around outside them, and then monsters leaped at her, claws black and bloody, their teeth serrated and their scales slick with oily, viscous substances she didn't want to think about. Once they would have terrified her; once they would have made her run like hell.

She had walked on the wrong side of madness since then. She had led people to their deaths, had taken lives from the undeserving, and decided who was deserving and who was not.

Her own monsters inside were just as frightening as anything Max carried. Worse, because she had birthed them.

You know nothing Max spat, even as he was laying his own current over hers, forcing them to integrate and work together. *You understand nothing.* The monsters grabbed onto her, digging their claws in, their bilious blood dripping into her veins, sending directions of what to do and how to do it directly to her core. It was a little like rape, and a lot like school, and entirely horrible. That was exactly the impact he intended, she was pretty sure. Bastard.

Her only consolation was the thought that whatever she was seeing, the guys after them were probably getting a taste of the same feedback in their unTalented skulls, under the force of Max's wild energy. She hoped that they did shit their pants, and then some.

Whatever they were getting, it was working. The bullets didn't so much miss them as decide to veer erratically away from them, zinging into trees and puffing up dirt where they hit the ground. If they could hold out…no, they couldn't. The goons might run out of bullets, and the cops *might* show up, but that wasn't going to solve the problem of getting the hell out of here.

Her brain formed the thought, but Max's finished it.

now was the only warning they got, and the ground moved under their feet, disappearing into the storm along with sound and sight, smell and taste. They did not exist, except in Max's overstimulated, current-overrun mind, his will the only thing holding them in reality.

And then the ground dropped in under their feet, their stomachs dropped in after them, and sensation returned.

Wren threw up.

So, she was oddly reassured to note, did the kid.

"Fool brat. Fool. Deserve to get herself killed."

Max was behind them, his clothing filthy, his shoulder-length white hair literally standing on end from the static he was generating.

"You're not listening. You never listen, you didn't listen and then you listen to someone else. You think that gets overlooked? Never diss crazy people, little girl. 'Specially when they crazy for you. You came back?" he spat. "You almost died. Brain's dead, there is no coming back. Back is the new front and front and center means get the hell back."

He was being typically cryptic, and she didn't have the energy to argue with him. Sprawled on the floor—tile, black-and-white squares, the smell of disinfectant in the air, she determined from the clues that the old bastard had translocated them into some bathroom somewhere—she didn't have the energy to do anything more than wipe her mouth and blink the tears from her eyes.

"You okay, kid?" she asked instead, turning her head to look at the boy.

He sat in a puddle of his own vomit, and looked at her with eyes that were huge, blue, and scared.

"No."

"Smart kid," Max observed, calming down a little, smoothing his hair down with hands that crackled with current and just made things worse. "Might actually survive to grow some hair, that one. Might. Maybe."

"I don't like him," the kid told Wren.

"Nobody does, kid," she said, hauling herself up to her knees and testing if she felt strong enough to get all the way up yet or not. "But he just saved our asses. Say thank you."

The kid looked up at Max and, politely, said "Thank you."

"Didn't do it for you. Or for you, either," he added irritably, when Wren started to say something. "Did it for…neveryou-mind. Just can't stand Nulls think they got the right to interfere in our business."

Wren shook her head, too tired to respond to that, either. Max had been a bigot when he was sane, too. The first time she had met him, Neezer had warned her…

Neezer.

For some reason, the "sense" of her old mentor was stronger than it had been in years. She had begun to forget what he looked and sounded like, over the past few years, but suddenly the memories were all there again, strong and clear. John Ebeneezer had been the one to tell her what she was, train her how to use current safely, had got her through most of high school without failing out or cracking up—and then disappeared when he felt himself start to wizz, rather than risk her safety with his madness.

She had yet to forgive him for that. Especially now, knowing what she knew.

She could almost see him, sitting behind his desk in the lab, marking papers, looking up to utter some annoyingly right bit of wisdom she was too much of a teenager to appreciate....

Wren froze the memory in midprogress, and turned to stare at Max. She sniffed at him once, twice, like a dog scenting a bone. Familiar. Familiar in a way the body never forgot, the mind never let go of.

The grizzled old wizzart took a step backward. The wrinkles around his bright eyes deepened, and his lips drew back from rotted old teeth.

"Where. Is. He?"

The words were growled out, her voice dropping a full octave, making the kid forget his own misery long enough to scoot away from both of the adults, his blue eyes wide.

She had the pleasure of seeing uncertainty and a smidge of caution flicker in Max's eyes. "I don't—"

"Max. Where. Is. He." A definite growl now, edged and hungry. She could sense the current-signature all over the old man now that she was looking, the specific flavor of someone else's magic. Someone not Max, and not her, but familiar all the same. Neezer. Neezer had been near him, had worked current around him. Recently.

In the bedrock, in those woods. Hidden, wizzed: but alive. Neezer was *alive*.

"Old man, you tell me…"

"No." He could growl better than she could. "Told you to go. Shouldn't have been there. Shouldn't have known. Won't go back, too late now. Gone. Keeps moving. Pissed at you, girl." Max glared at her, and like a sea change, or clouds moving, there was a spark of sanity in those eyes again, and his words were clear and to the point.

"He doesn't want to see you, brat. He doesn't want you to see *him*. You grok?"

Knowledge hit her like a brick to the head. Oh yes, she understood. Didn't mean she liked it. Or that she was going to accept it. "It doesn't have to be that way," she said softly.

"Yeah. It does. You escaped. Good for you, maybe. But you did it your way. Us, we are what we are. And we're dangerous, brat. You had your chance, maybe, and didn't take it. School's over. So stop looking for us."

"I wasn't looking for you, you fell over me!" she said, distracted by his comment, the way he had probably intended. Damn Max: crazy or not he knew how to play her.

"Pish." The sanity faded, and the wizzart was back. "Men's room. Pretty thing. You wanna see my dick, you're sprawled on the floor like that?"

If he was trying to shock her with being crude, he needed to work up better material than that. But the point was made: she wasn't going to get anything more out of him on anything useful, and going back to the site wasn't going to turn up Neezer—Max was right, by now he had moved on, or hidden himself again.

Besides, there was the kid to worry about. The handover had been blown, but she still had to deliver to get the final part of the payment. Assuming daddy dearest still wanted the kid. *Christ, don't borrow trouble, Valere. The client gets the goods, you're within letter of the agreement, everything's peachy. He's not a puppy you can adopt, damn it.*

"This isn't over, Max," she warned him, standing up.

"Yes," he whispered, his eyes level with her own, not blinking, not once, until her own eyes hurt. "Oh yes, it is. All over everything."

And with a manic grin and an inrushing of air that smelled like burned ozone, he was gone.

"Where he go?" the kid asked, looking around as though expecting to see Max lurking in one of the stalls.

"Hell, hopefully." She looked down at the kid, and sighed. "All right, come on, full cleanup this time. Grab some paper towels and get your disgusting self over to the sink...."

This was so not in the job description.

four

It took her almost half an hour to get the kid presentable again, including rinsing his T-shirt out and holding it under the air dryer until it was okay to put on again, if still, based on his grimace, a little damp. Wren, with more experience in being Translocated, had managed to miss her clothing when she threw up. She washed her hands and face, rinsed her mouth out and gargled with warm water, and figured that was as good as she was going to get, right then. But oh God, did she want that hot shower and a long nap. Not to mention that drink.

"Ready?"

The kid nodded, but looked less certain than he had since all this began. She didn't blame him a bit. In fact, it was a damned wonder the kid was still there, and not running for the first noncrazy adult he could find.

It made you wonder what the hell his home life was like.

Despite her concerns, nobody gave Wren or the kid a second glance when they walked out of the bathroom. She still felt horribly exposed and vulnerable, same as she did every time someone else Transloc'd her. The loss of control over your own molecules was disturbing, even without the throwing-up part. If she could do it herself with any kind of accuracy or reliability…

If you could, many things would be different. But since you only manage it under extreme stress and with massive stomach upset, let it go already!

Max had dropped them off in the men's room of a chain restaurant off Route 95 in Connecticut, just north of New York City. It was more than a hundred fifty miles from the aborted handoff site, far beyond what most Talent could manage. Showoff, Wren thought bitterly as she looked out the plate glass windows at the visible highway signs.

Then the white lettering on that sign really sank in, giving her a start. This was the client's hometown, where he lived and, more important, where he worked. Which meant that either luck had finally smiled on her, or—and this was the unpleasant thought—that Max had done some digging in her brain while he was hauling them around.

She strongly suspected the latter, and made a nasty promise to return the favor, if she ever got the chance, just on principle. She hated the thought of anyone in her brain. It made her feel…rumpled.

Despite her foul mood and worries, the smell coming from the kitchen of the restaurant made Wren salivate, and the look on the kid's face suggested he felt the same, even though he was too polite—or scared—to ask. She didn't want to stay here, though, just in case anyone—Max, or…anyone—decided to come back for them. Instead, she dragged the kid next door to a fast-food restaurant and dug into her sparse cash to get a burger and a kid's meal. They had little containers of chocolate milk, and she got three, two for him and one for her. It was milk, so that was almost like healthy food, right? She told herself to stop making like a mother; the kid wouldn't keel over from one junk food meal.

They ate as they walked, heading on instinct into the more crowded downtown area. The client, according to Sergei, was senior partner at a decent-sized law firm. Some questioning of local-looking people on the street finally got her an address. By the time their meals were done and the last of the chocolate milk slurped, Wren found the building.

"You ready?"

The kid looked less than thrilled. "I guess."

Kid of few words. And he didn't suck his thumb or throw tantrums or squirm, or anything that made her hate kids. Not bad, as kids went.

"I'm tired."

"Yeah. It's almost over now, kid."

He seemed to be thinking that through, then finally nodded and set his face into very solemn lines. "Okay."

She tossed the garbage into a nearby trash can, looked the kid over to make sure he looked as unmussed and untraumatized as possible, and then marched him into the lobby of the brick-and-chrome low-rise. There were only four companies listed: two law firms, a CPA firm, and something that didn't identify what they did but had five names on the masthead.

The directory sent them to the third floor, where the lobby was warm paneled wood and comfortable-looking chairs. If she ever needed a law firm she'd like it to look as upscale-comfortable as this one. Somehow she didn't think that they handled the kind of work she'd bring them, though; their criminal cases were probably more insider trading and whatnot. She put on an air of confident authority, best she could, and told the surprised receptionist—a large, elegant woman with glorious cornrows down her back—that there was a package for her boss. The kid seemed to know the woman, and more to the point actually like her, so Wren had no hesitation whatsoever in triggering her no-see-me lurk mode the moment he launched himself into the woman's arms. That was a handoff she felt a hell of a lot better about, yes.

Dad showed up a few minutes and a frantic page later, and while he scanned the lobby with an intent gaze, he didn't have a chance of spotting her standing in plain sight by the elevator doors. Retrievers were both born and made—you stayed at the top through training and skills, but you started out because you had the natural ability to go unnoticed. She suspected that was true for a lot of Null thieves, as well.

She studied Dad for a few minutes. Expensive suit and well-groomed hair, and he seemed really uncomfortable when the receptionist handed junior over. But the kid—despite his earlier statement—threw chubby little arms around Dad's neck without a second thought. The man's expression was one of guilty relief rather than annoyance or fear—or disappointment—and he hugged the boy back immediately, like something precious he hadn't expected to hold again. Maybe he wasn't such a shmuck after all. Maybe. Maybe he'd just made a mistake, had trusted the wrong people to do the right thing. It was a risk, but…

Take care of your son, she thought into the man's skull, making it into a pointed, current-driven command, and then went home.

The MetroNorth train southbound got her into Grand Central just in time to deal with the crush of early-evening commuters. The mass of people heading out of the city on a Thursday evening made it tough walking, but the irritation with crowds was a familiar thing, and she almost welcomed it, after the rest of the day. The subway downtown was packed as well, but she slid into the first train that came along, found a bit of wall to lean against, and was home without any significant delay.

As always when she had been away for even a day, the sensation of coming up out of the subway station and turning onto her street was akin to having someone lift a twenty-pound weight off her shoulders. *Home.*

The narrow brownstone was quiet—there were five floors, one apartment per floor, and most of her neighbors weren't the wild party-throwing type ever since the nudists on the third floor moved out and her friend Bonnie moved in…. All right, Bonnie threw parties, but they were clothed and respectable. Mostly.

Wren shook her head and shifted her backpack to the other shoulder as she climbed the stairs. Her thoughts were starting to get scattered, which was normal when a job ended. All that concentration fractured and the only thing she could think about was that strong drink, a hot shower, and going to sleep. Not necessarily in that order, either.

She lived on the top floor; normally that was a blessing in terms of privacy and air flow. Sometimes, though, that last turn of the landing was more than she could handle. She could use current to carry herself—or at least make her weight seem lighter—but the energy drain was too much to even consider. It had been a very, very long day, and that burger and chocolate milk was a long time ago.

Her apartment door was locked with multiple physical locks and a current-lock, primed with elementals, tiny creatures that gathered in electrical streams to feed. They weren't bright, but they could be trained—mostly—to respond to intrusions and report back. A quick touch indicated that none of the locks had been disturbed since she left that morning. She flipped two of the physical locks—the third was unlocked, and turning it would have secured the door against someone not aware of Wren's security quirk. The fourth lock was current-based; it only activated if a stranger tried to pass. Right now, it was keyed to five different people: two Talent—herself and Bonnie—and two Nulls—Sergei, and her mother, and one Fatae—the demon P.B., who was sitting on the sofa in her main room, bare feet propped up on the coffee table, reading the salmon-colored pages of the *Financial Times*.

She was too tired to even be surprised. How he had managed to get in without triggering the locks… He must still be using the fire escape and picking the lock on the kitchen window. Old habits died hard, apparently.

"Hey." She dropped her bag on the kitchen counter, threw her keys into the bowl, and went back out to hear why her former temporary roommate was back in her space.

"You got mail," he said, pointing a clawed paw to the pile of letters and catalogs on the coffee table by his claw-tipped toes.

"I often do," she replied drily. The furniture was new, and she had warned the four-foot-high demon what would happen if he scored claw marks in any of it. She had forgotten to warn him against shedding, but so far he seemed to be keeping his coarse white fur to himself.

"You know," she said to nobody in particular, "I have problems nobody else in this world does."

A snort was his only response: he had gone back to reading the paper. He clearly wasn't impressed with her trauma.

She went back into the kitchen and picked up the phone.

You have reached this number, I assume by intent. Leave a coherent message and I will get back to you.

"Your dossier was missing a rather important bit of information, Didier. But everything's copacetic, I'm home, I'm done, I'm going to bed. I'll talk to you tomorrow."

She hung up the phone, wishing not for the first or last time that she could use a cell phone without frying the innards seven ways from Sunday. Being able to call him from the road, and not relying on finding a working pay phone…

Might as well wish for another four inches of height, while you're at it, Valere. Besides, you as a Null? She couldn't imagine it, not even for a laugh.

Turning around in the galley space, she opened the fridge and considered the half-drunk bottle of wine—Sergei's contribution to last night's dinner—and the various beers, and instead grabbed a diet Sprite. Popping the top and slugging half of it, she went into the main room.

"You here for dinner?" she asked her uninvited guest, meaning it as a prelude to kicking him out.

"So long as you're not cooking." He snickered when she glared, then relented. "Bonnie came up and offered to cook dinner, if you got home before ten."

Bonnie, the other Talent who lived in the building, was a fabulous cook. Wren didn't cultivate a friendship with her for that—the younger woman was fun just to hang around with— but it was a much-appreciated benefit. Suddenly, staying awake a little while longer gained appeal.

yo she pinged downstairs.

A faint sense of awareness and busyness, and a tantalizing mental aroma replied.

"She's already cooking," she told the demon, sitting on the new brown-and-cream geometric pattern rug on the hardwood floor and gathering the mail onto her lap. As long as she was staying awake, might as well deal with the domestic shit. "Half an hour, we should go down."

"Gotcha." The demon didn't even bother looking up from his newspaper, turning pages with surprisingly delicate, claw-tipped paws.

What to do for dinner settled; Wren went to work organizing the pile. Catalogs were tossed, credit card bills were put to one side for paying, and anything that looked like junk mail was thrown back onto the table. One envelope looked like an invitation, and she slit it open and pulled out the card. A gallery opening. She didn't recognize the name, but that didn't mean anything—Sergei was the one in that field, not her. She didn't know from art, just what she liked. Often as not, it *wasn't* the stuff that sold well.

Because of who she was sleeping with—Sergei having reached a certain level of Impressive in the New York gallery world—she got added to the invitation lists at some of the weirdest places—and some of the toitiest, too. From the address, this one was on the upscale mark.

A few years ago she would have panicked, worried about what to wear, and then had a miserable time comparing herself to the inevitable models and high-gloss money-movers. Now... Well, she'd still worry about what to wear. Everything else got less important after you almost died a couple of times.

There was one remaining envelope, looking ominously business-like. She frowned at it, and took another slug out of the soda can. Slitting the envelope open, she removed a single sheet with a very severe-looking letterhead.

Dear Ms. Valere. We are pleased to inform you that we have acquired your building from Machi Management. In the coming year, we plan to make considerable improvements to the building with the goal of selling the units.

As a current tenant, you will of course have the first option to purchase your unit....

Wren stopped reading. She refolded the letter very carefully, placing it on the coffee table, and then went back into the kitchen and grabbed the bottle of wine out of the fridge. She didn't bother with a glass.

"Trouble?" P.B. put down the newspaper and looked at her, a worried expression in his dark red eyes. He didn't have eyebrows, just a faint ridge under the fur. She had never noticed that before, really.

"No. Not really. Sort of." She shook her head, then nodded, then shook her head again, not quite sure what she felt. Her demon's expression as he tried to follow her head motions almost made her laugh. "Maybe. My building's going condo."

The New Yorker's nightmare and dream, all in one. P.B. winced, his muzzle drawing back to show sharp white teeth and black gums in an expression you had to know meant sympathy for it to not be menacing. "Ow."

'Yeah, ow." Bonnie had to have gotten one, too. Suddenly, the offer of dinner made more sense. Bonnie was younger, with less money in the bank, and had only just moved in the year before. She was probably freaking more than a little bit over this letter.

"This has been a hell of a day, my friend," Wren said heavily. "A hell of a day. Let's go get us some home cooking. And a drink before dinner."

As expected, that proposed drink before dinner turned into two, and then more with dinner, and a late night overall, ending with human and demon staggering up the stairs trying to sing the chorus of a disreputable sea shanty in Norwegian, a language neither of them spoke—or sang—a word of.

When Wren finally crawled out of the bedroom some-where between oh God and semihuman the next morning to make coffee, there was a tall, well-built, reasonably good-looking man with a hawkish nose drinking a mug of tea at the kitchen counter.

"When'd you get here?" She knew he hadn't been here last night; the bed had been cold when she fell into it. Even drunk off her ass, she knew when Sergei was in bed with her. He was an excellent bed-warmer.

"The client was surprised that the handoff wasn't done as arranged," her partner said by way of greeting, without bother-ing to respond to her question. "And by 'surprised' I mean more than vaguely upset. You delivered the package to his *office?*"

Coffee was suddenly too much effort, if she was expected to talk coherently about business while figuring out how many scoops she had already put in. She waved a hand and muttered something vaguely in English at him, promising to return, then went to the bathroom and splashed water on her face. The re-flection in the mirror looked worse than she felt, which was saying something. Her shoulder-length brown hair was mussed and tangled, and her eyes were red-rimmed. Her skin, normally a healthy if pale color, was decidedly green.

Bonnie Torres could out-drink a demon, much less one slightly built Retriever. Someday, both demon and Retriever would remember that. Ideally, *before* the evil bitch pulled out the "after dinner, one last drink" brandy to toast the encroach-ing condo-ization of their building.

God. Condo. *Don't even think about it right now, Valere.* Her partner was waiting. He wouldn't thank her for skimping on her shower, though. Not if he needed her brains this morning.

The bathroom was old-fashioned, with a simple pedestal sink and pipes that clugged and clunked when you were waiting for hot water, but the heater did work and the pressure was fabulous, and a quick shower turned her into something closer to human.

"Client can bite me," she said, walking into the kitchen wrapped in a towel, in search of coffee. Her partner was dressed in his usual suit and tie; the suit a beautifully cut dark gray pin-stripe, the tie a nonregulation purple tie-dye. Friday morning, the gallery was closed; he must have a meeting with a new agent, or maybe a private client. Money, definitely. She took a good long look at him, just for the pleasure of it. His hair had more gray in it than even a year ago, but it was still full and swept back from a hawk's face; sharp brown eyes and an even sharper nose. She thought the nose was one of his better features. He didn't agree. "The guy who showed up had bought the kid."

That stopped the tea mug halfway to his mouth and raised a dark eyebrow. "I beg your pardon?"

She repeated herself, speaking slowly and precisely. "The guy who showed up had bought the kid. Cash on the barrel. I picked it up from him, clear and true. I don't know how much he paid, but it was a lot."

"From the father." His mouth tightened into a thin line and his entire body tensed. She reached up and patted him on one shoulder, and then shoved him gently out of the way so that she could get to the coffee maker, annoyed that he hadn't started it for her already.

If she moved, she could find a place that had a larger kitchen, with room for an actual table where people could sit down and eat meals together, maybe. That was something to think about. She could trade in the three tiny rooms at the end and maybe have a single bedroom large enough to turn around in. And a real closet? There were a lot of upsides to moving.

Maybe she could "forget" to give anyone her new address.

"Don't know," she said in response to his comment, going

up on her toes to try to snag a mug out of the cabinet. "Could be the mother—she's the one who did the initial grab, after all. Guy had contact with them both, I got that much from reading him. And Dad didn't…he didn't seem like the type. He was really glad the kid was back and safe." She had gotten details wrong before. Not often, though. Not at that level.

Sergei looked carefully at his partner's closed-off expression, then grabbed the mug for her and handed it down, not making a fuss out of his much greater height. "You picked that all up from one contact?"

"Yeah." Her voice said do-not-ask-how. He didn't. He wasn't sure he really wanted to know. He had been there for the results, when she'd been the recipient of a "battery" of current during the events of last summer, and he knew that it had changed her, changed her ability. That, combined with the pressures and stresses they were under, on a daily basis…

Admit it, to yourself if nobody else. She wizzed. She wizzed, and she came back, and she hasn't figured out what it all means yet. And neither have you.

The one thing he knew for sure was that her ability to channel current was stronger than it had been, which meant that she had to keep a tighter rein on it as well, or risk over-flowing into whatever was nearby—electronics, storm fronts, receptive humans….

Wren grabbed the sugar tin and a spoon, and placed them next to the mug, ready and waiting for when the coffee finished per-colating, and turned to face him. He knew that annoyed, sweetly inquisitive look, and braced himself for what was about to land.

"So. How was your session?"

As expected, and speaking of pressure and stress. She knew that he was seeing Doherty; she had in fact been the one to suggest, without much delicacy at all, that the therapist—as a Talent himself—would be the only person who might be able to understand Sergei's particular problem. She didn't know more than that, except that he was still going, and that was the way he wanted to keep it.

He was willing to do this, for her, but he didn't want to talk about it.

"It was fine." He gave back the do-not-ask tone and saw her bite the inside of her cheek, making her look like a chipmunk with a hangover, but she didn't press. For all of about a minute and forty seconds. Then her hand reached up into her hair, and curled a strand around her finger, sure sign she was about to say something she wasn't sure he was going to like.

Sergei felt a sigh building, and repressed it firmly. Once upon a time, he had been the senior partner, the guy with the answers, the one who had final say. After due consideration and a weighing of the pros and cons, he decided that he didn't miss those days at all.

All right, maybe a little. Sometimes. But if he never saw her finger-curl her hair ever again, it would be too soon.

"So why did you give the kid back?" he asked, not put off by her attempted change of topic, and not giving her a chance to dig further into the state of his mental or emotional health. "Isn't the guy going to sell the kid again?"

"Maybe." She didn't seem too disturbed by the fact.

"Genevieve!" He only used her given name when he was really annoyed. Or scared witless, but annoyed pretty much did the job right now. "Do you know what happens to kids who—" He stopped himself. Of course she did. More, she knew what happened to Talented kids who ended up in the wrong hands. No matter her personal opinion of kids, which was usually that they were best served braised on a bed of spinach—she would not keep from protecting the boy if she thought there was a need.

He fixed her with a Look, brows lowered, eyes narrowed, lips downturned, trying to channel his father's best "come clean now" expression. "Genevieve, what did you do?"

His father's look had worked much better on a preteen Sergei. His partner merely showed him an evil little smile and poured herself some of the coffee, yelping when a drop of it hit her rather than the pot. She shook her hand to cool it off, but her expression remained smugly satisfied. "Nothing he didn't deserve."

Good luck, you poor bastard, Sergei thought, managing to spare some sympathy for the client, whatever else he might or might not have done. Wren didn't just get even, she got *ahead*. Sergei suspected that if the guy even thought about being other than The Perfect Father for the next ten years, he would break out in a bad case of crotch-itch, or something equally attention-getting.

Since Sergei totally approved of such an action, he merely shook his head and gestured out the window at the blue sky showing. "I don't have to be at my meeting until this afternoon," he said conversationally. "You up for a walk around the duck pond?"

She wasn't fooled for even a minute, he knew, but he also knew that without distraction she would go back to sleep for the rest of the day in a classic case of post-job slump, and that usually was enough to throw her off schedule, which in turn made her cranky. Like jet lag, it was better to keep her up and moving until the evening, when she could then justifiably collapse. Plus, and he knew that she knew this, too, he wanted to be able to check out her mental state firsthand. There was something going on there, something she hadn't told him about. Something maybe more disturbing than an unexpected run-in with the Alchemist.

The name alone was enough to make him shudder. Talent was commonplace, the Fatae still unnerved him a little, but wizzarts... He had seen firsthand what even the least of them could do, had almost lost Wren to the bittersweet darkness of that madness. He would never be able to shrug it off. Never. And never the threat of a man as powerful as Stewart Maxwell.

The walk was as much for him was it as for her. He should have been there for her last night when she got home, and not left it to P.B, no matter how good the demon was at Wren-sitting. Until he was certain that everything was all right, that whatever she wasn't telling him wasn't something he needed to worry about, he didn't want to let her out of his sight again.

"Yeah," she said, obviously buying into his pretense for his sake, not hers. "Sure. I could use a good chance to get nibbled to death by rabid and unruly geese." She gestured with her coffee. "Lemme finish this, and go get dressed."

He still has trouble saying it, trouble going back to that moment.
And so, over and over again, they return to it.

"She almost died then. Worse."

"Worse?"

"There's worse than dying, and she was there, right on the
edge...."

"What happened? What put her there, on the edge?"

That was the question, wasn't it? What happened. He knows the
why, and they've figured out, mostly, the how, but...I don't know.
Not the details. But it was bad. It was...

It was hell. The memory played out behind his eyes whenever he
was too tired to hold it back: Wren splayed on the ground, her body
too still, too cold; her eyes bloodshot and staring, drained of all the
vitality that normally filled her body. She had gone in after the FocAs,
the Talent who had been trained and turned against their own people.
The Lost, they were called now. Lost, and then Retrieved.

"But that wasn't where it began. That wasn't where the
damage was done. All that came before, and then... She never
told me what happened, but I know when...when they attacked
her. Those men, those..."

"Take a breath. Hold, and now let it out, easy, the way we
talked about. She's all right."

She is all right. Except she isn't. His Wrenlet isn't a killer. He is.
He wants to be a killer again, even though they were long-dead already.
At his Zhenchenka's hands.

"The men who attacked her, who pushed her up onto the

razor's edge. They deserved to die?" *No condemnation, no offer of expiation, just the question.*

"Yes." *He has no doubt on that subject.* "But her magic should never have been used to murder."

"You feel that you failed her."

"I did fail her. And—" *The bitterness, here, and nowhere else* "— she *let* me fail her." *He still doesn't know how to deal with that.*

five

On that same morning that Sergei was dragging his partner out to decompress with the ducks, miles south from Manhattan, in a surprisingly well-known high-security building outside of D.C., other people were ignoring the glorious autumnal weather outside, trapped within four walls by professional obligations and legally sanctioned if not officially approved obsessions.

"Damn it, where was that file? Aha, there you are. Thought you could hide, did you?"

The office was reasonably sized, but badly designed and dark, despite the fluorescent light overhead. An interior space, there were no windows to bring any natural light or air in; circulation was dependent upon the old-fashioned air ducts, and an almost-as-old desk fan perched on the seat of a battered metal stool. One wall appeared to be held up by the number of black metal filing cabinets marching along it, the line broken only by a doorway. The frosted-glass-paned door was ajar, with hinges that hung in such a way as to indicate the door was rarely all the way closed. The other three walls were painted a standardized white that had seen better decades. Each of those three walls supported a whiteboard, covered in various scrawls in several different ink colors and handwriting styles, and a corkboard, filled with newspaper clippings, hand-written notes, and printed reports following half a dozen different cases.

It was an office built around and decorated by people who obsessed, and followed through, and then obsessed some more.

There were three desks crammed into the space, one for each wall, but only one figure was currently in the room.

That figure was sitting behind one of those desks, hunching forward in an expensive ergonomically correct chair, looking at the just-found file under the illumination of a battered office-issue desk lamp. In addition to the file, the lamp, a black in-box filled to the rim, and a matching plastic pen holder, the desk was covered with more reports, sheets of scrawled notes, a dozen red and black pens, and half a dozen pretzel sticks with the salt gnawed off and the remains abandoned in a pile.

A box with still-salted pretzel rods had been pushed to the side, as though the gnawer were aware of the addiction, and trying only half heartedly to break it.

The agent date-stamped a report, signed it, and filed it, then picked up a new pretzel stick and flipped through the remaining paperwork still awaiting closure.

Dismissing the pending cases, the agent got up and, current pretzel in hand, strode over to look at the nearest corkboard. The boards had the look of items tacked up in a hurry and riffled through frequently; the edges of the papers were tattered and some of the articles were faded, although the older ones had been laminated at some time in the past. But the pinholes were fresh, and the impression was of an overcrowded in-box rather than a layered archaeological dig. Things changed, progress was made, items were taken down and replaced by new ones. The newspaper clippings in the upper right corner were all from New York City papers, mostly covering crimes committed during the previous winter and spring, with the more violent and unsolved ones circled in red marker. A few of the more colorful tear sheets were from lurid magazines, proclaiming the coming of the Lord as evidenced by the glow coming down from the sky and landing in, of all places, Brooklyn, N.Y.

The tear sheets dated back to the 1970s, and some of the reports went all the way back to World War II, but the majority of them were less than two years old. It was these that the agent focused on, one well-groomed hand lifting the most recent to look below it at the one before then, silently comparing facts and observations.

A long strip of the remaining salt was taken off the pretzel rod, as buffed nails tapped the sheets in thought.

An observer would note that the reports were of a similar nature, following a track of murders and assaults, gang-related crimes and break ins. A blue and-red graph charted the rise— and the sudden decline—in those crimes over a two-year period. The chart ended on a flat line near zero, the most recent data point charted being last month.

Whatever it was causing the activity, it seemed to have ended.

The agent knew that sometimes cases were like that. You accepted the fact that you'd never get an answer, and moved on to the next, because the one thing you knew was that there would always be a next. The world was like that.

It was why there were people like them, in offices like this. To catch the ones they could, and not drive themselves crazy over the ones they couldn't.

And yet, something about this case still bugged the brain,

itched the instincts, and left questions hanging. You couldn't let those cases go.

The agent went back to the desk, dropping the pretzel stick long enough to reach for a yellow-tagged file, pick up a pen and jot down a new comment in the margin of one of the sheets. The motion held the weary but still determined air of someone who is no closer to a solution than a week before, but can't stop. It didn't matter that the search had been going on for almost a year now: if you are determined enough, the Bureau teaches, and you follow all the leads through to the end, luck will be on your side. Eventually.

A phone rang somewhere, outside the office and down the hall. Someone answered it on the third ring, and the echo of low voices carried faintly into the office and was swallowed by the shadows. The figure didn't even look up.

The annotated paper was returned to the file, and two photos were pulled out: one, of a tall, lean man in a dark suit, talking to two other men in the middle of a crowded food court. The other was of that same man, more casually dressed, in a subway car. A much shorter woman stood with him, their body language suggesting both familiarity and tension. Both photos were clearly taken without their knowledge, the angle and grainy texture suggesting a surveillance camera of some sort.

Two years ago she had heard whispers of something the higher-ups knew, of a group or organization in various American cities that the government might or might not consider a threat, a group that might or might not be causing those ups and downs in specific crimes. Of individuals who were more than human. Casual queries had gotten her stonewalled, left with the impression that this was a Secret only a few select were allowed to know.

Very few things got up the nose of an obsessive investigator like a Secret they were told they couldn't share.

Her first probe had gotten her a name, and that had led to another name, and she'd pulled enough strings to get a temporary watch put on those subjects, and who they interacted with. But the lead had faded and gone cold, and when there were no more incidents in that city, her line of investigation was cut off. Officially.

A man came to the office door, pushing it open just enough more to stick his head in. "The Old Lady wants to see us," he said.

"Uh-huh." The room's original resident didn't seem impressed with the news.

"I don't think it was a request, Chang. I think it was something like an order. As in, right now she wants to see us."

"I'll be there in a minute." Chang said, reaching for another pretzel rod, then being distracted midthought by a new possibility.

"Christ. You are trying to get yourself fired, aren't you?"

"She won't fire me. I work too cheap."

"Nothing's cheap enough for this place," the second agent said with mordant humor, then shook his head, coming into the office and looking at the papers on the desk. "Are you still working that lead? Give it up, already. I think someone's pulling your leg. All you're doing is wasting Bureau time, and you know how they feel about that."

The only response he got was the wave of one arm, middle finger extended in universal sign language. He shrugged. "Your funeral. I'll see you upstairs. Now, Chang. Seriously. The Old Lady is not in a good mood today."

The figure pushed the chair back with a squeak of wheels and a muttered curse, reaching with the right hand for one of the less-chewed pretzels, the left hand being preoccupied with writing something down. Numbers, possibly, or some sort of intricate code. The muttering was cut off as teeth slid across the length of the pretzel, harvesting the salt with the heedless competence of a beaver stripping bark.

The photographs were joined by several pencil sketches of another figure, this one much shorter and, at first glance, wearing some sort of furry costume under a trenchcoat. The only color in those sketches was the dark red used to indicate the eyes, and the comments written in navy-blue ink along the margins. Having recovered them from the pile, Chang was sorting through those now, shuffling them like some sort of static cartoon book as though hoping to see it suddenly start to move.

A phone rang, this time in the office.

"Agent Chang."

A familiar voice was on the other line; the same voice that had originally brought in the lead a year ago, off her half-joking comment about a seemingly impossible, almost supernatural event that had occurred on her watch.

He was an old friend, a trusted source, and a general pain in the ass. Chang half suspected that the other agent was right, and he was playing this out for his own twisted amusement, to see how far she'd buy into his claims of something powerful and weird just out of reach.

The thought that it might be true, that there might be a source of power—of information—out there that she might be able to tap into, to use, was the only reason she hadn't told him to take a flying leap, and his wild stories with him. But maybe it was time. There were other ways to climb the ladder, other sources she could cultivate, if she spent the time and energy…

"Either give me something useful or go the hell away," Chang said now, and this time she meant it.

Surprisingly, her source came through. "I can get you a meeting."

"Why now?" The timing seemed suspect; why now, just when she was about to give up? How had he known?

Her contact, surprisingly, answered that, too. "He wouldn't talk to you before, would have shut you down, hard. But things have changed. *If* you can convince him you're useful to *them*." A pause, and then, in a thoughtful voice that made her believe him, "I really think you two should talk. And soon."

Chang agreed to let him arrange it—as if she was going to argue?—and hung up the phone. Was it more of his game? Or was the situation, as he suggested, really reaching a point where the contact—one of these alleged supernaturals—might welcome a Federal ally?

Suddenly recalling the Old Lady's summons, Chang swore, then grabbed a thick file out of the in-box perched precariously on the edge of the desk and headed out the door, forgetting to turn off either the desk or overhead lights before heading upstairs. Despite her coworker's jokes, she wasn't obsessed enough to forget to handle the current caseload before going off on a wild-goose chase, no matter how interesting the goose might look.

six

Given her druthers, Wren Valere would prefer to spend her Saturday morning lazing around on the sofa with hot, quality coffee and fresh bagels, a *New York Times,* and absolutely nothing to do and nowhere to go except maybe the gym, if she felt like being good and dutiful.

Wren Valere did *not* want to spend her morning getting dressed up and going across the river to New Jersey. Wren rarely wanted to go to Jersey, except to meet with her mother, who still lived there in the town Wren had grown up in, although not—thanks to Wren's urgings—in the same crappy place Wren had grown up in. One of the benefits of being reasonably successful was that she had convinced her mother to move to a much nicer condo several years before.

"Over there. That building." She pointed, and they stepped off the curb in almost perfect physical accord.

Given her druthers, Wren would definitely never have spent her morning getting dressed up and going anywhere near a Tri-

Com meeting, in Jersey or anywhere else for that matter. But Sergei had suggested it, reluctantly bringing up the possibility during the postjob rundown that recent events were something that the Tri-Com should know about. Despite her initial, immediate, rather strong response, he was right. Damn it.

No, she absolutely did not want to be walking across the street, heading toward the second-to-last-people in the world she ever wanted to talk to again. But she would do it. Because she had stuff that needed dealing with, and that's what the Tri-Com was all about—taking care of loose ends and undealt-with problems.

Despite a long history of not playing well with each other, the humans and Fatae of the *Cosa Nostradamus* in the New York area had finally gotten their act together during the recent Troubles. Out of that had come the Truce Board, a joint program of street guards and organized information-sharing, a way to protect themselves from the Silence-funded human vigilantes who wanted them out of the city—on cold slabs, if possible.

The vigilantes had lost. So had Wren. Lost friends, lost faith, lost her way…and then gotten it all back, if shattered into a pile of bits and pieces. When the dust and blood had been cleared away, all she had wanted was to enjoy life again, work and love and figure out how all the pieces fit back together. She knew everything was stitched together like Frankenstein's monster, but she didn't know how well those stitches would hold, if she put too much weight on them. She didn't want to find out the hard way, either. So, walking delicate and not getting heavy in deed or thought, if she could help it. Not yet.

Meanwhile, the Truce Board had also collapsed in the messy, finger-pointing aftermath, and the re-cobbled-together remains dissolved soon after she'd Retrieved the Lost from the Silence's distinctly unpaternal hold. But when life came back to what passed for normal, some of the lessons they learned in the process sank in, and enough lonejacks remembered the benefits of hanging together to try and keep those lessons alive.

Tri-Com—the Trilaterial Communications Group—was the result, created to facilitate the flow of communications between the Fatae breeds, the human Talent, and the human Null community. Direct quote. A neat trick, that, considering that most Nulls didn't know that either the Fatae or Talent existed. But considering the rather high-profile and public— and messy—events during the Troubles, enough people who did know had started to get nervous. "Head small problems off now, and we have fewer nasty problems later," Bart, one of the leaders of the Truce Board had said, when he told her what they were planning, and he was entirely correct. After Burning Bridge, the entire *Cosa* had nothing but distrust for any and all Nulls, even ones they had known for years, even members of their own flesh-and-blood families. Even Sergei, who had done more for them than most.

That might have become a fatal rift, doing the work of the Silence after the fact—except that during the last of the Trouble, the night now just referred to as Blackout, Nulls had gathered to protect the Talent within their ranks, most notably the firefighters at the Plank Street station. The smoke-eaters there had not only defended their Talent coworker, they had become a rallying point for the counterstrike, giving everything they had—and it was considerable—to help save the day. Or, in that particular case, the night. Bringing outsiders in had been a risk, but one she approved of—so long as they were careful about who they brought in. So far, brains prevailed, and rather than politicians, the Nulls chosen were taken from the working levels of the city—firefighters, sanitation workers, social workers. People who would actually be on the front lines, if anything happened again.

Wren herself had come out with a particular fondness for New York City's Bravest, as it was one of their trucks that had gotten Sergei and P.B. to her in time to keep her alive when the Silence and overrush combined to take her down. That fondness didn't mean she wanted to get involved again, though, no matter how good an idea this new oversight board or whatever was. She had paid her dues, damn it. So when Bart came to her with his new idea earlier that year, Wren had wished them Godspeed, and beat feet out of the room before they could "suggest" that she take part in the new organization.

They had respected her wishes; not once since then had they called, officially. The fact that she hadn't consulted or even considered any of the major players when she went after the Silence probably had a lot to do with that; some noses were still out of joint at being ignored. Unofficially, Bart sometimes called to see if she wanted to meet for coffee, and Wren had gone, a time or two. They talked about books and movies, bitched about New York City politics and the weather, and never once, not once, talked shop, or about any of the people they had lost in those days.

She would have been very happy to keep it that way. Unfortunately, that little walk in the park yesterday—and the discussion she and Sergei had about the job—now drove her, oh so reluctantly, to make a report. In person, because that was how lonejacks did things. You looked people in the eye, and lied to their faces.

"Stop shaking. They're not going to rope you into anything."

That reassurance would have been more reassuring if Sergei had sounded as if he believed it. They both had very clear memories of how they both had gotten roped into things before, by some of the same people. Things that had almost gotten them both killed.

"Go in, give report, get out." Wren shifted, thankful that at least the Tri-Com didn't have any kind of dress code. Bad enough she had to get dressed, hell if she had to actually wear a skirt and heels, as you did to get in the front door of the much more formal—and tight-assed—Council. Jeans and a dark brown pullover sweater, and clunky hiking boots that made comfortable, clunky noises on the hardwood floor made her feel slightly better about the whole deal.

What made her feel even better than that was the fact that, despite the clunky boots and her own not inconsiderable notoriety within some circles, people in the building were saying hello to Sergei and ignoring her—almost as though they couldn't see her standing right there.

Which, in point of magic, they couldn't. She grinned, feeling the current hum quietly under her skin, making her slide from people's sight without any conscious effort. After a lifetime of walking in shadows, it had made her deeply uneasy when suddenly she had been front and center and being noticed during the Troubles. This was better. This was much, much better.

So too was the hand Sergei had slipped into her own as they entered the building, palm to palm, fingers twined together. His hand was firm without being hard, calloused but not rough, dry and warm; the hand of a man who could turn that hand to just about anything he needed to do.

The hand of a man who was there, totally and without hesitation.

They'd been through rough times, the past few years: moving from business partners to lovers, with the added complications of divided loyalties and a war coming between them. But that was in the past. They'd survived, in all the ways that mattered. The only thing they still had to deal with was Sergei's kink about current-touch during sex.

It was her fault. She knew that, even if he was in denial. She had started grounding in him as an emergency measure, during some jobs that had gotten a little squirrelly and she'd pulled too much current, and neither of them had thought much of it. They had discovered, purely by chance, that it enhanced the sexual experience for him, when she let some of her current ground in him during orgasm, as well. In another Talent, that wouldn't have been a problem. But Sergei was a Null, which meant that the current was doing damage to his internal organs.

The thing was, it turned out not to be just a kink. It was an addiction for him, that pain-pleasure thing. Thankfully, it seemed to start and stop with her, and specifically during sex. She didn't have to worry about him being out alone among other Talent, or being on a job with her. But it was putting a serious damper on the physical side of their relationship, and that meant that the emotional side was hurting, too.

He couldn't stop asking, and she couldn't always resist. But not having sex wasn't a solution either of them was happy about.

Still. He was here. Holding her hand. It was sappy enough to make you sick.

She gave his fingers a squeeze, and then reached out with her other hand to push open the door to the conference room.

The Tri-Com headquarters was actually a surprisingly relaxing place; Sergei was impressed. Unlike his former employers, the late, unlamented Silence, the Tri-Com had no budget at all to speak of, and was renting the first floor of an undistinguished office building across the river in Jersey City on a middling-to-respectable block. The space was filled with basic metal and pressboard office furniture that could have come from any rent-a-desk store. Despite that, the feel of the office itself was homey and welcoming. Once you got past the generic lobby, the walls were painted a golden cream, the lights set to daylight-neutral, and there were huge potted plants in every alcove, leaves swaying gently under the air vents.

The receptionist checked their names against a printed sheet of paper, and sent them on to where, she informed them, "The pooh-bahs were waiting."

"Pooh-bahs?" Sergei mouthed, looking at his partner, who merely shrugged.

When they reached their destination at the end of the hallway, the expected conference room decor had been replaced by a much more domestic look, complete with sofas instead of a traditional table and chairs, and a small water feature that filled the background with gentle, soothing noises.

Someone had paid attention to the details.

Part of him was immediately alert and suspicious, looking for the hook. The other part felt the incipient stress headache fade away, and was grateful.

This was not an enemy. This was not an interrogation. There was no danger here, except what might—and might not—come out of what Wren had to report, and that danger was not to them. He hoped.

Bart was there to meet them, along with Rorani, a grizzled otter of a Talent named Eddie whom Sergei vaguely remembered meeting at some point, and a tall black woman he didn't recognize, who was introduced merely as Jane. Rorani turned from the window and smiled at Wren and Sergei both, the smile reflecting in her bark-brown eyes and the movements of her willowy body. It was, he realized, good to see the dryad again, like discovering a favorite aunt would be at a family gathering you were dreading. It might still be bad, but you had someone you could trust to keep calm and listen instead of just reacting.

He had come a long way from the Fataephobic Silence operative he had once been, yes.

"I'm glad you were able to come down," Bart said, once the greetings were done. Unlike everyone else in the building until now, the stocky lonejack's gaze went directly to Wren. Bart was a bastard, but he was a straightforward, straight-talking bastard, and he didn't waste anyone's time. Sergei didn't like the guy— a building contractor when he wasn't handing *Cosa* matters— but he'd do business with him any day. Bart didn't deal in bullshit, and he had stood with Wren on the Bridge, coming out of that battle with a shattered leg that would never fully support his weight again, requiring him to wear a metal brace, and use a cane. That hadn't changed his hard-ass persona a bit, though. "You said you had something important to tell us, and for you to actually call means it actually is important, unlike the rest of these two-bit wusses who want us to wipe the snot out of their noses. So, tell."

Wren hesitated, visibly steeled herself, and then took the plunge. "Two things, actually. One that's just an FYI, and one that's…for you to deal with, I guess. Because I can't."

Bart took a seat, and waved them to a spot on the sofa. Wren sat down with her legs curled up underneath her, clunky boots and all. In someone else that might have indicated comfort, but Sergei could read Wren-sign. She wasn't relaxed, but curled to spring, if needed. He understood: these people had that effect on him, as well. Even Rorani.

"So." His partner kept speaking, keeping everyone's attention on her so he was able to observe, unobserved. "First thing first. I ran into the Alchemist yesterday."

She said it so casually that, even braced for something of import, it took a few seconds for the meaning to hit them. When it did, the reaction was…satisfying.

"You did what?" Rorani leaned forward as though struck by a heavy wind, her face creasing in worry, her branches—her arms, he reminded himself—coming forward in the urge to hug Wren to her in protection.

Bart was more practical. "Is anything in the area still left standing?"

Eddie just let out a pent-up breath in a whoosh of air, as if he'd been sucker punched. Or was deeply impressed.

The black woman was the only one to ask "Who the hell is the Alchemist?" That confirmed to Sergei that she was, like him, a Null. Even he, reasonably plugged into the *Cosa Nostradamus*, would never have heard of the Alchemist if it hadn't been for Wren's previous run-ins with him—one of which he had the misfortune of witnessing.

The memory of her almost going over the edge of the cliff, him too far away to do anything useful, would give him nightmares even in his grave.

"I did, yes there is, and he is one of our elder wizzarts," Wren said calmly to all three questions, as though that weren't a damned mouthful and a half. "We managed to muddle through without damage to anyone, actually." She had clearly thought about how much to tell them—Sergei wasn't even sure that she had told *him* everything. He wasn't okay with that, but he knew better than to push. Right now. They weren't pushing each other on anything, right now. There would be time later to coax the details, and see how much damage had actually been inflicted. "I was on a job, and he warned me off the site. I think…" She was clearly filtering what she would and would not tell them, but nobody was about to challenge her. "I think that he's claimed that area."

"Where?" Bart asked, and she told him. He nodded, making a note on a small pad of paper. That area would become off-limits not by order—the Tri-Com had no authority to issue such an order, even if the lonejacks as a whole would honor it—but out of courtesy and common sense.

The rule in the *Cosa,* as far as Sergei had been able to learn, was "live and let live" when it came to wizzarts, with a large dollop of "and stay the hell out of their way." Care for them when you can—the more organized and financially able Mage Council actually had halfway homes for those still able to function in society—and avoid pissing them off in every other way. Like bears and cougars wandering suburbia, your only other option was to shoot them, and unlike bears and cougars, they could and would shoot back faster, with higher-powered weapons.

"One wizzart, however disturbing, isn't enough to get you down here," Rory said, settling herself on the sofa next to Wren. Her fingers were long and gnarled, but gentle on Wren's arm. The dryad was one of the oldest Fatae in the city—she might even be one of the oldest in the country. Her oak had been growing when Central Park was planned around it, and she could rattle off the histories of every Fatae clan known to the *Cosa.* It occurred to him to wonder if Wren had specifically requested that she be here today, for this. Not for the news about Max, but what she was really here for.

Wren licked her lips, and slanted a glance sideways toward Sergei. He nodded, but didn't say anything. This was her call, but he would support her, either way. They had the advantage in that it was unlikely the client would ever discover what she had done. Unlikely, but not impossible. And even if they never found out, she would always know that confidence had been broken.

Therefore, her choice.

"No. It's not. There was a child." She carefully didn't say why there was a child, or how she knew about it. Nobody asked. "Young, about four. Parents were Null—highly probable the mother, definitely the father." She recited the facts mechanically, as though someone else had told her them a long time ago. "No history of Talent in either family tree, up to four generations back." They had checked, using Bonnie's mentor, a man with some standing and even more pull in the Council, late last night. Wren leaned back and delivered the money shot. "This kid? He's Talent."

"That's not possible," Jane said. Sergei was obscurely pleased that her reaction was the same as his own, on first hearing it.

"Except it was." Wren stared off into the distance, carefully not looking at anyone. "Believe me, it was."

Nobody in the room had any desire to doubt her certainty. Talent appeared unexpectedly, occasionally. Very occasionally. Mostly, there was trace within two generations, even if the grandparent or great-uncle wasn't ever identified as such. To come out of nowhere, strong enough to be recognized at such a young age, was…improbable, if not impossible.

"The child was adopted?" Rory suggested. Sergei could see the wheels churning in her ancient memory, trying to come up with an explanation.

"Not unless they hid it, with the complicity of the hospital staff." Sergei had a copy of the birth certificate in his possession, along with some other useful and official papers. Wren might not worry about the legalities, but if she were transporting a minor across state lines, he felt better knowing that she had the permission and blessing of the actual custodial parent, even if they obviously had no written contract or agreement for the job.

"Wrong parent?" Bart countered.

Wren grinned tightly, her gaze landing on him. "Nicely put. But no. Custody battle, DNA tests were ordered, came back positive." She hadn't known that at the time, Sergei had seen no reason to put it in the initial briefing, and he was right, at the time it had no bearing on the actual job. Still didn't. "Kid is blood offspring of two non-Talent, in a family tree of non-Talent, and yet is Talent. Possibly a pretty strong Talent, to be showing this early, without any training or examples…"

"And you are telling us this why?" Jane, the newcomer asked that. Her expression was intrigued but still doubting. She might not understand the importance of what Wren was saying. No reason she should, if she was Null, not tied into the *Cosa Nostradamus*. Yet. She would learn. You had no choice, when you got involved with all this. That he knew from personal experience.

Wren gave an eloquent shrug, as though to say that if this woman couldn't figure out the implications, it wasn't Wren's problem. "Maybe because the kid's caught in a custody battle, and the person who was set up to receive the kid for the custodial parent did not have the boy's best interests at heart." She paused to let that sink in a little.

"It's possible that one or the other of the parents just trusted the wrong person with what their little boy could do—for money or mistake, I don't know—but leaving a cute little boy unwatched, with parents like that… It's not a thought I'm comfortable with. Are you?"

The woman had the grace to look embarrassed.

"I took care of it this time, and I think daddy dearest learned his lesson, but someday this kid might need us." The "us" was clearly meant to mean not the Tri-Com, but the *Cosa*. "It's not enough to contact social services and file a complaint that might or might not be followed up on. He's a Talent. We've lost so many, it seems a crime to let this one slip through our fingers just because he wasn't expected or identified."

Because we need to replace the ones we lost. The ones who died. She was clearly thinking it, and they were clearly thinking it, even Sergei thought it, but nobody said it. Some scars were still too raw.

"This is the name of the custodial parent," she said, handing them a slip of paper, folded over. Printed off a printer in a Kinko's down the street, so there was no handwriting possible to trace, no home-office machine to track down. If anyone let anything slip, there was nothing to bring the trail back to her. Nothing to prove—or support—the suggestion that The Wren might have broken contract with a client. His suggestion: still looking out for the business side. It was still what he did best.

"Keep an eye on the kid," she went on. "He'll be safe enough for now—like I said, I made sure of that. But he's going to need training. Plus, the custody battle might get ugly again, and I can't protect him from that. You can."

And that was the crux of it, and why Wren—and he, yes— had agreed that it was worth breaking client confidentiality. Kids were known to be stupid. Talent just upped the odds of that stupidity being dangerous. That's why they had the mentorship program. Like fostering, it put the onus of training on someone who wasn't a parent, and could be trusted to be brutal as and if needed.

More important to Sergei's way of thinking was putting the Tri-Com on alert in case whatever *push* Wren had put on the dad failed. Kids weren't the only ones who could be stupid, Talent or not, and Sergei had less faith in human nature than his partner did. Or maybe had had more, and it was all bad.

"We could always take out the parents, and bring the kid in," Bart said thoughtfully, and ducked just as Rorani's slender arm swung at his head. Despite the grin on the man's face, Sergei was pretty sure the Talent hadn't been joking. From the glare Jane sent him, she didn't think he had been, either.

Wren just looked quiet and thoughtful, which was never a good sign, and Sergei was reminded, suddenly, that she had been raised by a single parent with no idea about Talent or the

Cosa, as well. That she had not known what she was until she was a teenager, and her mentor took her under his wing.

There were a few more exchanges, and the meeting was over. Rorani, ignoring Bart, reached over and hugged Wren, her brown lips whispering something in her ear. His partner smiled a little, and shook her head, but seemed pleased.

And then they were out, down the hallway and onto the street, and Wren let out a heavy sigh, the tension even he hadn't been able to see in her flowing out into the evening air.

"You're all right with this?" he asked. The kid was taken care of, no longer her responsibility, which was what she had wanted, and Max's territory would be respected. She'd done everything possible, but something was still bothering her and he didn't know what it was, or how to kill it for her.

"Yeah. Yeah. It's…" Her voice strengthened. "I want ice cream."

He nodded gravely, and tucked her hand onto the crook of his arm, escorting her across the street toward a strip mall with a Baskin Robbins sign. One of the things he was learning in therapy was how to not control everything, how to let go and see what the moment brought.

At the moment, it seemed to be bringing ice cream.

She broke the news of what else was on her mind over chocolate-chocolate-mint chip.

"Building's going condo. Do I have enough in the bank to cover it?"

Sergei put his legs out in front of him, under the café-style table outside the ice-cream shop, and licked a drip of ice cream off his spoon. He was, she told him, a philistine for insisting on cup instead of cone. He claimed a long-ago traumatic incident with a dog and a double scoop; she claimed he was afraid of going to a meeting with ice-cream stains on his tie.

A building conversion wasn't enough to put that faraway look in her eyes. Not when it was something she'd thought of, before. But she knew him: he'd let it run that way for a while. Until she was ready to tell him everything.

"You can't just check your own accounts?"

That wasn't fair. Yes, she could, but that would involve either finding time to stop by the bank when it was open, which she never could manage to do, or booting up her computer and checking online. The latter might work for the majority of the population, but Talent had this tendency to kill electronics they came into extended contact with, and while she had surge-protected her computer every way she could think of and a few others besides, her increased flow made even that risky. It was much easier to ask her business partner.

She licked her own cone, and glared at him over the top of it. Bastard laughed.

"All right," he said. "The market's recovered from the last tanking, but there are still a lot of open units available at the high end"—he should know, since he lived in one—"which means that it will be tough for them to get top dollar. Assuming nothing changes drastically, you should be able to swing it with a minimal mortgage, if you choose to stay there."

Wren wasn't sure what made her tense more, the "assuming nothing changes drastically" or the casual "if you choose to stay."

"That was always the plan. It's why I've been shoving money into the account instead of buying new shoes every month or taking cabs everywhere."

"I know." He was still casual. Too casual. Her eyes narrowed and her gaze tightened on his face. "But things have changed a little since then."

Oh. *Oh.*

"Are we about to have That Discussion?" She made sure that he could hear the capital letters in her words.

"That Discussion?" His damned manicured eyebrow raised in the way she was constantly trying to imitate, without success, and his pale brown eyes widened in innocence.

"The 'your apartment or mine' discussion," she clarified, trying to decide if she should be really annoyed or not.

He shrugged, going back to his ice cream. "Eventually, it's going to have to be dealt with," he said calmly. "Either when your lease came up for renewal, or now. I already own my place."

The fact that he was right didn't make her stomach feel any less twitchy. She'd rather face down a hellhound than have That Discussion.

"You really think that we're in any shape whatsoever to live together, 24-7?"

Sergei ate another spoonful of his ice cream.

"No."

Wren was bemused to discover she was disappointed by his assessment, despite the fact that she agreed with it.

"Ignoring the other things we're still working out…"

Like ignoring a cockroach in the bathtub; it could be done, but you didn't enjoy the shower.

"I like my space," he went on. "You like yours. You like quiet and I'm playing music most of the day. You're tolerant. I would throw P.B. out a window the first time he mooched the prime rib."

She laughed, the way he intended her to do.

"And yet, you raise the question—" she started to say, when he interrupted her.

"Because we do need to discuss it. We need to discuss a lot of things we've shoved under the table until there was time. And there's time, now."

He was right. Damn him. There were some things they could avoid until a better time, and some things…some things, the time was now.

Then he took the pressure off as suddenly as he had applied it. "Building conversions don't happen overnight. We don't have to make any decisions right now. I haven't thought this through, anyway, and neither have you. So eat your ice cream before it drips down your chin."

Part of That Discussion included progress on his therapy, she suspected. He wasn't ready for that, either. But closer. They were getting closer. It was good.

She wiped her face with the back of her free hand, and took an icy bite that sent shock waves through her teeth. *Ow.*

"What kind of *push* did you put on the guy, to protect the kid against daddy undearest changing his mind?" he asked, switching the topic back while she was recovering from the brain freeze. "In a purely professional, cover-our-asses-if-needed way of requesting."

She grinned again, remembering. "Dad didn't seem like a bad guy, and was genuinely glad to see the kid. So I figured if he had been the one to sell off the kid, he hadn't done anything out of malice but maybe stupidity or scaredyness."

"That's not a word."

"It is now. Anyway, I figured if he was scared it was because he suspected what the kid could do and didn't know what it was, and if it was he was stupid it was just 'cause he hadn't had the chance to learn better."

"Wren. Point?"

He ruined all the fun, sometimes. "I put a spell on him. Not anything harsh," she rushed to reassure her partner. "Sort of the type Neezer used to use." Just the mention of his name made her flinch inwardly, but she kept it all inside. "Like Neezer used to suggest to a kid that he could too pass the test, if he only studied? I suggested that the kid would be useful to have around, as he grew into his skills. That maybe keeping him home and safe was in Dad's and kid's best interests."

She could see her partner relax a little at that. Her mentor had been an amazingly kind and moral man—far more so than either of them ended up being—so anything he did passed the uh-oh test.

The truth wasn't quite so clean; that was what Wren had *intended* to do, but as seemed to happen more and more often, her current-use had more oomph than expected. Instead of a suggestion, she had planted a compulsion.

Neezer would *not* have approved.

She was spared further questioning by the sound of her partner's cell phone ringing. He put his almost-empty cup down on the table and, with an apologetic shrug in her direction, removed the phone from his pocket. Normally he turned the electronics off when he was going to be around Talent—either he had turned it back on after their meeting without her noticing, or he was slipping and had forgotten to turn it off in the first place. The first was bad on her; the second was bad on him.

"Didier," he said crisply, then his entire body language changed. Alerted, Wren sat up in her own chair, dropping her cone ice-cream down into his cup for possible fast movement.

"What happened? Slow down. Damn it, man, in English, I don't speak German! Dutch, whatever."

He reached out and patted her on the shoulder; whatever was happening on the other end of the phone wasn't going to require immediate fight-or-flight, apparently.

"Right, yeah, she's with me. You're at her apartment? All right. We'll meet you there."

P.B. Something had happened to P.B. Something had happened to P.B. and the demon had called Sergei, not her.

Kid and condo crisis both forgotten, Wren had tossed the remaining ice cream into the trash, grabbed her bag, and was ready to go before Sergei had the chance to snap the cell phone closed and put it back into his pocket.

"He's okay," he said, reassuring her with words and a hand back on her shoulder. "No blood, no fire. It's only that something's gotten him spooked."

She wasn't reassured, and from the tightness around his eyes and mouth, neither was Sergei, despite his words. The demon was not the type to spook easily; even when she was down and bleeding, he was the one who kept calm and focused. More, he dealt with his own shit; he did not bring it to someone else.

He was bringing it, now. Specifically, he was bringing it to *Sergei*, a Null. A Null with experience in mayhem and bloodshed.

They took a cab home back into the city, and damn the expense.

The very first session, months ago, the digging had begun.

"You've been together for a very long time."

Understatement. He had met her when he was on his last assignment for the Silence, already negotiating his exit. Someone in the organization had taken that exit badly, and tampered with his car with deadly intent.

She, still a teenager, merely a bystander, had used current to save his ass, not knowing anything other than he was a stranger in danger. He had tumbled out of the wrecked car headfirst, dazed and confused, and seen her, and...and he had seen potential dollar signs of a profitable partnership. Nothing more. Not for a few years, anyway.

"Not really. Not that way. We were partners first, before the sex."

"That doesn't count as being together? Was that relationship any less intense for being platonic?"

A valid point, and one he sometimes forgot, now. "No. If I screwed something up, she could die, or get caught. That made for intensity. She had to trust me entirely."

"And she did."

"She did. She doesn't any more."

"Are you sure about that?" *A pause, to let the question float between them.* "She let you back in, opened the door back to her life, to the *Cosa.* That would seem to indicate at least a certain level of trust, wouldn't it?"

It was a trick question. He knew it was. He just couldn't figure out what the trick was.

seven

P.B. might have been rattled, according to Sergei, but he was still P.B.—always hungry. By the time they arrived, the cabbie having taken one look at Wren's face and taken the "I know you're locals" route directly from point A to point B without arguing about the cost of going through the Tunnel, the entire apartment smelled of Chinese spices and the nutty fragrance of brown rice: the demon had taken the time to stop by Noodles and order dinner to go. Even after the ice cream, and with her stomach tied in knots from nerves, the moment the smells hit Wren's taste buds, she was salivating. She supposed everyone had their own addiction. Hers was Chinese food. Especially good Chinese food, and Noodles was the best in town.

P.B. knew that it was her weakness. She was immediately suspicious and expecting the worst from him.

"I told them to put it on your tab," the demon said, busily unpacking cartons onto plates.

"You have a tab?" Sergei asked her, both eyebrows rising in astonishment.

"I guess I do now," she said, and then turned to P.B., the difference between her six-foot-plus partner and the four-foot demon giving her a crick in her neck once again. She supposed someone better at interrogation or someone more sympathetic would ease into the conversation, but she wasn't either of those people. "Demon. What's going on? You okay? What's wrong?" Oh God, she sounded like her mother. The urge to run her hands over his body just as you'd examine a dog for injuries was checked, mainly because she wasn't sure she'd pull back an intact hand if she tried it.

"Not yet." The demon wasn't a chattermouth at the best of times, and right now, despite his earlier urgency on the phone with Sergei, he seemed particularly reluctant to speak. Was he regretting saying anything? Or was what he had to say that bad, or that painful? Wren watched him move food to the plates, not missing the way his thick white fur, normally carefully washed and groomed, looked matted and disheveled in places, or the fact that one claw on his left hand was splintered, as though he had been chewing on it.

Sergei was right, the demon had been spooked. And now he was trying to butter her up for something. That was very much not normal; P.B. didn't butter up any more than she did. When he did have something to say, he was as blunt in attack as the animal he got his nickname from.

"Food first," P.B. said, noticing her evaluation and turning away from it, physically and emotionally. "Crisis later."

That, at least, was classic P.B. He and her mother had a lot in common, not that she would ever tell either one of them that.

You're keeping stuff to yourself, too. Put down that stone and step away from the glass house, Valere.

The food dishes were quickly spread out on the low coffee table in the main room, the rice dumped into one large bowl and placed in the middle so everyone could reach it. Wren and the demon seated themselves cross-legged by the table, while Sergei, out of deference to his much longer legs, pulled over the dark gray cloth hassock and sat on that. He should have looked foolish, balancing a plate on one knee and chopsticks in his hand, dressed in slacks and a shirt and tie, but he didn't. She wasn't sure her partner could ever look foolish, and she had seen him in conditions that would have devastated more flappable mortals.

Kung pao chicken for her, shrimp in garlic sauce for P.B., and hot ginger beef for Sergei. Not that anyone's chopsticks stayed on their own plates: Chinese food got shared around, in this apartment.

Wren moved the rice toward her to scoop up the last bit, and was struck by the sight of three small objects that had been half-hidden behind the bowl. It shouldn't have been a surprise; where there was Chinese food, there were fortune cookies. And when the food came from Noodles, then the fortune cookies were impossible to avoid. She knew, she had tried: the Seer had merely hunted her down on a street corner and handed her the cookie.

She wondered if P.B. had gone to Noodles out of habit, if he really was trying to butter her up, or if he was actually looking for specific guidance via fortune cookie. It wouldn't be like him, but then again, neither was this.

"I got a letter today," P.B. said finally, and placed the item in question on the table. Wren's hands were occupied with her chopsticks, so it was Sergei, who was finished eating, who put down his plate and picked up the letter. It was in a heavy-looking, cream-colored envelope, the kind that fancy stationery stores sell, not the five-hundred-a-box kind Wren used.

There were a couple of interesting-looking stamps on it, not ones she recognized, and it was battered enough to have come through the Pony Express, not modern airmail.

Sergei reached into his shirt pocket and pulled out his glasses, settling them on his nose in order to read better, and investigated the writing on the front of the envelope. Both eyebrows went up again, and he looked at P.B.

"Faas…Faasradberaht?"

"Yes." The demon didn't sound thrilled. "That really is my name."

Wren giggled, despite the apparent seriousness of the moment. She had been the one to give the demon his nickname, years back. They had only just met, in less than auspicious circumstances, outside a church she was casing for a job. A Null, coming out of the rectory and catching sight of the short, white-furred, black-clawed, red-eyed entity, had screeched out to whomever might be listening, "Dear God, it's a demon!" Wren, being the only person actually within listening distance at the time, had been unable to resist, retorting "no, it's a damned polar bear."

The name stuck, and for cause: his given name was unpronounceable, in her opinion, no matter the good-faith effort her partner made with it.

But the fact that it was used on this letter meant that whoever had sent it had known him for a long time, and not recently, because nobody in Manhattan had used anything other than "P.B." in over a decade now, if they'd ever even heard another name.

As far as she knew, anyway. P.B. might qualify as her best friend, and they might be bonded now in a way she didn't quite understand—and neither, she suspected, did he—but he didn't tell her everything, not by a long shot.

Sergei opened the envelope and pulled out a single sheet the same weight and color as the envelope. Real stationery, the kind you used for a thank-you note, or a love letter. Somehow, Wren didn't think it was either of those things. Although, again, he didn't tell her everything.

"It's...what language is this?" Sergei asked. "It looks like German, but it's not—Dutch?"

"Yes. Mostly."

That must have been what P.B. had been speaking before, on the phone when Sergei had to remind him to use English. She had always known that P.B. was an immigrant, although one that had arrived on American shores long before she had been born. She hadn't asked much about his life before they met, and he had volunteered little.

Clearly they were about to learn more. And it wasn't going to be good.

P.B. took the letter back, the matte black claws of his paw gentle with the delicate material. Those paws had slapped at humans, drawn blood and ripped skin. They had also wiped her forehead when she had a fever, held her hand when she woke from bad dreams, and fought with her over the last re-maining sparerib in the take-out box.

He was demon. It meant less and more than most people knew, and Wren owed him a debt of service that could not be repaid except in kind.

She could touch the letter, use current to find out who had written it, if not why. But this was P.B.'s story. He would tell it, as he chose to, and as much or little as he chose. And whatever he needed from her, she would give. It had become that simple between them.

"It is a letter from one of my...brothers, for lack of a better word," he began, looking down at his plate of food as he spoke.

"A brother I never knew I had—I've never met him, and I don't know how he found me, except there are not so many of us still around that news would be so hard to find, if you know where to look." He paused, his snout wrinkling in an expression of annoyance. "I used to be better about keeping my head down and staying low-profile. You've been bad for me, you two."

Wren could have argued the same about him, for her, but kept silent.

"This letter…he asks about certain papers, documents that he suspected might be in my keeping. There was a time I was…favored by our creator, and it was thought I might have…that when the old man died, I might have taken his files with me."

"You didn't." Sergei sounded pretty sure of that.

"No. I took nothing from him." The demon's eyes closed, heavy lids hiding those dark red eyes from sight, then he opened them again and shook his head. "Nothing physical, anyway."

"So what's the problem?" There was a story there, too, and not one with a good ending, but it could wait until the immediate stuff was dealt with.

"My brother says, there have been…inquiries about these papers. By humans. It is subtle, in his wording, but I think… I think that this letter was written under duress. That one or more of these humans forced him to find me, to contact me."

"That's never good," Sergei said, and Wren nodded her head in agreement. No two demons looked alike, except for the dark blood-red eyes that marked their breed, but none of them were lightweights in any sense of the word. Coercion of a demon meant heavy guns, not flowers and candlelight. Chasing the last bit of shrimp around on her plate suddenly lost its appeal, and she put plate and chopsticks down.

"By humans, I assume that he means Talent?" she asked.

"Most likely," P.B. agreed. "A normal human…these papers would not mean anything to them, except as an oddity, a fantasy. Only ones with magic in their system would be able to use them."

"What sort of papers, P.B.?" Even as Wren asked, she thought, maybe, that she already knew.

Wren had learned, the hard and personal way, the secret demon kept from the rest of the *Cosa Nostradamus*. The reason *why* they kept it secret: to protect themselves from slavery—or worse.

"Papers that detailed…how we were created. And why."

Yeah. That had been what she was afraid of.

"Created." Sergei looked from one to the other of them, clearly aware there was a loop that he had been left out of, and not sure where to begin, or how. "So it's true, you're not…"

"Natural?" the demon asked.

Sergei let out a bark of laughter. "After everything we've been through, 'natural' and 'normal' are pretty much useless as descriptors, unless you add 'relatively' in front of them. I was going to say that you're not actually a demon, it's just a name someone stuck on your kind?" He caught the look Wren gave him, and shrugged. "I'm still—relatively speaking—new to the *Cosa* and the entire concept of Fatae, remember?" They had been working together for more than eleven years now, since Wren was a teenager, and she thought that would have been long enough to figure things out. Then again, before they had partnered up, he had known only that Talents existed, not that there was an entire society, human and not-human, with its own cultures and histories.

As usual, he knew where her thoughts were going. "Wrenlet, 'why are you called a demon?' is not the kind of thing you walk up to someone and ask. Not without looking for a fight, anyway."

True. Even she didn't know all the breeds of Fatae that were living in New York City, much less those hiding in pockets and enclaves outside the United States.

P.B. shrugged, a tight-muscled little jerk. "I'm as much a demon as the Angeli are angelic." That was to say, not at all. The Angeli were tall, good-looking, and winged—and total arrogant, species-centric bastards, as a rule. "Most of the names groups have for themselves translate to 'the true people' or something, anyway," P.B. went on. "At least we never had a chance to become egotistical enough to think we were part of God's master plan. There was always someone there ready to remind us what we were. So demon is as good a name as any. Made people think twice before messing with us."

"The claws probably had something to do with that, too," her partner said drily.

"We don't all have claws," P.B. said, laying his paws palm down on the table so that all ten of the thick black half-moons were visible. "We were designed according to need, and what was available, and what our creator's whim was that day." A pause. "We are all pretty tough, though, one way or another. Yeah."

"Your...creator." Wren couldn't bring herself to say father, or parent, or anything that might imply any kind of emotional attachment that, it was clear, didn't exist. "How many of you did he make?"

"I don't know. He wasn't the first. Magicians had gone that route before, created servants—golems or demon, same difference different terminology—but he was the only one of his generation to succeed, and even he didn't, all the time. High failure rate, when you're playing God.

"I know there were at least half a dozen made before me, that had either been given away or abandoned. I...was there for seven that survived; don't ask me how many didn't make it. There weren't any…after."

After what, neither Wren not Sergei asked. The word had a certain finality about it that dissuaded follow-up by even the most curious, or callous.

"And these papers… Could they have been stolen? Or did he have someone he might have passed them along to, an inheritance of sort? Could he have shared this knowledge, did he have a student, or an assistant?" Sergei's mind was churning now, and Wren was torn between the desire to sit back and watch, and the feeling that if she didn't get answers about the past out of P.B. now, the door would soon slam shut.

"They might have been stolen, a lot of his things were probably looted. Things were chaotic, after." There was that word again. *After.* After what? *Mind on the immediate stuff, Valere. Don't let him or you get distracted.*

"He didn't have an assistant, not a human one, anyway—that was what he kept me around for. I wasn't particularly agile—" and he flexed his paws again, emphasizing their strength "—but I was—am—smart. He gave me brains, whether he meant to or not, and he used them, the way he used the rest of me."

The bitterness that was always an undertone in his voice surfaced like a storm, dark and violent, and suddenly the words poured out.

"Brilliant, he was brilliant, was my master. Nobody denied that, not even his detractors, and he had a lot of them, people who thought he was a fool, a nutcase, and just plain dangerous. And he was, believe you me. Dangerous to himself, to us, to everyone. For all that brilliance? He was a crap Talent. They all were, all his group of magic users."

He didn't call them Talent, Wren noted.

"All of them so focused on their obsession they didn't understand how much more they could be capable of." P.B. clearly wanted to be disgusted, but his voice just sounded sad. "My creator wanted to be more, but he couldn't manage it, not even with us, because all he could think about was playing God. So he kept trying, kept creating newer and better models, something that would be the right one, the final result, the grand prize."

Sergei was looking like a man who knew he had catching up to do. Rather than make him ask, Wren took point.

"The thing between me and P.B." And by "thing" she meant the bond that had allowed him access into her brain, and her into his—the thing that allowed her to ground in him— without the physical stress or damage that Sergei risked when she did the same thing to him. The way her partner's jaw set, almost invisible but absolutely clear, indicated that he knew what she was referring to. It was stupid that he was jealous, and he knew that, and yet...

Maybe this would finally put it to rest, once and for all. Once he understood the nature of the connection, and why it was both a blessing and a curse.

"The link wasn't an accident, or some kind of freak twist of Talent. It was what he—what all demon—were created to do. To be grounding posts for Talent."

Her partner was no dummy; it took him all of three seconds to figure out what she'd needed spelled out for her. "A demon-connection keeps Talent from wizzing when they use too much power for too long, because there's additional protection. In the demon. That's what this guy was trying to create. What he did create."

"Yeah." She and P.B. spoke at the same time, with the identical tone of doom.

It was a good thing, in theory. In theory, it was a gift of the heart, a sacred bond, if your philosophy went that way.

In theory, it might save lives. In practice, it had sent her friend running for decades to keep his mind and his soul his own. In practice, in the wrong hands, it was nothing more or less than slavery.

And now someone wanted those papers. Which implied that someone knew, or suspected, what demon could do.

"Can you all do that? The demon he created?"

"The failures didn't survive." A blunt statement. "The earlier generations, Kolchyia and Mainyu and the others...probably not, or not as well. He didn't keep all his own; like I said, he gave them away, abandoned them when he changed workshops, or let them escape. The ones after me...he sent away. To others in his circle. But there weren't many of them."

His dark red eyes were almost black, the pupils wide. "Even one was too many."

Wren scrunched her eyes shut, then opened them, feeling a headache coming down hard and fast. There were maybe half a dozen demon in the United States that she had seen or heard of, in her life. She'd met a few, herself. She had no idea how many of them were earlier, and how many were later models, if any of them were P.B.'s brothers or just distant relations. Not that it mattered. If these papers got into the wrong hands, it wasn't as if anyone would be able to tell the difference until it was too late: Until after someone had tried to take what should only be given. Until, in self-defense, the demon fought back. That was what P.B. was preparing for, why he had called Sergei instead of her. To discuss options...battle plans.

There had been too much battle already. Too much blood.

She looked at P.B., eye to eye, skipping the verbal back-and-forth they might otherwise be stuck in, excising Sergei from the negotiations and cutting to the kill. "All right. I'll Retrieve the papers for you."

★ ★ ★

A few hours later, P.B. was sitting on the sofa, having second thoughts about the entire thing. "Maybe we should just forget it. Hell, I don't even know where to tell you to start. I don't even know if they exist. I don't even know if this brother exists, without asking around. It might be bullshit, someone trying to play me, get you on the hunt, maybe they expected you to do exactly what you did. You've got the ins with the community, or maybe they think you already know where the papers are, and then they can swoop in and take them away. This other demon might be in on it, even if he really exists. Not every demon's a nice guy, even before we do what we have to do. Just 'cause someone's got your blood doesn't mean you can trust 'em. And even if it's true, just because someone somewhere thinks maybe the papers might still exist doesn't mean it's our—"

"Hey."

For a normally taciturn Fatae, he was getting downright mouthy. That made her nervous. She put a hand on his paw, stilling the nervous tapping of his claws. "Stop denting my furniture. You're right—we have ins with the community, and skills nobody else can match. So Sergei's gonna ask some questions, nose about. It's what he's good at. It makes him feel useful. If he comes back with anything actual, then we've got us a Retrieval. If not...then odds are, ain't nobody nowhere gonna find anything, either."

He snorted. "Your mother would so kick your ass if she heard you abusing the English language like that."

"My mother's in Alaska with Mac, on a ship that doesn't get cell phone signal, and she's lousy at picking up e-mail, so forget about even trying to threaten me with her." Her mother was also a Null's Null, and P.B. could have—and had—danced a jig in front of her and she would have barely noticed, forgetting two minutes later there had been anything odd at all going on in her daughter's apartment. It was a gift that let the older woman sleep soundly at night. Although she doubted her mother was getting much sleep. Mac had shown up a couple of months ago, short, scrawny and surprisingly dashing, and totally swept her normally practical and grounded mother off her feet. Unlike the guys Wren remembered from her preteen years, Mac wasn't exactly daddy material. Wren had hopes for him—her mother had been alone for way too long.

The thought diverted her to another. "Hell, my mother can't even remember my father."

"What?"

As she had hoped, that admission distracted the demon from his own paternal-problem musings. He looked—not shocked, exactly, but astonished, his muzzle-length jaw hanging open slightly.

"Yeah." Wren sat down in the chair opposite him, and placed her mug of coffee on the table. "I pushed her on it a while ago, just on a whim, and she told me he was a one-night stand, and not a very memorable one at that."

The demon stared at her, then shook his head. "Okay, you win. And man, your mom was a slut. Who'da thought it?"

She used random current to spark him on his stumpy little tail for that, and he jumped and snarled at her. She snarled back, her own much less impressive except for the current she had to back it up. You didn't insult a Talent's mother, not even in jest, not without paying for it.

"Bitch."

"Furry."

Byplay finished, he settled back down onto the sofa, ostentatiously adjusting his backside on a pillow. "Seriously. She can't remember? Not at all?"

Wren wasn't quite as amused by the whole thing as he was. "She remembers meeting him, and she remembers going off with him, and she—apparently—remembers the occasion with fondness, enough that she decided to keep the kid that came of it. But no, she can't remember anything about him, not his name, not even what he looked like. Although he was tall, she remembered that."

"So you're a sport." Wren's mother might not be impressive, height wise, but she had considerable inches on her daughter's five-foot-not-much.

She ignored that comment entirely, her mind wandering off on another tangent, triggered by the topic. "You ever wonder where it comes from? Talent, I mean. I've asked, and nobody's ever been able to tell me if it's genetic or environmental or some weird virus in the womb, or…"

"You never cared much before now," P.B. said, not unreasonably. "All this from just my story? Or are you…"

"I'm not pregnant, no, bite your tongue. And I'm not thinking about it, either." The thought was a horrifying one. She was lousy with kids, and the thought of a baby…God, no.

"Part of it's all that, part of it's…the kid yester—two days ago, my Retrieval. He's Talent, but neither of his parents have even a smidge, and none of his grandparents were, far as anyone can tell." She held up fingers, counting off examples. "My mom is like the anti-Talent, and my dad, I've got suspicions he was one of us, but no proof. Sergei, he thinks his mother might have had a hint of Talent, from what he remembers, but he's got nada likewise." She shrugged. "It seems so arbitrary, random, but then you have families with generations and generations of seriously strong Talent like it was a dominant gene, no other way to explain it except heredity. Even old magic, where almost anyone could do a little bit if they had strong willpower, but some people could use easier, better, with less effort or cost, because of something inside them."

She ran out of breath, and stopped, not having planned on saying anything, much less so much. She hadn't even been aware that it had been bothering her, beyond what was said at the Tri–Com meeting. Apparently, something had struck somewhere sensitive.

P.B.'s dark red eyes narrowed as he considered her question. "And my creator could manipulate tissue to create something that wasn't Talent, but could handle current nonetheless. So there's something there that can be identified...."

"Bonnie thinks that it's goo."

"What?"

She nodded. "*Cosa* goo. There's a theory someone came up with that she likes way too much, that we've got this mucousy lining in our system, acts like a slide conductor, keeping current from damaging our system at the same time it lets us siphon it off and use it." Wren stroked the fabric of the chair she was sitting in, the texture seeming to ease the flow of her thoughts. "It's got basis in the animal kingdom, the way some things use electricity as a defensive weapon...."

"Yeah, I always thought you guys were a lot like electric eels, all slippery and shocky and lousy to eat."

"Hah. Hah."

"So Didier's got no mucous," he went on, thankfully letting go of the joke.

"Maybe. Or enough that he can remember what he sees, but not actually handle it." Dry or mucous–y wasn't much to choose from, aesthetically speaking. She wished, not for the first time, that Bonnie had used a less evocative term.

The demon got up and started pacing again. "Ow. That's gotta burn him."

She winced, and he realized the indelicacy of what he had said. "Sorry. I mean, he's…"

"Never mind, I got it. Yeah, it's a problem."

That was something that only the three of them, and Sergei's therapist, knew: that Sergei was addicted to the pleasure-pain of current, specifically when she grounded her overflow in him. That hadn't been a problem when she did it only occasionally, when something went wrong on a job, when she pulled down too much and needed help. But sex made it even more intense, and…

You can't tell him no, even when it's bad for him. You enable the addiction.

"Are you two, um…still doing the horizontal bop?" P.B. only knew about the problem, not what they were doing about it. She thought. She sure as hell hadn't told him anything, but she wasn't sure how deep the bond let him into her head. She didn't want to think about that too much, either. Better to pretend there were limits, even if there weren't.

"Nicely put," she said, instead. "Delicate as always. So nice to see you back in your usual fine form."

"I take it that's a no."

It had been a year. Not total abstention—they had tried, tentative and cautious, after the craziness died down and the Silence, the organization behind the vigilantes, had effectively fractured and disappeared. But while things weren't getting worse, they weren't getting better, either. Having to worry each time you had sex if something was going to go wrong didn't do a lot for the mood. And then one night a few months ago he had ended up in the emergency room of St. Vincent's, his bladder spasming, of all things embarrassing, and she had drawn the line. She would do whatever she could to help, but he had to make the first steps to understanding *why* he kept reaching for her current. Some of it was the whole pain-pleasure thing, yeah, and she mostly got that, but not when he didn't seem to care that it was killing him. That, she couldn't help him with. But a professional might.

He had gone to see Joe Doherty the next week. A Talent, and a trained psychologist heading the team working to reacclimatize the Lost to life outside the Silence, Doherty was one of the few people Wren could think of who might be able to understand, and to help, and could be trusted to keep it quiet.

She had no idea what they talked about, but Sergei kept going, and as time went by the sense of urgency she felt from him when she used current was starting to ease.

But only starting to. Starting wasn't enough.

That was why she had never given him the details of what P.B. could do. Jealousy on top of everything else…not good. He knew the generalities—he had been there when it started, and at the time was only thankful that the demon had been able to pull her back from wizzing. If he had wondered further about the bond, he had never asked. Not until tonight.

"Valere, no offense, but you guys need to either get it together or break it off. And since I don't see you guys breaking it off any time soon…"

"He wants me to move in with him. Okay, no, he doesn't. But he says we need to talk about it. I guess to just get it off—or on—the table." She got up and poured herself another cup of coffee, dumping a spoonful of sugar into the thick liquid to make it drinkable. "You want anything, while I'm up?"

"Coffee?"

"Not a chance in hell. I don't have any decaf." P.B. and caffeine were okay in small doses, but things got ugly when he had too much, and tonight he definitely didn't need it. Neither did she; between the job, reporting to the Tri-Com on the kid and now this, her nerves were definitely starting to twitch. It was something familiar to do, though.

"Bonnie calls it a Manhattan Marriage," she said from the kitchen. "When you're long-term, but keep your own place. Because we're so used to being able to retreat, get some space to ourselves, and nobody can afford a place large enough for two people to do that, in the city. She swears it's the only way she'll ever settle down."

"Sounds reasonable. The term I mean. Not that I see her ever settling down."

"Yeah." She came back in, leaning against the door frame and taking a sip. It tasted sour, even with the sugar. That was usually a sign, not just that the coffee was too old, but that she was seriously tired and should go to sleep already, not pour more caffeine into her system.

"You're not convinced." He was studying her, his head cocked slightly and looking, perched on the sofa, like something that might be sold at FAO Schwatz for goth kiddies.

"You've lived all over, haven't you?" she asked him, finally giving in to her curiosity.

"All over for a wide range of 'over,' yeah. Why?" He looked at her, really *looked* and, as usual, followed her unspoken thoughts. "Valere, are you thinking about leaving the city?"

For the first time in their long friendship, the demon actually sounded truly shocked.

Wren sighed. "I don't know." It had been a long damned day after a damned long day, and she wasn't thinking straight about anything any more. "Maybe. Probably not. But maybe. Right now, I'm not ruling anything out. Not anything. But I'm not going to decide anything until we get your situation settled."

And with that, she put her mug down on the table, patted

P.B. on the flattened top of his head, between his ears, and went to bed. He could let himself out or crash at the apartment; she was too tired to care.

eight

It was cold in Amsterdam; winter was still a few months away by the calendar, but the air already had a chill in it that rose off the port and the water of the canals and settled in the bones of the residents. Old men stretched aching muscles and muttered about dire forebodings and wicked storms, but there was no ominous taint to the air; simply a reminder of what would come.

On a small patio off an even smaller café by one of the canals, two men and a woman in their late forties sat talking over their midmorning coffees, so intent on their conversation that they barely noticed when the sun came out from behind the clouds to warm the air and sparkle off the water. The waiter walked around them carefully: wizards did not announce themselves, but a wise man of a certain age recognized the warning signs. The brightness of their eyes, the turn of their hands, the way they looked at you and saw into your soul....

Unaware, or uncaring of the waiter's superstitions, the three drank their coffee and plotted. The woman and the man to her left spoke Dutch, while the man to her right spoke French, but they all seemed to understand each other well enough for the bilingual conversation to proceed smoothly.

"It is merely a rumor," the Frenchman was saying. He rubbed his hands around the clunky ceramic mug as though warming himself on the liquid inside, chilled despite the warmth of his wool suit jacket. "One sighting is not confirmation, no matter how plausible the report. There have been too many frauds, too many disappointments. We have no proof that this time it is for real…."

"There is never proof. We have spent years chasing after sightings. We arrive after the fact, and it has already moved on, become legend. We arrive too soon and the reports are merely rumor, vapor spun by those with their own agenda. Waiting for proof has gotten us nowhere." The woman wore her dark red hair in a severe knot at the base of her neck, as though to counteract the lushness of her features. She looked younger than her companions by at least a handful of years, but her mind was as sharp for all that she lacked their experience—and patience.

"Legends and rumors are not truth," the other man said in the tone of a lecturer. Slightly older than the other two, his dark hair was only now beginning to silver, but his skin showed the tracings of lines and wrinkles beginning to cut into his sharp features. Offsetting that, he had dark eyes that had the alert look and inner glow of a fanatic held in check only by practical considerations. "Truth is physical. Truth is verifiable. The tool we found was useless, its limited brain unable to respond, and its information must therefore be considered suspect. It knew the same things we knew; that demons have gathered there, in numbers unheard of since our great-grandfather's time. It is highly likely that the tool extrapolated from that, saying what it thought we wanted to hear before it died. We cannot afford to waste our resources chasing every wisp of news, every sworn-on-Bible lead. The funds we have are limited enough, and must be carefully husbanded."

The woman was scornful of such caution, resting her hands on the table as though she were about to push away from the other two in disgust. "To win all, sometimes we must risk all. That is as we were taught. Is not the prize worth it?"

"If it even exists," the Frenchman said, clearly annoyed at her grandiose language, and then looked up defensively at the stares the other two gave him. "After all these years, all the dead ends and the failures... You have never doubted? Never once wondered if we were not chasing down the wrong road? If the legends were merely that? If the experiments were dead ends after all, the trials destroyed and scattered for a reason?"

The other two looked at him as though he had just suggested that the Sun, and not the Moon, were made of green cheese.

"Never," the woman declared, and the older man nodded his head once, firmly. In this matter they were in total agreement. "Our great-grandfathers were men of courage and intelligence," he said. "Their legacy is still in the world, and it is our responsibility—our destiny—to recover it."

"And use it." The Frenchman's blond hair and fair skin were touched by the shadow of a cloud overhead, making it seem as though he paled slightly. The whites of his eyes were slightly pinked, as though he had a cold, or had not been sleeping well.

"Of course," the woman said. "Are we not their inheritors? That magic belongs to us! Else what was the research they risked their lives to complete for, if not to put to use?"

Risked their lives, and lost them. They all knew the cost. Every member of that circle of magicians and scholars generations ago had been hunted down and killed over the years, their libraries burned and their experiments destroyed. The entire

Magischer Kreis, wiped clean off the face of the earth by fearful minds and lesser, weaker souls, their lives' work reviled and forbidden, punishable by death even to speak of it. And yet, the stories persisted over the later generations, among the children of the children who had been left behind. Stories of experiments that had succeeded, of papers that had been preserved, of legacies waiting to be reclaimed. Of magic that waited for the inheritors: magic, and power.

There were seven of them now, the grandchildren and great-grandchildren of the *Kreis,* gathered together cautiously through friend-of-a-friend-of-the-family, drawn together by that long-ago connection, held together by a fascination and reverence for those stories, for the promise of something greater in that knowledge, of the hint of wisdom and power their forefathers had accumulated.

It was their legacy and their goal, a holy grail of a more scientific sort, almost two decades old in the searching. It could not be a dead end. They would not accept it.

"And the newest information says that the legacy is in the United States?" the darker man said, asking for confirmation rather than responding further to his companion's doubts.

"Yes. In New York. The tool assured us that it was spotted there a few months back." The woman had a small PDA on the table next to her coffee cup, but she did not reach for it to check her notes; there was no need. She had been one of the three who had questioned the creature, and was confident in her facts. Facts, not rumor, this time. The tool had been an older one, identifiable by its appearance and low intellect, and no match for them in wile or determination.

"Did it have a chance to warn anyone?" A reminder, that despite their stronger will, the tool had still managed, in the end, to escape them for a short time.

"No. It died alone. Who would aid such a thing as that?" Her scorn was both clear and understandable. Even its own kind chose not to remain in each others' presence. "Without our guidance, it was a lost, helpless thing."

"But you trust the information it gave you?"

"It was unable to lie to us." That had been the first thing they had verified. They had no true training, and limited power because of it, but some old spells still worked, with the right ingredients, sacrifices, and chants. She was confident of their results.

He sighed, the oldest of the seven and as such, the one who made the final decision. "It is folly to leap—and more folly to hold back. The power must be reclaimed, before we forget what we once were, entirely. We will go."

Air seemed to be let out of the other two, even though they had not been aware of holding their breath. "Who is closest?" he asked. "Dara? No, Rog. He holds a U.S. passport, so he will be able to travel without incident. Call him today. I want him on the scene as quickly as possible. We cannot wait for others to arrive. If this is truth…" He looked down into his coffee, and the years suddenly seemed to weigh more heavily on him. "If it is true, we cannot let it slip from us. We cannot—*will* not—allow someone else to take what is ours."

"Breathe. Breathe, damn you!"

Despite the shouted command, the pile of dark brown fur on the wooden table lay still, inanimate. The eyes were closed, the muscles slack, the organs nonfunctional.

"Damn." A world of frustration was packed into that one word, frustration, and anger directed both outward, and in. The temptation to respond was too great for the third figure in the small, lamp-lit room.

"This would be a bad time to say I told you so?"

"Yes."

The word was snarled, and the third figure flinched, but kept his tone even, almost light. "I shall refrain from saying anything, then."

Despite his irritation, there might have been a faint smile flickering on the man's face. Or perhaps not. "You are a pestilence and a plague and dare too much," he told his assistant, his ire fading back under the civilized tone of an educated man, even as he moved away to allow his assistant to deal with the remains of the experiment.

"As you say, Master." The dirty white head bowed in acceptance, but his clawed paws flexed and released in tension he could not otherwise show. Moving forward out of the shadows where he had been waiting, the assistant reached down and drew a sheet over the motionless form, all the while keeping his back to the human. If Master saw his expression, there would be punishment for certain. Insolence might be permitted, occasionally even encouraged as amusing, depending on Master's mood; doubt or hesitation was forbidden.

"Dispose of it," his master ordered, as expected. "We'll try again tomorrow, after I've had a full night's sleep. Ensure that the blood is fresh, this time."

His assistant looked down at the dark splatters on the leather apron wrapped around his squat body. This time, his claws did not flex, and his voice was no longer daring, but resigned. The blood was always fresh. The failure was not the blood, but the flesh. It would not end. It would never end, but badly. "Yes, Master."

After a dream—a nightmare—like that, you either lay in bed staring at the ceiling until dawn came, or you got up and got busy. Wren was the sort to get busy.

The windows were open throughout the apartment, letting in the 4 a.m. sounds of a city that did, occasionally, sleep. She could identify an off-key car horn now and again, the distant wail of a siren waxing or waning, and a steady white noise that Wren had never been able to identify as a specific source, but merely accepted as the city's contented heartbeat. Occasional random thumps and the sound of water running through pipes suggested that others in the building were also awake.

If they were, they were probably doing the same thing she was doing: studying financial records, shuffling papers, and running numbers. Unlike her, they were probably using a computer, not an old solar-powered calculator, and sheets of scratch paper. The stronger a Talent, the closer to "pure" they were, the more trouble they had using electronics—every time you accessed your core, even involuntarily, you sent out sparks that looked for similar sparks to play with. And current didn't always make the distinction between other current, and electricity. Wren had destroyed half-a-dozen of Sergei's cell phones and PDAs back before she overrushed; now, unless she was careful, she could wipe out even her backed-up-seven-ways-from-Sunday home computer just by turning it on. And forget about ever getting a cell phone of her own.

Sometimes, she really hated being her.

The dream had woken her sometime around 1:00 a.m. Although she would have loved to have written it off to general anxiety, she knew better. A quick pajama-clad prowl through the apartment had told her that she was alone, P.B. having indeed gone home. She had thought about reaching out to him, but decided against it. The dream was already fading, leaving behind a bad taste in her mind and a deep sadness in her soul. How much worse must it be for P.B.? The bond they had formed to protect her life and sanity had been a gift between friends. There was no need to let him know that it had also cost him the privacy of his innermost, obviously deeply painful memories. And they had to be memories, they had too much of a concrete, solid feel to be anything else.

If he spoke of it, she would tell him. But not otherwise.

Unable to get back to sleep with so many things knocking around in her head, she had decided to make use of the relative quiet. She started with the basics—sorting and clearing out the desk in her office. The third bedroom, a library/storeroom, was in more need of organizing, but she had thought the desk would be an easier thing to accomplish. Bad idea—she had been avoiding the computer desk for months, and the debris was breeding at a scary rate. She had made it through two drawers into the old laminate-top desk when her hand closed on a small hardbound notebook that had been tossed in there, probably the week she had moved in. She pulled it out and looked at it, trying to remember what it was. The cover was a thick green suedelike fabric, and the spine was sturdy, but the corners were battered, as though it had been carried around for a long time. She stared at it without opening it, then placed it carefully on the corner of her desk and slid the drawer shut.

"Avoidance never got you anything good," she said, echoing one of her mother's favorite sayings. When she had been a sulky teenager, that phrase had annoyed the hell out of her, as she suspected it was meant to. Now, it had the ring of depressing truth to it.

So she turned to the thing that should have been number one on her hit list anyway: her bank statements.

Two hours later her head ached even worse, her ass was sore from sitting, and she was sick unto death of her own financial health. The picture she had put together was reassuring, though. Sergei had trained her well, and she'd been making a nice, if careful living for a bunch of years now. If she wanted to, if the asking price wasn't too insane, she could buy out her apartment when the new owner made the offer. Or she could move somewhere else, if she decided not to buy.

She could even afford to move somewhere else. Another city,

another part of the country. A different region, where Wren Valere might still be a name for the *Cosa* to conjure with, but they might treat her with wariness because of it. Might give her the space to breathe she so desperately needed.

Space without memories. Space without reminders. Space without guilt.

Space without Sergei?

She wasn't quite ready to poke at that thought yet. If ever. Maybe he would come with her. He had been talking recently about expanding, maybe handing the day-to-day gallery stuff over to Lowell and spending more time hunting down new artists instead of drowning in the paperwork. It would be good for him, too, to get out of the city, away from the memories. Maybe they'd buy a place together, somewhere large enough that they wouldn't be living in each other's pockets and getting on each other's nerves. She tried to imagine a place—a house— the two of them might each like, and failed, utterly.

Cart, horse, she reminded herself. And making plans for someone else was always a bad idea.

Getting up to stretch her legs, she walked out of the office and down the hallway, the new pale brown carpeting rough on her bare feet. Her apartment, like all the others in the building, was laid out along a T: three small, shoe-box-shaped bedrooms were lined up next to each other—her bedroom, her office, and the library/storage room/closet along the top crossline, with the bathroom, tiny kitchen and main room arrayed along the downward stroke. It wasn't what the Realtors called an open floor plan—in fact, it was downright crowded and crappy. But that had been what allowed her to afford it in the first place, and since she didn't like to entertain, and the long, carpeted hallway was good for pacing, she was fine with the layout.

And, even better, the building had over the years apparently built up a sort of current-signature of its own, current enough to resist a psi-bomb set outside her window during the early days of the Trouble. She had known the vibes were good the moment she walked into the place, she just hadn't realized *how* good. Now, if she paused and concentrated, she could almost feel the building's quietude, its grounded sensibility.

Like P.B.'s mental scent, in concrete and brick. Solid, comforting. Familiar.

"You really think you could leave this?" she asked herself.

Still. If there was a building in Manhattan like this, odds were good there were other buildings in other cities that felt the same, had the same protections, the same safety. She just had to follow her instincts to find them. Considering how much more she knew now than back then, it should be a simple matter to find a new refuge.

Buildings where ghosts of friends dead-and-gone didn't haunt her, waking or sleeping. Cities where whispers didn't follow her, where she could go on a job and not worry about anything except the job.

The *Cosa* was everywhere, yeah. The Mage Council, the organized branch of the Talent, was set up in localized groups, each major metropolitan area in North America—and major cities around the world—having their own mostly independent leadership. But a lonejack like herself, a freelancer without ties or obligations, should be able to slip by them without comment. Not every Council was run by someone like the late, unlamented KimAnn Howe of the New York Metro Council, on a power-mad membership drive.

Most Councils would leave her alone.

Other cities didn't have a Tri-Com, still thinking of her like some kind of last-ditch hero or savior. The dryad's parting words still echoed: "Any time, you'd be welcomed back."

Thinking hard, her brain let her feet take her down the hallway and into the main room, doing a circuit. She used to keep this room empty save for a chair and the stereo. That had worked fine for her, when she thought of it. Now there was a sofa, a coffee table, and an ottoman in addition to those things. When friends came over, they could make themselves comfortable. She had a folding table she could use to serve dinner on, and chairs that went with it, stored in the library.

She had fresh paint, courtesy of Bonnie and her coworkers— not the gothy purple sparkle P.B. had warned her of, but a lovely, neutral cream—and a scattering of artwork on the walls, and a new carpet underfoot, chosen for how it felt under her bare feet, exactly the way it did now. There were three handprints in dark blue paint on the wall just inside the front door: one large, male; one smaller, hers; and…well, there were two handprints and one paw print. She had staked ownership in this space, damn it.

She had…

Fortune cookies, sitting on the table where they had eaten dinner.

Oh. She had forgotten about them. But not so forgotten that the damn things had been thrown out; when they cleared the dishes from dinner, each of them had avoided even touching the cookies, as though denying they were there.

"Damn. Also, damn."

They sat on the table, wrapped in twists of waxed paper. She should throw them out. Just scoop them into her hand and toss them in the trash with the rest of the debris.

Most people treated fortune cookies like stale jokes, hoping maybe to get something rude or particularly funny, playing the "in bed" game with the fortunes found on the little slips of paper. Her? Hers came straight from an actual Seer, nine times out of ten, and like all Seers' pronouncements, were usually less than models of clarity and straightforwardness.

But trying to avoid them never worked. Maybe embracing Fate would bring a better result.

It couldn't hurt, anyway. She hoped.

She was pleased to see that her hand didn't shake when she reached down and picked a cookie at random. Three cookies, one for each of them. So which one was hers?

You're all tied together. What's for one is for you all.

Wren didn't know where the thought came from, but it felt annoyingly true.

"All right then, Seer, tell me what I don't want to know."

She pulled the white strip of paper from between the folds of the cookie, and turned it over.

"'Take no blood from stone, save you give it back.' Nicely useless. Next?" She placed the fortune on the table and picked up the second cookie. This one she had to break in order to get the fortune out. "Take no blood..." Her voice trailed off, and she dropped the second cookie in her haste to get to the third. The fragile dough crumbled in her hand, and she didn't bother to wipe the crumbs off before reading the slip of paper. The words registered, and she began to laugh, if a little hysterically.

Unlike the second fortune, which merely repeated the first in bold print, this one read: "You no like fortune, stop reading cookie."

Nobody had ever claimed that Seers didn't have a sense of humor.

P.B. had woken that morning aware not only that he had been dreaming—his sleep was often filled with memories in the shape of nightmares—but that he had not been alone in the dream.

"Damn it." He could taste the Retriever in his mind, like

the lingering flavor of garlic: not unpleasant, but unmistakable. Any moment now, she would show up at his door, demanding to know what the hell it meant, insisting on an explanation.

"You knew what would happen," he reminded himself. Although, in actuality, he had only suspected. The one time he was forced to act as conduit to a Talent, it had been his creator, and that miserable excuse for a human had been, at best, half Wren's skill. Plus, the bond had been formed unwillingly on his part, forced by the human's control of him, allowed by his fear of his creator. This time he had entered with full consent, and even if Wren had been ignorant of what she did, she had trusted him enough to follow without question.

He might deny it, might hate it, but this was what he had been created to do. It felt…right.

Had any of his brothers found someone like that, someone they could open themselves to? Or were they all as he had been, scarred and bitter…

All right, he was *still* scarred and bitter. That was who he was, now. Scarred and bitter…but with hope, dangerous though it was.

Falling out of bed, he padded over to the window and looked up and out. His apartment was, in Wren's words, a crap-tastic craphole, but it suited him; the view was eye level with the sidewalk, which meant that he could see out but someone would have to get down on their knees to see in, and it stayed cool enough even in the worst of Manhattan's summer heat that he didn't sweat too badly.

In the winter even he, fur and all, froze, but that was what Valere's heat-included-in-the-rent-and-actually-delivered apartment was for.

And speaking of whom…no current-ping in his brain. No phone call. No knocking on his door. She might still be on her way over, but…maybe not. Maybe she was doing exactly what she had promised: to not take anything more than what he offered. He was still scarred and bitter, but…he trusted Valere.

So trust her some more.

He checked the street level for an idea of the weather. No open-toed shoes, but no heavy slogging boots, either. A good day to stay in bed and read, except that he had things to accomplish, not the least of which was a courier job. It had arrived the night before, in his usual drop-spot, with directions on where to pick the tube up and where he was to deliver it. Boring work, for the most part, but that was how he, and most of the demon-kind, made their living: as couriers. Not many folk in their right mind or left wanted to tangle with a demon, and those who did had barely a thirty percent chance of getting away intact, much less with what they came for.

But there were ways to take down a demon, even one who knew you were coming. If they didn't know…

He had told Sergei the truth: he didn't keep track of how many demon there were, total, how many had survived or what they had done with themselves. It had been safer not to know too much, for a long time. Safety in staying off the radar, out of sight. But the ones in this country, those he could find, with a little work. And maybe they had kept in touch with others. A word in the wind: who knew how far it might carry?

After he finished the job; that was what he would do. He might not know them, might not like them or them him, but his brothers deserved a warning.

That decision made, he sniffed at his fur, and decided that he didn't need to shower this morning. Grabbing the orange juice out of his rickety old fridge, he drank it directly from the carton, finishing the last of it and tossing the empty container into the trash. His kitchen was even smaller than Wren's, not even qualifying as a separate galley, but rather just a linoleum-floored corner of the main space. The fridge had to be older than Wren, the sink leaked, and the stove might or might not work, he didn't know. But the rent was controlled at an almost obscenely low level, the landlord never bothered him, and the place was surprisingly free of cockroaches. So he didn't complain.

He went into the bathroom and brushed his teeth, put saline drops in his eyes to protect them from the daily pollution, and—in a concession to grooming he would deny if asked—spritzed himself with a liquid detangler and ran a flat-backed brush through his fur. Done with his ablutions, he grabbed his slouch hat off the wooden rack next to the sofa, and headed out the door and up the stairs to the street, mentally reviewing the job specs to make sure he hadn't missed anything.

The moment he hit the pavement outside his apartment building, he stopped, the fur on the back of his neck—and pretty much everywhere else—tingling slightly, although he wasn't prone to the human experience of gooseflesh. He sniffed at the air, the black nostrils opening and taking in more information than human, or even canine, noses could process. The normal smells of the city sped through his brain, nothing that should have alerted him to trouble. His dark red eyes scanned the street, while he leaned back against the wall and tried to look as though he was remembering if he was supposed to go uptown or downtown today. Three teenagers loitering, two older women gossiping with the grocer outside the bodega, a man in a semidecent suit walking as if he knew he had nowhere important to get to, and a young woman sitting on the stoop four buildings down, talking into a cell phone.

His rounded ears twitched, and her voice came to him, plus the strains of whomever she was talking to, those tinny tones almost but not quite out of his hearing range.

The moment he heard the accent, he knew why his fur had bristled, and the skin underneath had gone cold.

And why he had dreamed of the past so vividly, only a few hours before.

After decades of running, They had found him.

nine

After such a lousy predawn start to the day, it was almost a surprise to Wren when Sunday morning turned into a gorgeous example of Autumn, filled with bright sunshine, cool temperatures, and the slightly acrid smell of leaves beginning to turn, mixing with the suggestion of wood smoke and wool sweaters. She poured her umpteenth mug of coffee, crawled out onto the fire escape outside of her kitchen window, and pondered the corner of her street that she could see from that perch.

It was, she decided finally, a perfect day to take off and go apple picking, or take a boat ride around the island, or just take a walk in the park to hear the already-downed leaves crunch underfoot. If you had the day off, anyway. For people like her, it was just another workday.

Except that she had nothing to do, nothing concrete to work on. She could have waited for Sergei to get back to her about what, if anything, he had found out regarding P.B.'s story. Or, she could have spent the time going over everything she knew—very damned little—about demon and the history of the *Cosa*. Or she could have worried some more about her finances, and what she wanted to do—and where she wanted to be—when she grew up. Or, tempting thought, she could have gone back to bed and hoped to fall asleep again.

Instead, she crawled inside, laced up her boots, threw on her leather jacket over jeans and a long-sleeved T-shirt, and took a walk across town. The sun was warm, despite the cooler air temperature, and she welcomed the feel of the air on her skin. Walking, just simply walking to get somewhere, no danger lurking along the way or at the destination, was a strange feeling after the past few years, and she reveled in it. A handful of teenagers were hanging out on the steps of an old brick apartment building where a number of Talent lived. Two of them raised their hands to say hello, and then hesitated, as though not quite sure they had really seen her. Wren laughed to herself. She could have gone entirely no-see with just a flicker of current, but there was no need. Nor was there any need to become entirely visible. Half-seen, half-noticed, unremembered. She had always been most comfortable in the shadows, even walking under full sunlight.

"Two new calls came in," Sergei said without surprise when she finally walked through the door of the gallery. She was sweating slightly from the trek, but her skin was flushed in a good way, and she had worked off the worst of the morning's weirdness, leaving her with a sense of physical and mental calm she hadn't felt in a long time.

She dropped her jacket onto the coatrack that was normally reserved for potentially paying customers. Sergei's assistant looked up and glared at her; she resisted the urge to glare back and instead smiled sweetly, because Sergei had told her the blond man was more annoyed when she was nice than when she fought with him. Wren stopped and—with her good mood—considered the man behind the counter for just a second. Being completely fair, Lowell wasn't a bad guy as things went; Sergei thought highly of his abilities, and trusted him with a sizable part of the day-to-day running of his baby, the gallery. So there had to be something there that she didn't see. Part of it was that she just set Lowell on edge, somehow, and his reactions always made her want to poke his pompous WASPy, arty facade until it popped. Plus there was this whole tug-of-war over Sergei's attention that she had won, hands down.

All right, maybe Lowell got a pinkie of attention. But no more, and only in the office, and only about gallery stuff. The one time she had seriously faced off against Lowell here, Sergei had, verbally if not literally, spanked them both.

Trying not to remember that incident, she followed her partner through the gallery and into his private office, taking probably too much pleasure in the door sliding shut behind them, shutting Lowell out. Knowing that Lowell was resisting the urge to stick his tongue out at her direction made it all the better.

There was only so much maturity either one of them could manage without straining something, after all, and their part-time receptionist—Carole, her name was, wasn't it?—wasn't in today for him to harass.

"Business is definitely picking up then," she said to her partner. If he was telling her about two calls, odds were good there had been at least three. Maybe more. Someday she was going to start demanding to see everything that came in, just for a laugh and some egoboo.

Then she thought about how much work that would be, and remembered why they had started the "filter" system in the first place. Maybe not.

She sat down in her usual spot, tucking her denim-clad legs underneath her rather than letting them dangle like a little kid's. Stupid new sofa. He had gotten rid of the old leather sofa and replaced it with one covered in a soft, nubby dark gray fabric. She had to agree that this was going to be a lot more comfortable to sit on when the weather got hot and sticky, but she missed the old one, which had been low-slung enough for her to sit on normally.

"Anything good?" she asked, referring to the slips of paper he had picked up off his desk as he sat behind it. Good used to mean money. Now it meant anything that might give her a challenge.

But not too much of a challenge, she amended quickly, even in the relative privacy of her own mind not wanting to tempt Fate or God or anyone else who might need a laugh at her expense. The fortune cookie was still fresh in her mind, and blood in a fortune rarely added up to anything good in her experience, especially if they were talking about *her* blood.

Not that she was really worried about any jobs he might suggest. That was part of the filtering process Sergei went through before bringing anything up to her, clearing out the ones that smelled obviously of trouble. Post-Silence, that included any jobs that smelled of third-party interests or unwanted complications. They got turned away at the door, now, no matter how much of a challenge they might be. She didn't need to get burned twice to be three times shy. Her mother raised her smarter than that. She hoped.

Sergei didn't even bother to look at the slips, having committed them to memory even as he was writing the information down, as usual. "One smash-and-grab—our old friends at The Meadows recommended you to another private museum up in Toronto." It was strange and yet reassuring, seeing Sergei in manager-mode again. "Are you interested in going to Canada?"

She shrugged. "Hey, I've got a passport now, seems a shame not to use it every few years." Her first and only trip out of the country had been to Italy, a few years back. She had enjoyed meeting the local *Cosa*, and that was where she and Sergei had first hooked up, so she was willing to look favorably on travel overall, despite what happened on the rest of that trip. So long as she didn't have to take an airplane, anyway.

And a smash-and-grab—a basic Retrieval of an object, usually artwork—was nicely nonmagically soothing. Of course that's what she had thought about the last job, too, and that hadn't worked out so well.

"The other is a government gig," he went on, sliding the paper toward her.

"What?" Okay, *that* was new. The only time she had ever done any work for a government official, it had been to Retrieve blackmail material, and that was done on the civilian side, not through his office, for obvious reasons.

"Karl called, wants to know if you want to help him with a little problem down on the docks."

"Ah." Karl was one of Sergei's many useful contacts—he divided them into "useful," "may-be-useful," and "charity"—who worked for the U.S. Customs Service. They had met through Sergei's legitimate side, clearing artwork for sale in Sergei's gallery, but a mutual if cautious admiration had given rise to an equally cautious, casual friendship. They had, on more than one occasion, called on Karl's experience during a job.

Now it seemed the mitten was on the other paw.

She didn't bother to even look at the slip of paper, trusting to Sergei's evaluation. "Would I actually get paid by the government?" That was an interesting thought. She wondered what the invoice would look like, and if she would have to file a tax return on it. What budget would they pay her from? The Office of Miscellaneous Affairs?

"I'm not sure there would be payment as such," Sergei said. "He suggested a trade-in-kind."

Her first instinct was to reject it out of hand, then she paused. Sergei had brought her this job, and it couldn't be just because it was from a pre-existing contact—Sergei had no problem saying "no" to friends, relatives and...well, she didn't think he actually would be brave enough to say no to her mother, but then, not many people did. Margot Valere was lovely, charming, sweet, and had a spine of steel. Wren remembered her grandmother, Margot's mother, and could only be thankful that, unlike that woman, her mom had gotten charm to go over that steel.

Oh. Charm. Right. "He's got something in the back room?" Occasionally, things came through Customs that should never have been let out from whatever Aladdin's Cave they were found in. Karl was a Null, but he had a pretty good sense for things that were maybe-magical, without actually naming them as such, and no hesitation about turning them over to the folk as could deal with them, no questions asked, no answers wanted. The back room was, as Sergei put it, where "things went to get lost."

"So he says, although it's actually still on the ship, which is where you come in. He happened to be there the night it came in, and it gave him, and I quote, 'the jeebies.' There was no mention of an actual trade, but rather the implication that he had done enough passing along of questionable materials, and that he was now owed some services in return. There may also have been a passing reference to the authorities looking more closely at identification in the future, before allowing shipments through, especially ones of dubious trade value, like, oh, artwork. Although nothing was actually overtly said."

Wren placed a palm to her chest, fingers spread, and blinked coquettishly at her partner. "Mister Didier. Is the big bad Customs man trying to blackmail us?"

"I do believe he is, yes," he replied, straight-faced, his eyes heavy-hooded and his silvering hair slightly ruffled so that he looked even more than usual like a sleepy hawk.

"Oh dear." She feigned a swoon straight out of a bad pastiche of *Gone With The Wind*. "Tell him yes, of course. Such aptitude must be rewarded."

His thin lips quirked upward in a quick smile that was just as quickly quashed. He was being Serious Sergei right now. "And the other job?"

Wren sat up straight again and flicked through her mental checklist. Normally she was all about writing things down— her brain wasn't quite the catch-all Sergei's was—but she'd gotten lazy, recently. She would have to take care of that; leaving things unwritten too often ended up leaving them undone, which often led to chaos later. "If it's not urgent, I'm inclined to take it. But I'm starting to feel a little pressure, too many jobs in a row."

Sometimes, especially recently, it became easy to forget that they were running a business. You could only take on so many projects and since there really wasn't an option of expanding their services—Retrievers weren't thick on the ground, even if she could find someone both she and Sergei could trust, and have him or her trust them in return…nope. Wasn't going to happen. Lonejack weren't good at taking orders, and even the best guy in the Council was still Council and owed loyalty to them first and foremost, no matter who was signing the paycheck. Amazing what a retirement policy and medical could buy.

"I'll check," Sergei said, "but I think they were giving off 'me-first, right now!' vibes."

"Bother. Then no. See? I'm learning to say no." It hurt, though. Probably hurt her partner, too: Sergei had a pretty expensive lifestyle he worked hard to maintain, starting with that lovely uptown condo of his. But the final call was always hers.

"Good." Sergei took that strip and tore it in two, then dumped it into the recycling bin. "Next, we'll teach you how to take a vacation."

"Hah. Mr. Pot, is that your pager going off?" The last "vacation" he had taken in her memory had been a business trip for the gallery, where he spent every day hopping from workshop to workshop trying to decide who to bring in for a show and keeping her from bringing anything home "accidentally." Still, she supposed that for him, that *was* a vacation…"Anyway, lonejacks don't get a vacation. It's in our charter."

He wasn't going to let her get away with that. "You don't have a charter. None of you could agree on anything long enough to write one."

"Nitpicker." She grinned, settling herself more comfortably on the couch, seeing him wince as her boots came into contact with the upholstery. Tough, too much effort to take them off. And anyway, they were new, and clean. Mostly. "And that's not entirely true any more, anyway, thanks to the Tri-Com. And you're stalling on the important stuff." She leaned forward, letting go of the easy, casual dialogue they had been maintaining. "What do you have for me?"

The advantage of Sergei's other career, and the reason it dovetailed so well with their work together—his resources were varied, and international, and always could be counted on to come through, one way or the other.

Now, he pulled out an entirely new set of notes, these jotted on pale yellow index cards that she recognized from the desk in his apartment. For these he pulled out his glasses, looking up as though daring her to make a comment, risqué or otherwise. She looked back as innocently as she could, considering the sight of him in those things always sent a flicker through her that wasn't current-related at all.

"P.B.'s recollections of his earliest history were quite accurate," he said finally. "The folk at the Amsterdam Historical Society would very much like to talk to him."

She snorted, picking up a sofa cushion and rubbing the nubby surface absently. "Yeah, good luck with that. What did they tell you?"

"Let's see." He glanced down at the notes. "In 1890, a noted naturalist and certified loon—their words, by the way—named Herr Doktor Zee left Amsterdam by boat a few hours ahead of a lynch mob armed with the legendary pitchforks and fire. He was reportedly part of a small group of, and again I quote, 'rather progressive crackpots and theorists' who made the mistake of actually talking about their theories where too many people could hear them. The term 'heretics' and 'grave robbers' were reportedly thrown around, although much of that may have been fueled by desire for Herr Doktor's reportedly extensive collection of art rather than any doctrinal conflict."

He put the notes down and looked up at her, speaking from memory now.

"Anyway, he and much of his household was spirited away in the night, ending up in Traansval, in South Africa. Interesting place, back then. A few years later he was reportedly killed in a particularly pointless and otherwise unnotable battle during the Second Boer War. His body was never recovered, but the house he was renting was burned to the ground."

Wren didn't think it smart to interrupt his recitation to ask what a Boer was and why they had two wars. She'd look it up later.

"The sole remaining member of his family, a nephew who had remained in Holland, sold everything that survived to a small museum there, without ever investigating what his inheritance might be. A few decades later, the museum closed and the contents were sold off."

"Dead end?" She didn't think so. Not the way Sergei was holding back, as though he had something he wanted to tell her, but only after a proper setup. He'd dug deep into his contacts for this one, playing all the strings he had out there, and she had time, so she let him grandstand the delivery. It was good to see him play again.

"A lesser man might conclude that," he said, practically smirking. "I, however, do not conclude so easily. Karl gave me the name of someone who gave me the name of someone who turned out to be Council and maybe had heard of me."

He paused, and she smirked. Her name might be one that made Council double-check their valuables, but Sergei'd gotten in their faces a few times, too.

"Fortunately he saw no harm and some possible good in sharing seemingly useless information with me. The contents of that museum were sold off to individual collectors. After that, Herr Doktor's legacy disappeared for a number of years, probably into some good citizen's attic. The trail went cold for at least fifty years."

She waited.

He lowered his head and looked at her over the tops of his glasses, the gleam in his eye suggesting that he was about to drop the proverbial whammy on the table. "Further investigation, with the aid of Karl's antiquities database and an intern—did you know he had an intern? I think we need an intern—revealed that in the 1960s, several papers and various scientific objects of undetermined provenance or usage bearing our man's name on it appeared in auction. Since he wasn't anyone of note, they didn't go for much—another small museum bought the entire packet, exhibiting it as part of a crackpot science display, before they too went belly-up."

He paused, clearly expecting her to say something. So she did.

"And the contents of that museum were bought by…?"

"Nobody. They were put into storage for another fifty years or so, the fate of things too interesting to simply toss but too unimportant to preserve."

She decided that she had given him enough playtime. "Sergei. Where. Are. The. Papers?"

Mischief peeked out again from behind the businessman with another glance over the rims of his eyeglasses, and she braced herself. He was going to rock her world.…

"In 2000, a researcher in Cape Town came across the storage facility while working on a novel about the Boer Wars. The museum having long ago abandoned them, the contents, including Herr Doktor's papers and some, and again I quote, 'disturbing artifacts' were sold off…"

He paused dramatically then took pity on her. "To the Museum of Historical Science and Nature."

Wren felt her heart lurch like a drunken sailor, up into her throat and then down into her gut. She sat up, feet flat on the carpeted floor.

"*Our* Museum of Historical Science and Nature?" she asked cautiously, not willing to make any assumptions. It couldn't be that easy. It just couldn't.

Sergei grinned, the refined businessman's veneer cracking entirely to show the predator underneath. Apparently, it was that easy.

For impossible values of easy, anyway.

The HSN-NY. The museum she had spent half of her

lifetime wandering in and out of, fascinated by the old-fashioned displays of early technology and dioramas of exotic and extinct—and occasionally thoroughly debunked—creatures. The museum she knew practically blindfolded, top to bottom and side to side. One of the best-funded, most esoteric small private museums in a city filled with them, at the edge of the so-called "Museum Row" along the eastern edge of Central Park, living forever in the figurative shadow of the grand dame Museum of Natural History, but no less fascinating for it. A museum that took its security seriously. A challenge.

"Oh dear and kind God. Tell me it's not on display." She thought she might have noticed that, but there had been so many special exhibits over the years they all sort of ran together, and she'd been a little busy lately. A challenge was one thing, but temporary exhibits tended to be extremely well-guarded even inside those parameters, with lots of people paying attention to them, in the novelty of it all. A smash-and-grab from a temporary exhibit was a showboat gig, something you did for maximum splash to advertise how good you were. Wren didn't want any splash at all; she wanted to get in and out without anyone even noticing anything had been taken. If they were part of a permanent exhibit it might be easier, although she had never actually cased their security system; she tended to have more work around fine art collections, not dinosaur bones and six-foot-tall stuffed penguins. And there wasn't enough money in the world to entice her to try for the exotic minerals exhibits. She had it on good authority that the last time that was tried was in the 1940s, and the Retriever who took the job was never heard from again. Not the museum's responsibility—there was a meteor in their collection that was less than obliging about being stolen.

"Well now. That's where it gets…interesting," her partner said slowly, leaning back in his chair and letting his long legs stretch out under the wooden desk. He looked every inch the smug corporate boss, and she resisted—barely—the urge to move his chair out from under him with a swipe of current.

"You know I hate that word." She really did. It never made her happy, not in that context. "Spill."

"Nobody knows what was done with the acquisition."

Yeah, she knew it. She wasn't happy. "They…lost the papers."

He kept leaning back, and she had a passing thought that if he fell over backward and cracked his head, she was going to laugh, no matter how inappropriate or cruel it might be.

"Not only the papers, and not so much lost as…misplaced," he corrected her. "Nobody's really sure, since most of their moth-balled collections are stored due to their space restrictions, where the boxes were actually placed after they were purchased. The person who bought them died soon after—nothing suspicious, he was in his eighties by then—and nobody else had any real interest in that sideline of research, to put it kindly."

"They didn't throw it out?" She had a horrid vision of having to go through decades-old landfills, cursing all demon, Talent, and Null partners as she did so.

"Museums never throw anything out, Wren. That's what makes them museums. But according to the information I was able to dig up, the file cabinet with those records seems to have gone missing in a recent office move."

"Great. Remember what I say about coincidences?" Suddenly she had a throbbing headache. And Sergei's expression of almost unholy glee wasn't helping. "I'm good, but I'm not that good, Didier. Unlike some people, I don't believe my own press."

"Oh, it gets better."

She squinted at him. "And by better you mean worse, don't you?"

"The clock is ticking. We're not the only ones to have queried about Herr Doktor and his estate in the past six months. Which, by the way, is about when those files went missing: six months ago."

The headache had officially become a full-blown crawl-back-into-bed-and-die throb. Despite herself, and the pain, Wren felt flickers of interest, exactly the way Sergei had anticipated she would, damn him.

"Somebody knows what's in there? But how? Who? Why now?" Even as she asked, Wren thought she knew the answer. Because of her. It had to be. It all went back to their bond, the one P.B. instigated in order to save her life last year. Someone had found out about it, had realized how it connected to P.B.'s origins, and started hunting. Someone who knew what demon had been created for. That was the only thing that made any sense, and would explain the letter P.B. had gotten.

He had been right, that letter was real, and it was probably written under duress that was almost certainly fatal.

Her fault. Not that there were people out there with evil intent, she wasn't that much of a guilt-ridden egomaniac. But that they knew there was a reason to go after demon, that P.B., specifically, might be a target...that was her responsibility.

In the moment of truth months ago, torn up and worn down by events around her, Wren had gone beyond her limits, not caring what it did to her system so long as she could strike out against those who had harmed her and those around her. She had done it to end, once and for all, the fear and distrust that was shattering the *Cosa*, to end the efforts of the Silence, who had decided that the modern world had no place for magic, to rid the city of that "abomination."

She could not have done it alone, not even as Talented as she was. But the sudden infusion of current from the Fatae, through a tricky bit of electrical manipulation that she prayed would never be repeated, had allowed her access to the power.

And, already three-quarters of the way into wizzing, that jolt sent her over the edge.

In the darkness that tried to eat her, in that instant, she had been lost…until she heard not her own voice calling out, but two others. Sergei…and P.B.

She had never told a soul, not even those two, exactly what had happened inside her that night. But rumors spread, expanded, and became, somehow, more believable than the truth. Spread…and were heard by the wrong people.

She didn't know for sure that was what had happened, but the guilt weighed just as heavy, proven or not.

"Everyone wants their own damn personal demon." Exactly what she had promised P.B. would never happen.

"Not everyone." Sergei came around to sit next to her, his much larger hands capturing her own, stilling their restless fidgeting. "Even among those who might suspect, mostly they either don't care, or they're not strong enough for it to matter." You had to be at a certain level in order to channel enough current for wizzing to be a danger. Most Talent were blocked, could only use fifty or sixty percent of what was available. Wren had a few blocks—she couldn't Translocate herself without being ill, even now—but she figured she was maybe eighty percent unblocked.

Maybe more, now.

"It won't matter," she said. "He'll become a status symbol, a way to show you're Pure enough…even if you're not." And not just P.B. Her demon protected himself even before the events of the past year made things dicier. But other demon, ones who didn't have his experience, or weren't as savvy—even the strongest of bodies could be captured. Given enough muscle, even P.B. could be taken down, despite his precautions.

Her hands were like ice, and all she could think about was the promise that she had made to P.B., before she even knew what he was, what he could do.

I will never take anything you do not willingly offer.

And yet, to stop anyone from ever wizzing again…to keep people from the madness that had claimed Max, Neezer, so many others who could have given so much good to the world if they hadn't…. Again the thought came to her: to save Neezer, would she… No. Not ever. She felt sick inside, as if sudden vertigo mixed with a gut full of too much sugar was making her feel light-headed and sweaty. To choose between her father and her brother…

"Wren. Wren!"

Wren

Sergei was Null. That ping hadn't come from him.

Wren. Are you all right?

P.B. didn't use magic. None of the Fatae did; they *were* magic. That was how they had been able to gift her with the power to destroy the Silence, like giving blood at the scene of an accident. No, not blood: marrow. Prime and potent and nearly overwhelming with power.

Demon were not like the rest of the fatae, nor were they like humans. Somewhere in between, created to be a living bridge. The strength P.B. gave her blended into her own, rather than overpowering. Someday they were going to have to figure out exactly what that meant, and how far it could be pushed. Today wasn't that day.

I'm okay. Bad day. she sent back, and cut the connection. He would have to know the deal, know her guilt, but not right now. Not until she was sure what the deal was, and how much trouble they might be in.

Her attention returned to her partner, all business now. "I

need you to get me the blueprints to the museum and every single damn storeroom they have—everything and anything available, and the stuff that's not available, too. Plus the name of anyone working there who might be even slightly bribeable, influenceable or on vacation at any point in the next month." And then she had to convince P.B. to get in touch with his fellow demon, no matter how he did it. They needed to know if anyone else had been approached, if anyone else had gone missing. If she had competition in this Retrieval, and it sounded as if she might, she wanted to know who, who, and when, as well as why.

She reached over and picked up one of the slips of paper off Sergei's blotter. "Meanwhile, it looks like I have a favor to pay back. Joy."

ten

"Dear universe. Why does paying back favors never seem to involve lying on a towel somewhere on a beach with sweet-tempered cabana boys rubbing tanning oil all over hard-to-reach spots?"

She wasn't really expecting an answer. She didn't get one.

Instead of warm tropical breezes scented with coconut oil, the air was cold, and filled with the less-than-delightful smells of a working sea-wharf and the wind coming off Newark Bay. Moreover, there were absolutely no cabana boys of any temperament, anywhere to be seen. Port Newark wasn't exactly a hopping social spot on a Sunday night—correction, early Monday morning—for a reason.

Despite that, there was a steady if slow rumble of activity behind her, from the Container Terminal. The city might occasionally sleep, but the ocean never did, and dawn would arrive to find the 930 square acres of the Port already hard at work.

Wren leaned against a damp wooden post, shivering in her

jacket, and tried not to think about how damned tired she was. Soonest started, soonest home, soonest back in a comfy, warm, *occupied* bed.

With that pleasant thought, she pursed her lips and whistled lightly, the sound carrying a filament of current with it. It was a trick she had learned purely by accident, trying to whistle along with Billy Joel's "The Stranger." Sound conveyed current, of course; that was the point of cantrips; that the words helped focus and direct the magic. But a whistle, the pure sound without words, was even better for that. It just wasn't always practical, and not everyone could whistle well enough to hold the focus. She could.

And since when did you start thinking in terms of "magic?" That was Old Time, old ways, abandoned since the nineteenth century.

Probably since you started using old ways, too, her brain thought back at her with a touch of snide superiority. *Or are you going to pretend none of that ever happened?*

No, she wasn't. Not when touching on the old ways had— might have, she amended—saved her life. Fatae-magics. Sex-magics, blood-magics, sympathetic magics. She didn't have to like it, though. Old ways were unpredictable, unreliable, lurking underneath the psyche, within reach of anyone who had enough willpower to touch them but controllable by very few. You never knew what results you might get, with old magic. That's why Founder Ben started experimenting with his keys and kites in the first place, to find a better way. A more reliable, repeatable way.

Magic was a science, after all.

That thought led her back around to her discussion with P.B. about genetics, and inheritance, and goo, and father-creators, and the thoughts almost derailed her whistle.

Stop that. Don't you dare get distracted!

She came to the end of the passage without further stumbling, and started again, patiently. Some things were less about flair or finesse than patience. Most of the job—like standing in the darkness whistling—was boring, and that was good. Boring meant according to plan. Excitement meant excrement. Lots of excitement meant excrement in the air-conditioning.

After the third rendition of the whistle-touch, something broke the dark waters just off the pier, rising about a foot above the surface. In the pre-dawn blackness, it was difficult to make out any details, but she thought she saw the gleam of eyes looking her way.

She whistled again, a slightly different tone, letting it rise and decline before it faded away. She wasn't much of a singer, but she could whistle up a storm.

She almost laughed at the phrase. She probably could, at that.

The shadowy shape sank back below the surface, but the ripples indicated that it was still there, and heading toward her. Wren left the security of the shadows, and walked out along the dock to meet it, kneeling down at the edge even as the surface of the water broke and a figure rose three feet straight out of the water.

"Hello, *Cosa*-cousin," she said, thinking hard about her request. The serpent merely blinked at her, the large, pale eyes definitely glimmering in the lamplight coming down from overhead. From the size of the triangular head, and the thickly muscled neck flowing back down into the water, she estimated it to be about thirty feet long, and maybe five feet across. Not quite full grown, which made sense; very few of them hung around the shoreline once they got their full size. Not enough to eat, and too many chances of being spotted by someone with a decent camera.

hunger

Serpents, unlike their airborne cousins the dragons, weren't much for conversation, but they knew how to make their needs known. The wave of fish-scented hunger that hit her brain made Wren glad that she'd skipped breakfast that morning. Thankfully, forewarned was foregifted.

"Will this do?" She lifted the shopping bag she had been lugging and let the serpent scent the aromas, or whatever it was serpents did.

pleasure came back to her, and she tipped the bag open and dumped the contents onto the dock. That great triangular head dipped almost faster than she could follow, and she took an involuntary step back. Thankfully, the beast had no interest whatsoever in her. The loop of pastrami, however, disappeared almost before it hit the planks. Her informant had been right, bless his pointy little nose. New Yorkers, apparently, were New Yorkers, no matter where they lived. Wren supposed she should be thankful he hadn't been craving an egg cream or something a little more difficult to carry on the subway.

"All right. You know what to do?" she asked it as soon as the offering had been consumed.

A sated sense of satisfaction and agreement answered her, and the serpent slid beneath the waters again, leaving an oily ripple on the water's surface, and the scent of pastrami-burp in the air.

They weren't the smartest of the *Cosa*, serpents, but they were trustworthy. Most snake breeds were, she'd found. So much for that stereotype...

Right. She had about ten minutes, she estimated, before minor hell broke loose. Best not to waste any of it.

The empty bag stirred at her feet, and she looked down at it, half-surprised the serpent hadn't eaten that, too. She was tempted to leave it there, but a combination of good citizen training and common sense made her stoop to pick it up. *Leave nothing behind.*

"Recycle," she told it, barely even reaching for current, and the paper bag shimmered and dissolved into powdery wood dust. Close enough. She dusted off her hands and walked back off the pier, toward the more active part of the docks.

Her goal was the batch of most recent ships, the ones still in quarantine. There was a container in one of the ships docked there, she had been told, specifically the *Becca Sims.* Customs hadn't had a chance to go through the invoices yet, but they'd gotten wind of something hinky stored in the hold.

How hinky was still subject to debate. What wasn't, apparently, was the fact that it would embarrass a number of people, including the United States government, if there had to be any kind of formal investigation or, God forbid, arrest in the matter.

Wren had no problem with the government taking one or two on the chin, but she'd learned enough about politics in the past few years to know that sometimes you had to cover even for people you didn't like, to keep things from getting too ugly. And since she didn't happen to have a horse in this particular race, she'd shut up and do the job, discharging a favor-debt in the process and leaving the slate nice and clean.

Besides, quiet and sneaky was her stock in trade.

The moment she heard yelling coming from somewhere, drawing the attention of everyone who might otherwise be paying attention, Wren slipped up the gangway of the *Becca Sims* and, no-see-me firmly in place, ghosted up into the ship, through the bare metal hallways, and down into the cargo hold.

"Don't come out, come out, whatever you are" she called in a quiet singsong voice, ignoring the thudding against the hull that was her bribed buddy making like Nessie on a bad day. She was lucky he—she? How did you tell?—was young and still thought this would be a good prank. An older, wiser serpent would have told her where to get off, probably. Or would have taken this as an excuse to eat a sailor or two.

Hoorah for intra-*Cosa* relations. And she didn't have to play on that "hidden Cousin" thing, either. Notoriety was fine when you wanted it, but inconvenient as hell the rest of the time.

The container she was looking for was in the very back, of course. Most of the boxes were taller than she was, and several times as broad, but this one was barely up to her shoulder and wide as her arm span. Plastic; she had somehow expected everything to be wooden, but she seemed to be surrounded by a Tupperware farm. Made it tougher on the rats, she supposed.

"All right. Let's see what we got here." She didn't touch the container; she didn't need to, not yet. Instead, she let her eyes unfocus, and then looked with her current, instead.

Nothing. Not even an erg of a come-hither.

Another heavy thump almost managed to knock her off her feet, and she glared at the steel wall as though the serpent could see her through it. "I said distract, not sink, you stupid eel."

She turned her attention back to the container, still not touching it. Because she had never done this before, she took refuge in a familiar cantrip to focus her thoughts.

"friend or foe
water carries true;
tell me now."

It didn't have to be good poetry; it didn't even have to be poetry. She just happened to like the simplicity of the haiku structure. Plus, poetry was easier to remember. Sometimes, in dicey situations, that mattered.

The words merged with the current in her core, rising and swirling in a faint blue glow. She could see it, faintly, rising from her core, up her spine, out along her arms and out through her fingertips, sparking gently as it reached toward the container in question.

"Holy fu—" The word was stolen from her throat as she *felt* what was in there. Not animal, mineral or pharmaceutical; not even chemical, the way the unimaginative assumed.

She pulled her current back into herself, wincing as it snapped unpleasantly into place, like a thick, neon, rubber band. What was in there was *alchemical*; elements primed and ready for the final touch that would turn them into…whatever it was that it was supposed to be. She didn't feel any sense of malice or anger to it; not that it couldn't still be dangerous, but generally speaking things that had the touch of current to them also carried the emotions—the *signature*—of their user.

This just felt…greedy. Anonymous greed, but no less disturbing for that. In fact, it was even more disturbing for being faceless, unconnected.

She felt a shudder run down her spine that had nothing to do with current. Greed wasn't good. In her experience, greed caused more trouble than anything else, depending on what you were greedy for. Candy, minor. Blood, or souls, or life…

But nothing had been triggered yet. Everything here was just potential, the parts not yet assembled. She wasn't sure how she knew that, but she did, gut-level.

Problem was, she had no idea what the trigger was, or who was supposed to assemble it. Someone, anyone might come by and, intentionally or not…

The not-knowing was what killed you. Sometimes literally.

There was shouting, and the sound of a lot of boots running overhead. Her serpent had shifted his point of assault to the other side of the boat. That boy was having far too much fun.

Something skittered with her in the hold, against the far wall, and she wondered if modern cargo ships had rats, despite the Tupperware. Probably. Some things never changed.

Her job assignment had been vague. *"Do…whatever it is you do. I don't want to know. Just, if there's anything there, get rid of it."*

Get rid of it. Right. From Retriever to garbage detail. Still, she supposed she was within the realm of her job description—removing something from the premises without the possessor of the item knowing….

She started to slip into fugue state, and caught herself. No need to give herself cramps for this. Instead, Wren kept her physical eyes on the container, and touched the core of current within her. As always, it felt like a pit of vipers, scales dry-slithering and sparking against each other in neon brights. There was a hint of darker colors, too; a purple-black that alternated between shimmering and matte. The sludge of old magic, waiting for another chance at her. She ignored it, an act of purely human stubbornness and denial, and focused instead on the glimmers of scarlet winding through the mass.

Her core, her own personal current-store. Modern theory— and stories of old magic—suggested that everyone had it, but most humans lacked the ability to touch and mold it. It wasn't just the will and the word, apparently. *Goo,* she thought again. *I am filled with goo.*

All right. Back to the box. The bits individually were…not innocent, but not dangerous, not right now. So the trick was to make sure that they couldn't be joined.

Destroying something when you weren't quite sure what it was—stupid. Especially when on a boat, on water, with no easy access away from any major explosion, implosion, or other kind of boom.

A scarlet snake separated itself from the rest of the pit, rising to her command. It flowed out into the container as distinct threads, splitting off and then splitting off again. Not that Wren could see it, not using her physical eyes, but she knew it was there, doing her will.

Five threads, each one wrapping itself around a piece of the puzzle. Light, gentle layers, barely noticeable. Her arms raised as though conducting the movement, laying the threads by hand. Focused on the task, she barely felt the thuds that meant her *Cosa*-cousin was still at the job…or when the thuds stopped.

Bind, there, thus. A lesson in the back of her mind: John Ebeneezer sitting in the back of his classroom, still wearing the white lab coat he used during class over his jeans and Oxford shirt, teaching her how to thread a needle with current, each eye progressively smaller and smaller as her skills grew. Eye of the needle. Eye of the storm. Bind and close off, enclose, insulate.

Removing the items would require her to use current directly on them, and where would she send them, anyway? She sucked at Transloc; they'd probably end up in some longshoreman's breakfast, or a kid's backpack. And what if that was enough to trigger?

Thinking too much. Focus.

"Hey!" A voice, a man's voice, coming from behind her, echoing in the hold.

Oh damnittohell. Too much to hope for, that it wasn't directed at her…

She kept a light touch on the current, letting it continue as it had been started, and turned to deal with the intruder.

Technically, you're *the intruder.…*

Oh, shut up.

"What are you doing down here?" The speaker was a man, about fifty or so and hard-worn with it, from his shaved head to the gut hanging over his belt. But he also had the look of a man who knew how to throw trespassers off his boat—and maybe not worry about them hitting land.

He squinted to see her better; the Retriever's no-see-me trick was still working then, he was just used to being suspicious about shadows in his cargo hold. That should have made her feel better. It didn't.

Current-snakes slithered and hissed, demanding to be used. She fought her instinctive urge to run, needing to stay and make sure that the job was done.

"I'm not here," she said. Current rose again, but this time it stayed within her, humming in her bones, sliding just under her own skin, shimmering greens and blues. She felt tight, wound-up and ready to roll.

"What the hell?" He took a step closer, and she saw the short metal bar in his hand.

A body, crushed and beaten, bleeding out in a dark alley, once-white wings crushed and soiled. That was how it had all begun...one of the Angeli brought down low and dead.

She knew it wasn't the same. The Silence was broken, the vigilantes driven back underground. The only Silence member they knew was still alive was the researcher Darcy, who had helped them, in the end. Darcy had sent Sergei a postcard from somewhere in the Andes, about three months ago.

This guy? He was just a union joe doing his job. Wren held on, kept control until she felt the binding take over, the elements within the box rendered if not harmless, then at least useless.

"You, get out here! Don't make me hurt you!"

Wrong words. Oh so very much the wrong words. The job was done, she could let go, slip past him and be gone, but the emotions would not subside. *Don't make me hurt you!*

Bile rose in the back of her throat, and the hold she had on her current trembled, broke....

And held, held, if only by the tips of her shaking hands. P.B.: silent and supportive. Simply not trying to block him out allowed him in, not so much intrusive as preexisting. She could feel him in her, that bedrock of strength that could not be moved by mortals, nor broken by even her own current. She wiggled virtual toes, trying to ground herself in that strong comfort, but he was too far away, or she couldn't reach far enough down. The bile came back up into her mouth, and the bedrock receded and disappeared under the floodgate memory of rage and fear.

...hurt you...

No. She tried to quiet it, but the waves surged and swamped her, trying to drag her under and suffocate her in the tarry wash.

There was a buzzing hum in her ears, surprisingly gentle for the forces she felt assaulting her, a sound like a thousand black-and-red butterfly wings beating inside her head. Shaking with the need to control, to flee, to strike out against a threat, to *not kill*, she did the only thing she could do.

She Translocated.

"We've got to stop meeting like this," P.B. said.

Wren finished dry-heaving, and wiped her mouth with the damp washcloth he held out to her. Her limbs felt like Jell-O, and her skin crawled as if there were bugs on it. Worse, *under* it.

Teenagers with less Talent than she had in her palm could Translocate entire rooms with perfect accuracy, and she couldn't even send a pin into a pincushion without heaving her guts. Life was not fair.

"Seriously." P.B. squatted next to her. "What happened?"

Rage still controlled her brain, and she wanted to snarl at him. She didn't owe him any explanations. She didn't answer to anyone.

Then again, when you appear in someone's bathroom, puking your guts out into the toilet while they're taking a shower, they do have a right to know why. That thought was cold water on her, cooling her brain and washing away the bugs.

"Situation went bad. I had to get away."

"And you came here." He stood up and toweled himself off with a larger towel, his shower-wet fur giving off a pleasant, herb-scented smell. The demon used No More Tears, she knew that from previous visits to his bathroom. He usually had a slightly muskier, greener scent, too. Did demon wear cologne? He sure as hell didn't use an aftershave….

She felt herself start to get the giggles, an aftermath to the rage, and clamped down hard.

"Damn it, Valere…" The demon sighed, and sat down on the edge of the tub, his rounded body wrapped in the towel less for modesty than protection from the wet porcelain. "You only Transloc when you panic. What happened?"

"Not only when I panic," she said, sitting back on her heels and noting, absently, that she'd managed to ruin yet another pair of jeans. "Sometimes it's because I'm screwed, otherwise." Usually, no matter what the circumstances, her arrival results were less than pinpointed. Except when she panicked. Then she always came here.

If "always" translated into "twice now."

"This have anything to do with you cutting me off, earlier?"

"I did not…" Her sentence trailed off. She had, hadn't she. "No. Nothing to do with that. You caught me at a bad time." How much to tell, how much to withhold? "Sergei and I were…"

"Mamboing in a horizontal fashion?" he asked hopefully.

"Arguing," she had to admit.

P.B.'s bear-shaped face wasn't really suited to showing expression, but she could see the sorrow and frustration in his dark red eyes. "About me?"

She reached up to pat his knee, annoyed that her hand was

still shaking. "No." Then she paused, needing to be honest with him. "Not exactly."

"About the…job. That I asked you to do. He doesn't want you to do it?"

"He knows why, he was there, remember? And you didn't ask—I offered. If he'd had objections he would have voiced them there and then." That much was entirely true. It was also true that she wouldn't have listened, and he knew that, so wouldn't have bothered.

P.B. had an expression on his snouted face that suggested he knew all that, too.

"Look, can we not do this now?" she asked. "I'd really like some coffee, and—" she paused, testing her stomach. "And maybe some breakfast? Come on, I'll even buy. Least I can do for the unexpected drop-in."

He didn't want to let it go. "You have to trust me, Wren. Your body knows that—that's why you keep coming here when you're stressed. You can feel it. I ground you, and more to the point, I ground you safely, something Didier can't do. But your brain's not getting with the program, and that's dangerous."

"You're overstating—"

"Wren." He cut her off. "You wizzed. I can smell it on you, *feel* it on you, even now. Especially now. When those bastards attacked you, in the tunnels under the theater, you reacted…normally. No, I mean it."

There was nothing normal about what she had done. She had killed them. Worse, she had used current to rip them apart and scatter them into burned clumps and ash. She had murdered them.

"They were going to kill you. They were going to rape you and kill you, and they had done it to Talent before." She had never told him that, had never told them any of the details. P.B., apparently, didn't need to be told.

"You did a good thing, cleaning the world of that scum. The only problem was, you went into the dark storm, the wild, to do it, and you *liked* it. You crave it now."

She did. She craved it…as Sergei craved current-touch, the old sex-magics.

"That's what wizzing is, Valere. And you almost went there again today. Because you were scared."

She wanted to deny it. She couldn't. "It makes me sick. Every time I go too far, I get doubled over like I'm going to die." She had to force the words out of her mouth, and saying them wasn't the relief she'd hoped for. You couldn't be weak. If you were weak, the current took control. If it got the upper hand, you were toast.

"It's not the current that's making you sick," he corrected her, as though she were a student again and he her mentor. In this, she supposed, he was. That fact didn't make the lecture easier to bear. "It's the fact that you're controlling so much of it, keeping it in check, that's making you feel so ill. You're eating your body up from the inside, holding too much power in you. If you had actually wizzed, you'd feel just fine. You'd be mad as a hatter, but feel fine. It's the constant control that's killing you."

That was supposed to be his job: to supply the needed grounding, the fuel for her to work from. It just went against everything she'd ever been taught.

He didn't bother with subtlety or roundabout sweet-talking. He wasn't Sergei, to be delicate about her feelings. "Valere, I'm what stands between you and the crazies, now and until you die. It's not going to go away. Not ever. Not once you've been there. Not when you know how to make the scared, the uncertainty, go away. It's too easy, too tempting."

It was. Damn him. Damn her. It was so seductive, to dip into that dark storm—the maelstrom she felt when Max was around, the home of monsters—and make everything except the power go away.

"That's why you have to use me. Whenever, however you need to, without asking, without worrying. You can't get scruples about that, not now. Not without failing. And failing is not an option."

Hammering the point home, he hunched over her, reminding her once again that for all that he looked like a four-foot-tall polar bear cub, his solid bones and rock-hard muscle were fueled by human-level smarts and a truly scary level of Fatae indifference to the rest of the world.

"You don't get to protect me," he went on. "You never did. Doesn't matter that you didn't know what you did, that you didn't mean to. I let you in. I made a conscious decision. Because if I'm not there when you start to overrush? Your instinct's gonna be to ground in Didier, the way you used to. And he will let you.

"And how you gonna live with yourself when it kills him?"

"And how am I gonna feel when someone kills *you?*" she asked back, still wanting to snarl but lacking the energy. "Have you thought of that? People are actively hunting those papers, P.B. Word's out what you've—what *we've* done. You've become valuable. They might be hunting *you.*"

He looked annoyingly...smug? Yes, smug. "They can't break our bond. I won't serve anyone else. It's a choice, I can be tricked out of it, but I can't be coerced. It's the only reason why I can't hate my creator—he gave us that much freedom, whether he meant to or not. Freedom to choose."

Wren looked him in the eye, her seated position putting them almost nose to nose. "You're assuming these people give a damn. You're assuming they're thinking of you as anything other than a means to an end, that they want you whole. You're just as valuable—more valuable, maybe—as a vivisection model than a servant."

She had hoped to shock him with that. He didn't even blink. "I know. I was sort of hoping you hadn't thought of that, though."

Despite herself, she had to laugh. Her nose started to run, and she swiped at it with the washcloth. "No such luck. I'm just as bloody-minded as you are. It's why we get along. Now, breakfast?" Amazingly enough—or not, considering how much current she had used already that morning—she was suddenly ravenous. "Or are you going to let me starve to death on your bathroom rug?"

"Finish cleaning up in here, and let me dry off and call Sergei, let him know you're okay. *Then* breakfast."

Fair enough.

"Why are you here, and she's not?"

"Why should she be?" *He is defensive, knows it. They're starting to hit bone.*

"This is a joint problem, isn't it? You take, but she gives. She doesn't say no."

She's trying. She has other things she has to worry about first. Like her sanity." *Which he wasn't helping, being like this. That is why he's here.*

"You're protecting her."

"I'm her partner."

In the end, it comes down to that. He is here because he has to get the same kind of control she has. Who better to teach him than a therapist who is also a Talent?

Not as though he would bare his soul to some stranger. Just Joe Doherty, who had been there when the hell came to earth, and everything fell apart and came back together again. Sergei had seen his touch with the damaged then, working with the Lost, the children—the teenagers—Wren had stolen back from the Silence.

"Why are you here?"

"Again?"

"Again."

"I'm here because I need to understand my own kink, and how it's going to kill me some day." *Her own words, not his.*

"You can do better than that." *They've been down this road before, in the weeks and months prior. It's rote, but not comforting. Nothing about this is comforting, except the chair he sits in. He may buy one for his own office. Having clients put at ease is a plus in his business, too.*

"Why are you here, and she's not?" *Joe asks again.*

This time, the words come. "Because I don't trust her to be here, when I talk about this."

"This? What this are we talking about?"

"This...my being here. When I admit that I...that I blame her."

"Ah."

Sergei seriously goddamned hates that ahhh.

eleven

Wren stared at the flat cream-painted ceiling. There was a crack running through the plaster she had never noticed before. She should do something about that. Or not.

The dark green drapes were drawn across the windows, not allowing any of the afternoon light in, and she was naked on the bed, her skin prickling slightly from exposure. A single white candle burned on the old mahogany dresser, its squat beeswax reflection still and unwavering. Her mind was still, her thoughts open to the lesson from so long ago.

Flames are the traditional focus. Why is that?

Neezer's voice, teaching a bored fifteen-year-old. They were sitting on a picnic table in the park. Textbooks were open in front of them, to all intents and purposes an impromptu tutoring session. But what he was teaching had nothing to do with biology.

Because they're cheap? She'd had no idea, then, and blustered her way through it.

Because fire burns as well as warms. It is our servant—and can master us if we are not careful.

Like current? She had learned that much, at least. Knew what she was, and how she could do what others couldn't—and how very much it set her apart.

Like current. Look at the candle, Jenny-wren. Look, and become not the flame or the wick or the wax, but the entire thing. Flame and air, ash and scent.

Look at the candle. Focus. Remember.

John Ebeneezer. Oversized hands, so delicate when he handled the equipment in the labs, when he turned pages in a book. Fingernails perfectly trimmed, cuticles groomed, without a single ragged edge. She remembered his hands more than she remembered his face, or even his voice. He'd been a baritone, she thought; his voice had been low and deep, and it carried to the end of the classroom without him even trying. Some of the girls had had a crush on him. Maybe some of the boys, too. He'd been a born teacher, coaxing even the most reluctant student into some enthusiasm for his chosen subject.

She had been barely seventeen when he started to wizz. He disappeared a few months later, abandoning job, house, and her in one giant leap, and even knowing that he had done it out of fear for her safety, fear of what he might do to her in his inevitable madness, had not softened the blow of abandonment. If he had really loved her, if she had been a better student, if she had been more of what he wanted in a student, he would have found a way to stay....

Wren exhaled, and tried to refocus on the lesson. All right, so she had a few issues. She'd made peace with most of them years ago, even if they hung around in the back of her brain, mostly quiet and unnoticed. Neezer wasn't her father, he had never tried to be her father. He had been her mentor, though, and that had been more important in a lot of ways. And he had done what he had done in order to protect her, by his own standards, no matter how it hurt at the time, or now.

She missed him, even now. Even years after she had started to accept the fact that he was likely dead.

But he wasn't. Her thoughts crept back into the stillness she was trying to cultivate, drawn by the memory of the man who had taught her with such loving attention. *He wasn't dead and there was enough of him left in his madness, like Max, that he remembered her. Remembered her—and hid from her. What had he become? What scared Max so much that he played bullyboy with such sadness in his eyes?*

It was madness of her own, but she had to know. She needed to know. She couldn't afford *not* to know.

If the only difference between that and her was P.B....

Setting her gaze on the candle once more, Wren let herself feel the flame from across the room. She could feel the hiss of oxygen through her lungs, the softening of the wax in her bones, the shiver of heat on her skin, as if it *were* her lungs, her bones, her skin.

"John Ebeneezer."

The bond between mentor and student was the only one the lonejacks recognized. Not peer to peer, not parent to child, or sibling to sibling; the sole unending, undying, undeniable obligation was with your mentor. Only death could end it.

Death, or wizzing. That was the understanding, anyway.

Nobody said what happened to that bond when both mentor and mentee wizzed. Wren had decided that was an oversight she was going to correct.

"Neezer. John Ebeneezer. Where are you?"

The sense of him, the memories and sounds and scents and that most recent fleeting touch of him, before Max swept it all away. She gripped them tight, and *concentrated.*

It wasn't quite like fugue-state, but it wasn't unlike it, either. The candle became her, and she melted like wax, slipping from the grasp of flesh and scattering into the atmosphere on thousands of threads of wild current.

So very cool. Out-of-body exploration was something she had studied, but never actually done. She was more about the actually being there, not just looking on. Plus, you couldn't actually *look* without eyes. It was difficult enough to keep thoughts together, much less form retinas.

But for this kind of searching, broad-based and very specific all at once, there was nothing like an out-of-body experience.

Underneath her the East Coast spread out, crowded cities and sprawling suburbs, green expanses of farms and forests, and blue spreads of water. Current flickered in everything, bright and dark and sizzling. Nulls couldn't see it. Most Talent didn't bother to look deeply enough to find it. But it was there, breathing in the air and the water and the living flesh of the universe. She wanted to gather it all in her hand and take it into her core, so much so that she could feel her own tendrils stir, back in the bedroom, trying to reach out and consume.

Stay. she told it. *Be still.*

The trick was to know what you were looking for, and not get distracted. Get distracted, and…well, she didn't know exactly what might happen. But she didn't think it would be good. And probably wouldn't help finding what she was looking for.

Somewhere down there, in the speck of the map that was Manhattan, P.B. waited, as he promised. Breakfast in a tiny little café, apple pancakes drowning in real maple syrup and little cups of thick sweet coffee, the smell of tobacco lingering from decades past in the walls, and he had promised that if she did this, he would be there. Bedrock, if she needed it: the solid underlying foundation, the safest place to dig in and ground. She might slip, her control might fail. His never would. There was a tiny spark inside her that recognized that, held on to that, clung to it, letting it sit under her skin, under her bones, deep inside her core.

That bond wasn't sexual, or fraternal, or any sensation that she could identify. It simply *was*. She trusted it to keep her safe, and forgot about it.

Neezer. *Focus on Neezer.*

As though the thought was a rope, Wren felt tugged downward, her essence diving like a falcon toward one specific spot in the blue below her.

Water? she thought, just as she struck the surface and went underneath.

Out of body meant that she couldn't drown, of course. She wasn't even really wet; her body was safely back home, in her own bed. But the immediate reaction was one of flailing panic.

Jesus wept, Valere! She straightened herself out, arching like an arrow down farther into the water, following that hint deeper into the cool lake waters.

It wasn't possible that he was there; he was crazy but still human, still needing air to breathe. Right? But the scent was so strong, she couldn't not follow it.

The bottom came up fast, smacking her on the nonexistent nose. It was gravelly and disgusting, and she decided she must be in a man-made swimming hole of some sort. Hopefully not a reservoir, from the amount of junk thrown into the water and left to rust: the mess turning the water into an odd shade of green. Tires and old beer cans and the carcass of an old car off in the distance…she wondered, idly, if there was a body in the trunk, and the thought froze her in place.

He was alive. Not dead in the trunk of a Caddy like some Mafioso fall guy. She knew that.

But she had to check, anyway.

There were no fish in the murky waters, but she was pretty sure she saw/sensed something moving on the other side of the car. No sooner had she thought that than she was there. Her hand—her image of her hand—rested on the rusted trunk, and she could *see* inside.

There was a body there, but it wasn't Neezer. Wren didn't know how she knew the rotting skeleton was too old and too female, but it was.

Someone threw granny into the lake? Nice.

But Neezer's scent was still nearby. Wren let herself dissipate into the water slightly, and traced the currents of current to the object of her search.

Hiking boots. Old, battered, size-ten brown leather boots, worn down at the heel and tied with thick rawhide laces that had broken and been reknotted several times. There was nothing about them to say that they had belonged to any one specific person, and the odds were almost impossible, but she knew. They had been Neezer's, and not so very long ago, otherwise the water would have erased all trace of him. That was what water did; it cleaned and cleared and wore impressions away to nondescript blankness. That was why witches and warlocks traditionally feared running streams, because they were one of the few things that could wear down a spell once it was cast. Simply run through the stream and do what water did.

She reached for the boot, then jerked her entire body back as a tentacle came out from the boot's top. She had no idea what kind of pseudopod might live in water like this, in the cast-off shoe of a wizzart, but she suspected it might have either teeth or a sting.

And you don't have a body here, moron. It can't sting or bite you.

Feeling rather remarkably stupid, Wren reached out again and touched her not-there finger to the boot, not sure what to expect. If she didn't have a body, could her psychometry actually work?

Frustration. Immense amounts of frustration, and a bitch of a blister on his left heel. "You should have worn socks" except he didn't have any, not any more, and he kept forgetting to find some. He had a little money left, they had made sure of that, but he couldn't remember what he had done with it and the thought of going into a store—too many people, too much noise, too much everything—wasn't one he could contemplate for too long.

His feet hurt, but everything felt better as he stood barefoot in the mud and watched the boots go sailing out to splash splish splash thunk into the water and sink down down down and never be worn again....

That was all there was. No sense of when; it might have happened yesterday, or a year ago, or the day after he first disappeared.

No. Even as Wren felt herself leaving that spot, rising back up into the atmosphere, her current sparking and reshaping itself, she knew that it had been more recent than that. Neezer left when he was still mostly sane, was only starting to slip away. The man who had thrown those boots was more than a cracker shy of a full barrel.

And someone had given him money. Max? Or someone else? The Council maintained safe-homes, places with limited electrical power, where their wizzarts could rest if they wanted to, not distracted or tempted by easy access to current. But Neezer had been a lonejack, like her; the Council didn't take care of freelancers.

Someone was, though. Someone a little more together and coherent than Max was taking care of her mentor.

Wren should have, she supposed, been relieved. Instead, she was livid. Hurt, and angry, and mainly just pissed off.

That should have been *her* job, damn it. She was his student, his only student, and she should have been the one to make sure he was all right. Not someone else, not Max who barely held it together himself, who killed his own dog, for God's sake! Was that who had sent Max after her, this person or persons who had taken over her obligations, her responsibilities?

Or was it Neezer himself, denying her, cutting that final tie? Why?

She tried to catch another scent to follow, but her emotions screwed with her control, and she felt her concentration *snap* and fling her backward, ass over teakettle, knees over ears. She fell up and sideways, then was tumbling without any sense of direction or distance, her nonexistent body breaking under the stress until her sense of self started to disintegrate and dissipate, as well.

She reached out, grabbed at nothing, found a fingerhold somewhere of something hard, warm, accepting and unyielding at the same time. Bedrock. She clutched, felt it shake, as though undergoing seismic seizures, and she cried out in fear and loss. The cry echoed, and as though in response the bedrock stilled itself, like a horse shuddering to a heaving halt.

Once the virtual ground under her fingers stabilized, she could feel it slide under her, trying to support her, but the panic—and the crumbling loss of self—remained, making it impossible to stop the disintegration.

If she didn't stop it, she would not be. Not here…and not there. Trapped, forever.

Home she thought wildly, grabbing onto the word and hugging it tight. *Safe-home.*

Safe-words were like cantrips. You didn't really need them, but it made it easier to focus. *Safe-home* landed her, like Neezer's boot, solidly thunking back into her body on the bed in her apartment in Manhattan.

Feeling as if she had been beaten with bamboo rods by a mad percussionist, Wren lifted one eyelid and was dismayed to discover that the room was dark, much darker than even her blackout curtains could make it. *Was there a blackout? Oh shit, am I blind?*

The bed shifted under her, and the darkness moved a little. She squinted until Sergei's shadowed form came into focus. Her panic subsided, and she let out a little gasp of relief.

"I'm going to turn on the light," he warned in a low, rough voice, and she braced herself. He had placed something over the lampshade, though, and so the light was filtered. Her eyes watered anyway, and when she went to place an arm over them, to shield them from the glare, her entire body screamed a protest against moving.

"You scared the hell out of me," Sergei said, his voice still that same unnerving quiet roughness. "I came in and you were just lying there, naked, and I couldn't tell if you were breathing…. Your skin was cool and damp, and you didn't *move*."

"How long?" Her voice was cracked and dry, and she almost didn't recognize it.

"Since I got here? Two hours."

Wren would have sworn she was only "away" ten minutes, tops. She rested her head back down on the pillow and sighed. "I'm sorry. I didn't know it would take so long." Or that she would hurt so much. Fuck, it hurt.

"What were you doing?"

"I… I was doing a scrying." Her voice still sounded bad, but talking was a little easier. "Sort of astral projection, kind of."

"I didn't know you could do that." Still too tight, too rough, his voice.

"Me, neither," she admitted. "I mean, I knew about it, but…" It had been a scrap of an idea she had pulled from memory. Not every Talent could do everything—there were distinct strengths and weaknesses, and by the time you were an adult you usually knew your skill sets. Wren didn't know if it was wizzing, or being the focus of that damned battery, but she was finding new things every month that she could do, or do better. This…not better enough.

"You were looking for the papers?"

"No. I…I was trying to find Neezer. I think he's alive. I think Max was hiding him, or helping him to hide." Her voice dropped to a whisper, less because it hurt than because she felt foolish.

Sergei shifted on the bed, and sighed, years of history in that simple sound. "Wren, why? What difference does it make, if he is alive? He's not the man you remember, not any more. Why can't you just let him go? "

It was a valid question. She wasn't sure she knew why. A year ago she had thought he was dead, and the memory of his voice was fading, and she had been okay with that. Things came and went and she didn't love her mentor any less for his not being there. She had P.B., and Sergei, and her mom, and it wasn't as though she needed a mentor any more.…

And then the shit hit the fan with the vigilantes; she nearly went all wild-eyed Dark Side, and was blasted with the battery-current of the Fatae, and the carefully constructed mental boxes she had been keeping things in got shifted in the resulting shake-up, shifted, yeah and some of them got busted open.

Part of the resulting mess led to her insistence on Sergei getting help. Part of it led her to consider leaving the city. And part of it…part of it was jostled loose by the encounter with Max, and suddenly it was important that she know.

Know what?

I don't know.

Maybe she was the one who needed to be in therapy.

"It's almost nine," her partner said cautiously, as though uncertain of her temper. Or her sanity. "Do you want dinner?"

Nine? As in, p.m.? That bit of information shocked her out of her funk. She had been out-of-body much longer than two hours—more like six. No wonder she was exhausted. And no wonder he was freaked—they were supposed to have met almost four hours ago.

"I don't…soup, maybe," she suggested. The thought of anything heavier than that—or more effort to eat—made her just want to close her eyes and float away again, but something told her that would be a very bad idea. Her head was fuzzy and her body felt weightless and leaden at the same time, and although the last thing her stomach wanted was food, using current burned an amazing number of calories, even if the body itself wasn't doing a damned thing. Between the crap at the docks, and now this, all in twenty-four hours, she was seriously scraping the tank. If she didn't eat now, there would be hell to pay, later.

"Stay here," he said. "I'll see what you have in the kitchen, or I can order in."

"There's some canned stuff. I think." She had no idea how old it was, though. "Call Caesar's and get a quart of their daily special. Their kitchen's open until ten."

He nodded, and some instinct made her reach out an aching arm and grab his wrist before he could get up off the bed.

"I'm okay," she told him.

"I know." But his voice still sounded awful.

"I'm really okay," she repeated. "But it wasn't fun, and if I ever do that again, which I hope I won't, I'll make sure someone's here with me." Here, at her side, connected, not in his own apartment halfway across the city. She let that surrender drip through her body and soak into the psychic bedrock. There was no answering response, but she suspected the demon heard, and understood.

She wasn't sure that was enough to reassure the human listener, but some of the stiffness left Sergei's posture, and when he leaned down to brush his lips against hers, just a brief caress, his whispered "thank you" was in his normal toffee-smooth tenor.

Wren closed her eyes again and listened to the sounds of her partner moving around the apartment, and the muted but still-busy traffic on the streets below, and felt a warm tear prickle under one lid. It might have been exhaustion; she was tired enough to cry. Or it might have been frustration; all that, and the only thing to show for it was an old boot.

Or it might just have been for all the things lost, that could never be found again.

No answers. No closure. No absolution, no assurance that she had been a good student, that he was proud of her, that she'd done right by his teaching...

"Let it go," she told herself. "Focus on what you can do now. All this is just muck that's been stirred up by that damn kid. You'll feel better when the job's done."

For a minute, she even managed to convince herself.

Museums at night were always, by their nature, a little spooky. During the day, the past was just another artifact, something gone and dead, by its nature an object lesson rather than promise or threat. At night, however.... Hallways that during the day were filled with hundreds of thousands of soles tapping on the tile fell silent, save for the sound of the occasional night guard walking his route or talking on the phone while monitoring a bank of remote cameras. Artworks normally lit for ideal viewing now lurked in half-power shadows, and red lights came on in the place of incandescent white, giving structures an unearthly glow. Worse than all of that, though, was when the normal hum of conversation was replaced by the inaudible whispers of history.

In some museums, the whispers are genteel, civilized, the passions of their creation now aged into a more mellow and fond remembrance. The two renovated mansions that housed the Museum held more immediate energies; mankind forgot, Nature did not. Old ills, slights, and catastrophes still lingered, hot and raw as the instant of occurrence, until the floors and walls and windows were saturated.

Most humans never noticed. The Fatae had no use for museums, carrying their past with them unforgotten, so they never visited, and if they felt it outside those thick walls, they never told anyone.

The exhibits on display at least had the chance to be seen and admired. It mitigated the worst of the ills, softened the pain of misfortunes, and brought more positive energies to the front. For every child who smeared the glass, or every teenager who lost their poise or cool, the saturation came down a notch. Below, in the basements and storerooms, where every major and most minor museums locked away the items they were not using, had no space to show or had not yet identified the provenances of, there was less room for positive energy flow.

Some items moved in and out of storage. Some spent weeks, months, occasionally years being examined and studied, placated.

The rest sat in the dark, numbered, cataloged, and all too often forgotten. Large or small, all things became dangerous when ignored.

A figure slid through the door from the upper floors of the museum just as the final closing bell was rung. He paused to wave a thin electronic wand over the nearest camera, freezing it in place, and then casual street clothing was shed, revealing a thin, black nylon catsuit underneath covering the lithe body of a tumbler—or a thief. Now that he was dressed head to toe in dark clothing, exposed skin was powdered with a dark substance out of a palm-sized vial, in order to reduce any unfortunate reflection of light. Hands were gloved, head covered with a surgeon's cap under a black silk hood. The street clothing was folded into a small plastic bag that, at the touch of a button, squeezed itself into an impossibly small package that was placed carefully into a half-filled trash can by the doorway.

If the figure felt anything other than the usual burglar's caution, it was not evident in his smooth glide as he moved from the entrance, deeper into the storerooms.

Whatever the wand had done soon wore off, and the security camera overhead moved in its usual pattern of scan-and-pan up and down the hallway. The figure flowed one step behind the lens, obviously having timed it to precision. Every step was choreographed, even the side step from one door to another, designed to avoid an alarm trigger for the unwary. The museum might not know what was in these particular storerooms, in terms of provenance, but they had paid enough to acquire these items that spending a little more to protect them made sense.

Handwritten and computer-printed labels pasted on each door were ignored, the figure clearly having a specific goal in mind. Down one hallway, turn left at the branch, then turn right. Two doors down that hallway, then the figure swiftly jimmied open the next door, fitting something into the lock mechanism and closing it gently. The next camera tracked up and down the hallway, and the thief took a breath to judge the pattern, determining the difference from the other camera, before starting in motion again.

That unmarked door led to yet another short hallway off which there were two more exits. Without hesitation, the figure went to the nearest door and, rather than opening it normally, jerked the handle upward.

The door slid up into the ceiling, and the figure disappeared into the darkness within. There were sounds of boxes moving, the muffled noise of a toe hitting something, and a small blue glow appeared, lighting the interior for brief seconds before going out. The intruder reappeared a moment later with two objects: one a small metal box the size of a Manhattan phone book, and the other a slightly larger and longer object, wrapped in oilcloth.

Job complete, the thief turned to leave, but came face-to-face with an unexpected problem: he was unable to bring the door down with both hands already in use.

There was an instant of hesitation as though the figure was weighing the possibilities. Everything was to be left as it had been found, those were his instructions. But once he laid hands on his prize, he never let go, not until it was handed over to the client. That was how he worked.

Deciding that the one door, so far inside the labyrinth, would not be noticed until well after he was safely gone, the thief paused to gauge the timing of the camera, then ducked back out into the hallway, prepared to resume the choreographed hide-and-seek.

No sooner had the figure turned, however, than a light flashed, brighter than sunlight. He was blinded, but reacted without panic, dropping low and crawling toward the exit, the layout as memorized as the motion of the cameras. Every exit option was anticipated and planned for, well before he ever entered the site. At no point did either object leave his grasp, even though it undoubtedly slowed the thief's escape.

Slowed it enough that when the jimmied door opened from the outside, the figure was only halfway there.

The two security guards who entered were off-duty cops, well-armed and in no mood to play games. One of them gave a command and the other circled around to make sure that there was no one else in the room, while the first one held a gun aimed at the thief's torso. Even if the rent-a-cop missed the heart-shot, the odds were good that he would hit something significant.

The thief, being a professional and a pragmatist, rolled over and rested the objects carefully on his chest, waiting for them to bring out the cuffs. You never wanted to get caught, but the risk was always there. There was a plan for this, too.

twelve

It only took Wren half the morning to track her quarry down, and when she found him, he merely looked up and cracked half a smile. "Of all the java joints in the city, you had to walk into mine."

"Can it, willya? Too tired." Wren dropped herself into the booth opposite Danny, folded her arms on the table, and rested her head on top. Was it really only Wednesday? Tuesday was a blur of sleep and being spoon-fed soup and listening to Sergei's blues music playing low on the stereo in the main room. She was back on her feet now, however battered she still felt, and the world wasn't waiting on her exhaustion.

But God, she needed a weekend. She needed the week to end, period. Not that she had anything even remotely resembling normal work hours. And she was starting to spend too much time in this coffee shop. It was probably safe to go back to Starbucks. Probably. Then she looked at her companion and remembered how that last foray had ended. Maybe not. They might still hold a grudge about the broken tables.

"Long night?" The ex-cop-turned-investigator waved the waitress over, and ordered another pot of coffee, extra strong. In his dark blue jeans and cowboy boots under a chunky black sweater, Danny—the former Patrolman Daniel Henrickson, and still in damn fine shape—could have been one of the less-pretty cologne models Madison Avenue used to use, or maybe the hero of a B-grade Western romance. Until, that is, you looked more closely and saw the small horns peeking through his crop of brown curls, or pulled off his boots to see the hooves inside.

Rumor had it that fauns also had nubby—and cute—tails that could and did wag, but Wren didn't know anyone who had ever seen one. For a member of a breed that were reportedly randy and rude little bastards, Danny was almost annoyingly discreet. Words failed to express how thankful she was for that.

"Oh," he added before she could respond, "Bonnie says hello."

"Now is really not the time to change your policy of not kissing and telling," she muttered from her face plant on the table.

"Hah." He sounded amused. "She and I ended up working the same investigation, Valere, that's all. I saw her last night, and she said she hadn't made it home in almost two days, and to tell you she was alive and okay."

"Oh. Right." Bonnie was a PUPI, one of the private, un-affiliated paranormal investigators working on cases that involved the *Cosa*, and couldn't be brought to justice through normal channels. It made sense the two of them would run into each other in a professional capacity on occasion.

Wren was seriously hoping she never ran into Bonnie, or any of the other Pups, on anything other than a social basis. Retrieval was a traditional and respected career in the *Cosa*, but that didn't make it any more legal than it was in the Null world, something she occasionally forgot. She was pretty sure she was better at her job than they were at theirs, but the Pups were damn sharp as a pack, and Bonnie—who had moved into the apartment two floors below the year before—had gotten familiar with Wren's habits and, worse, the signature, or "taste" of her personal current. No, much better to never come to their professional attention. But she should stop by and say hello, see how the other Talent was doing, if she'd come to a decision about what to do if the building did go condo, thank her again for dinner, all the other things people did when their job didn't consume their damn life....

"You on a job?" Danny asked.

She didn't even bother lifting her head to ask in return, "You asking in what capacity?"

"Jeez, you're getting suspicious in your old age," he said, tsking mournfully. The waitress appeared with the fresh pot of coffee, and then Wren did lift herself up from her face-plant, accepting the cup with heartfelt thanks.

"I just wanted to know if this was going to be two friends getting together to talk about the bad old days, or if I should expense it."

She relaxed a little, even more when the coffee made its way down her throat and into her system.

"Just came off one day before last. Or the day before that. It starts getting blurry. Right now I'm here purely in the capacity of an old friend...who has nosy interests." Technically, that was true. Who could be an older friend than her ownself, and she *was* nosy. And this wasn't a job, really. Just the offshoot of one. Something to maybe shut her brain up, maybe once and for all.

"Ah," Danny responded. A wealth of meaning in that one

sound, most of which translated to "I don't believe you for an instant, but if that's the way you want to play it, you can pay for the coffee."

"I was on a job last week," she started.

"No! Say it ain't so!"

Danny was many things, mediocre wiseass among them, and the memory of when work was scarce was still fresh enough to make her wince. She shot him a glare until he subsided.

"There was a kid involved."

"Blond, innocent eyes, Talent out of nowhere," he supplied.

The *Cosa* gossip line was a thing of beauty.

"You hear anything useful in that line?" She took another sip of coffee and decided that being strong was its sole virtue, the taste being unfavorably compared to hot tar. She was probably drinking too much coffee, anyway. Her nerves were beginning to vibrate like the middle rail just before a train arrived.

"About the theories of how and why, or the kid's status?"

"Whatever you've got." She added more milk to her coffee, trying to drown the overburned taste, and settled down to listen. Danny's gossip, like Sergei's briefings, were worth getting comfortable for.

He leaned back and gestured with his coffee spoon. "Theories are split between you've finally gone 'round the bend and were hallucinating, or worse, and the idea that the kid is proof that Talent is expanding in the gene pool, like red tide or something." Danny's Brooklyn accent became more pronounced on the last, indicating his personal opinions on that.

"You don't buy it?"

"You hear the new theory goin' around, about how Talent is just a biological thing?"

"I've heard it, yeah."

"I don't buy that. You got magic in your soul, or you don't. If you don't, you can't. Simple as that. So how can it be genetic?"

For a die-hard pragmatist, his statement was surprising. She reminded herself that for Danny, one of the very, very rare half-breed Fatae, pragmatism had to fit in somewhere with a sense of the impossible. Apparently, that was how he did it, and to hell with all the implications of modern current.

He was Fatae, not Talent, she reminded herself. If you didn't use current yourself, she supposed that you could ignore the to-her obvious connection between the electrical pump of her heart, and the currential flow of her skills, the biological suggestion that made about how and why things worked.

Then again, she was no scientist. Hell, she broke alarm clocks and PDAs just by standing next to them, like most Talent. There was a reason most of them went into the Arts or craftsman trades, not technical ones. Even Neezer, who *had* been a scientist, or at least a teacher thereof, had never suggested that there was a genetic connection, and he had taught biology, so he would have at least had thought about it. Wouldn't he?

She reminded herself that he had wizzed before she was done with her mentorship. Who knew what he might have said, once they were peers rather than student and teacher? The thought brought sadness, and a touch of uncertainty to add to her pile of preexisting questions.

"By that line, though," she said to Danny now, playing devil's advocate; "isn't it possible for a sense of wonder, for magic in the soul, to spread? Even more easily than a gene pool mutation? Isn't a sense of wonder communicable?"

He shook his head, one hand absently sliding his spoon back and forth on the table. "Easier to lose than to find."

"Easier to drop than to bind," Wren finished up automatically. Every mentor worth their salt drummed that into their students' heads, first day. Interesting that Danny would quote it. She filed that bit of information away as pointless now, maybe pointy later.

"Look at you," he continued. "Serious, significant Talent. Nobody gonna gainsay that. Far as I've ever heard you peep, nobody in your family's got a hint of it. It's all in *you*, not them."

"What about my dad?" she heard herself say.

He opened his dark eyes wide, making them seem even rounder than normal. "What about your dad?"

"Maybe he was a Talent?"

Neither of them talked much about their fathers. Wren because she had nothing to say, Danny because he had nothing good to say about his; fauns were, well, fauns. Sexy, but useless. His human mother had been unusual in catching, much less in keeping the baby after that encounter.

"Maybe," Danny agreed. "Any way to find out?"

She thought about it barely a second. "No."

"Well then." And like that, the topic was dropped. That might have been why she felt comfortable enough to bring it up, here and now. Danny understood.

Truth was, even with all the questions starting to run around in her head she wasn't sure she wanted to think about it; her mother had said her sperm donor was a one-night stand, a guy she met, liked, had sex with, and then never saw again…and now couldn't remember a thing about, physically.

Sounded as if she got her no-see-me Retriever skills from somewhere, at least. But was it Talent, or merely being visually forgettable? Where did one move into the other? And why was all this—kid, and Max, and her long-absent sperm donor—suddenly such a big deal?

Is your biological clock ticking? She could hear her mother's voice in the back of her head, sounding way too happy at the thought, and shuddered.

"As to the kid," Danny said, dragging the conversation back to the original topic, "he's fine. His old man's keeping him close to home and pretty much wrapped up in cotton batting. I guess he doesn't want to have to send out a search party again."

Or maybe he was waiting for another chance to sell the kid to a high bidder. She didn't think so, though. The compulsion she had put into his mind was strong—far stronger than she had admitted to Sergei. Stronger than she had intended it to be. Daddy dearest would protect his kid properly, this time.

Kid was Talent, untrained, and beautiful. Bad combination in a little'un. She had the thought, and shuddered at the implications it carried on its back. She wasn't a hero. She couldn't save everyone.

"You ever regret...not having—" she almost started to say "your dad" but changed it midbreath "—a dad-figure? When you were growing up, I mean?"

"Hey, I had Mister Rogers. What else did I need?"

Well, that gave her an idea of how old Danny actually was. Fatae all aged differently.

"You?" he asked, sounding as though he really wanted to know.

"I had one. Neezer."

Except that was a lie; she hadn't, even if she'd wanted him to be her dad, because he came into her life when she was already a headstrong teenager, and left before she was an adult, and she knew, when she admitted it, that the scars of that abandonment— however well-meant and wise it might have been—still festered.

Max had torn open some of those scars, she supposed. That, and the kid, and any thought of genetics...healthier to acknowledge that there were issues and deal with them, right? Isn't that what she'd pushed Sergei to do?

"And anyway," she continued, "my mom was constantly on the lookout for potential dad-types for me. I think she would have done better looking for husband-types for herself, but that's my mom for ya." Understatement of the year.

And she really needed to set up another lunch, soon, as soon as her mother got home. Otherwise the older Valere woman might show up on her doorstep, and God knows what she would find. Wren's mother still wasn't all that happy about Sergei, even if she couldn't remember meeting P.B. from one minute to the next...

Well, if her mother could remember anything about her encounters with the non-Null, Wren's life would probably be a lot different.

"Mothers," Danny said in fervent agreement, and she laughed.

"And now, lovely though it's been to see you when people aren't howling for our blood or body parts, I gotta scoot. Pay the nice lady with the check, willya?" Danny shoved his mug away and picked up his hat. Today it was a dark brown baseball cap with a snarling goat picked out in bright red on the front. "Oh, and tell your man I said hello."

"You can't pick up a phone and call him yourself? Go out for beer or catch a game or whatever it is guys do." Wren tried to visualize that, and failed utterly. The two of them had bonded somehow, during the night of the blackout, but she had never gotten any details of when or how, and she wasn't sure she really wanted to know.

The faun smirked, and left. She was spending too much time in her brain on this, she decided—"this" meaning the entire tangle with the kid, and genetics, and the question of daddies. Neezer had hidden himself away on purpose, and Max had sent her away, making it clear they were over and she was on her own; her genetic father was a dead end, and the kid was taken care of. You didn't hang on to the shit from the past, especially shit from past jobs. Do the deal and move on. Anything else…

Anything else meant distraction, usually when she could least afford it.

Anything else meant tangles and ties and giving in to that last time had almost gotten her killed. It *had* gotten other people killed, and never mind they had deserved it. Wren didn't want the reminder of how good she was at killing; how terrifyingly easy it had been to do.

No. She was a Retriever. That was all.

Wren waved the waitress over and asked for the check, then drank what was left of her coffee. Time to get back to work.

Wren was halfway home when she changed her mind and went uptown instead. Sergei's apartment was a sleek steel-and-glass high-rise with its own emergency power generator, and every time she got into the elevator she had the urge to suck down a hit or three off of it. That might have been why they spent so much time at her place. He knew what that elevator did to her.

"Hey, Ms. Valere."

He also had a doorman—an entire staff of doormen, in fact, twenty-four hours a day, and most of them knew her by sight. Privacy did not happen in an upscale high-rise; you just paid extra for the *illusion* of it. She liked her place better. For all her building was like a small town, and you knew everyone and everything about them, nobody noticed anything they weren't invited to notice.

"Is he home?" she asked, leaning on the counter and looking up at the twenty-something manning the desk.

He checked the console, then nodded. "He is, yes. Should I call you up, or do you want to surprise him?"

Technically they weren't supposed to let her up without Sergei's approval. It was a measure of how often she was in and out, she supposed. Also, not her worry.

"Might as well call me up," she said, heading for the elevator. Keep him on his toes, if sometimes she called up and sometimes she didn't. You took your amusements where you found them.

The elevator was empty save for her, and she leaned against the back wall, letting her control slip ever-so-slightly. The comforting hum of electricity swam into her awareness, and for an instant overwhelmed all her other senses. You learned how to block it out, except when you were actively trolling for current, otherwise living in any kind of civilization would drive you mad, like a gourmand faced with a never-ending buffet. Especially her: especially now. But every now and again, when it was safe, she liked to open up and soak it in, a reminder of how glorious the world looked, when you looked at it with Talented eyes.

She wondered if anyone was teaching the kid how to look, and what would happen to him if he didn't learn.

"I wonder if my dad knew what he was," she said when Sergei met her at the door of his apartment. No lead-in, no hello kiss, just a plunge right into deep waters, despite her decision not half an hour before to put it aside, damn it. "I wonder if he'd been mentored, or picked up bits and pieces on his own, or he totally didn't know and was this huge walking stack of coincidences and unexplained weirdness that freaked him and his friends out."

Sergei looked as though he wanted to say something, but wasn't sure if she wanted comforting, profound, or commonsensical.

That was okay; she didn't know, either.

Then she took another look at his face, and braced herself. "What?"

He let her into the apartment, backing up rather than letting her follow him in. "There has to be a what?"

"When you have that face, yes." It was what she had come to think of as his Silence face, after the organization that had caused them so much trouble. It meant that shit was up.

"Danny called me."

"I just saw him!" she said, protesting.

"Yes, I know, he said that. After he left he says he got a phone call."

Any phone call that caused that face was not something she was going to be happy about.

"And?"

"Someone's been in town, nosing about, asking after us. You, me…and P.B."

Wren's mood, already off, plummeted like an elephant taking a nosedive. "Oh, *great.*"

At her insistence, they called P.B. in before she let Sergei say anything more. If the person poking around was including the demon in said poking, he had a right to know. Also, she really didn't want to deal with another lecture about trust or sharing from an annoyed demon if she could easily avoid it. While they waited, Sergei made a pot of tea, and Wren built a card house out of the deck he had left on his coffee table.

The demon took the news about as well as Wren expected. "Someone asking about us, about me. Bad enough to start with, yeah. But for it to happen right when I get that letter, and Mister Research here starts checking into things long-ago and far-away. Coincidence?" P.B. was pacing the length of Sergei's apartment, his clawed pads clicking on the hardwood in a way they never did in her mostly carpeted apartment.

"There's no such thing as coincidence in the *Cosa*," Wren

said. She was curled up on the sofa, a square cashmere throw tucked around her bare feet, watching him pace. It was making her dizzy, but she didn't think he would stop even if she asked. Or if he did, that nervous tension would go somewhere worse.

"Not just someone," Sergei clarified, repeating what he had already told them. "A government someone. The guy wasn't showing a badge, but the car was apparently unmistakable." Sergei had pulled a silver case from somewhere and removed a slender brown cigarette from it, rolling the cylinder between his fingers. He hadn't smoked in years, far as she knew, but he always carried the cigarettes with him, like some kind of nervous talisman. It had gone away for a while, but it was back now. She didn't know if that was a good sign or not.

"Someday they're going to start using random rental cars, and really screw with people," Wren said. "All right. Does this guy being government make it better, or worse? The government's never bothered us before—the ones that are willing to admit the possibility that maybe something outside of their rules, regs, and tax codes exists, anyway. And the ones that don't, don't bother us because we don't exist." It wasn't a perfect solution, but it had worked so far.

"This person not only believes, he has photos."

"What?" P.B.'s ears, normally rounded and flat at a 90° angle to his head, twitched upward. If Wren hadn't been equally shocked by the news, she would have made a comment.

"That's what Danny says. The Fed was showing around a picture of us. Me and Wren. And P.B."

Wren was flabbergasted. She didn't think even her mother had any photos of her. For a brief moment she let herself wonder if she looked good in the photos, and if so, how she could get her hands on a copy.

"Do you think it's the Council?" P.B. stopped pacing long

enough to ask her quietly. "Slipping word to the authorities, their way of getting revenge?"

The immediate NYC Council, led by KimAnn Howe, had tried a few years back to convince the local unaffiliateds, or lonejacks, into joining. By force, as needed. That attempt had failed, at least in part because of the three of them.

"KimAnn hasn't been heard from in over a year," Wren said, just as quietly, as though speaking her name might summon the woman from whatever depth of hell she'd been sunk to. "I think that the Council Proper—" the entire organization as a whole "—took care of her for us. She was getting too big for her Ferragamos, and they hate that. Anyway that's a line I'm not sure they'd take—it's too easy for someone snooping around to jump from knowing about lonejacks to knowing about the Council and then the fat's really in the fire. We've survived this long by not drawing attention—even KimAnn wasn't crazy enough to do that."

"Feds or local?" she asked her partner. "The local cops have always had a little more know—"

"Feds," he said definitely. He was sitting in a straight-back chair, having turned it around and straddled it, his arms resting on the back, his long legs out in front of him. His hair—that dark, wavy hair that she used to love running her fingers through, was streaked with gray, and cut too short to properly rumple, but her fingers still itched to tangle in it. Like any big, dangerous cat, you always wanted to pet him.

Inappropriate thoughts, she told herself with an inward smirk. *Focus on the problem, not the petting.*

"Federal's not good. Not good at all." She did not have warm-n-fuzzies about federal-level knowledge. Like Council membership, she left that for those with a taste for game-playing.

"It's not the Silence," Sergei said now, beating both of them to the question neither wanted to ask. "I checked."

His former employers had tried to wipe out magic in the world, starting with the users based in New York City. They had been wiped out instead.

Not wiped out, Wren corrected herself. *You don't kill a hydra with one swoop, and you don't destroy a hundred-year-old organization with one defeat, no matter how hard it hit them. In some form, under some other name, they're still out there, somewhere. Just not now, not here, not our problem. Yet.* Like the New York Council, the Silence had been led by a single person with ambition beyond what he already owned. Like KimAnn, he, too, had disappeared.

Unlike KimAnn, Wren suspected Duncan was very much dead. She had no proof…except the way Sergei slept more soundly at night, now.

That was enough for her.

"The fact that it's some stranger, some new crisis, does not make me feel any better about all this. In case anyone was wondering." P.B.'s voice was dry as a morning hangover, and about as brittle. His ears were back against his skull: like a cat's ears, that meant he was feeling defensive.

"New day, new troubles," Wren said, parroting one of her mother's refrains. "So we have a Fed on our tails, asking questions at a particularly suspicious and inauspicious moment. Assuming the worst, 'cause it usually is, what sort of questions? I mean, are we talking about 'have you seen this demon?' or 'are you interested in a million-dollar reward for bringing me their ears and tails?'"

"I don't have a tail," P.B. said.

"It's a saying," she told him in exasperation. What was it with Fatae and tails, anyway?

"I know. But I don't have a tail, not really."

"Oh for God's sake…"

Before they could get into a stress-driven wrangle about Fatae prejudices against the tailed, Sergei came back with the details.

"He's showing the photos around—and it's only a drawing of you, P.B., although reportedly pretty accurate—and asking if anyone knows anything about any of us. No specifics. Danny didn't sound too worried, but…"

"He's on a fishing expedition, this Fed," Wren said, not sure if that was a good thing or not.

"I think so, yes," her partner agreed. "But the question is, what is he fishing for? Is it tied into the recent events here in the city, or P.B.'s letter, somehow, or one of our older cases, or something, God help us, we don't know about yet?"

P.B. looked at Wren, who looked at Sergei, who looked at P.B. who looked up at the ceiling to indicate his total lack of an answer.

Sergei turned back to his partner. "Wren, do you think this is something that should be taken back to the Tri-Com?"

"No." Her reaction was immediate and definite; so much so that she had it out of her mouth before she could think about it. The guys both looked taken aback, so she paused to consider why she felt that way, trying to explain it to them.

"If I keep running to them…they're used to me dealing with the big nasty shit. If this turns out to be nothing, or just localized to us three, then they'll think I was crying wolf. And that would be seriously bad for my reputation."

It was a logical explanation, and had the benefit of being true. But it wasn't her real reason. The real reason, not-so-hidden deep in her gut, was the fear that the more contact she had with them, the more the members would think about trying to rope her back in. The lonejacks were still not as bad as the Council, they still remembered that life was every woman for herself and watch out only for those you choose to care for, but the entire idea of the Truce Board first and now the Tri-Com was scratching away at that independence, and it made her uneasy, even more than some unknown crazy person from P.B's past, or some unknown Federal nose.

No more. No matter how many tendrils she felt wrapping around her ankles, pulling her back in.

"You know what?" she said abruptly, uncurling off the sofa in a single smooth motion and sitting upright. "This could be nothing. We don't know, and we can't do anything, and I'm not going to worry about it."

"Where are you going?" Sergei asked, no, demanded, his voice sharpening.

She was slipping her shoes back on and lacing them up. When she finished, she looked up at her partner and shrugged. "The gym, first. I've been crap at keeping up and it's going to bite me, if I'm not careful. Then I was going to go to the store and actually buy groceries, since someone used the last of the eggs for breakfast when I wasn't home. And then I thought I might go break into a few houses, just to keep in practice."

They might have thought she was kidding, except they knew her better.

She thought Sergei was going to protest, but instead he nodded. "Good idea," he said. "When I know more, I'll let you know."

Amazing how those words eased the tightness in her chest. She shouldn't have doubted him. That was how the partnership had been established. Why screw with the part that still worked?

She grabbed her coat, and leaned over to give Sergei a rough but thorough kiss. "Dinner tonight?" After recent events, the two of them were keeping her on a tight make-sure-she-eats-food-watch. She didn't have any basis—or desire—to complain.

"I'm too busy to cook anything. I'll meet you at Mari-anna's, sevenish?"

She grinned in agreement, flicked a finger in farewell to P.B, and was out the door.

In the silence after the door closed: "Is she okay?"

Sergei gave the demon a sour look. "Why are you asking me?"

"Don't start with that shit," P.B. said, equally annoyed. "There are things she tells you, and things she tells me, and if we don't pool that, we're going to be outclassed and outgunned for the rest of our lives."

Sergei Didier was well into his forties. He was a former covert operative for an even more covert organization that he had, by their standards, betrayed; had established a second career as a successful legitimate businessman, and an equally successful third career as the manager of a not-technically-illegal-because-nobody-knew-to-make-it-illegal Retriever partnership. He should not have been shut down by a midget in a bear suit, no matter the midget was apparently over a hundred years old, and had claws and teeth to match the fur.

Some people might look at P.B. and only see the physical. Sergei had always been aware of the brain inside. That didn't mean he had to like it being used against him.

Even if he was being a shit.

"She's still not sleeping well. But I don't think she knows."

"Nightmares?"

Sergei nodded, feeling the tension of those nights creeping up on him again, of waking at three in the morning to the sound of his lover crying in her sleep, begging for someone not to go. Or, worse, the morning when he woke to a bundle of current in his arms, her skin crackling with so much power even he could feel it, his own skin craving for the touch. When she was awake, control had the upper hand. But in her dreams, the dark abyss could reach her, entice her. The siren call, Doherty called it. The desire to reach for just that much more current, and be damned the risk to system and sanity.

"You think the doc could help her with that?"

It was the first indication the demon had given that he knew Sergei was in counseling, and the human couldn't even find it in himself to be annoyed or invaded. He was getting therapy because Wren needed him to deal with the shit inside, if she was going to keep him, and anything that involved Wren involved the demon, as well. Sergei didn't like it, but he didn't try to deny it any more. That had gotten him exactly nowhere except a bad case of, he was told, useless and pointless jealousy.

"I doubt it." He got up from the chair and headed into the kitchen, his voice easily carrying back to the living area. "I'm not sure it helps much with anything, except giving me a place where I can put my fist through the wall periodically."

"Useful, that," P.B. agreed. "So the heart-to-heart gutspill's not doing anything?"

Sergei put the kettle on to boil, and got down a mug and the tea canister. He measured out the black leaves and set the infuser into the mug, then waited patiently for the water to be ready.

"That a no, a yes, or a mind your own damned business, fur ball?" P.B. asked from the kitchen's arched doorway.

"It's not hurting," Sergei said, not looking at the other male. "I don't know if it's helping. But it shows I'm trying."

"Yeah." The demon shook his head, and showed sharp white teeth in a sudden grin. "Used to be, to win a girl, humans would go kill something. Now you go sit in a comfy room and talk about your feelings. That's civilization for ya."

The water started to boil, and Sergei was saved from having to make a comeback by the whistle that filled the chrome and tile kitchen.

★ ★ ★

Across town, the day's judgment was that it had been long, irritating, and filled with penny-ante bullshit. In other words, your usual Tuesday for New York's Finest. It was almost end of shift, and there was one last transport to make before it was time for booze and a snooze.

"You think you're being a tough guy, huh?" The cop, a ten-year veteran who had spent all of those years working the streets, didn't push his prisoner out the door, but the manhandling made it clear that, were he the type to rough up a prisoner, the prisoner would be in no position to prevent it. The cop walking in front of them laughed. "He's not tough. He's already working a deal. Smart guy, figures the longer he holds out, the better the terms." They reached the squad car, and the speaker opened the back door, moving out of the way so that his partner could ease the prisoner into the seat without any unfortunate bruises.

This had not been part of the plan, but the prisoner remained quiet, as he had since they caught him, and throughout his incarceration, even when his lawyer didn't show. He had been told that he would be taken care of, and he trusted his employers. And if they failed to come through…well, he had a plan of his own, worst-case scenario. He felt no desire to share it with these two yahoos, however.

"Only problem is," the second cop continued, "we're not an airline, we don't up the offers to empty out the seats. More of you scum off the streets, better our job gets. So hold your breath all you want, pal. Won't break my heart."

"Excuse me?"

The first cop turned at the voice, his face dropping into pleasant "dealing with the public" lines even as his hand rested close to his holster, just in case.

By the time he had finished turning, he was already falling, his knees giving way under the low-handed blow. His partner shoved the prisoner into the car, slamming the door shut to lock the thief in while he dealt with this new threat. He started to shout for help, the precinct door only a few yards away, but never got the chance. A hypo was jammed into his bicep, and he joined his partner on the pavement, down and out for the count. The assailant stepped over the prone bodies, kneeling briefly to inject the first victim with another hypo, tucking both empty vials into a plastic bag and dropping it into a black leather briefcase. The thief, who had been watching all this from within the locked squad car, turned his face up to the newcomer, hope mixed with anticipation and a hint of fear.

The hope turned to excitement as the newcomer reached for the car door, opening it and allowing the prisoner to escape. Finally.

"You told them nothing?"

The former prisoner held out his hands for his rescuer to unlock the cuffs. "I was hired because I am a professional" he said, indignant now that things were happening. "I don't roll on my employers. You don't last in this business if you're scared of a little jail time."

"True." The cuffs came off, and were dropped onto the ground. "Come with me."

The thief stepped over the cops the way his rescuer did, not being quite as careful not to tread on fingers as he did so. They walked down the street, casual and slow, to all intents and purposes a well-dressed lawyer and more raggedly dressed client out for a stroll before their turn in the court house.

"You failed."

"I know." He was, as he had said, a professional. Part of being a professional was owning when you had screwed up. "If you wish me to make a second attempt, there will be no additional charge." Normally a client would merely have posted the bail money, if they did anything at all. He had expected better treatment from this employer, and being broken out in such a clean and bloodless manner boded well for a continuing relationship. He was smart enough not to want to screw that up, if so.

"No. Your services will not be needed on that project again. However, I would like to discuss another service you could provide to us."

"Of course."

They turned the corner, walking away from the busy streets around the precinct house, and headed into a quieter, less-inquisitive area of town, even as the injured officers were being discovered, and an alarm was raised for the missing prisoner.

I don't have time for a session. *They don't have set appointments; he stops by when there's a moment. Joe's not in active practice; he teaches, and sees very few patients beyond his students. The office, a shared space, is more for tax purposes than anything else.*

But you still stopped by. Have you thought more about what we discussed last time?

We didn't discuss anything last time. You shoved me into saying that I blamed her. But I don't.

No?

No. *He doesn't. Except he does. Not for the addiction—he hadn't known about the pleasure-pain kink before, but it was in him, was part of him, and she wasn't to blame for bringing it out. He didn't even blame her for not being able to say no to him; how could he be upset about someone who cared enough about him to want him to be happy?*

Then why did you say that you did?

Because I do.

He knows it doesn't make any sense. None of this makes any sense.

Is it blame? Or anger?

Sergei stares at Doherty, and his tense features relax just a little. I thought mind reading didn't actually exist, outside of stories.

You knew better than that. I'm not reading your mind, just your body. You're angry at her. Why?

Because she's what she is, and I am what I am, and there's nothing to be done about it. There's no point to any of it, because nothing's ever going to change. *He hadn't understood, before talking to P.B. He still didn't understand. But at least now he knew.*

You could leave her.

For the first time ever in that office, Sergei laughed.

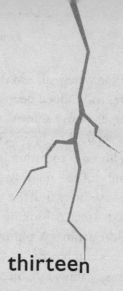

thirteen

"I have something for you," the old man said.

They were seated at a white-clothed table in Eddy's, a very exclusive restaurant midtown, where the waiters knew your first name but never used it, and the wine had its own level for storage. Sergei had eaten there three times in his entire life, and each time was with the old man across the table from him.

"I assumed you had," he replied calmly, making careful but appreciative work of the pear and foie gras appetizer in front of him. His companion never called except when he had something, and never spoke of it until after the formalities of ordering their meals and wine had been observed.

The Old Man wasn't a Talent, and he didn't, like Sergei, have ties to the *Cosa* of either personal or business nature. What he did have was money, more than he could count, and contacts everywhere, in every conceivable organization. That, and a fascination with the supernatural that bordered on the obsessive. Sergei had been the one to confirm the man's suspicions that the Fatae were real, and that the girl he had loved and lost, years before, had indeed been one.

Sergei wasn't sure if he had done the old man any favors, but it seemed to be working to their benefit, so far. The call from him this morning just after Wren had left his apartment, a summons to lunch, was proof of that.

"I have been hearing whispers of a group—small, but well-funded—that is looking for something of a physical and yet mystical nature. A philosopher's stone, of sorts, but one that breathes and bleeds."

Sergei calmly cut, lifted and chewed his appetizer, then took a sip of his wine. An Italian white, and surprisingly good. He made a mental note of the producer to buy for his own cellar, if it wasn't wildly overpriced retail; Wren might like it.

"A philosopher's stone? And one that lives?" His tone was politely dubious. Not everything the old man came up with was useful. Having massive amounts of money and knowing everyone worth knowing didn't make you not a crackpot. It just ensured that nobody called you a crackpot, not even behind your back.

"Yes, that was much my reaction, as well." The old man finished his wine and a waiter was there to refill it soundlessly. He waited until the server had finished and left them alone before continuing. "However, it appears that this is a different sort of stone. Rather than transmuting base metal into precious, it turns inert into active. It gives life."

All of Sergei's warning signals were chiming quietly, not quite at full alert but completely aware and quivering. A magical item that could convey life? You could interpret that a lot of ways, none of them good for them, right now. Wren joked about it, but it was true: Once was an accident. Twice was not-a-coincidence. Three times meant fecal matter was in the air vents.

"A valuable thing, if it's true. And they came to you, thinking that you might have some word of it?"

"And I come to you, knowing that you have a reputation as a man who can determine if something is truth or falsehood." The old man never asked where Sergei got his information from, and vice versa: it was one of the reasons they were able to do business.

"There is, to the best of my knowledge, no such thing as the philosopher's stone." It might exist. It might not. Sergei knew too much to say he knew everything about the supernatural world, but neither Wren or P.B. had ever even implied that any such thing might exist, not even in the most wistful of wishings. And he had heard them wistful and wishing—mostly about money—many, many times. A stone that might give life...that he would have heard mention of. Sergei was certain of it. So, he could say without any falsehood that there was no such thing as a philosopher's stone, flesh or otherwise.

He prayed that was enough for the old man.

"You're being cagey. When you are cagey it means that there is something under the words that intrigues you, but you don't want me to know."

Damn. He started to frame an explanation that said nothing, and was stopped by the old man's laughter. He waved a fork at Sergei, still chuckling. "I have no need for any such stone. I have more money than my advisors know what to do with, and more grandchildren than I can spoil with that money. Wealth and flesh have already been kind to me, I desire no more."

The two men looked at each other across the white linen and white china, and neither one of them blinked.

"I would like to know if such a thing exists, merely to have something to discuss with the good Lord when I go," the old man said. "You will find out, and you will tell me. And I will carry that knowing to my grave. In return, I give you the names of the men making the inquiries, and the specifics of what they claim. Agreed?"

Sergei trusted the old man as far as he could throw him, but he could probably throw him a reasonable distance. And this…sounded as though it might be what they were looking for: the names of whoever had coerced the demon who had sent P.B. that letter.

"Agreed."

They raised glasses at each other, and sipped in perfect accord.

He should have gone directly back to Wren with his information. Should have, and didn't. Sergei left the restaurant, having turned down the offer of an excellent cognac, and found himself walking up Fifth Avenue, covering ground at a steady pace, moving past casual pedestrians without even seeing them.

He should be heading downtown, not up. There was nothing uptown that related to this situation.

Maybe that's why he found himself heading there.

Somewhere in the sixties he realized what he was doing, and made a left turn, heading into the green space of Central Park.

Almost immediately, the change of atmosphere soothed him. He left the roadway and strolled much more slowly along the curving paths. Joggers and the occasional mounted rider went by and while he could still hear the traffic outside, it seemed miles away rather than yards. More than eight hundred acres, all for free, and the last time he had been here purely for pleasure was…

He couldn't remember. It had been summer, but he didn't remember if it was last summer, or the year before, or…

That had been the last time life was quiet enough to just take a walk for pleasure, no pressing needs or life-threatening crisis.

And you didn't have anyone to walk with, then, he reminded himself. Would you change it?

No. He was not the sort of man meant to go through life alone, no matter what his earlier years had brought him. Much as he'd fought it, Wren, and P.B., and the rest of their insane extended community was his community now, too. Which meant that their problems were his problems.

The philosopher's stone. Creating life, not wealth. People would pay well for such a thing. Pay—or kill.

Sergei felt a sigh building in his chest. It was possible, entirely possible that the information he had in his wallet had nothing whatsoever to do with P.B., or the materials that Wren was set to Retrieve. Possible, but probably not probable. One, two, three things intersecting. There was no such thing as coincidence where the *Cosa Nostradamus* was concerned.

"Hey. Partner-man."

Sergei felt the pinecone hit his shoulder the same instant the guttural call caught his attention. He looked up and was greeted with the sight of a small, grayish-green figure sitting on a tree branch about a foot above his head. Wild orange hair—a color not found in nature or supernature—spiked madly around the ugly little face, and one thin arm was wrapped around a squirrel, who was watching him with equally bright black eyes.

It wasn't the first time he had been addressed directly by a piskie, but it never felt comfortable. Piskies actually liked humans as a species, being one of the few Fatae-breeds who did, but they liked them as subjects for their practical jokes as much as anything else. As a Null, Sergei was well aware of the fact that he had few defenses against those pranks, or anything worse.

But then, he really only needed one: he was The Wren's partner-man. The Wren was friends with the demon P.B. And the piskies, for whatever reason, adored P.B. Wren had asked the demon about that once, and gotten a very vague hand-waving shoulder-shrugging response. If Sergei didn't know the demon better, he would have said that it was embarrassed.

"Partner-man," the piske said again, more urgently. He knew they had individual names, but personally couldn't tell one from the other. They all looked like Kewpie dolls to him.

"Yes?" He was cautious, but polite in responding. He really didn't want any more pinecones—or worse—thrown at him.

"You be careful, partner-man."

"Any particular reason why, or just a general warning?" It could be anything, knowing piskies, up to and including a prank they themselves had planned.

"Whispers. Whispers in the ground, rising on the wind." The piskie made a face, as if it couldn't believe it was saying what it was saying. "Old history, blood and stone. It should have been left in the old world, but it's coming here. Bad cess."

"Could you be a little less obscure?" Sergei couldn't resist asking, and the piskie grinned, showing small sharp teeth. "No," it said. With an impossible leap, it disappeared into the higher branches.

Abandoned, the squirrel stared at Sergei for another moment and then, with a scolding chrrruup chrrrruup, disappeared, as well, if not quite so gracefully.

"Great." Sergei kept walking, not even bothering to keep an eye out for further interruptions from above. The piskie had said what it wanted to say.

"Whispers in the ground, rising on the wind." It sounded like something one of Jimmy's fortune cookies would say. "Blood and stone." That had him more concerned. Stones again. Was that the same as the philosopher's stone the old man had mentioned?

"It has to be. Coincidence and *Cosa* don't go together, never have."

He took the sheet of paper out of his pocket, and fumbled for his glasses, putting them on so that he could read the hand-written notes without holding the paper at arm's length.

Two names: Rogier Kees and Jef van Deuren. Dutch passports: Dutch nationals, although the first, Kees, had arrived a week ago from Canada. He had taken a room at the Midtown Hilton. Despite the high-ticket room, he wasn't splashing money around: the room had been booked using points. Interesting. Van Deuren showed up only the day before, and his room was paid for with a credit card. The two of them met for breakfast each day since then, and then went their own ways. Kees would return to his room and work the phones and computer systems all day, while van Deuren appeared to be making a more direct approach. According to the information Sergei had been given, he was making personal calls to every veterinarian in the city, working a sweep pattern from the Upper East Side across and down to the Financial district, asking about any unusual animals treated lately. Specifically, white-furred animals.

Sergei felt his lips twitch, despite himself. If they were looking for P.B., they really had no clue. A veterinarian? The demon had a massage therapist he saw every few months; Sergei had heard Wren teasing him about that once, but otherwise the entire concept of medical attention was nonexistent. In fact, Sergei wasn't even sure if it was possible to damage the demon with sheer brute force; his bones were so solid you could drop him out of a third-story window and he'd probably bounce up and land on his feet without a bruise, and any flesh wounds could be healed by a halfway decent Talent. They were crap at healing internal injuries, although he'd never quite understood the explanation why, but mending cuts and breaks was nothing. Even Wren could manage that, and she had trouble applying a bandage properly.

But they were clearly looking for P.B., and with bad intent. What the demon had to do with the legend of the philosopher's stone, Sergei didn't know; it was enough that these Dutchmen made a connection to make him worry. Creating life—or possibly *saving* life, against the ravages of current? Did they think that *P.B.* was that stone, that his ability to bond with a Talent…? Possible. Very possible. Damn.

The demon might be physically tough, but anyone could be killed, if you brought the right tools to the party and he would not go quietly if someone tried to shove him into the back of a van.

Outsiders, and Fed, and *Cosa*, oh my. Bad combination. This might be the one to finally give him an ulcer.

"Start with the immediate problems and work out from there," he said, focusing his thoughts. That meant the job they had been hired to do. "If this creator was a Frankenstein of sorts, creating life from random bits, then it might make sense that someone might assume that he had a magical object that allowed him to do this." The ironic thing was that, according to P.B., Mary Shelly had it right: there was less magic and more science involved, although only if you assumed that it was electricity rather than current that had animated the monster….

"This *dermo* makes my head hurt," Sergei muttered, refolding the paper and putting it back into his pocket and looking at his watch, a wafer-thin gold indulgence that had somehow managed to survive several years of close contact with Wren. "Almost quitting time," he said, although he had told Lowell this morning not to expect him back at the gallery the rest of the day. "Maybe I'll—

"Sergei Didier?"

It was nice to know that his reflexes were still what they used to be, even if his eyesight wasn't quite. The small pistol he had started carrying again—despite Wren's silent but pronounced distaste—was out and aimed at the speaker by the time the last syllable of his name—horribly mispronounced, Sergei noted in passing, was uttered.

The sight of his handgun triggered an instant reaction—the woman reached into her own jacket, and then froze, as though realizing how that kind of motion could be interpreted.

"You are Sergei Didier, then," she said, not moving. "I am going to take out my identification, all right? Please don't shoot me."

He nodded, alert to everything going on around them, in case anyone else happened to stop by, either to "help" his would-be assailant, or misguidedly attempt to protect her from the guy with the gun.

She took out a thin wallet, and offered it to him, letting the flap drop open.

Sergei sighed, and put his gun away, but didn't relax or let down his guard. "How can I help you, agent…Chang?"

"Anea, please."

Sergei eyed her carefully. "Agent Chang. Your reason for accosting me in the middle of my walk?"

She was tall, for an Asian woman. The last name suggested Chinese, but her features made him think Thai, and her eyes, huge and dark, were almost Amerindian. Her hair was short, thick, and had interesting reddish highlights in the blackness. And her first name…

"Heinz 57," she said, obviously used to people trying to size her up. "Chinese father, Irish-Cherokee mother. Like yourself, proof that the genetic pool works better when stirred regularly."

He grinned. She was attractive *and* sharp, apparently.

"Please. A few moments of your time."

Attractive and sharp didn't automatically earn trust, especially when they came with a badge.

"A few minutes may be more than we need. Am I in trouble of some sort? Did Lowell screw up a customs invoice?" He put on his best Important Businessman face, his voice promising dire results for any peon who ruined his afternoon with misfiled paperwork.

"This isn't about the gallery, Mr. Didier."

"Di-dee-eh," he corrected her. She took it in stride.

"Thank you. Please. I would like to ask you a few questions about your other business. And your associate, Ms. Valere."

Any pretense of sociability evaporated as his suspicions were confirmed. Agent Chang had been the government sniff Danny warned them about. Idiot, to have made the assumption the agent was male. The fact that Wren and P.B. did the same was no comfort.

"Genevieve? What has the girl gotten herself into now? I'm afraid that while we are close, I'm not—"

He stopped. Agent Chang was smiling at him and he got the feeling that she was resisting the urge to applaud.

"I'm not here to bust you, Didier." She got the pronunciation right, this time. "Or your partner, for that matter. If I wanted to do that I would not have come alone, or without the appropriate paperwork without which you would be savvy enough to shut me down. I'm not interested in either of you as such, and have no intention of causing trouble."

"Officially."

She smiled again and shrugged. "Officially, I'm not even in Manhattan." The smile faded. "That can change, if I feel the need. But I'd rather keep this all...civilized. A mutual friend of ours suggested that I contact you. He seemed to think that we could be of...shared benefit."

There was the sound of a pine cone dropping, somewhere behind him. Sergei resisted the urge to look up. He had a pretty good idea what was lurking overhead, and while he appreciated the implicit offer of help, somehow he didn't think that an aerial Piskie attack was going to help matters.

"This mutual friend...he wouldn't happen to—" He was about to ask if he had horns and hooves, but stopped himself in the nick of time. Danny wasn't outed to everyone, despite what it seemed like sometimes. "To be a former NYPD officer, currently masquerading as a pain in the ass?"

Her smile became a little warmer. "That would be Danny-boy, yes."

Sergei relaxed, a little, at the same time making a mental note to throttle the Fatae for his miserable sense of humor. A Fed sniffing around—because that damned faun *set* her to sniffing! And the bastard had to move them around like chess pieces rather than making like a yenta and introducing them formally. Oh yes, Danny was going to suffer for this one.

Although, to be fair, it seemed unlikely he would have agreed to just meet, if Danny had suggested it. She must have been trailing him...how long? Never mind, it didn't matter.

"Do you think Uncle Sugar will float us a cup of coffee then, if we're being civilized?" he said, moving forward, out of the potential range of aerial assault by overanxious Piskies, and forcing her to keep her attention on him. No matter who sent her, she was still Federal, and therefore to be kept as far away from the *Cosa* as he could manage. For her own safety, as well as theirs.

She obviously knew she was being herded, but thankfully kept her attention at ground level, casting a quick and almost-unobtrusive glance around before returning her full attention to him. She wasn't expecting flying small-and-uglies, then. A fact to remember.

"I'd rather not sit anywhere we might be overheard, Mr. Didier. And I suspect that you feel the same. So let us continue your walk, by all means. Merely two people joining steps on this lovely day."

He suspected mockery, but her almond-shaped eyes were clear and met his gaze without hesitation.

"You're leading in this dance," he said, if less than graciously, and indicated that they should proceed.

"It has, indeed, been a dance. I have been looking for you for several years now."

"I'm in the phone book. Well, the gallery is anyway."

"That is only useful if one has a name or an identity to start with. I did not. All I had was—"

"A photograph," he said, deciding not to waste any time tap-dancing.

"Yes." She took his comment with only a slight hitch in her step, and none at all in her voice. There were fewer joggers passing them by now; only an occasional mother with a stroller, or an older couple power walking. "Although those came later, after I had already developed an interest in, shall we say, a certain number of interesting occurrences, here and elsewhere in the States?"

"You can say whatever you want," he told her.

"Yes. Well, I started looking into those occurrences as part of my day job. You specifically only came into play when a number of eyewitness reports placed you and your companion on location during a number of incidents in which certain branches of the government have a more than passing interest in."

"Certain branches whose interests you represent?"

That surprised a laugh out of her. "No. I'm not quite that spooky. Mr. Didier, I am not your enemy. Our mutual friend would not have put us together if I were."

She had a point. He nodded, acknowledging that.

"The official position of my office is that you and your people do not actually exist, and anything you and your people may or may not be involved in does not exist, and therefore no investigations can actually be opened into that which does not exist."

"Officially," he said again.

"Officially or unofficially. We're in a political purge year, Mr. Didier. The books are open for audit and the consciences are clear. Next year?" She made a "who knows" gesture with her hands. "Next year may be a different story. But for now, this is entirely off the books."

"And what is this, off the books?"

"Curiosity. And an offer."

Sergei had been approached with offers before. The Silence had made an offer to him, not so long ago: bring Wren in as a freelance agent, in exchange for protection from the Council. In the end, the Council had turned out to be a much lesser threat than the Silence itself.

The desire was there to tell Agent Chang to take a flying leap off a short pier, Danny or no. Desire was clubbed with common sense, and stuck in a corner for the moment. "An offer of what?"

Agent Chang kept her poker face on. "I don't know. Yet. But I suspect that we can work something out. As we go along." She turned to look at him, her height allowing them to be eye to eye. "I'm curious by nature. That's why I ended up where I did, doing what I do. Very little is known, even un-officially about your...people. The people who do know are not talking. Being able to join that fraternity of knowledge is something I want, very badly. Badly enough to spend two years of my life on it, Mr. Didier. Two years of using my agency's computers and off-hours footwork, just to track down a name to go with the rumors. And even then, it took more time to be able to do anything with that name."

"That doesn't say much for your investigational skills." He meant the barb to sting.

"I've been a little busy" she said, properly stung. "This has been a side search. My agency does not merely sit on its thumbs watching radar screens and closed-circuit televisions all day."

"Rebuke taken. But you did finally track me down. Now what?"

"As I said. Curiosity. Perhaps the possibility of mutual aid: when, as and if needed. Our mutual friend agreed this would be a good time to offer that."

She seemed to be under the impression that he, Sergei, was a Talent. That amused him, but he thought it better not to correct the misapprehension. Not yet, anyway.

"Originally I meant to contact you simply to exchange business cards, if you will. In the past week, however, my contacts have turned up a new whisper. Someone else is looking at the…unusual communities in this city. Not for you, or Ms. Valere, but something that might be associated with you—or you with it."

"And you thought to warn us? How nice." Damn. They were all connected, then. That ulcer absolutely had his name on it.

She stopped, turned and glared at him. "I am not a fool, or a little girl to be patted on the head and dismissed, Didier." Her voice had gone cold, and her expression could have given P.B. frostbite. "If you didn't already know that something was up, you would be much less efficient than I expected, and a sore disappointment to me."

She started walking again, this time faster. He had to stretch his legs slightly to keep up.

"I came today to offer my assistance. Should you so desire it." She shrugged. "If you don't…I walk away, having gotten what I wanted—verification, and a contact with someone who is—how shall we put this?"

"Bluntly usually works."

"Bluntly then. A contact with individuals who have proven to be significant players in a game I'm interested in."

"If I say no, you actually walk away, no strings attached?" He was deeply dubious.

"Oh for the love of God. I'm not the bad guy here. I'm not even a player—yet. Right now all I want is to know what the game pieces are, and how they can be moved. In case I ever have a reason to join the game."

"Unofficially."

"Or otherwise. I am a government agent. If you know something that can aid me in my sworn duty, I won't not ask. I am presuming that a warrant might inconvenience your day-to-day activities but not disrupt...whatever else it is that you do."

The government could kill his gallery, and she knew it. Especially now that he had broadened into non-American artists and imported works. But no, he didn't think long-term she could do anything to hurt Wren. It would make Margot, Wren's mother, furious, though.

Given otherwise even odds, he'd back Margot Elizabeta Valere over Agent Chang. No hesitation.

But...the back-scratching could go both ways, too. Danny, damn him, had been right.

Sergei had to sell his decision a few hours later. "Your mother could take her. In a fair fight, anyway. I'm not sure FBI agents play fair."

"Neither does my mom, when she's pissed," Wren said. They were sitting at the back table at Marianna's, the chalkboard menu of specials off to one side, ignored. There had been a time they ate here so often the waitress knew their quirks individually. It had been a while; when they came in tonight, they didn't recognize the waiter, a young, slightly hyperactive Latino man who seemed to be wearing uncomfortable shoes.

Time passed. Things changed, even in your own backyard. Wren was depressed just thinking about it. She hoped that Callie had gone on to better-tipping venues.

The waiter came back, and hovered. They had been talking too long.

"I'll have the veal piccatta," she told him. "And a glass of the riojo."

Sergei nodded approvingly at her choice of wines, and she felt the urge to kick him. She hadn't been drinking Ripple when they met, after all. All right, she had been under legal drinking age when they met. But she wasn't Galeatea, he wasn't Pygmalion, and he could keep his damned approval to himself

Even as she got cranky, Wren recognized that she was overreacting. It had been a long day: the workout at the gym had left her feeling achy rather than invigorated, Karl had left a note for her saying that the debt was paid off except for his having to listen to an afternoon's worth of wild fish stories, and he'd get her for that, and every attempt to find a place to practice her break-ins had been too crowded to really consider, if only for the risk of tripping over someone. And now, when she'd hoped to be pleasantly wiped out and smug in victory she was instead being told that they had a new player in the game and her partner wasn't even sure what the damn game was.

And Callie wasn't here to snark at them.

The food had better still be good, was all she was thinking.

"I'll have the New York strip with tamarind, and a glass of the same," he told the waiter. "And could we have some more bread, please? Thank you."

The bread, at least, was still good. Wren allowed herself one more stick, refusing Sergei's offer of the tiny pot of garlic butter, the memory of the gym still fresh in her mind.

"And she wants to meet with us."

"That was strongly implied. She's curious. She wants to be counted among the Players in her office, and she thinks that knowing us will get her there. Or at least be a building block to where she wants to be."

"You're the one with all the people skills. What's your take? Is she playing straight with us?"

"No." He didn't hesitate on that. "But whatever game she's playing, she's treating us like teammates. Right now, anyway."

Wren waited, chewing on the bread, but he left it at that.

So. This was in her lap, then.

"Danny thought she'd be useful to us, otherwise he would never have given her our contact info, prank or no prank. And you think her information is solid." If he didn't, he wouldn't have told her about the meeting. Or maybe he would have; things had changed in the past few years, a lot of it at her insistence. Something like this, she'd have been pissed if he didn't tell her. And he knew that.

"I think she believes that it is. But someone might be playing her playing us."

"You're just so appallingly cynical," she told him. "Very sexy."

He just smiled at her, and she felt an answering smirk rise up. For a moment, just a moment in these familiar surroundings it was light and easy and the only stress was trying to keep one step ahead of her monthly payments and dodging her mother's attempts to match-make with a nice boy from home.

Then the moment faded, and she was back in today's reality again.

"What do you think?" she asked him, pointing what was left of her bread at him like a baton.

"I think it's a risk. And I'm not sure if we can take on any more risks right now."

"Okay. Point taken." They were treading into deep water with P.B.'s job, and maybe not the best time to be juggling new uncertainties, when they were still recovering, and so much else was on the personal plate. But... "Not every new ally is dangerous. Sometimes they're just annoying." He raised his pale brown eyes to her in query and she shrugged. "And sometimes they're damned useful. If not now, then later."

"That was the gist of her offer, as well. That we might be useful to her later."

"You normally appreciate that kind of long-thinking," she said.

Their wine came and the conversation paused until the waiter went back to hover over the other couple in the tiny restaurant, who still hadn't decided what they wanted for dinner.

"Normally yes. But I prefer it be us who thinks forward, and everyone else be short-term and shortsighted."

"You don't like her?" Wren frowned. "So you don't think I should meet with her?"

He was primed to agree, to say that he thought that Wren should keep her distance; that any government agent who wanted to know a Talent personally had an ulterior motive he didn't like.

Then he had a sudden flick of a switch and was thinking less like a business manager and more like a partner. If he said no, and Wren ever did meet Agent Chang, her first thought would be to wonder if that woman's looks had anything to do with his desire to keep them apart.

It didn't. It really didn't. But convincing Wren of that after the fact...he might as well just slice himself open now and save the time later.

"Yeah actually. I think you should meet. I'd like your take on her, before we dismiss anything out of hand."

The food came then and the conversation was put aside in favor of eating. The food was as good as previous visits, and for a while the only noises were that of satisfied diners, interrupted occasionally by the waiter coming around to offer to refill their glasses.

"I think I'm tipsy," Wren said, after they'd agreed to a glass of port instead of dessert. "I haven't drunk this much since…New Year's, I think. Mister Didier, are you trying to get me drunk to take advantage of me?"

"The thought never once crossed my mind," he protested, all innocence. "Since when do I need to get you drunk?"

She looked at him with a sparkle that hadn't been in her eye for a very long time, and Sergei almost broke his fingers getting his credit card out of his wallet to pay for the meal.

Her breath was scented with red wine and coffee, and her skin smelled like baby powder. They were only a few blocks from Wren's apartment and they held hands the entire way, strolling in the crisp night air like newlyweds, or a third date couple. On the third landing Sergei threw caution—and common sense—to the wind and picked Wren up in a gentle fireman's carry, taking the rest of the steps two at a time.

"Oh God, Sergei, crazy man, what are you doing?" she squealed, which made the effort worth it.

He was panting so hard when he reached her landing, he had a moment's fear he was about to have a heart attack. *Idiot macho ego.*

She took pity on him, and as they came to her front door, current snapped the locks open and invisible hands pulled the door open.

He hadn't known she could do that. Then again, he hadn't

known she couldn't, either. He didn't much care. His mind was on other things right then.

The door closed behind them, the locks snicking shut one by one, and he carried her down the hallway to the dark green warmth of her bedroom, not bothering to turn on the lamp.

He fell onto the bed first, bringing her down on top of him, and even as they hit the mattress she was squirming free, her hands reaching for his shirt, flicking open the buttons one by one.

"Careful, *Zhenchenka,* that's a good work shirt."

"I'll be gentle," she promised, and he grunted, his own fingers sliding under her top, fingers stroking the warm flesh there, feeling the male satisfaction when she had to stop what she was doing to deal with the shudder that ran down her spine at his touch. A good shudder, deep and thick, and he knew without even looking at her face that her eyes were heavy-lidded, her head tilted back slightly, her lips curled in the tiniest of smirks.

Blood surged into his cock, and the weight of his clothing against his skin was suddenly too much. But first, Wren.

She was wearing basic cotton; he had dated women who brought him to his knees with silk and lace, and she did it with a cotton knit sweater and a practical cotton bra, and he was thankful, actually, because he could toss them on the floor without worrying too much about what shape they were in come morning.

And then his hands were on her skin and he wasn't thinking about any kind of clothing at all. Her body was supple and smooth above him; he could feel the muscle moving beneath the flesh, but there was enough flesh to pad out her hips and ribs pleasingly, and her breasts, *thank all the stars in the universe for her breasts* he thought, as close to a prayer as he normally got. He cupped their weight in his hand, the nipples hard against his palms.

She got herself out of her pants while he was otherwise

occupied, and straddled him wearing only a wisp of panties. Cotton again, maybe, but they were barely there as she stroked his crotch with her own, riding him like a pony, a tease of what was to come.

His shirt was finally open, but it was too much effort to shrug out of it, when it was so much more important to get the hell out of his pants.

Her hands were at his belt, opening his fly, urging his hips up so she could tug the pants down, taking his underwear with it. Only to discover, with a snort of laughter that he was still wearing his dress shoes.

He tried to kick them off, but they were well-made, with good laces, and stayed put on his feet.

She turned, leaving his hands bereft, to deal with the laces, and his hands were presented with a new object of fascination: her rounded cheeks.

"Slap me and regret it," she warned, without even looking back, and he restrained himself to merely caressing them. There was a cool breath on his toes, and the sound of shoes dropping to the floor, and he pulled the cotton panties off her and pulled her back onto him with such speed that she let out a little squeak of surprise.

Her ass brushed his erection, and then she wiggled a little, opening her thighs for him. He groaned with pleasure at the sensation, and with his hands on her hips, carefully guided them both home.

"You're…"

"Shh."

Thankfully, she shushed, spreading herself wider on his lap, and he was able to slide into her with relative ease, only a little awkwardness trying to find her entrance. God, she was tight, as though it had been months instead of weeks since they'd had any kind of physical contact. He went hilt-deep, her weight solidly on him, and he rocked forward, drawing a groan out of her that was sweeter than honey.

They were normally face-to-face lovers, finding comfort in open eyes and whispers, tasting and touching. But this position felt right deep inside her, Wren's knees drawn up, her controlling the pace while he held on for the ride, letting go and falling into her, all over again....

They came together, her startled yell and immediate collapse backward matching his own explosive "whoof" and reactionary melting of muscles that had been so tense up until then.

They lay there both supine on the bed, covered in sweat, until she started to giggle.

"Get off me, woman," he commanded. "You're dripping."

"Whose fault is that?" she asked, but obediently rolled off him, and he could breathe again, already missing her weight on him.

"Nice," she said, her voice already soft and drowsy. "Very nice."

She was like a guy in that; sex always made her sleepy. He'd take offense, if it didn't match his own preferences perfectly. They could talk in the morning. He gathered her up next to him, sweaty skin sticking to sweaty skin. She curled against his side and before he could even think to ask if she wanted to get under the blanket, they were both asleep.

fourteen

Wren woke up with a grin on her face. Not a smile, not a smirk, a full-wattage, canary-feathered expression of satisfaction that made her jaw hurt. It took her a while to figure out why.

Bed, check. Her own bed. Warm and cozy. Nice, but not grin-worthy, exactly. She had slept in, judging from the sunlight managing to get through her dark green drapes; again, nice but nothing of real impact. Achy legs and abs—some of that from the gym workout yesterday but more from the workout last night. That was grin-worthy, oh yes, but it felt as if more was behind it, somehow.

So. Sex. With Sergei. Nice sex. Very nice sex, in fact. The thought warmed up the already-comfortable temperature in the bedroom slightly, better than any furnace could. For the first time in—she didn't want to think about how long since they had done more than cautious mutual hand-and-mouth-play, actually. So, nice. Made nicer by the fact that it had happened not when she wasn't so tired she could barely stir current, but when she was rested and alert. All right, maybe "alert" wasn't the right word. But even better than that, in fact: it had happened when she was slightly drunk from the wine at dinner. A drunk— or even tipsy—Talent typically had less control over impulse-reactions. It should have been a recipe for disaster. Instead, there had been no overflow of current, no loss of control. No need to ground in Sergei, because even with more flowing in and around her core, she had been able to control it all.

And, more to the point, he hadn't seemed to feel the need for her to ground in him, either. Her partner had a good time—she had a very clear memory of how good a time he'd been having and the finger-bruises on her hips to prove it— without the need to enhance it by having her ground current in him. He might have wanted it, might have thought about it, but that want or thought hadn't limited his participation, or put a strain on their mutual satisfaction.

That was—cautiously—grin-worthy.

It didn't prove anything was cured or solved or whatever. But it was more progress than they'd had in months.

Of course, waking to memories and no actual body was less than thrilling. She felt the space in the bed next to her: cool. If it was as late as she thought, he would already be up and showered and having breakfast—or even gone off to work. Drat. She moved enough to look over the side of the bed. Her clothes were still scattered there, but his were gone. Shoes, too.

Oh well.

She collapsed back into bed, pulling the covers up over her bare skin and snuggled down into the pillow. As long as she was in bed, she might as well sleep a little longer.

And then of course, the phone rang. Wren considered letting the answering machine get it, but the fact that it was already midmorning made her throw the covers off and pad, bare-assed, down the hallway and into the kitchen. There was another phone in the office, but her instinct was always to go to the main line.

The fact that the coffee was there, as well, probably had something to do with it.

The coffeemaker was on and there was in fact a full pot waiting, hot and strong-looking. She picked up the phone in one hand and reached for a mug with the other.

"Hello?" Her voice was scratchy and she had to clear her throat and try again. "Hello?" She got the mug, and put it on the counter, then turned to reach for the coffeepot. Her kitchen was small enough that everything was more or less within arm's distance no matter where you stood. She looked out the window to check the weather, and was annoyed and then thankful, considering she hadn't put on her robe, that the shade was pulled down.

"Oh good you're awake." It was Sergei on the other end of the line, sounding far too chipper. She twisted the phone cord with her fingers and tried not to grin even more widely.

"Barely. Bless you for turning the machine on."

"Figured you'd need it."

They were both very blasé, very casual, very matter-of-fact. Wren wasn't going to mention the fabulous noncurrentical sex if he wasn't. No damage, no mention, no jinxing, no big deal. But it *was,* and she knew that he knew it, too. Not saying anything didn't make it any less.

"I've arranged a meeting," Sergei said, and it took her a minute for her brain to catch up and remember what he was talking about. The Fed. Right.

"This morning?"

He laughed a low, amused chortle. "Valere, it's two in the afternoon."

"Holy mother of God." Wren actually looked at the new solar-powered clock on the wall—a replacement for the old battery-operated one she had fried on a particularly bad day—and shook her head. "I guess I really was tired. Or tired-out."

He ignored the comment. "Can you make yourself presentable and get over to the coffee shop near the gallery by three?"

Thank God, a different coffee shop. She didn't want to start getting so predictable her enemies—or even her friends—could target her movements or probable destinations. A little paranoia was never a bad thing. "Yeah no problem. Any suggestions on who I should be?" She rarely met with clients, or even anyone who might be tempted to hire her; not so much to keep herself unknown, since few people ever remembered what she looked like anyway, as to not get involved in the hiring discussions or negotiations. The few times she did she deferred to Sergei's opinion as to what sort of look she should project, depending on how he was selling her.

"Comfortable," he said. "Oh, excellent, Lowell has a large fish on the line. I need to go close the deal. I'll see you in a bit."

"Okay," she said, but he had already hung up, hot on the scent of money. Wren finished pouring a cup of coffee into the oversized yellow mug she had stolen from a store in Grand Central Station and carried it with her to the bathroom. "Comfortable. I'm going to assume he didn't mean pajamas." Although that would certainly set a definite tone for the meeting, absolutely. "Hi, I'm The Wren. Trust me, I'm Comfy." She grinned again. Probably not, not even for the look on Sergei's face.

He really was fun to tweak, though. She hadn't been doing enough of that lately, caught up in the seemingly unending sturm und drama of their lives. They deserved a break, damn it. Hopefully the recent bits of playfulness from both of them, like last night's vanilla-but-tasty sex, were a good sign.

She put the coffee mug on the edge of the sink, balancing it with the casualness of long practice, and turned the shower on. While she waited for the water heater to kick in, she finger-combed the snarls out of her hair, wincing periodically. Sergei was a finger-tangler when he was in the moment, and her hair tangled if you looked at it wrong.

Detangled, she got under the shower head and let the hot water take the edge, pounding into her skin and raising a mottled flush. It wasn't good for her, probably, but it *felt* good. A quick shampoo and rinse, and she turned the water off, standing there dripping in the tub a moment.

"Awake. Yeah," she decided, and reached for a towel.

In the end, she settled on a pair of unripped, reasonably unfaded jeans and a dark blue v-neck sweater. Her hair, brushed out but still damp, hung past her shoulders and made her face look very young, if not innocent. She used blush and a pale lipstick, just enough to give a polish that contradicted the youthful look, and then added a pair of brown leather boots that added another three inches to her height. She had bought them on a whim when they were on sale, and never had a place to wear them until now.

By the time she was done it was almost two forty-five, and she had to double-time it down the stairs, grabbing her battered leather jacket and shoulder bag as she went out the door. A bus happened to be going past as she hit the nearest stop and she madly flagged it down. The driver must have been in a good mood, or maybe someone on the bus had pissed him off specifically, because he stopped and let her get on. Nobody glared at her from the few seats that were occupied, so maybe it was just good karma day.

The traffic wasn't horrible, and she ended up walking into the coffee shop only a few minutes late.

All right, ten minutes. For mass transit time that wasn't too bad, she thought. Sergei was already seated in a booth in the back, facing the door so that he would see her—or anyone—as they came in. She noted that he was also able to see the entrances to both bathrooms and the kitchen, as well, and didn't know if she should be impressed that she noted that he had done that, or unnerved.

The woman with him had black hair and good posture, and that was all she could tell from here. Dodging a waitress balancing two pots of coffee, one with the terrifying orange handle of decaf, Wren crossed the space and joined them. From the way the woman started as the Retriever slid into the booth next to Sergei, the agent hadn't seen or sensed her coming. From the way she collected herself after that start, she hadn't been expecting to see or sense Wren, or was really good at public recovery.

"Agent Chang."

"Ms. Valere."

Wren took the other woman's measure quickly. Damn. And also, damn. Gorgeous, yeah: and if Wren could read people at all, not entirely thrilled with the fact. Like Wren she was low on the face paint, her sleek black hair cut bluntly at chin length so it was easy to care for, dressed more formally than Wren in a pantsuit that skirted being standard government issue by being a dark forest-green herringbone rather than navy blue. Summation: A woman who knew what worked for her, and what was expected, and how to make them work together, but didn't take anything nature had given her too seriously. The kind of woman Danny would know, yeah.

Wren liked her immediately, but didn't let any of that show.

"I'm told you wanted to be able to say you knew me." She caught the agent's gaze, one pair of brown eyes and one pair of black watching the other carefully.

"I suspect you were told no such thing," Chang replied evenly.

Sergei looked as though he was going to say something, but a light tap on his foot from Wren's boot silenced him. Danny'd had his fun, now she was going to have hers.

"Not in so many words, no. But it all comes down to bragging rights, doesn't it?"

"I try not to brag. It gets in the way of actual accomplishments."

Wren snorted, and broke the gaze-hold by turning to attract the waiter's attention and asking silently, in universal coffee shop sign language, for a menu.

"So now that you've…accomplished this, what now, Agent Chang?"

"I would like to pick your brain, if I may," she said. "About what it is that you do, who you are. How many of you there are."

"There's only one of me," Wren said, fully expecting Sergei to chime in with a fervent "Thank God." He remained silent, however.

Chang sized her up again, clearly thinking through her words before asking the next question. "You are not the only person with extraordinary abilities, even if you are deeply extraordinary. How do you refer to yourselves?"

P.B.'s comment, that most groups merely called themselves some variant of "true people" came to Wren's mind, but she wasn't sure how far she could tweak this woman without her getting pissy, so she decided to mix things up a little with straight truth and see how she reacted.

"We're not very original. Talent."

"Talent." Nope, she didn't sound impressed.

"Well, it's a talent, what we do, and we are what we do, and so…Talent." Truth, all truth, as far as it went.

"And there are a lot of you." That wasn't a question, the way it was said, so Wren didn't feel the need to respond. There were a lot, by some standards. By others, their population was depressingly small. Certainly they would qualify for minority status in any census. "And you are all…human?"

"The way you ask that implies that you think that we're not."

"You're human," Chang said.

Some devil made Wren ask "Are you sure?"

Chang blinked at her, and Wren thought she felt Sergei quivering with barely suppressed *something* next to her. Hopefully, it was laughter.

"You're close enough to pass in a crowded elevator," Chang finally said. "If I was to start determining what was human and what wasn't, I'd have to back out half the population and almost everyone I work with."

Sergei did laugh, then.

"What do you already know, Agent Chang?" Wren leaned back, resting one arm comfortably along the back of the banquette, behind Sergei's shoulders. Not that she was being territorial or anything. But Agent Chang *was* damn gorgeous.

"Anea," the other woman said. "My name is Anea."

"Genevieve," she offered in return, acknowledging and accepting the no-poaching, no-foul discussion without anything more being said. "What do you already know, so I don't waste your valuable time repeating anything?"

What she really meant, and what Chang understood she meant, was that Wren wasn't going to risk giving anything away she didn't have to.

"Our mutual acquaintance didn't tell me much. I know that you…your people, are able to manipulate electrical power for rather impressive results, up to and including blacking out entire cities. And that you, yourself, have a reputation for being able to lay hands on items that others have not been able to obtain."

Well, that was one of the more diplomatic ways of describing her job, certainly. Agent Chang—Anea—could go into advertising, if the Fed thing didn't work out.

"And that you were involved in a recent fracas here in Manhattan that resulted in a rather impressive body count and absolutely no publicity, no charges filed, and no repercussions."

The idea that there had been no repercussions would have been funny, if it weren't so painful. Wren's humor in the situation faded slightly.

"I admit to being…very interested in the details of that, and earlier, incidents, as a law enforcement official, no matter that they were never formally investigated."

Wren's amusement faded a little more. That was what she—and pretty much every other lonejack in the city—had been afraid of: official attention.

"I also know—" and the Asian woman hesitated, playing absently with her coffee spoon in a way that suggested that she didn't actually know, but was fishing "—that you have…associates who are *not* human. Specifically, an individual known as Polar Bear?"

Hearing P.B.'s nickname actually said in full took Wren a moment to process, but she didn't lose track of the question.

"I know someone who is called that, yes. I'm not sure I'd call him an associate, though." Friend, yes. Mooch, occasional roommate, protector, *demon*. Brother, if she was going to be sappy. But not associate.

"He is not human, though. What is he?"

"You don't need to know that, Agent Chang." Wren's words were casual, friendly even, but they were made of steel.

"Actually, I do," Chang said in tones of matching steel, but her body language remained open, and those almond-shaped eyes were good-natured. "Curiosity, you see." She let the question drop, though; they hadn't forbidden her to dig for answers on her own, after that implied challenge, even if they weren't going to spoon-feed her what she wanted to know.

Oh yeah. Wren liked this woman a lot. Be damned if she'd show it, though. Interesting or otherwise, she was also a Fed. Wren didn't need those sorts of complications, no matter what Danny thought.

"Could I...could you show me?" the Fed asked. "What it is that you do?"

Sergei seemed taken aback, but Wren had actually expected that to be one of the first questions asked. It was what *she* would have asked, anyway, were the positions reversed. And if Agent Chang already knew this much, a little more wasn't going to make the situation any better, or worse.

"It's really not all that impressive," she warned. "Like watching someone turn on a light switch, mostly." If Anea thought it was electricity, Wren was perfectly willing to continue with that metaphor. It was as close as she wanted to explain, anyway.

The waitress came with the menu, finally, and Wren took it from her, but didn't open it. "Watch," she said, once the waitress had moved far enough way.

She tapped a thread of current, letting it rise up through her arm, down out through her fingers. It was a simple trick, and one that used to drive Neezer crazy when she did it as a teenager: rearranging the ink molecules on a printed sheet. She used to change the wording of Neezer's tests when she didn't know the answer—which was often; biology had never been one of her strong points.

All she intended to do was rearrange the name of the restaurant. But the gasp Anea let out before anything had even happened made her startle, and the words instead faded entirely off the page, leaving a large blank spot on the menu.

"Wow."

"You saw that." Interesting. The ability to see current was far more common than the ability to use it—maybe a full third of the human population could see some aspect of it or another, especially if they were already aware and looking for it—but that meant that Agent Chang wasn't entirely Null. *Gooey,* she thought, and squashed the thought. She was so damned tired of that word, and cursed Bonnie for ever putting it in her brain.

"That was…"

"Magic. Yeah."

"Wow." Then the agent looked at the menu. "Wow." Her voice sharpened. "You can put the letters back, too?"

Wren did so, going back to her original plan and making the lettering read "MaliWho" rather than "Malibu" Diner.

"An interesting skill. Definitely something that could be useful."

Wren cocked her head, not sure what Anea was talking about. It was a parlor trick….

"Very few of the Talent are criminally minded," Sergei said, his voice dry, and Wren finally clued in. The ability to alter words on laminated paper—or unlaminated but otherwise specially treated—would indeed be of interest to a government agent. Oops.

"Jesus wept," she said. "I never thought of that. That is really…sad." Her money worries would have been over a long time ago, if she'd just gone into counterfeiting instead of Retrieval.

"It's refreshing, actually," Chang said. "I think you may have just restored a drop of my faith in human nature."

As though Wren's words were in fact the sign the other woman had been looking for, she reached down into the battered leather portfolio case at her feet, and extracted a number of sheets: two printed reports, and a grainy, black-and-white photograph.

"As promised, my share of the exchange. This photograph was taken four days ago, during an attempted break-in at a certain privately operated museum here in New York."

Both Wren and Sergei sat upright at that, and Agent Chang smiled grimly. "I see that gets your attention. Our mutual friend thought it might. Transcripts of the post-arrest interview"—a nice way of saying the interrogation—"seemed to imply that the burglar was hired by a member of your community."

A Retriever? Wren was amused at how indignant she felt, that someone would hire an out-of-towner for a local job. Then she looked again at the photograph, and shook her head. "He's not one of ours."

"You recognize him? Or is the community so small that you would know everyone?"

Oh, Chang was good at this, yeah. But Wren was just as good.

"I don't know him, but that doesn't mean anything. But he's not one of ours."

A Retriever in work mode would have fritzed the camera, just off the no-see-me vibes he or she would emit, plus the natural tendency of Talent to wreak havoc on electronics in their vicinity. But there was no need to mention that right now, if the agent didn't already know.

"Do you know what he was after?" Sergei asked.

"The Museum declined to give us any more information than the rooms were used to store odd bits they had picked up over the years and not yet determined a provenance or display use for. They tend to keep their noses clean and their paperwork in order, so we didn't push for details." She shrugged, sipping her coffee and wincing at the taste. People apparently came to this diner for convenience, not quality. "Truthfully, normally we would never have been involved, save that it pinged on my radar screen."

"And you didn't want to push for fear of alerting someone that you had found something of interest."

"Have I?" Anea asked, her expression one of cautious anticipation.

Wren looked at her partner, who nodded, ever so slightly, his eyes half-lidded but alert. She would spill and he would survey the reaction, then.

"We have reason to believe that they are after the belongings of…a Talent from several generations ago, in another country, who dabbled in things he should have left alone."

"Things." Chang had the gift of packing a lot of questions into one word.

Wren tapped her fingers on the menu, trying to decide how to phrase what little she was going to tell, without leaving too many openings for the other woman to pry at. Finally, she gave up and went for the kill.

"He created a form—a living battery of sorts—that would allow a Talent to increase his or her abilities, and possibly bypass our…call it a surge protector." Wren was pretty proud of that last analogy, actually, especially done on the fly.

"And this is a bad thing?"

"Bad for the battery," Wren said. "The *living* battery."

Agent Change was not slow on the uptake, no. Her eyes widened, and her mouth opened in a silent "oh." "These belongings…they were in that storeroom? And included, perhaps, directions on how to accomplish this little parlor trick?"

"Possibly. Probably, based on your information."

"And the person who tried to steal them…"

"Hired by a group of people who should not have their hands on this material." Wren was definite about that. It had to be them—the timing was too damned coincidental—and absolutely they should not get them. No matter who they were, any group that wanted those papers that badly should *not* have them. The *Cosa* had created a battery of their own—a nonliving, non-sentient one—and destroyed it, and the plans, after one use. For once in her life, she really did hold the high moral ground.

"Who should, then? You?"

Sergei jumped in at this point, taking Chang's fire. "We have been retained by a legitimate heir to the original author to reclaim possession of the papers."

Lovely, legitimate, and the added benefit of being true. Mostly.

"If these papers are that dangerous, I could use my own contacts to pry them from the Museum—it would be simpler to—"

"No!" Wren reacted immediately, and with more heat than she had been expecting. Chang looked taken aback, but Sergei was already nodding his head in agreement. Wren felt better about her instinctive response, then.

"No?"

"Whoever has these papers…they'll be a target. Allowing a N—a non-Talent to handle them opens that person to too much risk. We—our client—will be able to protect them." She hoped. They would have a better chance than a Null—even a partially Null government agent who, no matter her possible good intentions, still had layers of bureaucracy and political animals to report to. While she liked the other woman, you had to earn trust, in Wren's world.

Chang looked from Wren to Sergei, and pulled out another photo. This one was also black-and-white, but it wasn't grainy. It was, in fact, crystal clear. Wren swallowed hard and looked away. Sergei didn't blink.

"The thief, I assume," he said, referring to the body sprawled faceup on the pavement, the face hacked into shreds, the dark stain across his throat proof to how he had been killed.

"As he was being transferred to another holding facility, his police escort was ambushed, and he was taken away. The assumption was that his partners, whoever they were, had staged a rescue."

She shrugged, clearly not broken up by the man's demise. "The body was found seven hours later, dumped two blocks from the site of the ambush."

"The police officers?"

"Banged up, lightly sedated, and pissed off, but otherwise all right. Whoever these people are, they knew better than to become cop-killers."

"Too much heat on them, then," Sergei agreed. "Tying off a loose end, someone nobody will really miss…that would be investigated, but not hunted with the same dedication."

"Exactly." Some lives were of more value than others. Nobody was arguing that. Probably why they had chosen a Null thief, whoever They actually were. The death of a Talent—local or imported—would have been noted and followed up on. Especially now, when the community was still reeling from recent events.

"And you waited to tell us this until you were confident that we had nothing to do with it." Sergei was moderately pissed-off himself. "How can you be sure?"

"I suspect that your bodies tend not to show up," Chang said evenly.

Sergei's eyes showed the wince his face was too well-trained to let escape. Wren wondered if Agent Chang had caught it, or not.

She hoped not.

"Thank you for your help," she said, trying to distract attention from him, and the thought of dead bodies, necessary and hidden or otherwise. "We'll handle this, going forward."

"And you will call me, if anything changes, or I can be of assistance?"

"Sergei will. I tend to be…least in sight."

The agent-facade disappeared, and the woman Anea appeared, smiling in appreciation at the joke. "Thank you," she said, and seemed to mean it. "For trusting me. I can only imagine that it is difficult. I will protect your confidences to the very best of my ability to do so."

Wren believed her.

The agent looked at her watch, then swore and tapped it as though to resuscitate its workings. Wren felt a twinge of guilt, and quickly squelched it. If Agent Chang—Anea—wanted to hang with Talent, she was going to have to learn about things like watches, cell phones, PDAs and whatnot. Hopefully the Federal budget was up to a few replacements here and there.

"Damn." Chang cast her glance around the diner, finally finding a clock. "My train leaves in an hour. It's been educational meeting you two, and my thanks for both your candor and your assistance. Here's my card—the number on the front is my office line. If I'm not there it will transfer to the main line, and they will be able to reach me wherever I am." She pushed the business card across the table and left it there for Sergei to pick up, while she shuffled the photos and reports back into her briefcase. Wren let her fingers rest on the sheet she had lifted from the pile, and didn't say a word as farewell handshakes were exchanged and Chang left for Penn Station and her train back to D.C.

"We'll take care of it?" Sergei said, after the door closed behind the agent.

"We have no choice, now. Even if the museum had no idea what they had in that room before, someone's going to be a bright bunny and wonder about it, now. And all it takes is one really bright bunny poking around and maybe running a few experiments, and all hell could break loose. Remember the Nescanni Parchment?" That Artifact had been a soul-eater, and a friend had lost his life in the struggle to contain it. From the look on Sergei's face, he remembered that, and the fact that the damned—literally—thing had almost eaten *him*. Only admitting that she loved him—that she *needed* him—had kept him connected to this world, and even that had been close.

A tough couple of years, yeah. They had lost so much—and gained a lot, too, yeah. New friends, renewed ties among the old, mostly but not entirely offsetting the costs they'd paid. Seemed like the way life went: you had to pay before you got the goods, no credit offered.

The fortune cookie came back to her, the way they tended to. *Take no blood from stone, save you give it back.* They'd bled enough to get back the entire damn city and half the 'burbs, by now. Somehow, she didn't think that was what the fortune meant, though. If it were straightforward, it wouldn't need a Seer to see.

She pulled a sugar packet out of the holder and played with it, pushing it around on the Formica table. "For years, generations, this stuff's been hidden. Now, it's not so much hidden, because—" she shrugged. "—because things like this tend not to stay lost forever. So odds are good that this thing gets out of holding, maybe into hands not ours. You want someone playing amateur Doctor Frankenstein? Or worse yet, holding an all-comers auction for the papers?" Wren pushed her point, wanting to make sure that he understood. "I don't believe in coincidences, you know that. These people looking, I'm sure they're the ones who took Geinga—the demon who sent P.B. the letter," she clarified at his puzzled look. "The demon who, by the way, hasn't been seen since about a week before P.B. got the letter. I put out some feelers into the *Cosa*, and it's like he never existed. Nobody knows nuthin', nobody saw nuthin', nobody wants to talk about nuthin'. And it's not the usual don't-talk-to-strangers routine, either. These are Fatae that see everything, and don't scare easy. But they're scared now.

"I wasn't bullshitting Chang," the Retriever went on. "Even just being in proximity to those papers isn't going to be safe, if they are what we think they are, if they have the information we think they do. And even if they're not, if other people think they are what they think they are they'll show up sooner or later." She tried to decide if that made any sense, decided that so long as Sergei was following her, pronouns were irrelevant. "The only way to remove the risk is to Retrieve the papers, to make them disappear again, this time forever."

She paused, contemplating that. How did you erase knowledge forever, once it was known? Just burning paper didn't do it, when magic was concerned. "We were hamstrung before by not knowing exactly where the papers were. Now, thanks to our competitors doing the gruntwork, we do."

"We did, rather." Sergei pointed out. "As you said, one bright bunny, of which the museum has plenty, and they'll take another hard look at what the thief tried to steal. He or she will start to poke around, take the rest of the material out of storage and move it somewhere else. Maybe even send it elsewhere to any expert in the country—or outside. We're back to step two, only worse off, because more people have gotten their eyes on it."

Wren touched the report in her lap, the one with the full, classified theft report from Chang's briefcase, and smiled at her partner. "Not exactly…"

Anything not nailed down was a Retriever's toy. Anything she could pry loose was not nailed down. Agent Chang would have to learn that about the *Cosa,* too.

There was too much going on in her brain, so after she left Sergei to do his thing with blueprints and backgrounds, Wren went to the one place where she knew that she would be able to put it aside for a while, let it simmer while she worked out different muscles.

"Twenty-three. Twenty-four." She paused, before continuing. "Twenty-five."

"Valere. We got problems."

So much for no distractions. "Twenty-six." This was a news flash? "We always got problems. We got heaps of problems. Twenty-seven."

"This is a new problem."

Wren was doing crunches, and her hair was flopping into her eyes, annoying the hell out of her. P.B. reached out and, with surprising delicacy, tucked the strands back under her sweatband.

"Thanks. Twenty-eight."

"No problem."

She raised her torso again, and then stopped midmovement. "I've lost count now."

The demon hunkered down beside the padded exercise mat, the mirror opposite them reflecting the incongruous sight of the white-pelted demon kneeling beside a woman in a red jog bra, black sweatpants, and sneakers. "Valere, trust me. Least of our problems."

"Not a problem for you. You're built like a damned brick. Me, doesn't matter how many calories I burn, still doesn't do a damn thing for my abs. You'd think current could do something about giving me a six-pack. But no…"

"Valere, you're babbling."

"You're interrupting my workout. A workout I need so my brain is free to work through the details of *your* job, by the way, so interrupting me isn't in your best interests. How did you get in, anyway? This gym's females-only."

"Same way I get in anywhere," he said in exasperation. "I

walk in and nobody stops me because if they stop me they have to admit that they saw me. Valere, I don't have much time, my shadow's probably downstairs getting a temporary membership right now."

"Shadow?" That got her attention.

"Shadow. Female, hence the guard downstairs not stopping her. Been following me for a couple-three days, I'm not sure how long, exactly, just when I noticed her. There may be others, but I haven't smelled them."

His leathery black nostrils flared as though remembering the scent.

Wren went back to doing her crunches, counting again from the beginning. "What does she smell like?"

"Memories. And blood. It doesn't matter. She's one of them, or more likely working for them, because her sweat smells like she's been drinking local water for longer than a month, and she's been following me. I've spent the past twenty-four hours trying to stay as much in public as I can, to throw her off, and it's starting to drive me insane."

Wren gave up on her workout, and sat up, taking off the sweatband and wiping her face with the back of her hand. "Why the hell didn't you come to me when this shadow of yours first showed up?"

He stared at her as if she had lost her mind. "Valere, you're slipping. Why would I show them exactly where you were if I had any other choice? You think I want to hang a target around your neck that says 'here's my weak spot'?"

"Oh. Right. And here I was worried about bringing them to you. We really need to work on our communication."

The demon bared his teeth in a gesture that wasn't supposed to be a smile. "Next job. Let's survive this one, first. They're using magic to tag me, I can feel it whirling around on my skin, so yeah, they're Talent. Not much, compared to what you haul around, but enough."

"You can feel current like that?"

"When it's directed at me, yeah. Especially now."

"Can they…are they able to pick up the thing with us?"

The demon shook his head. "No. Someone would have to know both of us, and be looking, and know what he or she was looking for, to sense it. I think."

"You think."

"It's not like there was a damned instruction booklet!" His voice rose in annoyance, and the older woman on the treadmill nearest them looked over curiously, then looked away quickly when P.B. glared at her.

"Sorry. Look, you knew they were in town—you have a plan?"

"Yeah. No. Maybe." Wren bit her lip, uncertain.

"That's reassuring. Any minute now, my shadow's gonna work her way in here and see us—what should I do?"

She thought hard, fast. "Go home. While there are still people around on the street. Lock the doors and stay there."

"That's your plan? Putting me under house arrest?" He wasn't impressed. "You've done better."

"I need time. We knew someone was in town, two guy-types specifically. We didn't know about this woman, we don't know if there's anyone else, hired or otherwise. And we need to know if she is just a hireling, and if so, if she has access to high-powered Talent or if they're all low-res like you say. Either way, if you're home, at least one of them has to be there to watch you, so that person's not my problem going forward. And I know where you are and I can have someone watching you."

"Nobody watching me!" the demon protested. "Nobody can know about this, that's the deal!"

She could almost see the wheels turning in his head. It was

one thing to let his human know he was freaked out. And okay, her human got to know, because this was a tag-team deal. But anyone else.... No.

"My job's based on being a tough guy, Valere. Word gets around I'm trapped in my apartment by a chickie, I'll never work again."

"A chickie?" She didn't know if she should be amused or insulted on this woman's behalf.

"Grant me my age and my slang. This female of lurking—damn it, there she is!"

She risked a look over her shoulder, at where he was looking. "Go. Go home, P.B. Be obvious about it! And stay there, until one of us tells you it's safe!"

Grumbling, slamming his battered fedora onto his rounded head, the demon went.

The woman, a slender dirty blonde wearing a denim jacket over jeans, and indistinguishable from a large chunk of the population, was walking up the stairs behind one of the gym reps, who was giving her the guest spiel. The blonde saw P.B. walking toward them and halted, staring as P.B. walked right past her, turning his head in order to give her a full long look at his face, and then he grinned, deliberately showing all of his rather sharp teeth.

The woman took an involuntary step back, then turned to watch him go down the stairs, forgetting—as P.B. had intended—to look for who he had been talking to. Wren used the opportunity to move to another mat, just in case the woman had seen where P.B. had been squatting.

By the time the host turned to see how the guest was reacting to the gym, the blonde was gone, down the stairs and after her target.

"Why is it the jobs that pay crap always get so damn complicated?" Wren wondered out loud, then went back to doing her crunches, starting from the beginning again.

Another player in the mix, and Wren could feel the noose getting tighter around P.B.'s neck. If she didn't get her hands on everything his creator—he should rot in a seventh hell—had ever written, the demon would never be able to relax again. Crap hell, this job wasn't paying anything except in headaches.

She had to know who she was dealing with, and fast, and one hundred percent accurate.

Tomorrow, she'd swallow her pride and go see Morrie.

fifteen

She was up on her roof the next morning before the sun rose, standing on the tar papered surface, wearing a ragged pair of back sweatpants and a tank top, thick socks and sneakers on her feet. The sky was filled with narrow wisps of clouds that told any Talent with basic weather forecasting skills that there was damn little electrical energy to work with in the upper atmosphere. The view almost made up for that lack: pale red glints of sunlight reflecting off hundreds of glass-fronted buildings and the pale blue of the rivers bordering her island. At that moment it *was* her island; she could have been the only living human anywhere.

Then the blare of an early-morning taxi rose from the street, and the sounds of the city were back, if slightly muted, and she had to share the city with almost two million other bodies, human and otherwise.

Wren breathed in deeply, and stretched her hands over her head, fingers pointing into the sky, then brought them together, palms touching, and bent at the waist, fingertips now reaching down to her toes. Her spine cracked, not unpleasantly, and she felt the muscles pull from her calves to her forearms.

Holding that position, she let her palms rest flat on the tar paper surface of the roof, feeling the vibrations of the building rumble through her. Somewhere down there, Bonnie was dreaming, current weaving around her restlessly. Wren skirted around it, slipping deeper through the building, letting the vibes of the building itself guide her to what she was looking for.

Ley lines, some people called them. Convergence points. Mystical alignments of energy. Current was lazy; given the option, like water it followed established paths rather than creating its own. Ley lines ran through this building, in the structure of it, roof to foundation, after fifty-plus years infusing every brick and timber with a tinge of natural current.

"Hello, darlings," she said to it now, but didn't touch it. She wasn't looking for a quick skim, but something a little…deeper. A little harder.

Down through the basement, past the building's boiler, the masses of wiring coiled and simmering to a Talent's eyes.

She remembered the feel of the deep bedrock underneath it all, the foundation of Manhattan itself. Living. Breathing. Imbued with current that had been building since before Europeans came to these shores, when local Indian tribes walked the woodlands and paddled the creeks and rivers…

If she let it, the history would pull her down and hold her, the inanimate current turning her into stone, as well.

Not this time. Not now. I just need a touch, a touch…

Somewhere, a hundred miles away, she felt a resonance in the stone. A cave dragon, twitching on its pile of treasure, thinking someone was stalking it.

Not you, cousin, she reassured it.

Hidden cousin came back the sleepy, reassured acknowledgement, the nickname the Fatae had given her for once not pissing her off. *If you need, take.*

The casualness of it floored her. Not the generosity—dragons never gave anything away without cost to the borrower, but they did give—but the fact that it was offered without the asking.

Thank you. But not today.

What she wanted was deeper than living things. Stronger. Sturdier. More still.

Bedrock she thought, and let the stillness of the rock, the natural current baked into the rock by the heart of the earth itself, trickle into her. Blood from stone. Slow, so slow. But *strong*.

She was going to need that strength, today.

"You like to challenge me, don't you?" Morrie glared down at the Retriever as though expecting her to be intimidated. Seven feet tall and three feet across, with a face like a hardened, semisuccessful prizefighter, Morrie probably looked intimidating as hell. If—and this was a big if—you didn't know that underneath that granite facade beat the heart of the biggest show-off on the entire northern continent.

Wren knew. It didn't always help.

"I live to challenge you," she said in response. "It's what gives my life meaning, my lungs breath, my loins heat, my—"

"Oh for fucks' sake, stop. You'll make the cat laugh."

The cat in question, a smooshed-face orange Persian, didn't even bother to look up at either one of them, being more intent on napping in the sun-filled window seat, on a black velvet cushion.

It was just Morrie and the cat in the entire house, an old Victorian at the far tip of Long Island, about as far away from everyone as he could get and still be considered a local celebrity of sorts by Manhattan's *Cosa,* if by "celebrity" you meant "the guy everyone wanted it to be known they knew, but nobody actually wanted to know."

Once, Wren had been told, his kind had lived all up and down the East Coast. Now, he was the only one left. Or, at least, she amended to herself, the only one who still had contact with the rest of the *Cosa*. Like pandas, stone giants were secretive, shy, and really not good in crowds. There could be a dozen of them in the area, and they just never felt the need to come down and mingle.

Like demon, actually, except that demon tended to make a living off others, and so had to be out and about, couriering and body-guarding. Giants never seemed to need to make a living. Morrie only did what he did because it meant he got to score points off lesser and less-knowing mortals. He didn't ask for money, or food, or goods of any kind, just the knowledge that people had to come to him to get what they needed.

He made it a point of pride to always deliver. But you had to beg, first. That was what he got off on, making people beg.

"Morrie. Come on, you're killing me." She jumped up on the table, a solid piece of wood polished to a high gleam, in order to be able to see him eye to eye. Or eye to chin, anyway. A stone giant might not be one of the big guys of yore, but they were still plenty big, in her book. "A simple, little favor. The kind you do better than anyone else." She waited, and he stared back at her, impassive. "You won't even tell me you can dig up *something* for me? Two easy-peasy names?"

Wren wasn't good at begging. She touched her core, and felt the cool immobility of bedrock, let it ooze a little out of her. Not overt, but enough for Morrie to feel, even if he didn't know why, or where it came from. Stone to stone.

He crossed his arms across his bare chest and scowled down at her feet. "Get the hell off my table. I can dig up anything. Tell me why I'd want to."

"Because I want to know?" She got down off the table, noting that her feet hadn't left a smudge on the wood. That was some serious high-gloss.

"Not good enough." He turned away and clucked at the cat, who continued to ignore them both.

"Because they're bad, bad people who need to be stopped?"

"By you?" A stone giant's snort was not a thing to underestimate. Wren had to take a full step back under the gust. She wasn't sure if she was supposed to take offense at his dismissal or take it as a compliment that she, too, was a bad, bad person— or at least someone who wasn't overly bothered by bad, bad people. Morrie was weird even for a giant; it was tough to know what went on in his head. Although he did have a few known weaknesses....

She sighed deeply, reached down into her bag of tricks, and played her trump card. "It would mean a lot to Sergei if you did this for us."

Morrie gave her a half glare from under his heavy lids. "Don't play me, Retriever. He's gorgeous, but not that gorgeous." He shifted in his chair, a huge, reinforced throne of hardwood that weighed about as much as a VW Bug, and stared out the plate glass window. He had a view of the Long Island Sound that was probably worth a midsized fortune, and all Wren could think about was how cold it must be in the winter, with nothing to stop the winds rushing in off the water. The wind off the East River was bad enough to knock her backward when she stepped off the curb downtown; this would probably send her flying.

Stone giants didn't have that kind of problem. The "stone" in their names didn't just come from the way their skin looked; they were rock-solid bastards, epidermis to marrow. Morrie was wearing pants—a leather job that must have cost a fortune to custom-make, unless he did the work himself—only as deference to her modesty, not because his skin needed the protection.

She had dragged her ass all the way out here, dealing with insane Friday-morning commuters, and the bastard was going to make her sweat even more. God, she hated dealing with the Fatae, sometimes. Most of the time. The clock was ticking, damn it, and she was doing this to protect one of their own!

Except most of the Fatae didn't really think of demon as one of their own; if they didn't like admitting tails, they liked admitting created cousins even less. Especially created-by-human. Wren supposed she understood that, but enough was goddamned enough. She could feel something inside her stirring, wanting to get moving, and it was becoming more and more of an effort to keep it tamped down, even with the aid of the bedrock-current. They needed details before she could move, and she needed to move *now*, without anyone else knowing what she knew or that she knew it. That meant that they needed Morrie.

The stone giant was still staring out the window when he finally spoke, and it took her a moment to realize he was talking to her. "Two names. Fine. Time frame?"

She didn't stop to wonder why he had finally agreed. She really didn't care. "They got into town last week-ish. Address and all known info I got, you got. I need to know who they know, who they're taking instructions from, who they're meeting with, what makes them jump. And I need to know now."

"Now as in, this week, or…"

"Now as in, I'll wait right here."

The giant grumbled at that. "You're not staying anywhere near me while I work, lonejack. Like as not kill all my tech. Go into the kitchen and make yourself a sandwich. Put some flesh on those bones of yours. Humans, phagh. No idea how to stay healthy, all over too skinny and soft, like jellyfish." He flapped one thick-fingered hand at her. "Go, out of my sight."

His kitchen was as oversized as everything else, and just as empty of furnishings. Giants weren't much on furniture, or any kind of normal-sized comfort. But there was a fresh-baked baguette in the bread bag, and some kind of fish spread and half a dozen cheeses in the fridge, along with the makings of a green salad. No coffee or soda, but there was overly tart lemonade that was surprisingly refreshing once she cut it with seltzer. By the time Morrie bellowed her name, Wren had managed to make a sizable dent in the food, and was feeling a postgorge satiation. If this were a fairy tale, she thought sleepily, sitting on the floor with the remains of her meal spread out in front of her, the giant would be in the other room preparing a nice toasty fire to broil her on for his dinner.

She wondered, just as sleepily, if she should have told someone where she was going, before she left the city, and if Sergei would find her bones or if Morrie would use them for toothpicks.

"Retriever! You want this information or not?"

She did.

The train ride back to the city seemed to take forever, but the alternative would have been to rent a car, and no matter what Sergei said Wren was shying away from any additional expenses right now. If her apartment was really about to go private-ownership, every penny counted. Besides, dealing with traffic on the Long Island Expressway would have made her so frustrated, she wasn't sure if the car would survive. Bad form to return a rental car with its entire electrical system melted into a nervous breakdown.

So she sat on the train and tried to get some sleep, despite

the chatty ladies-who-lunch in the seats behind her, talking
about the play they were going to see. Screaming children
were easier to tune out than Madge and Midge and Dolores.
Every time she dozed off, though, either one of the ladies
would hit an excited high-note screech, or the train would
jounce and knock her head against the window, waking her up.

Control, *Valere. You will not lose your temper. You will not fry
Dolores' perm, hotseat the train conductor for crap driving, or short out
the lights just because you want to be home already. Misery does not
love company, misery just wants to be left the hell alone to sulk.*

She was actually in a decent enough mood all things considered. Considering those things, though, she'd be happier
once she was home and could get things moving.

Dolores—or was it Midge?—hit another high note. Wren
stilled the tremor in her legs through sheer determination, and
practiced deep breathing exercises to calm the matching tremor
in her core, and only she knew how close the Ladies who
Lunched came to being squelched.

When the train finally pulled into Penn Station, only half
an hour late, she waited until the day-trippers had gotten off
the train. It wasn't courtesy but common sense: tourists moved
too slow, blocked aisles, and generally confounded and annoyed
those who knew what they were doing. In her mood? Better
to wait for the herd to thin out a little, and actually get where
she was going more quickly.

Once freed, she bypassed the warren of subways and tunnels,
and went up the stairs to the sidewalk level. It was nice enough
that Wren decided to walk to the gallery rather than waiting
for a bus to make it across town. Once out of the immediate
area, the pedestrian traffic became more manageable, and she
was able to lengthen her stride—as much as her legs could
manage, anyway. One advantage of hanging out with height-

gifted people all her life; she had learned how to walk taller than she actually was.

Blocks later, Wren crossed Houston and continued downtown, dodging the little tables of a café that was holding on to summer with both hands, and made her way to Blaine Street. The sunlight hit the stained glass front just so, and she paused, despite her hurry, to look at it. Sergei had commissioned the glass specifically for the gallery, and the soft blues and greens reminded her of the ocean outside Morrie's window. In the winter, the waters were often as not gray, but right now, with the sun hitting them, they had been those shades.

She forgot, sometimes, that Manhattan was an island, that Long Island was an island, that they were all just a bunch of little islands connected by bridges and tunnels and cable wires. Wire and tunnels. Blood and bone. Blood and stone. A living city.

Either you're getting deep, or you're getting stupid she told herself, and went inside.

The gallery was empty. Literally: all the artwork from the previous installation had either gone on to new homes or back to the artist, and the new show hadn't been brought in yet, so there were empty pedestals and cardboard boxes throughout the space, and a sense of echoing emptiness, otherwise. No customers, browsing or otherwise. The second-level catwalk still had a display of watercolors by a group of artists from New Mexico that Wren rather liked, but nobody was up there right now. She kept meaning to talk to Sergei about buying one of the smaller paintings but hadn't gotten around to it yet. She needed him to be with her when she chose, not because she didn't trust her taste, but because she was afraid to go up the narrow steps in case she accidentally came down with all of them in her bag.

She didn't just Retrieve; she *was* a Retriever. It went beyond training and into bone-deep instinct. When she was a teenager, she sometimes came home with things she honestly had no memory of taking. That hadn't happened in years, but she remembered how mortifying the realization could be—especially after Neezer and her mom made her return a few of the items they knew about.

No, better not to even go up there, at least not alone.

Lowell was leaning against the dark wood of the front desk, perfect as always in dark blue trousers and a paler blue shirt that set off his frat boy blondness. He looked as though he was surgically attached to the phone headset, arguing with someone about a delivery date. He looked up when she came in, prepared to deal with a would-be customer, but then just waved her toward the back office. No sneer, no scornful up-and-down dismissal that he usually gave, even when Sergei was standing there. The walk across town had mellowed her enough that she merely nodded in acknowledgement and went past him without comment of her own. Between this, and not snarking at each other earlier…maybe they were both finally growing up?

Perish the thought, she decided. It was just a temporary truce while they were both busy. She'd get back to him later.

"Morrie came through, as expected," Wren announced as she went through the door and saw that Sergei was alone, and not on the phone or otherwise occupied with uninterruptible things. The door closed behind her before she continued. "Our friends are from the right area, anyway. One is a naturalized American, born in Canada of Dutch parents. The other's a German national, travels a lot on business, is frequently in Amsterdam for gatherings he refers to as family reunions."

"Actual family members?" He was sitting on the edge of the desk and shuffling papers as he spoke, sorting them into two piles. One went back into his in-box, a hideous burlwood thing with carved gargoyle legs he had picked up somewhere, and the other pile was tossed onto the desk behind him.

"If so, it's a rather extended family. And it includes our Canadian-born friend. The last meeting was over six months ago. Yes, I know that's over our time frame. But—" when Sergei looked up, Wren held up a finger to forestall anything he might say "—just last week our Canadian-born friend, Rogier, got a phone call from one of those members. The very next day he was traveling down here. The woman who called him, a—" and she had to check her notes for this one "—a Sophia Roos, had met the day before with two other members of this 'family'—" and she used air quotes when she said the word, in case he missed her irony "—in Amsterdam."

"It's not enough to convict, but it would be enough for a warrant," Sergei said, putting the remaining papers away, and Wren thought that yes, he had been spending too much time with Danny the ex-cop, to think that way. The *Cosa* didn't have warrants. All right, the *Cosa* didn't have much by way of law enforcement, period; that was why the PUPIs were so useful, and so controversial.

She stuck to the business at hand. "Morrie also informed me that they have informed the hotel that their stay will be ending this week. Checking out in three days, specifically."

Sergei looked distinctly unhappy to hear that. "So whatever they came here to do, they've either run out of time…"

"Or they're confident that they've accomplished it, despite the thief having failed to actually get hold of the papers," she said, having already gone through the possibilities on her way home. "These guys came here with a plan, Sergei. They're not about to just crawl home with their tails between their legs." Not if these people were who P.B. suspected they were—offspring of the original creator, or some variant of heirs thereof.

Talent bordered on arrogant even in the best-case scenarios. Talent, or near-Talent, who had actual crazy mad scientists in their family trees? Going to be arrogant like nobody's business.

"They haven't gotten their hands on the papers yet. And won't, not for at least a day or two, no matter how good their plans might be." Sergei sounded certain, which was reassuring. He'd been working, and thinking, while she was gone, clearly. "We still have the advantage. They're not local, and they seem to be working without much of an infrastructure in place in this city. It's tough to move fast when you have to do everything yourself."

Wren nodded, feeling the twitch come back into her core. *Soon* she told it. "They'll want to keep it to themselves, too. I don't know how many of them are viable Talent themselves, but we'll have to assume at least a percentage, if they're true heirs of the original mages. Lonejacks could get away with roaming, but if they're European Council, they have to keep it on the quiet, otherwise not going through channels will earn them a load of hurt." Lonejacks could and did move around freely, and poaching was considered tacky, but not offensive. Council had rules and regs in exchange for membership benefits, and working in another Council's territory without permission…well, the punishment was a bit harsher than a slap on the wrist. And if they'd gotten permission, one of their contacts would have heard about it by now, and let them know.

"If this were Null-world," Sergei said thoughtfully, "I'd say they were neither. A small, obsessive group, bonded by an almost cultlike focus on something? They wouldn't fit with either lonejack or Council culture."

That thought stopped Wren cold for an instant. She tried to imagine being outside both of the two circles that made up human *Cosa Nostradamus* culture, and failed utterly. That didn't mean Sergei was wrong, though. In fact, he was probably right, and it explained a hell of a lot.

It didn't change anything, though.

"Their first—or first we know of, anyway—theft attempt failed, the objects were taken back by the museum, and our bad boys killed the thief, or had him killed. They also seem confident that they will have the objects in their possession soon. That means they either had someone as backup, which would be expensive and unlikely, or they have to hire someone new, fast. If the latter, and word gets out that's how they treat the hired help…" He paused, thinking hard, doubtless of how best to spread that word. Bad news might not make every decent thief shy away from the job, but it would jack the price way up.

"I don't suppose there's any way that you could get them to hire me?" It was a long shot, but man, it would make her life easier….

He looked at her, as if he was sizing her up as a stranger. "If they're desperate enough to trust a Talent outside of their group, risking discovery of what's at stake, maybe. If we had a little more time and you were a little less known, probably. Or a high probability, anyway. You want to risk it?"

If it were just her, she'd say yes—the fastest and most satisfying way to get a Retrieval done was to steal it by using someone else's heist, everyone knew that. Plus: getting paid by these bastards, even only the up-front half of the fee, *really* appealed to her. But what Sergei was really asking was if she wanted to bring these people even that half step closer to P.B. And the answer was an unequivocal no.

P.B. He hadn't been in touch, not by ping or phone, not since she saw him at the gym. And she didn't dare stop by his place or initiate a ping, not now that they knew for certain—near-certain, anyway—that these people were connected with his past. For now, P.B. was safe. Relatively speaking, anyway. After learning about his shadow, she'd asked Danny and a few of his friends to keep an eye on him—she didn't dare ask another Talent; right now, he needed to be associated only with Fatae, not Talent. If these lunatics discovered that P.B. had formed a connection, that he was one of the viable ones…

She refused to even contemplate the thought.

So they had to get to Herr Doktor's legacy before the others did, on their own, and leave no trace behind. Make it disappear, and hope that these modern-day Frankensteins didn't have a taste for reverse-engineering from an unwilling demon subject.

Thou shalt not kill.

She didn't want to. Not ever again. But she could. She *would*, to protect the people she loved. That knowledge left a bitter, metallic taste in her mouth.

Thankfully, they had—she hoped—a bit of information the others lacked, that would keep things from getting that far.

"How did your hunt go?" she asked her partner, crossing her fingers in anticipation.

In response, he reached down to the other side of his desk, and handed her a sheet of letterhead, with the Museum's masthead at the top.

She took it, and skimmed the terse, typewritten note.

Dear Dr. Allenby,

Thank you for your inquiry, and your offer of assistance. I am sorry to hear that your museum was also targeted by these thieves, and hope that it is not the beginning of another wave of antiquity black marketing. However, I am pleased to inform you that nothing was taken, and the thief in this case was caught. We have moved the items in question to another secure position, and will begin examining them soon to determine why they were targeted specifically. It may be that there is value here we had not previously been aware of. As soon as we have answers, I will, of course, pass our findings along, so that you may protect and enhance your displays as well. Sincerely,

Wren shook her head not in denial but admiration. "You are amazing, incredible, astonishing, and a master of the shmooze. Do I want to know whose ass you had to kiss to get this, and if there really is an Allenby, doctor or otherwise?"

He just buffed his nails, and looked smug. And to think that some people thought that *she* was the sneaky one!

"It's all about ego," he said. "They don't want to admit that they almost got robbed, but *almost* isn't the same as actually having anything taken, and discovering something of potential value, especially if they didn't pay a lot for it, and it turns out to be one of a kind—they won't be able to not brag on it."

"You think that they know the thief's dead?" She would have said dead and gone, once, except she knew better now. Dead almost mostly always meant gone, but not *always* always. The thought made her move her fingers slightly, as though to ward away the possibility. The last damn thing they needed right now was another pissed-off spirit trying for revenge. Although now that she knew how to redirect them where she wanted...

The idea was evil enough to consider, then she put it away as complicating things needlessly.

"They probably don't care." Sergei stopped buffing and got up, only to sit down behind his desk, shoving the chair back slightly to stretch his legs in front of him and rest his elbows on the chair's arms, lacing his fingers across his stomach. "Ego, remember. When dealing with obsessive people, always play to the ego. Their only area of concern is what concerns them, which is good for us. So we know they're holding on to the papers, and bringing them front and center rather than hiding them in a deeper hole. That means they're going to be in the museum proper, not some off-site holding facility." He looked up at her, a question in his expression. "Does that make it easier for you, or harder?"

Wren shrugged, taking her usual position on the sofa now that they were settling in for the long-haul discussions. "Depends. Won't know until I try for 'em. I'm more worried about what our European friends may or may not be planning." She looked at Sergei, and for the first time in her life, without any conscious effort, raised a single eyebrow at him. "Morrie can only do so much, in the time we gave him. I need to know what's going to happen, not just what already has."

"Right," he said without missing a beat, reaching for the phone. "I'll call Agent Chang."

sixteen

Agent Chang wasn't in the office, so Sergei left a message, carefully not specifying what he was calling about while giving enough information that he didn't sound like a crackpot who should be investigated.

"She gave us the office number, not her cell phone," he said, hanging up the phone. "Strange."

"Maybe she doesn't have a cell phone."

Sergei looked at his partner as though she had taken off her arm and handed it to him. "Everyone has a cell phone."

"I don't."

"You would if you could."

There wasn't much she could say in response to that, since it was true. Cell phones were far more sensitive to current than landlines, although both tended to go to static and die if used too long. "Maybe she keeps that for personal stuff?"

"I can't imagine field agents not having a cell. I wonder if she was worried about the line being compromised."

"So a line into a government office would be safer than a cell phone?" Wren sounded surprised, and Sergei grinned tightly, his eyes unamused.

"Landlines are always safer. Landlines that go right under Big Brother's nose are safest of all, because who's more paranoid than the paranoid in power?"

Wren tugged at her hair and blinked. "Oh."

"Go back to work, Wren. Let me worry about the tech, or you're going to start frying my entire damn office from just thinking about it."

She grinned at that, and did as he suggested.

Around five-thirty that afternoon, Lowell buzzed the inner office, asking if they wanted him to order in dinner, since he was starving. The sound of the buzzer broke Sergei out of his focused concentration, and he looked up across the office. His partner had been so quiet, he half suspected that she had fallen asleep. Instead, she was nose-deep in a small dark green notebook—reading, not writing in it.

"You hungry?" he asked softly.

"What?" Her head came up, and he realized that she had been so intent, she hadn't even heard the buzzer, or Lowell's voice.

"It's almost dinnertime. You hungry?"

He saw her expression change as she took an internal inventory. Talent burned calories at an insane rate, even when they weren't technically working; he would be very surprised if she didn't need to fuel the engine. He had never understood how she could be so unconcerned with food, when she needed so much of it. Or maybe it was just having food in the kitchen, as though if she had anything in the fridge, she might have to cook it…

"Yeah," she said finally, breaking into his musings on the eating habits of captive Talent. "Is the gallery too successful these days to allow Reggie's through the door?"

He winced, and she saw it. "All right, we can order from somewhere else."

Reggie's was a local pizza place, best known for being cheap, fast, and insanely heavy on the grease. He never understood why Wren loved it so much.

"No, it's okay." The last thing he wanted to do was stop her from eating when she needed it. "How about Raina's?" he offered as a compromise. If she wanted pizza, he was on board with that, but preferably without the heartburn. He wasn't as young as he used to be, and neither was his digestion. Neither was hers, for that matter, but it didn't seem to bother her. Too much time spent with P.B., probably.

"I can live with that," she agreed, fast enough that he got the feeling that he had just been hustled. "Mushroom and green pepper, please, with a diet Sprite and a side of fried mozzarella."

She really, really, should weigh two hundred pounds. Sergei felt a sudden kinship with all the women he had known over the years who complained about the male metabolism and dieting.

"You want garlic bread, too?" He was being ironic, but she didn't seem to notice, already back in the notebook, wiggling her fingers in a way that he took to mean "yes, please." He gave the order to Lowell, plus his own request for a green side salad and a Coke, and went back to the floor plans he had been studying. If P.B. wasn't going to be paying for this job, as seemed likely, the gallery had better pick up the bill-paying slack, which meant this new installation had to go flawlessly. So far, Lowell had been managing everything exactly as he, Sergei, would have. Unsurprising, since he trained the younger man, but reassuring nonetheless. He had trained people to shoot, to lie to officials, and to kill in the name of justice, but running a gallery was another level of complexity entirely.

"I've been thinking," she said, seemingly out of the blue.

"About what?" He looked back at her, but her gaze was still focused on the pages of the notebook.

"Moving."

Fair enough. He saw the quicksand under his feet, and moved carefully. "And where are those thoughts taking you?"

"Mostly around in circles," she admitted ruefully, closing the notebook over one finger and looking at him. "The condo conversion…it's sort of scary. Okay, it's very scary. Owning my own place? I'm not sure I'm ready for that." A strange expression passed over her face, barely a flicker and it was gone. "I don't want to leave my apartment…and then three seconds later I want to get out of the city, period."

"That's normal," he said, relaxing a little. They weren't back to That Discussion just yet. "You're being presented, not-quite-unexpectedly, with a decision, and that's opened up a whole round of choices you weren't letting in before."

"Sergei." Her mouth twisted as if she'd sucked on a lemon. "Don't psychoanalyze me. I took psych 101, at your instigation I might add, and I've read the self-help books." He was willing to bet that she had stolen them from the bookstore, actually, but figured that qualified as self-help, too, her helping herself to books. "I know *why* I'm doing it. I just don't know what to *do* about it."

"At the risk of sounding like an analyst, what do you *want* to do about it?"

She started to say one thing, then the words jumbled in her mouth, and all that came out was silence. She looked surprised. He wasn't.

"In a perfect world, we'd have options," he said, trying really hard not to sound like a patronizing bastard, aware that he was probably failing. He had been spending too much time in

Doherty's office getting his own head shrunk. "We don't, always. Have options, that is. There's not enough money to do everything, not enough time. And unless you've decided that you do want to go into counterfeiting, or someone's finally figured out a way to use current to rig the lottery—" it had been tried, more than once, and always failed "—then we still have to work. So. You need a place to live, and you need to have somewhere you can work. I can't see you being happy living out in the country—" and he had to laugh when she made a quick sign to avert such a fate "—and cities are expensive no matter where you go...."

"Might as well stay here, where all of our contacts are?" Her voice wasn't bitter, but resigned, and that hurt almost as much to hear.

"I didn't say that. And we have contacts other places. We just haven't been using them much."

True. Wren chewed on that thought for a while. She had friends out in California, and in the Midwest, and hell, she even had contacts Down Under, although she wasn't sure that she knew her IM buddy OhSoBloodyTalented well enough to presume on that friendship. And hell, Sergei probably knew people in every city with a population of over 50,000.

But the thought of leaving Manhattan was like a tug in her gut, and not the pleasant, anticipatory kind. She'd grown up across the river, thinking Manhattan was the center of the universe. She'd never been the sort to get hit with wanderlust, had never had the desire to see what was over the next hill just because the hill hid the view. So why now?

Because you're running. Or thinking about running. You can't shove things into little boxes any more, and your thinking space is getting too crowded, with everything out in the open. She hadn't been lying when she said she had taken psych 101. She could self-analyze like a pro. She just never enjoyed the results. Or the process, for that matter. God, she hoped Sergei wasn't turning into a therapy junkie.

"I'm not moving in with you," she said, and was almost insulted at how relieved he looked.

The phone on his desk made a soft beeping noise before he could respond; not the office line, then. She leaned forward as he picked it up on the second ring. "Didier."

He listened to the response, then nodded once at her, indicating that it was nothing she had to worry about but that he had to deal with it now. She relaxed back into the sofa, picking up her notebook again. It had been sitting on her desk ever since she found it, buried under the mail she tossed there but never quite hidden, the green like a flash in the corner of her eye every time she went into the office, until finally, in annoyed desperation, she threw it into her bag, meaning to skim through it when she was stuck on a bus or something.

Once she opened the first page, she was trapped.

I saw her again yesterday. Tiny thing, and if you aren't paying attention you'll miss her entirely. I haven't yet determined if she is doing that intentionally, or if it's a natural defense mechanism. Either way, I need to find a way to approach her. She can't be left to drift, alone. Too much could go wrong, and so badly.

Neat, precise handwriting, familiar to her from a year of tests and homework assignments with comments printed on the back. He had handwriting like a woman's, each curl and line carefully placed. He did what he said and he meant what he wrote, and his handwriting showed the planning behind it all.

John Ebeneezer had been a planner. He did nothing without

thinking it through, seeing all the possible outcomes and pitfalls, collecting data and details.

The notebook was like a gift, the past and present colluding to present it to her, years after she had gotten it and, sick with pain and loss, shoved it into a box, but it was a gift that she wasn't sure she wanted. Reading about yourself, seeing yourself observed and judged.... How much of that could a person take? How much was healthy, and where did it become masochism?

How much history could you ingest, even your own?

Still, she kept turning pages, and his voice came back to her, line after line.

I think she's using current to shoplift. That will have to stop, now.

The date on that page—two days before he had intercepted her in the Five and Dime. Two days before he had interrupted and changed her life completely, forever.

His voice, fading for so long, had come back to her, in full force. Damn that job, for putting her on an unexpected collision course with her past, all in one loosely wrapped package.

There were no coincidences. Didn't mean the Universe didn't have a nasty sense of humor.

Wren put down the notebook, using one of Sergei's business cards to mark her place. Suddenly, she didn't feel like reading any more.

The blueprints neatly folded on the floor next to the sofa were the obvious next step. She should already have memorized them, really. It wasn't any different from any other job…except it was. And she couldn't pin down why.

They had done jobs for other friends before. Most of them had turned out fine. Almost all, in fact. She went in, Retrieved, made client happy. The competition factor, of someone else trying for the same prize? Pffft. Yeah, she was worried about getting there first, but she also had the home ground advantage. Plus, Talent. Unlike Null thieves, she had that in her tool kit. If her competition tried to hire another Talent to do it? Unlikely, but if they did, unlike most other Retrievers she had met or read about, she had a full complement of traditional skills—lock-picking, gymnastics training—to round out her more esoteric skill sets. Best of both worlds made her the best in both, that was her theory.

So what was her trauma?

The stakes, came the answer, gut-deep and undeniable. This wasn't for money, or ego, or even reputation. It wasn't to save the world, or even to save a city. All those things were real and valid, but they were either petty enough to be tucked inside, or huge enough that you couldn't think about them.

This was for a friend. For a friend's life. For his freedom.

For P.B.'s freedom.

Wren reached over and picked up the prints, feeling their weight in her palm. *No time like right now to get things done.* Sitting upright and cross-legged on the sofa, she opened the plans and got to work memorizing the pertinent, the potentially pertinent, and the probably-never-pertinent-but-can't hurt details.

This time, the sound of the buzzer did break her concentration, and only then did she realize that the smell of something hot, greasy, and good was drifting into the office.

"Our dinner's here," Sergei said, somewhat unnecessarily. She folded the blueprints back into their square, and uncurled herself from the sofa, feeling the stiffness in her hips and knees. She wasn't twenty-five any more, that was for sure.

They left the quiet cocoon of the office, and joined Lowell, who had spread the pizza boxes and sodas on the counter, and was already opening up a container of what looked like fried squid. Wren bit her tongue and didn't say anything as she reached for her own eight-inch pizza. Lowell cast his own disparaging glance at her food, but was likewise restrained.

Sergei looked from one to the other as though suspecting a trick, but was wise enough to just enjoy the truce for as long as it lasted.

Wren passed him a slice of garlic bread and then, almost as an afterthought, slid the container across the counter to Lowell, too.

burp

The sound echoed throughout the office, followed by the faint aroma of cheese and anchovies. Both individuals looked surprised, as though it had appeared out of thin air, and not the depths of Wren's stomach, as though the meal of an hour before had been two days earlier, instead.

"Thank you, P.B." Sergei said, going back to his paperwork.

Wren chuckled, not at all abashed by her bodily functions. "Nah, his have more— what's the word? Resonance. His tummy's a little echo chamber or something."

"Nice. Thank you for sharing."

She moved the straw around in her cup, trying to get the last of the now-flat soda before admitting it was gone. "If you were looking for ladylike, I think you made a wrong turn at Pismo Beach.

"I think I know a way in," she said, changing the subject midstride even as he snorted in agreement with her previous comment. "It's not perfect, but it should avoid the mistakes their guy made."

"Like getting caught?"

Like getting killed, she thought, but didn't say.

"I trust you have—" The phone interrupted whatever trust he was going to impart, and he picked it up with a brusque motion. "Didier. Yes, this is he—Agent Chang, thank you for calling me back so quickly."

Wren sat up, ignoring the overfed ache in her stomach, and watched his expression. Her partner was a damn good poker player when he wanted to be, but times like this, she could read him like a newspaper. Something was breaking. Something useful.

"Yes, I am fine, thank you, and will be better if you tell me that your resources turned something up on the question."

She knew the moment he got what he was looking for, even before he reached over to flick two switches on his desk. One enabled a low-level electronic hum in the walls that served a dual purpose: to confound any Null who might be trying to listen in, and to distract any less-than-tight-focused Talent who was doing likewise. To Wren it was like smelling food cooking in another apartment, and—after enough practice—was easy enough to tune out. The second switch put Agent Chang on speakerphone.

"Wren is here, as well," he said.

"Heya Anea."

"Wren. I have news, I'm not sure if it's good or bad." The agent's voice was flattened by the speaker, and, possibly, by exhaustion. Wren wondered if the other woman took phone calls sitting upright at her desk, feet flat on the floor, or if she had kicked back, toed off her sensible shoes, maybe with her feet on the desk like a satisfied car dealer. Not that it mattered, but you could learn a lot about a person through their body language, especially when they thought nobody could see them.

"Let us decide that," Sergei said, impatient. Case in point— his body language was practically shouting, although she was the only one who was impressed by it.

Agent Chang was cool, but wound up. "Your boys are definitely up to something. I had a friend in the...in another
office check, and there has been some significant bank activity
in their names in the past twenty-four hours. They've been
transferring funds from overseas, clearing them in a local
bank, through an account that's about two years old. All the
legal T's have been crossed and the I's dotted. It's sort of
reflex for my friend to check for that sort of thing, but there's
no reason he could find to raise a red flag other than the sud-
denness of the transactions, and that wasn't enough to shove
through, without priors. Not without getting someone
coming down in their defense, or alerting them to the fact
that they're being watched, which I figured you didn't want
happening. Sorry."

The fact that Chang had even thought to think about that
impressed Wren—she supposed it came with the job, to think
like a criminal. Danny did the same thing.

Funny, really. She *was* a criminal, and she didn't think like one.

"They also bought airline tickets this afternoon. From JFK
to Gatwick. Three days from now."

The day their hotel stay ended. So they weren't planning on
moving somewhere cheaper, which had been a passing thought
in Wren's head. "Both of them?'

"Three, actually. Three seats, specifically. Requested all
three together in the center row, not aisle or window seat,
which is unusual."

Wren and Sergei exchanged looks across the desk. It
might be nothing. It could be they were taking P.B.'s shadow
back with them. They might be meeting another member
of their group here, someone already on the ground, who
planned to go back with them. It might be a girlfriend, a
boyfriend, a sibling...

An unwilling companion?

Sergei scratched something on a sheet of paper and shoved it across the desk at her. She took it, but already knew what it would say.

Is he safe?

She read it, and shrugged helplessly. Who knew? She told him to go to ground, and he had, but the demon was as stubborn as she was: when he said he was done with running that was exactly what he meant. The bedrock of Manhattan would be easier to budge, and she couldn't check on him without risking his security, and alerting his shadow to a possible connection between them. Even if they didn't make the demon–Talent assumption, it would still get their attention exactly when she needed them to *not* be looking at her.

"Anything else?" Sergei was more brusque than she would have been to a woman who'd just not only done them a favor but been really good about not even asking why.

Chang didn't seem to be offended by his tone, though. "They're booked on Virgin, the evening flight." She rattled off a series of numbers—their seat numbers. "That may change, though. I'll let you know if it does. They've arranged for car service to pick them up three hours before the flight—not near enough time to deal with traffic and security, but I tend to get there early, it's easier on my stomach lining."

Listening, Wren decided that Chang definitely had her shoes off, even if she was in otherwise perfect office posture. There was just that hint of "now you owe me" in her voice, and in Wren's experience that sort of smugness didn't happen if your toes were shoved into even the most expensively comfortable of shoes.

She looked up at her partner again and noted his own body

language, which had changed over the course of that brief exchange. Sergei had heard the same tone in Chang's voice that Wren noticed, and was now both resigned and amused. This was a game that he knew, and he knew that he was better at it than Agent Chang, but he didn't know how much better, and that uncertainty amused him.

If he would bet on her mother against Chang, she would bet on him...but not forever. She knew why he introduced them, and it wasn't because he needed Wren's take on the other woman; it was because he was worried that Wren might see her and be paranoid because the other woman was so attractive, and so totally his usual type.

Wren was pretty damn sure that Chang had enough self-awareness to know the reaction she got from men, and was enough of a gambler to bet how one Sergei Didier was likely to react to that reaction, specifically his reaction to her and Wren's possible reaction to that, and was not above using all of it to get her the direct introduction she wanted.

Her partner had been *played*.

Wren wouldn't mention that chain of probable to him, though. Not yet, anyway. It was more fun sometimes just to watch.

Chang and he exchanged farewells, and Sergei ended the call feeling as though he still had the upper hand, but not as much as he was comfortable with. He also had a feeling that his partner was laughing at him, although she had already gone back to the blueprints during the farewells, and was making quick chicken-scratches on a pad she had taken from his desk.

From the drawer in his desk, actually. And he hadn't even noticed. There were times he almost forgot what it was she did, what she *was*. And then things of his own appeared in her possession, things he knew he hadn't brought over, and he was reminded all over again. Wren wasn't a Retriever because she was good at stealing: she was good at stealing because she was a Retriever.

We are what we are. Human, Null, Talent, Fatae, demon. Are those racing against us as trapped in their roles as we are? He shrugged, dismissing the thought as irrelevant. They were threatening his people. He reacted badly to that, no matter why it was done.

He watched her, knowing that she didn't mind being observed, that she in fact found it comforting that he *always* saw her, unless she was using current to disappear. There was a sense of urgency to the way she was writing out her notes, a sense that he now shared. Chang's information had turned the "little time" to act into "no time." Whatever plan Wren had in mind, it had to be ready to go within the next twenty-four hours, if not sooner. It was a calculated risk: that the competition would not want to stay in the city any longer than they had to, once the papers were in their hands, but would not cut things so tight that anything going wrong might cause them to miss their flight or otherwise raise red flags. That gave the would-be Frankensteins a rather specific window to slip through. Wren had to be ready to slip through just before them.

Sergei picked up the phone again, and dialed the number of a friend of his who worked in the security industry. He had installed the system that protected the gallery, and did enough work for other galleries and private collectors that he was bound to have contacts among some of the bigger players, as well.

"Mike. Hi, it's Sergei. No, everything's fine here, why do you always assume something's wrong? That little faith in your own work?"

A pungent curse came back through the wires. Pleasantries concluded; Sergei began the delicate tightrope of trying to get information without actually asking anything. It helped that he didn't actually want to know anything about the system the museum had installed—they had the electrical specifics noted in the material he had already gotten for her, and if it was enhanced by anything magical, Wren was better suited to sniffing it out and dealing with it. No, he wanted to know about the museum itself, and the people who worked there.

You could tell a lot about a place from the gossip surrounding its employees. If payroll was late, or benefits had been cut, or the boss was known to be a tosser, or hip-deep in gambling debts, it all meant something he could use, something that could give them a better idea of the situation Wren would be walking into.

As he fenced verbally with Mike, he was making notes on a pad of his own. He'd rather use his computer, or his PDA, but those were out of the question with his partner concentrating so hard in the same room. He wasn't sure how much current she touched when she was preparing like this, but from what she'd said over the years he got the idea that she used it like a cat when she was stressed, petting it for reassurance. That alone probably wouldn't hurt his computer, which was surge-protected as though it were based in Storm Alley, or the phones, which were likewise grounded, but why take the risk? And his PDA…he knew better than to even bring it out of the case when she was around. He had gone through three in their first year of partnership alone, and they weren't cheap.

The shape taking place on his pad was a rough draft of the building shown on Wren's blueprints. He was working mostly from memory, but the museum was large enough that the basics were, well, basic; two old-style townhouses—mansions by most standards—on Museum Mile, also known as Fifth Avenue above 80th. They'd been bought over fifty years ago, renovated into one building for the sole purpose of creating a museum. A narrow alley still ran between them, for what looked like trash collection, with a walkway connecting them two stories overhead.

There were bus stops in front, entrances on these sides, construction there—he needed to double-check that.

Wren worked alone. He had gone in with her on a few jobs over the years, mainly when she needed a driver, a cover, or a body to help haul, but she worked alone. To suggest otherwise now would imply that he had doubts, and that was the last thing she needed—and the last thing he meant to say.

The doubts were on his side. About himself.

Doc managed to dig up doubts he hadn't even known he had, and now they wouldn't go away.

She used to ground in him, when there was need. Now, she had P.B., and that was better for everyone, all-around. He had gotten far enough in therapy to admit that, and to actually really mean it. She had proven that, in need, she could handle the business side of things, although she didn't like it, and wasn't anywhere near as good at it as he was.

She didn't need him. That was good, even as the awareness caused him an occasional pang for the days when he was the senior partner, the one who made the decisions. How could he not be pleased when his partner came into her own, became the woman he had seen in that mouthy, scared, Talented teenager so many years ago?

But P.B. might not be available. Whether or not the others knew that the demon was—what was the word, viable—they still knew that he was here, that he worked with Talent, and they were following him. If the Dutchmen failed to grab the materials, the third seat might be intended for the demon. Even if they did get the papers, they might want the additional prize, the living proof. From what P.B. had said and not said, it didn't sound as if any of the other demon were serving any Talent, at least not currently.

He winced at the pun, but kept to the line of thought. Despite Wren's hopes of keeping the connection hidden, enough people in town knew of the friendship between P.B. and Wren for him to assume that bit of information as known, and from there it was a logical jump to suspect that P.B. might be the only extant demon capable of serving—the only intact working model of the mad bastard's work.

He used a red pen to mark possible line-of-sight points, even as Mike was dodging his questions. Even if P.B. was safe and sound and able to be there, Sergei knew he needed to be on-scene for the Retrieval, as well. He had one advantage, if you could call it that, that she didn't. An advantage that he didn't want her to have.

When Wren wizzed, the final straw that had broken her, sending her spiraling down, was being attacked by several Nulls who thought that they would have some fun with a slight, slender female witch—their term, not his, although he suspected they used a *b*, not a *w*.

The anger and the hatred she felt, from them and from inside herself, piled on top of the stress every Talent in the city had been under for a year by then…she never said what happened to those Nulls, exactly, but he knew. He knew her well enough to know.

Just as he knew, even though she had never said anything, how much it hurt her to kill, both then, and later. How she never wanted to be in that situation ever again.

She wasn't a killer. Even P.B., for all that he was built for inflicting violence, wasn't a killer.

It didn't bother Sergei at all, to have blood on his hands. He slept better when his family was safe.

"Well. You're not who I expected to see here."

He had come in through the first floor window; he was good at not being seen by most people, if not anywhere near Valere's class of sneaky, but he didn't know if the doc's secretary was Cosa or not. Cosa might have spotted him. And there was always the matter of his friendly neighborhood shadow, who was still on his literal tail. He had been tempted more than once to turn and attack, but common sense stilled his paw. Forcing violence wasn't the name of the game. Yet.

"What, I can't have an existential crisis, too?" *he asked the doc, instead.*

"Are you?"

He had wondered that, himself. "I might be. But that's not why I'm here. I need you to do something for me. If I…if I have to disappear, or nobody can find me. I need you to promise to do something for me."

The words came out fast, and he didn't have time to slow down or explain. Doc had been through the Blackout, he was overseeing the reclamation of the Lost. He knew bad shit when it hit the fan.

"This has to do with The Wren?"

"Wren…and Didier. If I disappear."

Doc nodded. He either knew, or he knew enough to suspect. Either way, it made things easier. "What do you need?"

"You need to be there. When it all goes down. In case it goes down bad. And bring backup."

"You think that will be needed?"

"I don't think anything, Doc. That's your job, all the deep thinking. I'm just trying to keep everyone alive."

"Alive…and intact."

"Yeah." *Doc knew enough about what had happened to Valere to be worried about what might happen if she came unglued again. Good. That, too.*

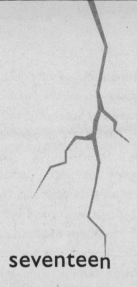

seventeen

This time, she woke up expecting to be alone. She had gone to bed alone, by her own decision.

Sometimes, the night before a job she liked sex-and-snuggle. This time she was twitchity, restless. Better to burn that out alone, running through the details, fine-tuning the moves, and put herself down early, get a solid night's sleep. She slept well after sex, but it was a...less restful sleep, and something made her think she was going to have to be a hundred and ten percent on, today.

Her precog was for shit, but she knew her job.

This morning, the air was comfortably cool on her skin when she got up. As she stretched in the darkness of her bedroom, bare skin feeling a slight burn but not sweating, yet, she let her mind run lightly over the details one last time, her eyes slowly adjusting to the shadows in front of her.

There was no reason to not have turned on the lights; she wasn't worried about anyone watching her apartment—their competition, as far as they could tell, was still focused on P.B., not her. When she finally got in touch with him late last night, through a conference call with Sergei and a one-use cell phone bought for the purpose, the demon had told them, with a heavy sigh, that he was still trapped. Despite his losing his shadow during the day, the woman had called in for help, and been joined by a male, trading off shadowing duties. "They're outside now. Looks like they're settling in for the night."

The demon didn't live in a great neighborhood. Wren might have felt sympathy for anyone else stuck on stakeouts there.

She had mentioned, without giving details, that she would be taking care of the problem they had discussed today, and the fewer disturbances she had to deal with, the better. Anything he could do to make them focus on him, *without,* she emphasized, actively putting himself in danger... He had laughed, a dry, barklike laugh, and told her his only plan for the next day was to, overtly and ostentatiously, sleep in, go down to the corner to buy the newspaper, and then come back home to sit on the sofa and read that newspaper. Maybe he would make a few phone calls to a few friends, about getting out of town for a few days over the weekend, meeting up in some out-of-the-way spot.

So she wasn't too worried about anyone watching her: she just liked doing her stretches in the dark, listening to her body as it came awake without being distracted by sight.

Lift the arm over her head, and feel the muscle pull all the way down the torso, down the leg. Stretch the leg, and let the spine lengthen in response. Bend, and let the body fold in on itself like a well-made fan. She might not be happy with her gym routine lately, but there was no question but that she was ready for whatever might come, physically.

"So long as nobody asks me to lift anything, anyway." She was lithe and limber, yeah, but she was still a petite-sized, light-boned female, and not all the exercise routines in the world were going to make her that much stronger. Not without taking away some of that agility, and that was too stupid to consider, in her line of work.

That was one "pro" to moving to another place. In a proper apartment—one the size of Sergei's, for example, with its open floor plan—she would have room in her bedroom to do full stretches, maybe even some yoga. She could even put in one of those compact weight lifting stations, and never have an excuse not to go to the gym.

Although she kind of liked her gym; it was low-tech and low-noise, with no chirpy aerobics types in spandex or gymborees for babies, just a weight room and another room for treadmills and ellipticals, and a pool and a racquetball court, and showers that made you bring your own towel.

Her palms flat on the floor, her spine not crackling at all from the effort, Wren tasted that thought in her mind. Shower. Yes.

Her muscles comfortably warmed up, and her brain starting to kick over at a more acceptable rate, she grabbed her robe off the hook on the back of the tiny closet and wrapped it around her, then walked down to the bathroom. She looked around, trying to see it the way a new renter might. Mediocre to moderate, on the surface. The bathroom was nothing fancy: white ceramic and aged chrome, with old-fashioned fixtures and chipped black-and-white tile, but it was as close to religion as she ever got; the application of hot water externally followed by hot water—coffee—internally. This morning, though, services would have to be abridged. A quick scrub under cool water with unscented soap rather than her usual hot-and-scented was the physical signal to send her brain into the right place, and by the time she was toweled off, her entire self was focused on the job to come.

"Museum opens at ten," she recited while the spray dug into her scalp and washed away the soap. "There aren't any new exhibits, nothing particularly hot, so crowds will be average. Security's solid but not so much of a worry." She could get past the usual front security check while running a fever, playing a trumpet, and carrying a bag full of contraband. Hired security guards weren't even a factor in her plans.

The first thief had come in from the main floors. It was a time-honored approach for a reason; there was no way to entirely protect any entrance that needed to be used on a regular basis, especially if your budget was limited by practicalities. She had done it a number of times, dressing like an ordinary member of the public and then sliding into work gear once she was past the initial guards.

In fact, normally she would use an entrance that was almost-but-not-exactly the same as the previous failed attempt, under the assumption that while they might be alert they would also be cocky that their security worked.

Not this time.

This time she was worried less about security than she was about running into her counterpart doing the same thing the same way. It was one thing to Retrieve an object under the competition's noses. It was another entirely to be actually *under* their noses. Who needed that kind of stress?

All right, it might be kind of fun. But not today.

Humming to herself, a tune she had heard in the subway, blasting through someone else's headphones, she bopped her way to her bedroom, where her slicks lay waiting on the dresser.

Turning on the single lamp, she went through the final rituals of preparation. Unscented corn powder went on her limbs, smoothing the skin and masking a little more of her own scent. She had learned that from an old deer hunter, back when she was twelve, and never forgotten it. Human noses were much less keen than deer. Even better, the thin black material slid over her powdered skin like an old friend's caress, covering her from ankles to neck, and down to her wrists. She left off the slippered feet and the hood this time; in the daylight, having your face shadowed attracted more attention than a cheerfully bright face front and center. The microfiber pouch strapped to her thigh, and a matte black plastic case, a smaller version of the ones bike messengers used to deliver blueprints, strapped to the small of her back. Black socks and black running shoes completed the picture; if she were, God forbid, stopped on the street, the slicks might pass for some kind of high-tech running suit.

Fully dressed, she stood in front of the mirror and combed the tangle of her hair back off her face, weaving the wet locks into a tight braid and securing it with a soft, textured clip against her scalp. Nothing that might set off a security scan. Nothing that might carry a clear fingerprint. These were things she didn't even think about consciously any more, except when she forced herself to stop and run through the steps in her mind.

She stared at herself in the mirror. Genevieve Valere. The Wren. Retriever. The shadow no one ever saw clearly. The one who could steal the shine off a pair of headlights: the lonejack who stood up to the Mage Council and made them blink. The one some folk said was the best Retriever of her generation.

The woman who went after the Lost, the young Talent who were stolen and brainwashed, and took them back.

It should have been over. But it wasn't. Nobody would tell her what happened to the kids—the teenagers, the adults, she had taken out of the hell of the Silence's training hall. She hadn't ever seen any of them on the street. None of them had ever come to thank her, or to curse her, or just to stare at her in silence.

In silence. Irony, yes. Oh, she knew where they were: in the home set up for them, trained professionals weaning them off the diet of self-hatred the Silence had fed them, bringing them back to some semblance of…something. That much she'd been able to learn, before walking away. They owed her nothing. She had not been kind to them; she hadn't had time or sanity to be kind to them, too busy ending a private little war. At least now they were surrounded by those who loved them, who cared for them. She took some small comfort in that, in the fact that some had been reunited with parents, siblings. Some might even have been able to forgive what had been done to them.

She held on to that fact and tucked it inside, like a warming stone.

Next, she pulled on her gloves. The same fabric as the rest of her slicks, but even thinner, their abraded surfaces for gripping, and backs textured for protection. Almost unrippable, no matter how roughly she treated them. Gloves of a thief. The gear of a Retriever.

It shouldn't matter if any of those kids hated her, or thanked her, or even thought of her at all. It didn't matter if the target was a piece of jewelry, or a cursed artifact, or a blond-haired blue-eyed kidlet with parents who didn't have a clue, or…or anything. You didn't form attachments to what you Retrieved, not the good, the bad, or the cute. Or the broken. Lonejack creed: take care of yourself.

She was what she was. She did what she did. Time to do it, and not look back.

Wren reached down and shook out two pills from a small brown vial waiting on her dresser, a new and unwanted addition to her job routine. She dry-swallowed them, then turned and walked out of the room, down the hallway and out of the apartment.

★ ★ ★

"Valere." The sky was only starting to lighten when she hit the street, but the streetlamps had already turned off. The Talent waiting for her was seated cross-legged on top of the mailbox. The shadow lurking behind him was no shadow, but Danny, cleaning his fingernails with a knife like some parody of the classic street hoodlum in his jeans and a leather jacket, his head bare for once, the brown curls not quite hiding his nubby horns.

"Tony," she greeted the Talent in turn. "Thanks for coming out. Danny, you pain in the ass, what the hell are you doing here?"

Danny ignored her attitude. "Body-guarding."

"I don't need—"

"Not you. Me."

Wren eyeballed Tony, who eyeballed her right back. "I'm too old to risk my hide on one of your crazy gigs, and don't even try to pretend, Valere, because everything you touch is crazy."

"Even when it works?" She was more than a little offended.

"Especially then," he said, refusing to take offense himself.

He had a point, damn him. "Just do this, okay?" Her nerves were starting to creep in, poking with needle claws for access, and the only way to deal with that was work.

"Did you take the pills?"

"Yeah." He had warned her, when she approached him, that there might be side effects, even at his best. The pills were supposed to counteract that. "Supposed to" being the operative term.

A bottle of water appeared in Tony's hand, and he handed it to her. She took it, noting that the seal was untouched.

"Drink," he ordered. "You need to be well-hydrated for them to work."

"I'll just chuck it when I get there," Wren muttered, but unscrewed the plastic cap and took a long swallow, then another, suddenly thirsty.

"Stay alert," Danny said. "Get the job done and come home."

"Yes Mother," she said, just as Tony raised his hands and started to mutter something in a language Wren had the feeling she should recognize, but didn't. And then the world disappeared in the sickening swirling nothingness of being Translocated.

I goddamned hate *this,* she thought, dropping to her knees and readying herself for the usual course of vomit. This time, though, she only dry-gagged a little, coughing up nothing but a little water. It might have been the pills, or the fact that Tony was considered one of the best, but she only felt slightly as if she wanted to die, not a lot.

She reached out to grab at the wall for support, then stopped herself, getting to her feet slowly but unaided. Her knees wobbled a little, and her throat and head ached, but otherwise she was okay. Her slicks were unmarred by vomit, for which she was doubly thankful.

Most talented Retriever of her generation, maybe. But shit at Transloc, even when she'd been flooded with Fatae-magics. Neezer had said everyone had a blockage on something, to keep them humble. She could do humble, as long as the vomiting part went away.

Tony was worth every damn penny she overpaid him, until then.

Her hand still gripped the water bottle, and she drained it, luxuriating in the cool water going down her suddenly parched throat. She started to toss the bottle, and then reconsidered, and shoved it into the pouch tied to her thigh. It just barely fit, alongside her tool kit and emergency supplies. Pity that bags of holding, like telepathy and fairy godmothers, were so much bunk.

Hydrated and alert now, Wren did a mental shakedown. She was inside the museum, down in the lower warrens, thanks to Tony's handiwork. It was an hour before the doors opened for general employees, and three hours before the public would be let in, among them Sergei with her change of clothing and a lead-lined box for the items she would be Retrieving. In through current, out through ordinary. Leave 'em guessing. With luck, she would be in and out before the other thief even arrived. Let him or her take the fall.

Clock's ticking. Get moving.

"He hasn't even gotten out of bed yet." It was still early, but the servant was normally awake by now, if not out and about. The break in routine was worrisome, and warranted a phone call to check for new orders.

Her contact, hours ahead in Zurich, was annoyed. "You may have been spotted, chasing it around all week. I knew that we should have left it alone until the last minute."

There was no response to that that would not provoke useless squabbling. What was done was done, and there was no way to undo it.

"Where is Julia?"

"Back at the Embassy. I did not think that we would require her services any longer." The woman, a longtime resident in this city, had been useful while they were here, but would serve no purpose once all the parts were collected. She was a granddaughter of the *Kreis*, but not skilled in any way, either in the sciences or magics. She was not part of the elite, and had not earned the right to be in on the Discovery.

"No, a good decision," Zurich agreed. "She would become a handicap at this juncture. However, we can't afford to wait much longer. We are ready to begin at this end. If it does not emerge within the hour, go in and get it."

"By myself?" The man sounded slightly taken aback, even though it was no more or less than he had expected.

"It is a servant," the voice on the other end of the line was thin with distance, and sharp with annoyance. "It will not dare resist."

"As you say." He bowed his head in submission, even though Himself could not see it. They might argue with each other in meetings, but once a decision was reached, his word was law. "I will collect it and meet Rog at the airport, on schedule."

Sliding the phone back into his pocket, Jef looked dubiously at the still-dark window of the basement apartment. An hour. Word as law or no, it was easy enough for Himself to speak of servants and collecting. He was the one who had spent the past week researching the creature, observing it, while Julia was the obvious threat. He was the one who had seen the creature up close. More specifically, he was the one who had seen the creature's claws and teeth up close. Fine for Himself to be casual about servants who served; he wasn't the one who had to go down and get the thing.

Fortunately, his discussions with local veterinarians had proven fruitful in one way, if not exactly as hoped. He checked his pocket for reassurance, feeling the capped syringe and capsules secreted there. He was assured that the sedative contained therein would put even a raging bear out, if needed. All he had to do was hit square in the flesh, and then get out of the way. It was important, vitally important: this servant was one rumored to be viable. They needed it, to test the Discovery.

He patted his pocket one more time, took a deep breath, ran a hand down his tie to erase nonexistent wrinkles, and took a better position to watch the apartment door.

Wren could feel the hum of her current, reacting to her mood. She slipped through the hallway, counting steps under her breath, making her movements almost like a dance. The ceiling-mounted cameras turned and tracked up and down the hallway but she ignored them, letting the crackle of current just under her skin do its job in hiding her. When she was just starting out it would have taken her a good ten minutes to prep that; now it was like slipping into bathwater. Nothing to do with her increased flow; just experience.

She could feel the energy pulsing around her, shimmering in the walls like a living thing, like a thousand living things, but it was purely electricity; the museum didn't use anything current-based at all. Either they had no Talent on staff— possible—or the ones they did have were smart enough to keep their current to themselves and out of the system. Some Nulls were cool with having coworkers who were different—there was that entire firehouse who had rallied to defend their Talented brother, had become the base of operations for the main stand against the Silence last year, and they'd probably get cookies every Christmas until the building was torn down, for that—but even with the Tri-Com working to improve relations, "outed" Talent in the workplace were still rare, as much because of the Cosa's hard-learned preference for obscurity as humanity's distaste for the differently abled, especially the supra-abled.

Still, it wasn't smart to get cocky until the job was done. She dialed back a little, dampened her current until it was merely what was needed to bypass the cameras, and let her own physical abilities handle the rest. Right now it was her memory that she needed more than anything, since she couldn't trust any of the signage on the various doors. A Null thief could commit plans to a PDA or microchip. Unless she wanted to haul around miniaturized blueprints and a magnifying glass, she had only her gray matter.

Thankfully, the layout of these rooms was simple enough, echoing the public rooms she knew so well, and once she had her bearings, it was just a matter of getting there. After the first, failed attempt, the inventory had been taken from cold storage and brought up to these rooms, where items of possible interest were poked and prodded, photographed, and deciphered. Exactly what they had hoped to avoid.

But there was a silver lining, even now. The active rooms were, well, active. People went in and out of them all the time. Therefore security would have greater holes to exploit.

Of course, she thought, there were also negatives to that too, as the sound of confident footfalls on the linoleum flooring alerted her that someone was coming her way. Slipping up against the bare white walls, Wren took a deep breath and brought up another layer of current. The worker—an early-morning curator? A janitor? Who knew?—passed within a foot of her, and didn't notice a thing.

Don't get cocky, Valere, she reminded herself, and started breathing again. *In, grab, out.* She moved on down the hall, running through the plans in her memory. Neither Sergei's contacts nor Chang's influence had been able to shake loose exactly where the materials had been moved to, only that they were under new scrutiny by the museum staff, to determine why a thief would be interested in that exact bin.

Wren never thought that she'd regret Retrieving something nonmagical. The truth was, in a situation like this, if the papers had been anything more than merely papers, she would have been able to open herself to the flow, and find where current was concentrated oddly indicating something more than normal or customary. Current picked up the signature of its user, and so did Artifacts and ritual objects.

That thought stopped her cold.

Duh. Idiot.

Herr Doktor had been a Talent, even if a low-res one, and he had spent his entire life, according to P.B., trying to perfect demon to a specific purpose. It was a madness—not like wizzing, but not unlike it, either. And madness was one of the strongest influences of signature there was…like finding Neezer's boots because he had been so frustrated, these papers should carry Herr Doktor's signature, as well.

Fainter, oh so much fainter, but they had much more of an emotional connection to him in the first place; his entire life's blood might have been used, rather than ink, to make those notations.

You're an idiot for not thinking of that sooner. Although to be fair, if you didn't have the inside scoop on the guy's focused single-mindedness, and the fact that he was a Talent, and the fact that he wrote them out himself, old-style pen and paper, it wasn't something that popped to mind right away. And there was no reason to assume any signature at all would remain after all this time. And no guarantee that even this close, in the same building, she would be able to pick it up, not having known the guy.

You didn't, no. But you know someone who did. Intimately.

Ducking into a broom closet in case anyone else had come into work early or unexpectedly, Wren leaned up against a mop that smelled rather disgustingly of ammonia and fake pine, and reached not inward, as usual, but out.

P.B.?

Fatae weren't usually able to ping, using thin strands of current like telegraph wires to speak to each other, but demon seemed to be a major exception to every "usually" she knew. Or maybe it was just their connection, hers and P.B.'s, working the way it was supposed to when she needed him.

Trouble? A sense of alertness, coiled and ready for action, marbled with a faint sense of boredom, waiting.

No. Need your memory. She shoved as much an apology as she could manage into those words, trying to impart what she needed. It was difficult, and foggy, and she could tell it wasn't getting through. *Him. His signature* she clarified. *Current. What did it feel like?*

Comprehension, and a reluctance to dig into that memory, then a surge of determination so fast the earlier reluctance was swamped and erased. For her, he would do this. The feel of heavy doors unlocking deep in his memory, so different and yet similar to her own mental storage boxes, and as simple as that she was brought down into the memory, and given what she needed.

You okay? she asked, once she had pocketed what was there.

Bored A stronger sense of frustration, being kept cooped up in his apartment, more than any injury from what she had asked. She chuckled, sending as much sympathy as she dared.

Over soon. Hang tough.

Shutting herself down, she cupped the sense of the old man. It wasn't at all what she had expected, braced for something slimy, maybe, or at least unsavory. Instead she got straight-backed and eagle-eyed, cruel and kind all at once, wise and foolish in his obsession but never once actually inhumane to those in his care, even the ones not human. Merely...careless of them, as one might be to a horse or dog that was not particularly beloved. Selfish, God yes. Astonishingly so. Talent, but P.B. had been right, more brilliant than Talented; driven and dedicated enough to make up for it in all areas...all except one.

She touched the memory of that Talent, felt it course through her veins the way it must have for P.B., when he was young and malleable. Felt the sting of unwanted intimacy, and the weight of slavery, even if it was called servitude.

There. That was it. She held the spark of memory, cradling it in her mental palms, and drew it out into a thin strand, copper-red with age. A strand of her own current, thicker and a darker blue, joined it, twining around it, and then she let them both go with a simple command: like to like.

Assuming there weren't too many objects with the creator's signature on it the strand should take her to wherever the crate of materials had been moved. Hopefully.

"And away we go" she said, feeling the tug somewhere in her gut. She slipped out of the closet, thankful to leave the smell behind, and moved down the hallway. The tug brought her to a stairwell, and up a level. From the change in the way the building felt, somehow, she thought that she had left one wing and entered another, where they had cobbled the two old brownstones together when the museum was established. She was still in the off-limit areas, though, she could tell that much.

The pull grew stronger, leading her up another level to a wider hallway where the doors, rather than being solid slabs, were lighter wood, with frosted glass insets. It looked more like…

Oh hell. She was out of the storage areas, and into the actual workrooms.

No matter how good the blueprints, there was something about museums, even the smaller ones, that just never translated from floor plan to actuality, and no matter how sure you were you knew where you where, most of the time, you weren't.

She pulled up that part of the plan from memory: one hallway, seven rooms, each separate from the other, like classrooms, or offices. Easier to search: also easier to be trapped in. At least there were fewer cameras here.

There. Behind the fifth door. She slipped inside, praying that nobody had decided to make an early morning of it.

Chaos greeted her: wooden crates on the floor, and plastic bins on tables, a whiteboard the size of her living room wall against one side, covered with boxes that she supposed were meant to represent rooms in the museum itself.

Damn it. She risked looking over some of the items that were unpacked on the tables, skimming the notes taped to the surfaces. *They're putting together an exhibit. Of Herr Doktor's work?*

The inked placard gave her an answer: Mad Science: Real Life Dr. Frankensteins and the Pursuit of Life.

Oh hell. Oh damn it and twice-damn it and three times more. Exactly what she had wanted to avoid: some bright thing bringing the material to the public view and banging a drum over it.

What, because you're afraid someone's going to figure it out? A little late for that, isn't it, considering they've already made a first grab.

But right now, the damage was limited. Once this was on display? All it would take was one wiseass Talent to come through and see the exhibit, and put two and two together to get five, and she knew damn well how easy it was for Cosa members to do that. And hell, if a Council Mage were to hear of it...

She glared around the room, furious at the universe that seemed determined to make this as complicated as possible, willing the specific material she needed to appear before her out of the organized mess.

"paperwork to file
buried deeply out of sight;
it must first be found."

The strand of copper and blue appeared in the air in front of her, quivering and pointing like a bird dog on the job.

"Come to me," she commanded, focusing not on the strand but the materials it had found. A heavy book, two rolls of paper, and a small notebook rose off their various desks, and an ornate, old-fashioned ink pen rose out of a small rosewood box.

Too much, more than she was looking for. Her irritation and

her enhanced current were working against her, now. *Ease back, clarify, and control,* she reminded herself.

Ignoring the pen—she wasn't here for memorabilia, even though it would probably get a nice price from a collector—Wren grabbed the scrolls and tucked them into the short carry-tube that was strapped to her left calf. She removed the water bottle from her thigh pouch, and tucked the small notebook there in its place, tossing the water bottle into the small recycling can under the desk. With luck, nobody would even think to sort through and pull one water bottle from the power drink cans and soda bottles already there.

"And what the hell will I do with you?" she asked the large book. It was the size of a phone book, hardbound and locked with a brass lock that had been carefully, almost expertly prised open.

"Give it to me," a gravelly voice behind her said. It wasn't phrased like a suggestion.

eighteen

Think fast, Jenny-wren.

This time, it wasn't an echo of her mentor's voice she heard, just her own awareness using his voice. Old habits died hard, even imaginary ones.

When Wren first went into partnership with Sergei Didier, she had been a small-town teenage shoplifter with some basic talent as well as Talent. Seeing potential in her itchy fingers, he encouraged her to stretch exactly the skills and inclinations her mentor had once despaired of, and found her teachers for the things she needed to know. But it had been Wren's own idea to work with a woman who trained agility dogs. The woman used to run her through obstacle courses that were similar to what the dogs trained on—up ladders and over jumps and through tunnels—with the added fun of throwing things as Wren did so. Wren's reflexes, always good, had gotten better.

Those reflexes were screaming at her to throw something at

that voice, but the only thing to hand was the book he was demanding, and that was the one thing she wasn't about to give him.

Should have paid Tony more to stick around, she thought with annoyance, even as her brain was running through possible responses. Translocating the hell out of here now would have been worth the price. Although maybe not—once, the pills seemed to work. Twice, in close proximity…the last time she tried that many Translocs, she was damn near incapacitated for a week.

Those thoughts took less than a second to race through her mind, and she was already moving by the time they finished. Rather than swing around to confront the speaker, or drop to the ground to try and escape, Wren went *up.*

"What the hell?" Gravel-voice asked, his voice squeaking in surprise on the last word.

Sergei had been right; they had gone to the Null population again for their thief. A Talent wouldn't have blinked at the sight of a Retriever clinging to the ceiling like some kind of real-world Spiderman.

The pull from the wiring in the ten-foot-high ceiling was just enough to make her palms and knees itch to draw more down, and Wren was careful to keep the touch of her own current light. The last thing she wanted to do now was overload the already stressed wiring of the building and cause a power outage that would bring every cop in the city wailing to the front door, sure a heist was in progress.

Especially since one *was.*

Carefully matching her drawdown to the flutter of current leaking naturally, using it like a spider's web to keep her attached to the ceiling, she scrambled over the other intruder's head, the large book pressed against her stomach like a mutant baby possum looking for mama.

Getting down was as easy as falling, which was pretty much

what she did—right on top of the other intruder, toppling him to the ground. As she hit, a weird, nasty feeling skittered over her skin, and she shuddered, rolling quickly to get away from him, and it. As she rolled, she got a look at the other intruder for the first time: Tall, dark, stocky, and pissed-off. Also, wearing a uniform, dark blue pants and jacket with a patch on his shoulder, and a walkie-talkie—but no gun—at his leather belt

Ooops. Not a thief. Museum security.

Where the hell did he come from? He was off his rounds, damn it. Nobody was supposed to be patrolling this floor for another twenty minutes!

"Sorry," she muttered, pitching her voice as low as she could in order to sound masculine, and used the spine of the book to knock him one across the chin, praying she didn't do any damage to the book. She wasn't trying to hurt him, either, just keep him down long enough for her to get away. Her gym routine paid off, giving her the upper body strength needed, and he blinked and fell back again, the back of his head clunking against the floor.

Reaching down even as she scrambled up to her knees, Wren touched the walkie-talkie and the cell phone clipped to his belt, and sent a surge of current through them both. With luck, when he came to, he'd spend a few essential minutes trying to figure out why nobody was responding to his calls before he chased after her.

"Follow me," she told the book, and it obligingly attached itself to her like a dog on "heel" command. Dashing out the now-open door, Wren left the guard ass-down on the floor, and fled down the hallway.

Time check. How much time had passed? Her internal clock was usually pretty good on these things—when you couldn't wear a watch, you learned how to estimate time to within a few minutes' accuracy. The doors should be opening for staff soon, if they hadn't already. And someone was going to find the guard sooner rather than later, even if he sat there fiddling with his now-junked radios until then. Why did he have to come in just then, to see her boosting the book? Damn it, she should have tied him up, should have—bingo!

Wren skidded to a halt before she reached the stairs. It wasn't a brilliant idea, and it had a high probability of failure, but it was better than anything else she could think of and had the added advantage of being simple. Simple sometimes was better than brilliant, especially under stress conditions.

She flicked a finger, and the book came into her hands. It was dark brown leather, scuffed and battered at the corners even before she used it as a weapon, as if it had been shoved into a lot of trunks and desks over the years. There was nothing written or embossed on the front or back, and the spine had lettering that was too faded now to read. The pages looked to be heavy paper, and had at one time been edged in gilt. The temptation to open the book and see what was inside was intense, but Wren resisted. With her luck, Herr Doktor had bespelled the pages to trap any Talent who dared peek. That seemed like the kind of thing a mad mage-scientist would do, didn't it?

A wizzart sure as hell would have. And it would have been a nasty spelling, too.

Beside, she didn't need to know what was inside for what she needed to do.

Sliding into fugue state, she dunked herself into her current, gracelessly surrounding herself with crackling, slithering thick-bodied coils of current. They rubbed up against her with dry static and set the virtual hair on her virtual arms pleasantly on end. The *idea* of the book appeared in her hands, and she concentrated for a moment to make sure that her memory supplied all the relevant details. Heft and weight and texture and color and smell...if she thought it would help she would have licked it, to get the taste. as well.

Deep inside her body, the pain kicked her in the gut. With sheer force of will, she ignored it.

"see it be
and make it be so:
book, appear"

Not here, not in her hands; she already had the real thing. Cantrips didn't need to be exact, so long as the caster knew exactly what they wanted, and focused all their control on it.

Will and the Way, they used to call it in the old days. Magical Visualization, if you were all New Age-y. Focus, if you were a Talent. It all came down to the same thing: making shit happen the way you wanted, not the way current would naturally flow in the easiest channel.

That was where old magic went wrong, most of the time. Just because you could chant and wave didn't mean you were directing the power. Current, like electricity, like people, was lazy. It wanted to go where it always went, not where you wanted it to go. Not unless you were trained specifically in directing it. You had to be tougher than it was, every single time.

Focus. Control. Training.

Wren Valere had been very well-trained, long before she ever became a Retriever. Her mentor had made damned sure of that.

Wren looked inside and out through her current, and Saw the room she had taken the materials from. The guard was still flat out on the floor, but he was groaning and reaching around with one hand for his walkie-talkie. She didn't have much time at all.

"see it be
and make it so:
book, *appear*."

The emphasis worked this time, and the book in her fugue-sight disappeared, reappearing with a satisfyingly solid thunk on the desk where she had found it. The guard should, if he bothered to look, think that everything was undisturbed, as would anyone who came in later, at least until they tried to pick the book up, and discovered the pages were blank.

Quickly, before she could give in to the pain trying to gnaw out her innards, Wren shifted her focus from the book to the guard. She had to keep him from following her, had to put him out of the game—without killing him. She knew how to do it, now. But she hesitated, something making her concentration waver.

It was wrong. What she was planning to do was very, very wrong, and she could almost hear Neezer muttering in her ear how wrong it was.

"Shut up, old man" she said. "You abandoned me, you dumped me, you gave my responsibilities to someone else, you miserable bastard, and I am angry at you. So you don't get to tell me how to live my life—or how to protect it."

A dark crimson lightning bolt of current shot up through her arm, making it jerk under the impact into a disturbingly salutelike gesture, the finger pointing back down toward the room—toward the guard. Wren *saw* the bolt leave her finger, thicker and darker than she had expected, zapping into the air and disappearing.

"wash him clean
absent all mem'ry
of today."

She'd love to have lifted only the memory of finding someone in the room, but the time for that sort of precision didn't exist, even if she had that kind of fine-tuned control. If she was lucky, her intent and her control was good enough that the poor bastard only lost everything since he woke up that morning, and blamed it all on the bad spill he took when entering the room. If nothing was overtly out of place, he would go for medical attention, and not report an intruder or trigger any alarm.

If she'd screwed up, hit him too hard…then God have mercy on the poor schmuck, whose only mistake had been getting ahead of his schedule.

She dropped out of fugue state, and her body wreaked its own revenge for overusing that dark current, dropping her to the ground as hard as she had dropped the guard. Hard, hot spines of pain slammed into her abdomen, ricocheting around to see how much damage they could do.

"Oh, fuck," she managed, before the pain made her black out.

The book dropped to the floor beside her, the noise echoing in the otherwise-silent room.

In the room down the hall, the guard twitched once, then again. A spangle of current darker and thicker than Wren's blast lifted off his skin, as though disturbed by her spell. It hovered bare seconds, then settled back down onto his flesh, sinking into the dermis. The guard twitched again, moaned, and then his eyes opened as though forced to do so by an external source.

★Valere!★

Confusion, annoyance, a sense of being kicked in the gut, and a splitting headache pulled Wren back into consciousness. She blinked, groggy, her arm automatically reaching out to grab where the book had landed even before she was fully alert to where she was.

"Shit." This was bad. This was very, very bad. How much time had she lost? No way to tell, now. Find a clock. No, first, listen for pursuit, sounds, anything to indicate the guard had remembered enough to set off an alarm. Her body ached as though she had been worked over by a sadist, but the pain made it easier, somehow, for her to listen. Probably because her ears weren't trying to move. If she'd had ears like P.B's, that flicked back and forth when he was concentrating...

Voices. Not near, but coming closer. Dress shoes, heels on linoleum. Conversational tones, not alarmed ones. Early workers, too early, damn it, for anyone to be coming to work. Not many, but any was too many. She had to move. Oh God, she had to move.

Once she convinced her torso to uncurl and her legs to straighten, the pain wasn't quite as bad as expected. Bad, but nothing she couldn't shove through. Time had passed, then. Enough time for her body to recover, enough for her to command her muscles to respond, and not have them give her a virtual finger in response. With the book cradled to her side, staggering bent-over and leaning against the wall, she moved down the hallway, looking for an unoccupied space to crawl into.

Hide. Stay undetected. Don't get caught.

But there was nowhere to hide, no empty closet or spare office. With her normal defenses battered and down, every room she touched the door of repelled her, filled to the brim with waves of anger, resentment, discontent, or sheer loneliness. The weight of those emotions bruised her, and only sheer stubborn annoyance of her own kept her moving.

It wasn't until she came to the third door that her brain caught up with her instincts, and she realized what was happening. Not people. Artifacts. Not magical, not particularly dangerous, but in her hyperaware, hyperexposed state, everything in the museum had an aura around it, everything was *projecting.*

That thought stirred something else in her brain. Something about P.B.? A voice, or a note, or something…. She couldn't remember, and didn't have the energy to spare to worry at it right then, anyway.

Up or down? She hesitated in the stairwell, panting like an overheated dog, confused and aching. Down…down there were no people. She could hide down there, have time to recover, complete the job. But one step on the stairs, and a tsunami of projections staggered her backward.

"I'm sorry, I'm sorry" she whispered, not sure who she was apologizing to, or why. Whatever was down there was *lonely.* Was *angry.* Everyone had gone and *left* them *alone.*

If she went down there, the way she was right now, open to every currentical influence, she would…

It would be bad. Whatever happened, it would be bad. She couldn't go back down there. Not alone. Not now. Not the way she was. Turning, she went up the stairs, instead, into the museum itself.

The halls were wider here, the ceilings higher, and her steps, even in her work gear, echoed in a way that should have been reassuring but wasn't. The oppression she could feel practically oozing off the walls, from every glass-enclosed exhibit and display, reminded her, oddly, of the Dark Space in the House of Holding, the current-null space in the hills of Tuscany. Which was worse? Given a vote, Wren would have said they were both scary-ass, and let her out now, thanks and bye-bye.

There was still a job to be done, though. Do it, get out, go home. Never come back here again, not ever. The litany went through her head until it filled the echoes a little. The footsteps still echoed too much, though.

Slipping off her shoes and socks, she went barefoot. The coolness of the tile against her skin was a shock, and helped bring her back to herself. The malice she felt was from things long dead and gone, their rage coming from the fact that they were trapped and helpless. And they were…less angry than downstairs. Less abandoned, less ignored. That helped her to breathe a little more easily, when a shadow fell over her brain, and a heavy step sounded behind her.

"Give it to me."

Wren blinked, and turned to stare at the guard. There was blood on the edge of his forehead where she had conked him, and his uniform jacket was off, revealing a white shirt that wasn't as bleach-clean as it should have been stretched over a paunch the size of a small keg, the sleeves rolled up to show beefy forearms.

"What you took. Give it to me."

The guard's voice was flat now, the accent odd, as though he were deaf and speaking for the first time. He wiped the blood off his face where it was running into his eyes, not seeming to care about it otherwise, and stared at her. He wasn't menacing, or angry. In fact, his body language was as flat as his voice. It was unnerving as hell, and Wren took an involuntary step backward. She had faced angry ghosts out for revenge, evil, soul-eating manuscripts, bigoted humans with guns, and an animated stuffed horse that predicted misfortune, and none of them had made her feel quite as heebie-jeebied as this guy did. Something had changed. Something…bad. Something worse than what was downstairs.

Because he wasn't there. Something else was working his brain.

Oh, merciful God. The nasty sensation she'd felt, when she hit him. Old magic. Bad magic. Worst magic. The old world mages, the ones after P.B., they hadn't sent in another thief. They had stolen one already on-site. They'd controlled him enough to get him off-rounds, sent him after the book, the rest of the exhibit, and when she had interrupted things... They had gone deeper. They'd *eaten* him. Oh *sweet Jesus I know I've been bad but I promise to be good, I will I will I will*....

Wren swallowed hard, turned, and ran like hell down the hallway, the mage-ridden guard, with his much longer legs, barely three yards behind and gaining fast.

nineteen

There was a coffee cart setting up shop on the corner, a middle-aged man and his teenage son, dreadlocked and sullen, working with smooth, practiced moves inside the close confines of the traditional metal box. There was one on every corner, farther downtown, where they multiplied in accordance with the number of office buildings, but in this neighborhood, filled with high-end apartments and higher-end doctor's offices, the cart was a welcome oasis on a cold morning. Sergei bought a cup of lousy coffee and a surprisingly good muffin, and sat on the bench on the corner, sipping and grimacing. A squirrel came to rest on the back of the bench, chittering at him. Sergei looked over his shoulder, expecting to see a piskie, as well, but the beast was alone.

Squirrels and piskies all looked alike to him, anyway. Except for the fur. And wings. And the intelligence in the face of the squirrel. He gave the animal a bit of the muffin, anyway.

An early-morning jogger went by, the woman giving Sergei

and the squirrel a curious glance, and he raised his coffee cup to her in salute. He supposed he looked like a surprisingly well-dressed homeless man, in his wool coat and dress shoes, sitting in the predawn light sharing his breakfast with a tree-rat. He should have picked up a newspaper on his way over, to pass the time. He didn't handle waiting well, not under these circumstances.

There was a reason he preferred to work behind the scenes and before the game actually started. And it wasn't, despite what Wren claimed, because he was afraid to muss one of his suits getting down and dirty. He was, at heart, a thinker and a worrier. And when a thinker started to worry, there was no end to the number of gone-bad scenarios he could produce during the length of time it took to, oh, drink a cup of coffee.

Sergei put the coffee down and took his cell phone out of his coat's pocket, hitting a newly updated #3 on the speed dial.

The phone rang, and rang. Nobody answered, not even an answering machine.

"Damn it." He closed the phone, cutting it off midring, and put it back in his pocket. Three times he had called P.B. this morning, and three times the phone had merely rung. He was supposed to be staying put, Wren had said, playing possum to draw off at least one of their hounds.

So where the hell was the demon? Why wasn't he answering the phone? Why did he even care? It wasn't as though the demon couldn't take care of himself. Had, in fact, been doing exactly that for at least fifty years—and probably closer to a hundred—before he, Sergei was even born.

That was then. This was now. Now, the demon had obligations beyond his own furry self. If something happened to the demon...

Sergei checked his watch again. Still an hour before they

expected the second thief, if Wren was correct in her assumptions. She might be wrong. She might have run into trouble inside, already.

If, if, if. If she had, there was nothing he could do, not out here. He was no thief to sneak in, no acrobat to get in through a high window, no Talent to Translocate inside thick walls. Until the doors opened and he could walk through, unless someone raised a fuss outside those walls, there was nothing he could do save sit and wait. And worry.

And drink crap coffee.

He hated coffee. He'd give anything for a decent cup of tea, but these carts used crap water that always tasted of coffee anyway.

He reached for the phone again, and stopped.

If the demon could have answered, he would have.

Something was wrong.

He cast a worried look over his shoulder at the museum. Five stories tall, from the street the facade of the building still looked like the two original townhouses it had once been, back in the days when it was an exclusive address rather than merely being oh dear God expensive.

The building was still and quiet, no light showing in any of the windows save the red emergency lights that glowed 24-7. There was no sign of anything, good or ill, happening inside.

P.B. was essential to Wren's continued well-being. More… Sergei was fond of the furry little freak. And, thick-skulled musculature or no, there were things even a demon couldn't deflect. Like a high-powered rifle. Or a kidnapping attempt.

Decision half made, he was already shoving the remains of the muffin into his other pocket and rising up off the bench, making the squirrel jump off the back of the bench and flee into the landscaping of the building behind him. Sergei brushed the remaining crumbs off his coat front, striding down the street toward the corner. At this hour of the morning, a cab would be faster than waiting for a subway train to come.

Forgive me, Zhenchenka. But he took care of you when I couldn't. He watched over you when I wasn't there. I owe him. I owe him this.

A turn and a skid down the overpolished stairs, grabbing for the handrail even as the soles of her feet slipped on a step, only her excellent reflexes keeping her from slamming down on her ass. She had lost track of what floor she was on, the twists and turns of the building confusing her, the unquiet stares of the exhibits, even those without eyes, making it even worse. The weight might be reduced here, maybe because so many people trooped past every week, but it wasn't gone entirely. She was wobbly in the brain, unsure of what was real and what was delusion, and what was a true illusion.

No wonder nobody in the Cosa *robs this place. Nobody could stay sane long enough to do the job.*

The guard—or whatever was riding him—seemed unaware of the pressure she felt, running at a steady lope she hadn't expected from his overweight form. A Null, then, although she had pretty well figured that out from the whole possession thing.

How the hell are they doing that? Old magic, has to be, there's nothing…vodoun? It was the only thing that made sense, as much as anything made sense, but even in a global economy the thought of Dutch mages using African magic…

Duh. Afrikaaners. She had looked up the Boer War, since she was doing research anyway. Late nineteenth century, English versus Dutch over land and mines in South Africa. Nasty stuff, but the important thing was that P.B.'s creator had been there for a couple more years by then, before he reportedly died there during the war. Plenty of chances to learn the local traditions— even the ones white men weren't supposed to poke around in.

Old Zee had been the type to be up to his elbows in all sorts of old magics, most of them bad, why would it surprise her that his would-be heirs were cut from the same cloth?

Idiots. There were reasons Talent moved away from the old magics. Blood and sex-magics ate more of you than current, and if you were stupid enough to invoke the oldest ones to help, you had to pay them. And they usually weren't the type to take AmEx....

Sergei was right. These guys were so ego-ridden, they didn't think past their own wants.

She was moving now through a series of small rooms filled with pottery shards. Useful bits, shattered and useless now. Regret and hopelessness, but all things built to be used are built to be abandoned, as well. The pressure was less here, knowing that, and she took a deep breath before plunging through the next display.

Weapons. Bow and arrows and stone knives and they were plunged into Wren's heart all at once, stabbing sharp and sudden. If she hadn't known it wasn't real, she would have died, then and there.

The power of the attack was too much: this wasn't just the snarls of history, pissed off at being passed by. They were using the exhibits, knowingly or not, to attack her. Bastards. That was what they did; they used things lesser than themselves, like tools, and never mind what it did to those tools.

The tube was chafing against her slicks, the material having to work overtime wicking sweat off her skin, the book clutched to her side. It would be easier to have current carry them both but she was afraid to let them go, afraid the guard would try to grab them, would get his hands on them.

"Let it go."

A whisper in her ear, a coaxing lure, twitching like a hook

in the water, glinting like gold. "You're so tired, so scared. Let it go, and you can rest, you'll be safe, he won't be interested in you any more."

Wren's eyes widened, her skin prickling under the sweat. Air caught in her throat and she hiccupped painfully. The nearest exhibit, a display of Native garb, swayed forward ominously— or was it her imagination?

"So scared, poor thing…" The voice was back, trying to pry open her scalp and climb inside her brain, painted fingernails and perfect teeth the image of concerned comfort and safety, if only she, Wren, would turn to her, give up, give in.

Wren almost laughed, and the deerskin outfit swayed back away from the sound. Idiots. They thought that she was scared? She was *pissed*. They threatened her demon, were fiddling about with her damned livelihood for their own damn egos, and using piss-stupid old magics they probably had no clue about, hurting this poor schlub who was going to have a heart attack from all the running they were making him do, and then they tried to mindfuck her into just giving up because she was, oh poor little her, *scared?*

Old magics had been abandoned because they were unpredictable, unreliable. Not weaker—stronger in some ways, especially if you weren't picky about the price you paid. Blood magic, sex magic, the exchange of power for power. That was what these bastards were doing.

Current was cleaner. It asked more of *you,* but the eventual price was less. And nobody else had to pay for what you took.

Wren had used old magics before, too, and had them used on her. She could play that game, if that was the game these bastards wanted to play. But she would take precautions, negotiate the price to be paid ahead of time. She just had to figure out how. And fast.

Take blood from stone. Give blood. Stone. Bedrock for strength, but more…what was it that she wasn't remembering?

She spun on her heel, the book dropping to the ground in front of her, and waited. The guard blew through the doorway, clearly expecting her to still be running, and almost plowed into her.

The conflict was clear on his face: the man, his training, said to grab the intruder, to arrest the thief. Whoever was riding him, meanwhile, was demanding that he grab the book. But to do so would require him to go down low in front of her, opening himself to attack, and he was a smart enough man, normally, not to do that willingly.

In the seconds it took for man and rider to wage a war of wills, Wren acted. Not outwardly, but inward, burrowing down deep into herself, into the core, through her core and into the bedrock of her life.

She didn't need old magics. She had something better.

There was no sense of doorways or windows, no sideways slip from one awareness to the other, but a layering of the two-into-one, like layers of onion skin: thin and crackling, but malleable at the same time.

Valere? a sense of—not surprise, but distraction.

She apologized for the intrusion, even as she was laying hold of the solid grounding that he represented. *just need to take a bit.*

She felt him brace for a blast of current, but instead she gathered double fistfuls of current inside her, the darker, tarry strength, the cobras of current, poison in their fangs and venom in their motions, and shoved them into him, cutting furrows in the bone, etching her own signature into his solid, stolid self. Stone, current running like blood, the poison leeching out in the stone of his psyche, coming out clean and strong, still dark but smoother, less poisoned.

Less wizzed.

Blood not from stone, but *into* stone.

This was what demon were for. This was his gift to her; her gift to him, to trust him with herself, utterly and entirely, everything inside, the shameful as well as the pleasing, the illness as well as the health. The hatred, as well as the love. Into stone, and stone would purify.

Understanding brought a deeper connection, and through that connection she saw, for an instant, through his eyes.

Sergei, his normally sleekly tidy hair a mess, knocked into a corner of P.B.'s apartment, his face bleeding and bruised, his eyes closed, lids heavy-shadowed and brow furrowed as though in pain. Another man stood over him, thick arms and heavy fists, reaching down as though to pick him up to administer another beating. Thick white-furred arms, holding—a chair? Part of a chair, at least, the ladderback of a former chair, bringing it down on the stranger's head.

bit busy right now

His thought came without alarm; annoyance, yes, and disgust, and a bit of fierce amusement.

so I see, she thought back at him.

Sergei's eyes opened, and the pale brown of them bypassed the attacker and went directly to her—no, to P.B., but she felt the impact, as well, the fierce delight of an all-out brawl. His internal energy surged almost like current, and half a city away her system responded, taking the almost-tangible crackle out of the air and bundling it up as though it was a live wire, channeling it—the demon acting as safe-conductor between them—and running it back down into her core, bright and alive, clean and sparking. In that instant, the three of them were one, complete and delighted.

Then the chair came down on the back of the stranger's

head, and as the man doubled over, Sergci gut-punched him with obvious, malicious relish in the act.

Boys, she thought, and left them to it.

Back in the museum, barely a second had passed, but it was long enough for the rider to have regained control of the guard and worked out some kind of compromise, controlling mind and ridden body. He scuttled sideways around her, kicking the book out of her range and then, rather than diving for it the way she expected, lunged toward her.

Current surged in reaction, the purified current carrying her outrage without rage, her disgust and horror under control but no less powerful for that. It twined, ribbons of color and dark forming one giant serpent so strong the guard saw it with physical eyes, forcing him back a half step in shock before his rider sent him forward again, clearly against his own wishes.

For that alone, Wren hated her opponent—if they did this to another human, an innocent, what worse would they do to a demon in their control? What would they do with that kind of freedom, that kind of power?

The current struck, and Wren had a moment of satisfaction as she felt it sizzle through his skin, and dropped him unconscious onto the floor. A shimmer of blackness rose out of him, kicked out of his system by the blow.

Poor bastard, she thought, reaching down to grab the book, *but you can't have this book. I'll burn it, first.* She must have said it out loud, or thought it loud enough, because the black magic expanded into a full-sized cloud of energy, fierce striations of no-color at its core, pulsing like a dozen hearts. Glass shattered behind her, and a roar—psychic, not physical, but no less eardrum-shattering for all that, filled the room and echoed down the hallways.

"You have got to be shitting me," Wren said, already running. No need to look back; she already knew what was gaining on her. A giant grizzly bear, half of his teeth fake and no digestive ability whatsoever inside his taxidermied body, but wanting to tear her flesh from bone anyway: not for dinner but because, suddenly, he *could*.

She had captured a stuffed horse once. More accurately, she had trapped the body of an old stuffed warhorse that had been inhabited by a pookha. But it had taken years of working the case part-time, chasing after a being with an agenda of its own. This was entirely different, and wasn't nobody paying her to do a damn thing except run.

The old-magic mages were *pissed*.

Around her, exhibits were moving, clearly feeling the effects of whatever spell her assailants were using, but the bear seemed to have taken the largest dose, as it was the only one actually out of its enclosure and doing more than looking and gesturing in her direction.

Safest place, where's the safest place? She knew this museum, damn it. She should know where to go. *Something without live-stock in the display.* The obvious choice would be the exotic minerals display, but it was too far, would take too long, and anyway, there was danger there, as well, that damned meteor, why she had avoided it originally. *Somewhere things aren't so angry,* she decided, almost losing her balance on an overpolished bit of floor, and knocking into the side of a water fountain. *Where things get what they think is their due, where people go oooo....*

Her mind was already there, calculating escape routes, even as she changed her direction mid-stride and backtracked right past the bear. It wasn't as agile as it had been in life, and took several paces to turn around and start back after her.

By then, Wren was already heading across the main lobby, and into the dinosaur exhibit.

By the standards of larger museums, the exhibit wasn't much. But it was enough, like jumping out of thick, humid summer air into a crisp wet stream, the difference in psychic pressure: for the first time since going into fugue state, Wren didn't feel anger or frustration but rather a smooth, almost mellow contentment.

Guess being dead and dust that long really does give you new perspective she thought, morbidly amused, before a baby T rex reached down as though to sniff at the top of her head like an inquisitive cat. Wren yelped, jumping forward and ducking under the outstretched arms of another, unrecognizable dinosaur skeleton, feeling the cool finger bones brush against her cheek. *Oh holy mother of God, get me* out *of here.*

In response, the roar of the *ursa major* returned as the furred corpse lumbered through the door and batted aside baby rex, letting the bones scatter across the floor like giant pickup stix. Wren barely had time to gulp before mama Rex's head swung around and down, looking directly at the grizzly as though she still had eyes.

Wren was pretty sure she wet herself. That was the thing about old magic. You could get it started, but you didn't always get to control where it went. Especially when you went riding someone without their consent, the way these idiots had. Everything was moving, like some damned Disney Animatronics ride, and it was a hell of a lot more fun when you got warned *before* it started that you were on a dark ride.

Wren put on another burst of speed toward where an unmarked emergency exit should be, according to the floor plan. Unlike the public ones, it shouldn't be alarmed from the inside—employees used it to take smoke breaks, during shift.

Even if it screamed in every alarm in every precinct in town, at this point she didn't care. If she could get outside, she somehow knew, the spell couldn't follow her. It was trapped within the confines, where the exhibits lived, bounded by their territory, their comfort zone. That was the limit to old magic, where current had none.

Fine by her. She'd done the job; it was time to go home. Let someone else do the goddamned cleanup this time.

twenty

Wren busted out of the museum's emergency side door and into the narrow—and thankfully trash-free—alley between the buildings. If anyone had been lurking for her, or if they had thought to post any kind of guard on the various exits, she would have been toast, but apparently the competition had focused all their talent—and Talent—on controlling the guard. She hoped they choked on their incantations and died purple-faced in embarrassing-to-explain positions.

Clutching the book and papers to her closely, she edged toward the street. Just because it looked and sounded clear was no reason to assume it actually *was* clear. Lots of jobs went south at the very end, because someone got cocky.

Barely shoving her nose out, she took a quick look. A woman in a long coat, walking a short-legged brown dog down the street: both of them looking bored to death by the process. A transit bus cruising down Fifth Avenue, lumbering to a stop. Nobody got on or off, and it rolled forward again when the light changed.

No police cars, no yowling masses, no anything out of place. No scent or sight of current in the air, beyond the normal flickers. If she went into fugue she might be able to find more, but...no. Not worth it. A woman and two men wearing business casual walked up to the museum, disappearing around to the main side entrance, where peons and delivery people went to be let inside. The admin staff was arriving. Time to be going.

No sign of Sergei.

Of course not. He was off having a bonding bar brawl with P.B.

Damn it, he was supposed to be here, waiting for the doors to open. He had her change of clothing! Not to mention a bag to hold her Retrieval, so it wasn't all quite so much out in the open. The tube could be carrying anything, bike messengers and couriers used them all the time, nobody looked twice, but the book was...not the sort of thing you lugged around Manhattan, as a rule.

The irritation flared, and then faded. He had a reason to go haring off, otherwise he would be here. She needed to finish the job, *then* worry about her boys. Anything else was counterproductive.

She had to get away from here, before the Dutch mages— and their magic-slave—found her.

"too tired
to deal with this shit:
safely home."

The words could have meant anything, in the mouths of any other Talent. Wren's intent shaped the cantrip into a heavy boost for her no-see-me, feeling it kick in and crank through her system until she thought she might be able to walk right up to a cop and kick him in the shins and not have him even feel it.

Not that she was going to test that theory. At least not until she was a few blocks away. Taking a deep breath, she walked out into the street, and strode away from the museum, the book and the tube clutched to her chest like a baby rescued from fire. Every step she took, the tension in her back grew less, but the weight of the book became heavier.

She had it. Now what the hell were they going to *do* with it?

With each step, as the adrenaline of the job wore off completely, Wren's entire body began to feel the results of the mad chase. She had a shin splint, and a pulled muscle in her side, a depressing number of bruises, and at some point she had conked her elbow hard enough that it still twinged painfully when she moved. Four or five blocks away from the museum a downtown bus pulled to the curb just as she passed by the stop, and Wren took the opportunity to slip on behind a woman with twin toddlers. One of them, a black-haired little angel with a devilish look on her face, caught sight of Wren despite the no-see-me spell, and looked as if she was going to say something, but was distracted by her mother urging her onto one of the plastic seats.

The incident made her think, again, about the kid she'd left upstate. Was his dad behaving himself? She hoped so. If not, the Tri-Com would do something. They understood; they had to take better care of their kidlets. There couldn't be a repeat of the Lost Ones.

She had a sudden vision of a dozen or so kidlets being herded by exasperated mentors, like some kind of demented *Cosa* version of a crèche, and started to giggle.

Fortunately, her stop came up next, before anyone noticed that an empty patch of air was having hysterics.

She made it through the streets and up the stairs of her apartment, flipped the door locks open, and locked them securely behind her. Then she stashed the book, notebook, and tube in the back of her overcrowded hall closet where only a trained archaeologist could excavate them safely, peeled off her slicks and tossed them into a corner, and crawled, almost literally, into bed, tears of exhaustion forming at the corner of her eyes even as her body touched the mattress.

"I'm getting too old for this shit," she told the apartment, and in her exhaustion she could have sworn that she heard the walls and floors hum with sympathy, before she passed out.

She woke when a weight dropped onto the bed next to her. Still exhausted, she reached out, expecting to touch Sergei's warm skin. The thick, scratchy texture her fingers encountered had her sitting upright, the covers sliding off her body as she scooted away from whatever it was breathing heavily next to her.

Current flashed like lightning, filling the room, and all the air was expelled from her lungs.

"Whoa, careful with the remaining fur!"

"You scared the crap out of me," she said, then did a double take as she actually saw what she had touched. "What the hell happened?"

P.B. tried to smile, but it came out as more of a grimace, the patchy skin where fur had been shaved away to allow for the stitches stretching the demon's face uncomfortably. Between that, and the bandages, and what looked like a black eye, the demon looked less like a cuddly stuffed toy and more like the tail end of a hard riot. "Your partner has a hell of an uppercut."

"Sergei?" She started to get out of bed, then remembered that she had striped off her slicks when she came in and not bothered to put anything on before collapsing into bed. "Demon, close your eyes!"

"Like I haven't seen it all before," P.B. grumbled, but obligingly placed one bandaged paw over his eyes and turned his face away. "Sergei's fine, by the way," he continued as she searched the room for her robe, wrapping herself in it and tying the tie firmly. "A few stitches here and there, and a hell of a headache, but he's fine."

"Stitches?" That got her to stop, half-dressed, and look at him. Stitches were okay, but if that was what he was *telling* her, there was more he wasn't.

The demon shrugged, as sheepish as she could imagine him looking, even with his eyes covered. "I kinda hit him with part of the chair, is the worst of the damage. And he wouldn't even have gotten bruised if he hadn't charged in like some kind of unhorsed knight to defend the honor of…I'm not sure whose honor he was racing in to save, honestly," the demon complained. "I was doing fine. I feel better than you look, anyway. Does he freak out that much when you don't answer the phone?"

"What?" She was totally confused now. Once the initial adrenaline rush had subsided, again, she could see that the bruises and scrapes were just that, and even the black eye was more of a brownish bruise than anything else. She was just so used to thinking of P.B. as invulnerable; the shock was always intense when he got banged up.

"They went after you?" That she remembered, when she had tapped him for a current discharge. Him, and Sergei, in the middle of a brawl…

The entire thing seemed as though it had happened a week ago, not…she tried to puzzle out what time it was, and realized that she didn't even know what *day* it was, at that point.

"Yeah. Wanted me to take a little trip with them, like you suspected. I declined, on account of my luggage not being packed and my passport gone missing."

That explained why Sergei hadn't been there when she hit street level. Wasn't that just like a guy, skip out on a date to get into a fight.

Then what the demon was saying sank in. Sergei had gone to P.B.'s aid. Unrequested, it sounded like. She felt her face twitch into a smile, and repressed it. Her partner, who had once referred to the Fatae as "bad special effects looking for a free handout," had abandoned her to go to the aid of a demon. She didn't think she wanted to know what had caused this about-face, she was just glad it had happened. But why wasn't Sergei here? What wasn't P.B. telling her?

"How long…" she started to ask.

"You've been sleeping around the clock. It's almost dawn. Sergei figured you'd be waking up soon, went out to get coffee and the newspapers."

Oh. The panic level dropped another few notches. Her partner had a thing about keeping up with a range of newspapers, and was accustomed to reading them online. Not an option in this apartment. Wren had a computer, reasonably fast and surge-protected to within an inch of her life, but she had been uncomfortable using it since she had wizzed. There were things on that hard drive she wanted to keep, not crisp out of existence with a badly timed sneeze. She missed instant messenger, and her mailing lists. Time to do something about banging together a new surge-proof system, if they could.

"You think he'll bring back bagels?" Now that she knew everyone was in one piece, more or less, she was hungry. No, she was *starving*. God knew how much energy she had burned during the Retrieval—the Retrieval!

"Oh my God, I swear, my brain leaked out with the first zombie hit," she muttered in annoyance, heading for the hallway, and the closet.

It took P.B. a moment to catch up with her. "Zombie? What zombie? Valere, there's no such thing as zombies! Is there?"

She was already at the closet, rooting through the debris of out-of-season coats, tote bags, broken umbrellas, and an old breakfast-in-bed tray someone had given her that she had never used. The hotstick Bonnie had loaned her was there, too, the current-weapon painted black and pink, and looking harmless for something so nasty. Wren was lethal enough, now, without amplification. She should give it back to Bonnie, who might need it someday on the job.

"Valere?"

"Hah. There it is." She reached in, relieved that the entire episode hadn't been some kind of particularly bizarre fever dream, and laid fingers on the tube of papers. The small notebook followed, being laid out on the carpet behind her, as the demon fell silent. She had to get on her knees to reach in and pull out the larger hardback book. It felt heavier than it had the day before, the leather of the cover less smooth, but she added it to the pile and then sat back, turning to see the demon's reaction.

He was sitting on his haunches across the narrow hallway, his back up against the wall, his dark red eyes very dark and wide.

"P.B.?" She looked from him to the pile of papers on the carpet. "I got them. I finished the job." She wasn't looking for an attagirl, exactly, but some sort of acknowledgement, more than that blank stare, would be nice, considering what she had to go through to get them—and for no pay, she could but wouldn't add.

"You got them."

She started to say "well, duh" but the look on his face stopped her. He looked…not scared, no. but…awed.

It floored her, unexpectedly. She had been so focused, she and Sergei, on the mechanics of the job, the details of outwitting the others and getting in and getting the job done, they had forgotten—or never really stopped to think—about what the job *was*.

These weren't journals, or blueprints, or scientific documents. They were origin stories. Birth certificates. Holy documents, if you were of that bent, proving the intentional creation of a sentient species.

In all the concern over what other people might do with the information in them, she had never stopped to wonder what they meant to P.B.

All that research, everything that must have gone into creating and perfecting the demon, to creating her friend… And she had been treating it like a liability, something to be destroyed, without even pausing to consider their real beauty, their real value.

"They're yours," she said gently.

"What?"

"Yours. Take them. Do whatever you want with them."

He held the book in his huge flat paws, and she could almost see the desire in him to stroke the leather, like a human might a holy text, or a childhood diary.

"You think I should destroy them."

She did, actually. She had seen the black sludge that was in her system, knew firsthand what she was capable of if she thought it was the right thing, the necessary thing. She had killed—*thou shalt not kill*—and she had tampered with a Null's brain—*for the good of a Talented child*—and she had done it again to protect herself from that security guard. She hadn't gone too far—not like those mages had, to destroy a man for their own use, but…. But she could still fall into that dark abyss. She could still go mad, if their connection, human and demon, ever failed.

If it did, would she want to create a new one? Would she be driven to, in order to survive? Would she do it, to save herself… Or someone she loved?

If it was now, if Neezer were still salvageable, would she…

It doesn't have to be this way. Her own voice; pleading with a madman for a second chance.

Better never to know. Better never to understand that much about what she was capable of.

Let the *Cosa* never know, either. Let them heal, and survive as they always had, and have illusions about their innate strength, and good intentions.

"Let them be myth," she said, not answering him directly. "Humans have no need to know. The Fatae have no need to know. Demon…someday, you may want offspring. Or you may not. But that's only for you to decide. Let demon determine your own species' future."

It was a speech, for her, and she didn't feel comfortable even as the words were coming out of her mouth, but some of the tension seeped out of P.B.'s body as she spoke.

"They're yours," she said again. It was all she could say, really.

"Aren't you…" His dark red eyes met hers in an unflinching gaze. "This could answer all the things you've been wondering about. The stuff you haven't been talking about."

He knew her too well. She wasn't sure if that was good or bad or just…maybe it just was. All the things she'd been wondering about, yeah. Genetics, and inheritance, and what causes Talent, what the "goo" really was, and how it could be manipulated, rechanneled, reinforced.

None of that really mattered, sitting on the floor in her apartment, her demon safe and her partner bringing back bagels, and the smell of coffee coming from the kitchen.

"I never wondered about the science," she said, smiling at him, feeling tension leave her own body with the truth of it. "Just the reasons. The causes. That's different. The reasons aren't in those papers. His reasons, his causes…aren't mine."

"No," her demon agreed. "They're not."

She left him there on the floor, staring at the pile, and went into the kitchen. As expected, the fridge was barren, with only a half-empty carton of orange juice, two bottles of her Diet Sprite, and half a carton of eggs. The coffee was too old, and after a sniff at it she dumped the pot and started another round, then ran water into the kettle and set it to boil.

A minute later, the coffee began to perk, and the front door opened.

"Hey," she said, sticking her head out of the kitchenette, even though she knew damn well who it was.

P.B. had definitely gotten the worst of their half of the brawl. Her partner had a bad bruise on his temple—courtesy of the chair?—and his left hand had a soft cast on two of the fingers, but otherwise he looked unharmed, the newspapers tucked under his injured arm, a bag of what smelled like fresh bagels held in his right.

"Do I want to know what the other guys look like?"

"Chang can probably get you access to their mug shots," he said with satisfaction. "Our boys missed their flight home, I'm sorry to say." He followed her into the kitchen, dropping the newspapers on the counter, the bagels going next to the toaster. "The Federal government apparently had some questions about the validity of their visas, especially when one of them was discovered breaking and entering a residence apartment in Manhattan for allegedly unlawful purposes."

"Awww. That's no way for tourists to behave. They should leave that to the locals." A pity there was no way to add unlawful control of a human to the charges. Or was there? That was something to ask Bonnie about, later. That was the sort of thing the PUPIs had been set up to deal with, after all—paranormal crimes, the kind of stuff the NYPD didn't have a clue on. In the meanwhile, she'd have to trust that Chang would do what she could. By the time it was straightened out, the papers would have disappeared again, this time for good. She found things, and P.B. could make them disappear. Not her problem any more. Not her responsibility.

That felt good. For once, it felt good to let it go, and not worry.

She let Sergei come up behind her, and leaned back against his broad chest, listening to the healthy thumping of his heart against her ear. If she touched him with current—lightly, so lightly—she could feel the electrical impulses of his entire body working the muscles throughout. That felt good, too.

One deeper touch so, and his heart would stop. But humans could and had damaged hearts without current, and healed them the same way.

They still could do damage to each other. Bad, nasty damage. That was the risk you took, when you loved someone.

But you could also save someone the very same way.

"I love you," she said, and felt his arms come up around her, his lips pressed to the top of her head.

"I ove you, too, Wrenlet."

Talent was more than genetics, more than goo. She might never know who her father was. It wasn't okay, it wasn't nothing, it would probably come back to snipe at her for the rest of her life, but she had lived this long without knowing, and she could live the rest of her life without knowing.

And in that realization, surrounded by her family, she was almost able to accept that she had to let Neezer go, as well. He had reached out to her in her darkest hour; had offered her the only advice his maddened brain could. *Wrenlet, no.* He had kept her from a reaction-killing, kept her from taking a—not an innocent life, no, but one she had no right to take. He hadn't forgotten her…and she had not recognized him in her own madness, had turned to others instead, to the bonds she had with Sergei and P.B.

That was as it should be. Mentors, like parents, were there to help you grow, to become self-aware. After that, you had to be on your own.

Neezer knew that, once. But his wizzed brain…she understood now, suddenly. He had never been able to let go, had still thought of her as his mentoree, his to protect. That turning away had stung, been something worse. When she had rejected him, moved on without him, without even knowing it, he had been angry. That was why The Alchemist had been scared, caught between Neezer's anger and love for her, and not knowing which would win, if his old friend would let go…or strike out, and in killing her, kill the last bit of himself, too.

She didn't know what impulse would have won, either. What impulse *would* win. Max had been right. She needed to stay away from Neezer. Forever. For both their sakes. They were in different places now. Different worlds.

She wasn't a student any more. She was on her own.

"Are you okay?" Sergei asked, his arms still wrapped around her, and she knew what he really meant was "are *we* okay?"

"Sometimes you get answers," she said in response to both questions. "And sometimes you just have to hope that it's all going to work out. But…yeah. I think I'm okay."

She thought about Neezer, and Max, and the little towheaded kid, then rested her head against her partner's chest, and looked up. "Do you think…maybe next time you go see Doc…I could come, too?"

Sometimes you were on your own. Nothing said you had to do it alone.

★ ★ ★ ★ ★

*Find out more about Bonnie and the origin of the
PUPIs in HARD MAGIC a PSI novel
Coming in 2010*

The dream was back. It always came back when I was stressed.

The site was deserted. I sneaked through the fence and into the house. Lucky for me none of the alarms had been turned on yet.

As usual, my brain was telling me that it was only a memory; that I already knew what I would find, that it was okay for my heart to stop pounding so fast, but the dream was in control.

The door called to me. I could feel it, practically singing in the rain-filled dusk. My flashlight skittered across the floor, allowing me to pick my way around the piles of trash and debris. No tools left out; the carpenter's daughter approved.

"Hello, beauty" I said to the door. Or maybe to the woman in the door: in the darkness, in the beam of light, she was nakedly apparent now, a sweet-eyed woman who gazed out into the bare bones of the room with approval and fondness.

Even now, the beauty of Zaki's work astounded me, and I mourned again for all that loss.

"Who are you, then? That's the key to all this. Who are you?"

The door, not too surprisingly, didn't answer. But I knew how to make it talk.

Or I thought I did anyway.

It was all instinct, but J. had always told me that instinct was the way most new things were discovered—instinct and panic.

I held my hand over the door the way I had with tools, carefully not touching it, and touched just the lighted levels of current, like alto bells sounding in the distance.

The woman's hair stirred in a breeze, and her face seemed softer, rounder, then she disappeared behind the leaves again.

I hated her, this woman I'd never known, never met. Hated her for being the reason my father was dead.

Zaki really had been an artist, the bastard. I could feel him in the work. But I didn't know, yet, what he had been feeling.

"Evidence doesn't lie."

Shut up, *I told the voice.* I'm working.

I touched a deeper level of current, bringing it out with a firm hand and splaying it gently across the door so that it landed easily, smoothly

Oh how I love her, such a bad woman, such a strong woman, and I cannot have her, but still I will show her my love....

Zaki, melancholy and impassioned, his hand steady on the chisel, his eyes on the wood, sensing even through his distraction how to chip here, cut there, to make the most of the grain. He was concentrating, thinking of his object of affection, the muse who inspired him. So focused, the way all Talent learned to be, that he never saw the man coming up behind him, the man who had already seen the work in progress, and recognized, the way a man might, the face growing out of the wood.

I knew what was about to happen, in my dream-mind, and tensed against the memory.

The blow was sudden and sharp, and the vision faded.

No, *I told my current.* More.

It surged, searched, and found...nothing. No emotions from the killer. No residue of his actions. It had been too long, or he had been too good, too quick. Or I needed to be better, sharper.

You were a kid, I wanted to tell my then-self. You did

what you could, and you did as well as you could. But you can't talk back to memories, only relive them.

"Damn it." My flashlight's beam dropped off the door; I was unwilling to look at the face of the woman who had cost my father his life.

"There is always evidence,

The voice was back. And probably right. I let the beam play on the floor, unsure what I was looking for. Scan, step, scan. I repeated the process all the way up to the door, then turned around and looked the way I had come.

"There."

On the floor, about two feet away. A spot where the hardwood floor shone differently. That meant that it had been refinished more recently than the rest of the floor, or been treated somehow... Zaki would have known. All I knew was that it was a clue.

I touched it with current, as lightly as I could. Something warned me that a gentle touch would reveal more than demanding ever would.

"The killer's actions, I beg you wood, reveal."

J's influence: treat current the way you would a horse; control it through its natural instincts. Current, like electricity, illuminated.

A dent in the floor, sanded down and covered up. The point of a chisel stained with blood? No. The harder end, sticking out of a body as it landed, falling backwards...

Oh, Zaki, you idiot *was all I could find in myself, following the arc of the body.* For a woman? For another man's woman when you had Claire at home?

And then I saw it, the shadow figure of the killer, indistinct even in his own mind—shading himself. That meant the killer was a Talent, if of even less skill than Zaki. Had that been a factor? The man— the foreman, I knew now—jealous not only of the carpenter's attraction to his wife, but of his skill to display it, driven to murder?

The chisel was removed, wiped down, and...

I still flinched, even years and dreams later.

The blood alone flared in the pictorial, a shine of wet rubies in the shadows as the foreman dipped the chisel onto a cloth still damp with the blood, laying the trace for me to find, a week later.

Find, and be unable to do anything about, save live with the knowledge that my father had been murdered, and the murderer still walked, unpunished....

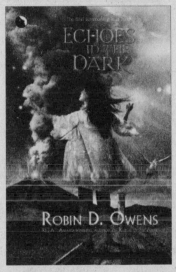

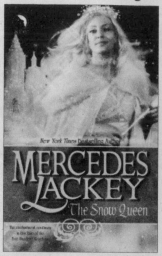